Anonymous

Life and Letters of William John Butler

Anonymous

Life and Letters of William John Butler

ISBN/EAN: 9783744717847

Printed in Europe, USA, Canada, Australia, Japan

Cover: Foto ©Raphael Reischuk / pixelio.de

More available books at **www.hansebooks.com**

William John Butler

1888.

LIFE AND LETTERS

OF

WILLIAM JOHN BUTLER

LATE DEAN OF LINCOLN

AND SOMETIME VICAR OF WANTAGE

WITH PORTRAITS

ἀμετακίνητοι, περισσεύοντες ἐν
τῷ ἔργῳ τοῦ Κυρίου πάντοτε,
εἰδότες ὅτι ὁ κόπος ὑμῶν οὐκ
ἔστι κενὸς ἐν Κυρίῳ.

London

MACMILLAN AND CO., Limited

NEW YORK : THE MACMILLAN COMPANY

1898

First Edition 1897.
New Impression 1898.

GLASGOW : PRINTED AT THE UNIVERSITY PRESS
BY ROBERT MACLEHOSE AND CO.

PREFACE.

THE late Dean of Lincoln was one of those whose lives seem especially to call for some record. That few men, certainly few men as uncompromising, have ever won more affection from their fellows, will be acknowledged by all who were present when he was laid to rest under the shadow of Lincoln Minster, and saw that vast building filled from end to end with mourners and sympathizers, the greater part of them being citizens of a city to which, less than nine years before, he had come as a total stranger. At the same time, few men who have done so much work in their lives have been less known by name to what is called " the general public." On both accounts therefore, that those who knew and loved him might have some permanent memorial of him, and that the record of a strenuous life in which Englishmen even of widely different schools of thought cannot fail to find a stimulus, might be made known to many who never felt its direct influence, it was thought that a memoir of him might without presumption take its place beside those of other men who did good service in the generation that is now passing away.

A few words seem to be called for in explanation of the absence of any author's name from the title-page of this book. When it became apparent that abundant materials for it were forthcoming, several persons, among them some of our approved writers of clerical biography, were approached, in the hope of securing adequate literary treatment for a narrative which was felt to be not unworthy of a capable hand. For one reason however or another none of those before whom the proposal was laid found himself at liberty to undertake the task; and it was resolved to try what could be done by the method of pretty wide co-operation. Various friends with whom in his life of many activities he had come in contact, responded most kindly to the suggestion that they should write down such recollections of him as were most vivid in their minds; and these, together with selections from his correspondence, were arranged, with just so much of connecting matter as was needed to give unity to the book, by a member of his family, aided by one of the Cathedral staff with whom he had been in constant intercourse. To the friends in question are due the warmest thanks of those by whom the memory of William Butler is most cherished. The greater part of them will be found named in connexion with their contributions; but besides these the names of Rev. H. H. Woodward, G. H. Drew, Esq., Miss Alice Ottley, Mrs. Arthur

Baker, and E. M. Hutton Riddell, Esq., may be
mentioned. Thanks are also due to the representatives of Mr. Keble, Canon Liddon, Cardinal Manning,
Bishop Wilberforce, and others, for permission to
publish letters written by them.

We are constantly being reminded in the intercourse of society that "the world is very round";
and the same holds true in a measure of the world
of books. For illustration of the biography of a
hard-working clergyman one would hardly look to
a school of fiction based upon the negation of all
which the clergyman morally and socially represents.
Yet those who realize that Wantage is the 'Alfred-
ston' of one of the most powerful, and repulsive,
novels which the English branch of that school
has produced, will find it interesting and instructive
to contrast the novelist's more or less conjectural
criticism of life in and about our smaller country-
towns with the results actually produced on that
life by constructive energy, informed and directed
by faith, hope, and love.

A. J. B.

CONTENTS.

CHAPTER XI.

LINCOLN.

CHAPTER XII.

THE LAST YEARS.

APPENDIX I.

APPENDIX II.

William John Butler.
1843.

CHAPTER I.

EARLY YEARS.

WILLIAM JOHN BUTLER was born 10th February, 1818, in Bryanston Street, Marylebone, the eldest child of John Laforey Butler and Henrietta his wife, daughter of Capt. Robert Patrick. His father was a partner in the mercantile house of Johnston & Co. in Bush Lane. His family originally came from Pembrokeshire. Mrs. Butler was of Irish descent, the Patricks having settled in the seventeenth century in the north of Ireland, in company with many other Scottish families, at the "Plantation of Ulster." Something must be said of the characters of Mr. and Mrs. Butler, to form some conception of the influences which surrounded William Butler's childhood. The father was a thoroughly upright, conscientious man, sensitive in disposition, extremely accurate and fastidious in language ; traits which were certainly inherited by the son. The mother's Irish blood brought with it the national characteristics of gaiety and open-heartedness, and a keen sense of humour. William Butler was baptized at

A

Marylebone Church by the Rev. Basil Woodd, who presented him with *Burkitt on the New Testament*, in unconscious anticipation of his future clerical career. After him were born two sons— Charles and Paul, twins ; and two daughters— Frances, who married Kirkman Daniel Hodgson, Esq., M.P., and Anna.

There is little to tell about his childhood. It was passed at Southgate, in the parish of Edmonton, Middlesex, whither his parents moved from London. He is reported to have been " a fine child, and forward for his age," which is evident from his having read Beckmann's *Inventions* and Bingley's *Animal Biography* when only five or six years old ; " a thoroughly manly boy, and very tender-hearted," " never frivolous or indolent, always fond of study and literature ; quite without malice or unkind feelings towards anyone"; such is the testimony of his surviving brother and sister.

He was brought up religiously in the school of old-fashioned, orthodox churchmanship, and one little incident of his childhood bears witness to it. During a thunderstorm, when he was between three and four years of age, he was heard to repeat the Collect, " Lighten our darkness." No one who knew his fidelity through life to the Prayer Book will fail to appreciate this early manifestation of it.

The village schoolmaster taught him till he was eight or nine ; he then went to a school kept by the Rev. Stephen Freeman at Forty Hill, in Enfield, a few miles from his home. No trace remains of

his schooldays there except a letter to his grandmother Mrs. Patrick, the joint composition of
himself and his brothers, who were at school with
him. From Enfield he went in 1830 to Westminster, where he was elected a Queen's Scholar.

One of his few surviving schoolfellows has furnished some recollections of these early days. He
writes as follows:

We were together at Westminster for five years as Queen's
Scholars, but until the fifth year we were not in the same
Election. College consisted of four Elections, and the boys of
the same Elections were associated as friends. If I had, in
the usual course, left Westminster at the end of my fourth
year of College, I should never have known Butler. For special
reasons I was allowed to stay there a fifth year, and so became one of the same Election, and I then began to associate
with him; but I had already a special friend in the same
Election, and I did not seek to make a friend of Butler.
My impression of him at that time was of a boy of more
than average ability and acquired knowledge, but too evidently
conscious of his acquirements, and disposed to boast of them,
and very confident in his own opinion. Such a character and
the fact of his having very short sight invited much mockery
and teasing by his companions, so that my recollections of
him at that time consist principally of absurd situations in
which he placed himself through attempting things in which
he failed, partly through defective sight, partly through natural
awkwardness.

Defective sight made him fail at cricket, football, and hockey;
but he learned to row, and when in 1836 a Westminster eight
rowed against an Eton eight at Staines, he rowed No. 4, I
rowing No. 8. Westminster was then a rough school, and I
recollect some special examples among boys of the Elections
above Butler's of low moral tone, but I have no recollection
of his ever following bad example, or that he ever was otherwise than well conducted both in and out of school hours.

In May 1836 he and I were elected scholars of Trinity

College, Cambridge, and we did not meet from that month till the following October, when we began to keep terms at Trinity. The rough discipline he underwent at Westminster was perhaps wholesome for him. At Cambridge his opinion of his own acquirements and ability were seldom manifest. His friends were of the best of the Trinity undergraduates, *e.g.* Vaughan, now Dean of Llandaff, Hodson, now Vicar of Enfield, Mathison, Lawrence, Webb, Philip Freeman, Farrer, and, in his last year, George Kennedy of St. John's. At that time no one was allowed to try for classical honours who had not taken mathematical. Butler had no taste for mathematics, and wisely, I think, decided not to waste time in learning what he disliked, but to prepare for the ordinary B.A. degree. He read steadily the subjects necessary for that degree; he also read higher Classics with Vaughan as a private tutor, and if he could have tried for Honours in Classics I believe he would have taken a high place. He also read Italian, French, and I think German, and History. He was a member of the Cambridge Camden Society, which implied some knowledge of architecture; he attended Professor Smythe's lectures on the French Revolution, and Professor Sedgwick's lectures on Geology. He was a member of the Union and occasionally took part in the debates.

Butler was in lodgings during his first year; then, until he left Cambridge, he had the rooms in the upper story of the gateway tower leading from the great Court into Trinity Lane, known as the Queen's Gate. M. T. Farrer, also a Westminster scholar, had the lower story.

When we went to Trinity in October, 1836, the Third Trinity (Eton and Westminster) Boat Club, which had once been head of the river, was very low, I think tenth, and we were persuaded to join in recovering its place. When we left it was second, and for some time Butler regularly took part in the practice and races; but after the first year he found it interfered with reading, and he ceased to row with the first crew. He was never a first-rate oar, but could always be depended on to do his best.

In January 1840 we took our B.A. degree; I then left Cambridge, and I believe that I did not see Butler again until 1844, when we were there to take our M.A. degree. In that interval each had married, and each had nearly lost his wife in her first confinement, and for that reason we were more drawn together than ever before. At his invitation I went with my wife to stay a Sunday with him at a place near Amwell in Herts, where he had a Cure. We went to Amwell on the Saturday, and I remember being taken by him in the evening to help in the teaching of a men's night school, and I began to understand and appreciate his real character and the energy of his work. I did not visit him again until he was at Wantage. Of his work there and since he left Wantage there are many who can tell far better than I can, and I do not attempt to say anything of it.

I feel that what I have written will help you little, if at all, to give any idea of Butler's life at Westminster and Cambridge; I wish it were otherwise. Since I knew what he really was I have always regretted that I did not take more pains to know him when I had the opportunity at Cambridge.

The Very Reverend C. J. Vaughan, D.D., who was his most intimate friend during a good part of his Cambridge career, writes:

It must ever be a pleasure to me to think of your father, so dear and kind a friend in the young life of Cambridge and Trinity days, and even in the later years of silence and separation not forgotten.

I can still see him as he was in the long vacation of 1837, the time of our closest intimacy, full of health and spirits, always brave and true, not yet developed into the devotion of his maturer life, but already loved by good men like our dear common friend G. E. L. Cotton, and already with many " shadows cast before " of what he was to be in due time.

I have little to say that is worth saying. But this is because our life together was uneventful and our friendship without breach or jar.

When we met forty or fifty years afterwards in Convocation, generally voting on opposite sides, the old alliance was still recognized both in speech and feeling on both sides. And

when I last saw him (in the Charing Cross Hospital) he was
the same cheery and joyful companion that I knew him of
old, only ripened into the man of experience, the man of
many toils and high attainments in the service of God and
man.

His friendship for the writer of these lines led
on one occasion to an affair which seems to have
made some stir in the University, and might, but
for the intervention of some sensible advisers, have
brought him into serious trouble. In the early part
of 1839, Mr. Vaughan was standing for the office
of President of the Union Society, and Butler
naturally canvassed with energy for his friend.
There was, however, a set, headed by some young
men of good family belonging to St. John's, with
whom Mr. Vaughan was personally unpopular. These
put up an opposition candidate, and party feeling
ran somewhat high. Butler, in common with a
large number of members, had signed a requisition
to the existing president, agreeably to the rules of
the society, calling upon him to reconsider some
decision, and this was lying in the reading-room for
signature. S——, one of the Johnians in question,
and some of his set, chancing to see this, added to the
list of names—in a not uncommon vein of undergraduate wit—those of certain race-horses. The
matter attracted some notice. At a meeting on
March 21st, Butler moved a resolution expressing the
society's disapprobation of this conduct. A stormy
debate resulted, in the course of which S—— used
some epithets that were thought to involve an

allusion to private and personal matters. Failing
to obtain from the president the protection which
he thought due to him, Butler then moved that
the house should form itself into a committee.
This was carried, and the chair was taken by a
fellow of Trinity, no less a person than the well-
known scholar J. W. Donaldson. S—— then observed
that "seeing the name of the honourable mover
among the signers of the requisition he had written
down the names of the five other brutes." Cambridge men of a later generation will recognize the
Unionic invective, as still employed occasionally by
heated orators. However, this was a little too much,
and S—— narrowly escaped expulsion on the spot,
the feeling, it would appear, being almost unanimous
against him. A demand for an apology only elicited,
as it would seem, an insolent reply, and threats
of personal violence were uttered by the aggrieved
party. It was, however, represented by cooler-
headed friends that the result of this might be
serious for both sides. At that time duelling was
not yet a tradition of the remote past, and the
penalty for taking part in a duel, even if no worse
consequences ensued, would inevitably be expulsion
from the University.

Ultimately the matter was put into the hands
of three friends, Trinity men of good standing, two
undergraduates and one B.A., the latter being the
senior classic of the previous year, W. G. Humphry,
in after years Vicar of St. Martin's in the Fields.
These prudent counsellors, to whose judgement

Butler absolutely submitted himself, decided, as
indeed they could hardly have failed to do, "that
it was only to the expression of public feeling that
he could look for redress," and "that on the manner
in which that feeling had been expressed by the
Union Society and generally in the University, he
had every reason to congratulate himself."

About a week later, S——, who had also in
the meantime taken counsel with a friend, wrote
acknowledging that the expressions used by him
"were unbecoming and unjustifiable," and the matter
seems to have blown over, though from a letter
written to Butler by his mother nearly a month
afterwards, it would seem that discords still sim-
mered. Among other things she writes:

> I myself wish you had amongst you all, one clear-sighted
> old Nestor who might, from his own wisdom, put down the
> whole quarrel, which in a few years will be seen by the present
> young actors as quite a ridiculous business; a Professor of
> Patience and Harmony being much needed there, I suspect.

The old story, *si jeunesse savait*.

Another letter written by Mrs. Butler to her son
about this time contains some sound advice on the
subject of bills.

> Your expenses are now becoming understood by yourself,
> and by a judicious arrangement you can get them into a nut-
> shell. Pray have as FEW bills as possible. Tradespeople are
> not always friendly to this, as amongst many a profit is obtained
> by the contrary practice. But it is so injurious to the honest
> feelings of a young person to be spending he knows not what
> of his income, and then temptations abound till the best
> principles are led to yield. Also the *doctoring* of bills, by which

I mean, the making an account out; but from an idea that
another can be subtracted from it, the endeavour to make
all appear SMOOTH becomes a perpetual source of artifice and
plotting which weighs down a mind, otherwise ingenuous, till
it becomes callous, reckless, and hardened, and is at last completely out of that strong firm path of integrity for which no
human pleasure can compensate.

W. J. B. TO HIS MOTHER.

CAMBRIDGE, March 30, 1838.

I have just passed that dreadful and difficult ordeal yclept
by the Dons "the previous examination," and by the Undergraduates "Little-go." I went in on Tuesday, the second day
of examination, in a most wholesome state of alarm, for it is
a peculiarity attached to this examination that every one,
from the best even unto the worst men in the year, are
frightened by the prospect of this. Paley's *Evidences* is the
great bugbear to most, but some unfortunate mathematical
men, who have never been at public schools, get plucked in
the Classics. However, my horror was greatly abated in the
course of an hour, and on finding I could floor eight out of
nine questions in Paley, it was changed to mirth. Well, in
the evening at nine o'clock my fate was decided, and I was
written down as "examined and approved," with sundry others;
forty went in on my day, and of these fourteen were plucked.
. . . A friend of mine goes in to-morrow; I have been
coaching him, as the technical expression is, for the last fortnight. . . . To-morrow, Sedgwick, the geological professor,
gives a field-lecture, *i.e.* a cross-country expedition on horse-
back, stopping at the various places worthy of his attention.
These he previously specifies, and I am going to walk with a
friend of mine and cut off corners, etc., and get to the different
points where he lectures, and so get what good we can. He
winds up at Ely. . . . Vaughan has just been bracketed
equal with Lord Lyttelton for the Chancellor's Medals, a prize
given to Classics. He was also put equal with him in the
Classical Tripos Examination, so that the two are as equal as
possible. Vaughan beat him two years ago for the University
Scholarship, and last year when Vaughan was *hors de combat*

Lyttelton got the Scholarship. This year Freeman of Trinity and Williams of King's got the two Scholarships. . . . Have any of you read Carlyle's *History of the French Revolution*? It is written in quite a new style, and, as far as I can judge, an exceedingly powerful one. I long to be able to read it satisfactorily through when I get home, for I have no time here.

In the summer he was at the Lakes with a reading party during the Long Vacation. Some brief extracts from his journal contain his impressions of some Oxford contemporaries.

Ambleside, July 11. Wednesday and rainy. Faber an Oxford Catholic and friend of Freeman came with two pupils. He teaed with us. Sufficiently conceited and donnish.

Friday. Faber & Co. dined with us including Whytehead. The mannerism of these people is intolerable.

Saturday. To my great joy the Balstons came, as it will perhaps relieve us from that eternal Faber & Co.

Balstons, Champernowne, Froude, Freeman, and I set forth to climb Fairfield.

Sunday, August 5. We walked to Troutbeck, a little village four miles off, to hear Arnold preach. He preached very well indeed. The church was most primitive, only one pew, and most extraordinary altar decorations. The real clergyman, Arnold told us, spoke in the regular Westmoreland dialect. The walk was most beautiful, and showed the mountains to perfection, Scawfell, Langdale Pikes, and the arch [?] of Mickledoor, to which Arnold compared the Greek μεγάλη θύρα, as being exactly the same in sound.

On this tour he is said to have taken a black-letter Chaucer for his private reading. Mr. Freeman took the *Christian Year*. Before long they exchanged books, and he expresses his admiration for the *Christian Year* in verses, which are given more to show his appreciation of its character than for any peculiar excellence of their own. He had indeed what Wordsworth calls the " Faculty of verse," and wrote it till the last year of his life, but he never considered himself in any sense of the term a poet.

CHRISTIAN YEAR.

Here are no strains of maniac devotee
    Blighting soft mercy with their uncouth lay,
Nor here the songs of Pagan revelry
    Unhallowed, darkening the pure Gospel day ;
But here the gentle streams of Heaven glide
    Rippling through caves of crystal, where the air
Is soft and pleasant, and the woodland's pride
    Of song is echoed from each distant lair.
Roses not thorns surround their path of love
While through their variegated banks they rove,
    Slaking the thirst of all who hither haste
    With ardent souls, the glittering springs to taste,
And ebbing now, now flowing, glancing bright
Where all before appeared but gloomy night.

Although a smoker in his College days, he entirely gave up the use of tobacco after he was ordained. The following verses amusingly recall his old attachment to the habit for which in later days he expressed antipathy.

A TRINITY CLOISTER INCIDENT.

Gently was the night breeze blowing,
    Tranquil light the fair moon gave,
Sleep o'er mortals' breasts was flowing,
    All was silent as the grave,
Save my footsteps' echoed traces,
    As through cloistered shades I walked,
Thinking now of lovely faces,
    Pleasures past, or pleasures baulked.

Sweet, though tinged with sacred sorrow,
   All my recollections were,
And I hoped the coming morrow,
   Like the past, would be as fair.
Puffing at my mild Havannah,
   Slow and grave I wandered on,
As on bank of Guadiana
   Stalks the solemn Spanish Don.
But a Cambridge Don drew nigher
   Filled with Euclid, filled with spleen,
When he saw the gleaming fire
   Anger turned his visage green.
"Sir," he cried, "what means this horrid
   Stench, what means this loose array,
Men come here to store their forehead,
   Not to blow their wits away."

·   ·   ·   ·   ·   ·   ·   ·   ·

A tragic event which occurred while William Butler was at Trinity is thus described by him in a letter to his mother.

I must now tell you the most distressing thing I ever heard. Poor F—— was drowned on Sunday morning at half-past one o'clock, under the most fearful circumstances. I knew him very well, and was to have breakfasted with him that very morning. I am so much shocked that it will be quite a relief to tell you the whole case. I had sculled to and from Ely with Arthur Shadwell and a Trinity man named Welby. On our return we went to Welby's rooms for some food, and while we were there in came F——. He sat down and joined us, and stayed there till near one o'clock, talking and laughing. We were, as usual, quizzing him, etc. Another man named B—— came in and said he was hungry. F——, the most good-natured fellow alive, said that he had provided food for his breakfast party next day, and B—— might have some then if he liked. But B—— [said] this would not be fair and asked him to get some audit ale he (F——) had. F—— went for the ale, the party broke up, and B—— thought no more of it, but went to bed. In a short time F—— came to his

rooms with the ale, but finding him in bed wished him good-
night, and returned for his own rooms, which are in the
Great Court, on the Chapel side. But going through the
screens, he met a tipsy man named H—— standing there with
some others. F—— said, We ought to go out of College to-
night; H—— agreed, hardly knowing what he said, and F——
being the most experienced, offered to show them the way.
Now the way out of College is round the extremity of a wall
which abuts on the river, at the back of the library. This
wall it was necessary to stride round from one parapet to the
other. F—— got round safely enough, but H——, being very
tipsy, missing his footing tumbled in. The water was up to
his waist, but he was very much frightened. F——, who was
a capital swimmer, called out, Can you swim? No, said H——.
So F—— took off his coat and hat, and walked down the steps
into the water to help him out. He got hold of him, and went
back with him towards the steps, but, owing to the darkness
probably, could not find them. He was heard to say, "Never
mind, I will take you across." He was seen to go across with
H—— for a little way, and suddenly both disappeared. There
was another man there named H——t, who had merely joined
them to see the climb round the wall. He rushed away for
help, and on returning they found H—— clinging to the ivy
on the wall, and saw nothing of F——. Knowing that he
was a good swimmer, they supposed he had swam across and
gone away for fear of being caught, and gave themselves little
trouble about him. H—— was far too flurried with wine
and horror to know anything about him, nor even how he
himself got to the wall. They let down a drag to him, and
pulled him [up] when he had been about twenty minutes in
the water. Ferguson met them in the cloisters as they were
carrying him up, and one of them said that they were not
quite sure about F——, but hardly supposing that anything
could have happened. Ferguson said that there should be
no doubt on such a question, and immediately climbed over
the walls to the Johnian Bridge to see for tidings of F——.
In the meantime others came; they got a boat and a drag,
yet hardly believing any mischief, and after dragging for nearly
three hours, struck on his body. It was carried into College
at five o'clock yesterday morning. Of course he was quite

dead. You may imagine the sensation which so appalling an event would cause. An inquest sat yesterday, and brought in a verdict of "drowned while endeavouring to rescue Mr. H——." There can be no doubt that going in as he did, flushed and heated, after eating and drinking heartily, and feet foremost, brought on a sudden fit of apoplexy. The affair is rendered more distressing by the fact that his brother was burnt to death at school about a year and a half ago.

Mrs. Butler was a thoroughly religious-minded woman, and her letters show it. In one she speaks in terms of high approval of Newman's sermons; but in another, dated 30th November, 1838, she gently reproves her son for neglecting to attend the funeral of the veteran leader of the Evangelical party at Cambridge.

I received your letter, and had great pleasure in so doing, perceiving the cheerful strain in which it was written; but before I proceed to one topic, in which I know you will sympathize with me, two or three remarks I will previously make upon your's. I should have felt better pleased had you on the day of Mr. Simeon's funeral made the attendance upon it instead of your water excursion.

She then proceeds to give a graphic account of a fire which had broken out in the house between one and two in the morning. The whole family had had a narrow escape of being burnt to death, and probably would have been had not Mrs. Butler been awakened by the smoke, and given the alarm. Touches that now look quaint enough are the allusions to the efficiency of the "New Police," Sir Robert Peel's recent invention, and, a small domestic tragedy, "the parrot burnt to a cinder."

She concludes, " All little matters now appear indeed useless, after so great a crisis, to dwell upon. To you I repeat, my dear boy, be steady, seek not company for company's sake ; a character of another kind I pray may be your's for the sake of many whose happiness is bound up with your's. Economy also, and not those vain amusements which end in nothing."

In 1839 he won the Trinity College Essay Prize. The subject was " The Colonial Policy of the Ancients." A complimentary notice in a Cambridge paper describes it as manifesting " ability, learning, and research." His mother, writing from Southgate, 23rd March, says, " I am glad we are so soon to enjoy a re-perusal of your essay, which for so deep a production of Greek and Latin quotations is as little dry as possible."

Some excellent advice as to the necessity of keeping accounts follows, and one sentence recalls a characteristic trait which distinguished him through life : " You are not extravagant, quite, I should say, the reverse, but from a born indolence averse to the routine of Bookkeeping."

He took his B.A. degree in January 1840.

W. J. B. TO HIS MOTHER.

CAMBRIDGE, February 12, 1840.

I got another present from Freeman. It was the large edition of the *Christian Year*, handsomely bound in morocco. I liked it particularly from him, because he first opened my eyes to its surpassing beauties. I write this letter while waiting

for my lazy pupil, I wish I could say pupils. This is the
second lesson he has skipped, and I am sure I read more for
him than he does for himself. . . . I just returned to
Cambridge in time to see Cotton, who departed for Rugby
the next day. I have agreed to pay him a visit at Easter.
. . . I am attending Professor Scholefield's Lectures in
Thucydides, and preparing for these together with coaching
my pupil, and preparing for it, pretty nearly occupies all my
time. . . . The Classical examination is going on, and I
instruct D—— as much as I can, but I fear that he is not
likely to do very well. Alfred Shadwell has done better
than I expected. Kennedy is one of the examiners, and I
am to read the papers to him this evening, while he marks
the faults.

The last remark implies a curiously slack method,
as it would now appear, of performing an examiner's
duties.

W. J. B. TO HIS SISTER.

CAMBRIDGE, February 24, 1840.

I have been assisting Kennedy to examine the papers of the
candidates for the Classical Honours. Drew, Shadwell, and
many of my friends are among them, and I feel sometimes sorely
tempted to cheat! I have also been correcting the proof sheets
of my essay, which will be out in a very few days, as soon as I
can get hold of Kennedy to look over it, and correct any errors
which may have crept in by negligence of the author, for when
printed it is of course irrevocable. I am looking out for a pupil
to go abroad with this summer, for I think that that would be
an agreeable arrangement for every one, both at home and at
Cambridge. I should like some one to prepare for Cambridge.
Last week I dined out every day. Never were such doings—
with Kennedy, Lawrence, White, and others, and in King's
Hall with the Fellows. . . . I think that Mr. Quin is a
great humbug. I recommend you not to argue with him, but
ask him, if the Roman Church be in reality the same as the
Anglican, why he goes to a Dissenting Chapel instead of the
Parish Church. I have no patience with such sophistry.

In July he started with a pupil for a continental tour. They went from Southampton to Havre; then to Paris, where they stayed till the 17th, and then visited Berne, Lausanne, and Geneva, passing on by Turin and Genoa to Florence and Rome, and seeing Ravenna on the way to Venice. He kept a journal during the tour, which is a good sample of the thoroughgoing industry he put into all his work. Public buildings, churches, and pictures he never allowed to escape his eye. At Lake Leman, after saying that one end of the lake is rendered classical by Chillon, *St. Gingo*, and Vevey, he adds in a note, "I never met with this saint except here and in the *Vicar of Wakefield*, 'by the living Jingo,' which oath evil disposed people have tried to explain away!"

The journal ends abruptly at Venice, September 22nd.

The year 1840 was destined to end in gloom, and a crisis took place which materially affected his prospects. Hitherto he had known no pecuniary cares. His father was a partner in a flourishing mercantile house, and although he was precise and careful in money arrangements with his sons, he does not seem to have stinted them. Suddenly, without any preliminary warning, it was discovered that a very large sum of money had been misappropriated, quite sufficient to put the credit of Johnston & Co. in jeopardy, if not to ruin them. Mrs. Butler had the unpleasant task of breaking this bad news to her son in a letter dated 5th November, 1840. After

a few lines on domestic matters she introduces the
painful subject as,—"the trial which I am now
wishing to break to you, the all but total ruin of
Bush Lane."

Having now broken the ice, I will enter more into detail,
begging you, darling son, to remember that no fault or error
attaches to your beloved father, who bears his share of the
calamity with calm and manly fortitude, feeling and relying
upon the affection of his dearest Will, Paul, and Charles, all
now approaching the age when their influence over his mind
and prospects can be felt.

No time was lost by her son on the receipt of
this bad news, in devising means by which he
might maintain himself, and so relieve his parents
of any outlay on his behalf. Till the fortunes of
the family began to recover he supported himself
by taking pupils, and he prepared to take Holy
Orders as soon as possible.

W. J. B. TO HIS MOTHER.

[Undated.]

As this is the fourth letter I have been writing this morning,
you must not expect it to be very long. I was very much
obliged for your long letter, which gave me a very good idea of
the state of things, and which I have duly forwarded to Paul.
I think Mr. J——'s a very timely offer. I had a most kind
letter from Mr. G——, who says that he is proud to be
called the friend of such a man as my father. He also sent
me an enormous brace of birds, and I took the opportunity
to send these to Aunt—with a letter, which brought me back
next day a most kind reply. I will enclose it for you, as I
think it may show you that her zeal has not, as you feared
it might, tired itself out. I have got two *whole* pupils for
the Christmas vacation, which puts £20 into my pocket. I

am sadly afraid I shall not be able to visit you at all pleasantly till after the 14th of next month, so that you must not expect me on Christmas day, though if it seem at all feasible or judicious, I certainly will be at Southgate. After that time I shall be free from pupils for a week or so, and my mind will be more unoccupied. At present I am as busy as a bee. I had an offer of a perpetual curacy of £70 a year at Halifax, but I think that this will not be worth my while, without the certainty of two or three pupils at £200 a-piece, and Halifax is so disagreeable a town, that I should not get them. The only spoke in the wheel for a Chaplaincy[1] is that to be eligible it is necessary to be in orders, so that I am exerting all my powers to get a title in or near Cambridge, or a Sunday duty within reach, and I have written to Mr. Gwilt on the subject. Mr. Barnett's is a most delightful letter. I have not had so much pleasure for a long time as in reading it. . . . I think that Mr. —— acts like a fool. It is very easy for a man to be thought an oracle, when he has plenty of money to enforce his opinions. I must now return to Bullinger and Transubstantiation, and with love to my dear father, Fanny, Anna, and Charley, I am, dearest mamma, ever your affectionate son,

W. J. BUTLER.

His father wrote to him at the end of the year.

December 30, 1840.

MY DEAREST WILL,—I have had so many events to meet of late that I have had hardly courage to sit down and write to you, nor can I do so now at length; but I cannot help now telling you how much I have felt the tender love and affection which you have shown me under the circumstances in which I have been placed, and what a blessing it has been to us all to be allied to one who fills in so exemplary a manner every duty of life. I leave to your dear mother and sisters the detail of passing events. My chief object in writing is to request you to address a letter to Messrs. H. & I. Johnston & Co., authorising them to pay over to me

[1] Of the College. (?)

the sum of £500 deposited in your name with the *late* firm
of Johnston, Butler, & Son, by Charles Shadwell; the meaning
of this I will explain more fully hereafter. . . . I am to
have a third instead of a half of the profits, which is as
much as I could reasonably expect considering the large sum
which I am unable to pay of my share of losses, and I can
only expect a very small income for some time to come;
still it is better than being cast on the world to struggle for
a subsistence. My health has kept up better than I could
have expected.

The fortunes of the house of Johnston & Co.
revived under Mr. Butler's able management, and
with the assistance of friends, who had the fullest
confidence in his integrity and ability, he succeeded
in placing it on the road to a higher level of prosperity than before.

CHAPTER II.

THE BEGINNING OF WORK.

IN view of his approaching ordination, as we have already seen, William Butler had begun to seek for a title for Holy Orders. Through a cousin he obtained an introduction to the Rev. Charles Dyson, Rector of Dogmersfield in Hampshire. Mr. Dyson was a man of great learning and ability; he had been a Scholar of Corpus, where he became the intimate friend of John Keble, Arnold, and J. T. Coleridge. Dean Stanley in his life of Dr. Arnold, says of Charles Dyson that his "remarkable love for historical and geographical research, and his proficiency in it, with his clear judgement, quiet humour, and mildness in communicating information made him particularly attractive to Arnold." But his religious views were those of Keble and Newman, and he was a firm though quiet supporter of the "Oxford Movement." At the age of twenty-four he became Rawlinsonian Professor of Anglo-Saxon at the University of Oxford, but he relinquished this post in 1816 when he took orders, and after holding livings in Yorkshire and Essex, he was presented to Dogmersfield in 1836, and there remained till his death in 1860. "He was an admirable parish priest, and a man of deep learning, though he shrank from authorship."[1] There can be no doubt that he exercised a great influence over William Butler's mind, and that to his example and instruction much of his curate's successful work was due.

THE REV. CHARLES DYSON TO W. J. B.

DOGMERSFIELD, February 9, 1841, HARTFORD BRIDGE.

DEAR SIR,—You will naturally have expected some communication before this, touching the curacy of Dogmersfield; but owing to my total inability to do anything personally during this unfortunate weather, we have had more difficulties about houses, etc., than I anticipated; and it was indeed only on Sunday afternoon that Mr. Lefroy (my present curate) gave me any information that we could act upon: yesterday, I am sorry to say, was one of my drooping days.

First, respecting the time of entering upon the curacy. I wrote to the bishop the day after you left us, to enquire whether he could grant letters dimissory in case his own ordination was too late. His answer was that his ordination would not take place before July, and that he never gave letters dimissory unless under particular circumstances, which did not apply to your case. Mr. Lefroy, however, kindly undertook to sound him again at an interview he was to have with him about other matters. This interview he had on Saturday last. The bishop was still firm in his refusal about letters dimissory; but good-naturedly said he would provide for the Sunday duty during Mr. Lefroy's absence in May. I believe we shall have no difficulty about the duty till the time of ordination in July. For in May I trust to be equal to the parochial charge myself.

[1] *Dict. Nat. Biog.* "C. Dyson."

Secondly, as to houses, we have had more delays about them than was expected. . . . Word was sent me on Saturday that we could have one at Odiham, which might do for pupils: and on Sunday Mr. Lefroy brought me information that he had found one at Crondall (the village where his family live) which he thought would suit you completely, at a rent of £24. This of all the houses that have been mentioned to us seems most desirable, as being nearest to the church and village; distant two miles and two miles and a half respectively. You have now all the information I can give you at present, and all indeed that is immediately necessary to your decision about your plans. I think, however, I should treat neither you nor my parish fairly if I did not set before you for very serious consideration a doubt that has suggested itself to my own thoughts, and, as I find in conversation, to the thoughts of others; it is this. Whether under the circumstances of your just entering so responsible a profession, with so slight a preparation for its demands and duties as you candidly acknowledged when here, it would be advisable to encumber yourself with pupils for the first year or two, during your professional engagements. I believe I speak the sentiments of experienced men, when I suggest that you will find it difficult to combine the management of pupils even with professional reading; a difficulty that will be much enhanced if joined with the care of a parish, however small, at a distance. For though I trust that during the summer months I shall be able to help you much, both in parochial and Sunday duties, I fear I cannot promise great assistance in the pulpit, that being the difficult matter to my weak lungs. In winter, I must if I follow the advice of my physician, leave the parish entirely to your charge, in all points at least that require personal attendance. If you would take this suggestion into your serious consideration, and decide accordingly to begin without pupils, you will find it less difficult to suit yourself with a residence, and what is more to be valued, more able to give up your time to your profession. Then after some experience of its demands, you will be better able to judge of its compatibility with the care of pupils. There is always much to learn in the entrance of any profession, and I do not know that this ought to be considered less exacting than

any other, where there is so much to be done, so much to
be accounted for. There may be circumstances of another
kind, however, that require you to decide otherwise; and it
would be an intrusion on my part to enter on any consideration about them.[1]

As a good deal of time has necessarily been disposed of in
our enquiries and difficulties here, it would be a convenience
to me if you could come to an early decision and communicate
it to me. If you decide to give me your assistance, such
decision will enable me to be useful on many interesting
points. If you decide against it, it will enable me to look
to other quarters for help. In either case the sooner the
better.

Butler wrote to a relation in January 1841:

. . . For the last two or three weeks my thoughts have
been mainly employed on the subject of Holy Orders, and the
deep and fearful responsibility therewith connected. Most
truly do I feel my own incompetency, though most desirous
and willing to do my duty, and the great advantage of beginning my labours under the tuition of Mr. Dyson. But
as I am entirely at present dependent upon myself, and as
I cannot say when those whom I love far more dearly than
myself may to a certain extent be also dependent upon me,
and also as it would be a sorry return for Mr. Dyson's
kindness to saddle his parish with a pauper curate, I was
anxious, before I gave a definite answer, to make myself sure
in the matter of pupils. . . . I am almost certain of having
two pupils, though if I have but one, I will not hesitate to
accept so agreeable a situation.

He was ordained Deacon at the ensuing July
ordination, and took a house in the neighbouring
parish of Crondall.

While here he became acquainted through the

---

[1] The straitened means of the Butler family were found to make
the taking of pupils a necessity, and in the long run this did not
interfere with his parochial duties.

Dysons with several of their friends who had taken part in the Oxford Movement, such as John Keble, H. E. Manning, Henry Wilberforce, and Charles Marriott. There can be no doubt that this had a powerful effect in determining the character of his religious convictions, and under Mr. Dyson he formed a very high conception of a clergyman's duties and the responsibility of his office.

A letter from one of his sisters describes his ordination as Priest at Farnham Castle.

CRONDALL, July 11, 1842.

We left this at a little after nine yesterday morning. The morning was bright and beautiful, but none of us talked much, as we were thinking of solemn things. . . . About half to eleven we set off for the Castle. It was an odd sight to see troops of men in gowns and hoods winding up the steep hill. (One deacon was lame.) When we got up the hill a laughable sight presented itself. *The* deacon out of the trap putting on his gown and hood under the hedge, like a professional hedge-preacher. The simple vestry work over, we four clomb the hill, the deacon following looking very grave. Then we marched through a long room, deacons and priests on either side in gowns and hoods, some M.A., some B.A., to the drawing room. There we (ladies) sat down and then Mr. Jacob came flitting about to arrange the candidates for ordination. . . . At eleven precisely the people were all settled in their places. I saw very well where I was placed. Mr. —— (who apes the bishop) read the morning service. Then Dr. Dealtry "praught" a long sermon with little meaning in it, but —— looked triumphant at intervals. . . . We had luncheon at the Castle, and then returned to Miss Barlow's, being too tired body and mind to go to afternoon service. They were most kind to us, and made us stay and dine with them ; at half-past six we went to evening service at Farnham church, and on our return we found William returned from the Castle.

In the course of this year he became engaged to his second cousin, Miss Emma Barnett, daughter of George Henry Barnett, Esq., head of the banking firm of Barnett, Hoare & Co. Mrs. Barnett was the daughter of Stratford Canning, and sister of Lord Stratford de Redcliffe, and of William Canning, Canon of Windsor, who afterwards presented his niece's husband to the living of Wantage. To make the connexion more intelligible it may be said that William Butler's maternal grandfather, Capt. Robert Patrick, was brother of Miss Barnett's maternal grandmother, Mrs. Stratford Canning.

His old friend C. J. Vaughan wrote on hearing of his approaching marriage:

May 16, 1843.

Do not be angry with me for offering you my heartiest congratulations on the prospect of your marriage, which I believe will be a real blessing to you, so far from thinking the contrary. And pray do not be above marrying with pupils. I am sure my brother is as happy as a man can be, though he takes pupils.

Shortly before his marriage he moved from Dogmersfield to the curacy of Puttenham, near Guildford, where he had the sole charge of the parish, and continued to take pupils. On the 29th July, 1843, his marriage took place at Putney,[1]

---

[1] The newly married couple visited Hursley on their way to France. Mr. Keble wrote to his brother, Rev. T. Keble:

H. V., Aug. 1, 1843.

. . . We are here quite in the bridal line. . . . Behold at church were Mr. Butler, Dyson's late curate, and his bride, Miss Emma where his eldest son, Arthur John, was born the following year.

In 1844 he was appointed as first incumbent of the newly formed parish of Wareside which had been previously part of the extensive parish of Ware. Through the exertions of a former vicar of Ware, the Rev. H. Coddington, a chapel dedicated to the Holy Trinity had been built at a cost of £1,800, to accommodate 400 people. The population was about 700. As there was no glebe house, William Butler took a house in the adjoining parish of Amwell. Some extracts from his private diary will give an idea of his life at Wareside, and of the spirit in which he devoted all his powers of mind and body to his parishioners' welfare, at the very outset of his life as a parish priest.

Things in my parish have now got into some train. Our schools are working. The people seem to feel that they have a minister and church. Our Clothing Club numbers 140. We have visited every parishioner, and on the whole there seems a fair spirit of obedience to the Church, and desire to be taught and act. My great difficulty is, of course, the lack of a dwelling on the spot, which, although I do not dislike the drive there and back, yet cannot but put me in a great degree in the footing of a stranger to those among whom I ought to be most familiar.

. . . This is the 1st [sic] Sunday after Christmas Day, the continuation, as it were, of the Feast of Circumcision. Of course, I felt myself bound to preach as well as I could, in allusion to that feast, but then came the difficulty. Here am

---

Barnett that was, who did us the honour of including us in their wedding tour ; so I shewed them round the parish, and very nice folk they be or seem to be.

I in a parish of which, I am sure, nine-tenths understand not
a single word of the event in question, intricate too to explain,
embarrassed with allusions to the Jewish Law, of which,
perhaps, all were ignorant. Yet it is impossible to pass these
things, these great feasts, carelessly over; it is really too much
for the conscience to be talking of irrelevant matters when
these great acts of our redemption are concerned. The people
here seem hardly to feel Christmas Day. I observed that they
wore their working-day clothes, and a very scanty attendance
at church in proportion to that on Sundays. This seems
to be the case very generally throughout the country. The
people have utterly lost sight of the great Christian feasts,
and with them the knowledge of the mighty events they
celebrated. The Popish ways may be all very bad, but at
least they teach something of the grounds of our faith
and salvation. The religion of the English peasant is all
confined to generalities. It consists pretty nearly in this:
A general notion that Christ died for sinners, but of Christ,
His Nature or Person, absolutely nothing, nor how He died,
nor for what kind of sinners; that it is all right to go to
church on Sundays, perhaps better twice; that we are all
sinners, none better than his neighbours, but as to any confession of particular sin it irritates them to be exhorted to it;
utterly no notion of self-denial for almsgiving, no notion of
earnest hearty prayer, nor of giving the attention, and striving
to make out and practise the preacher's words. I do not
mean to say that this, even this, is the worst temper of mind
with which a minister can have to deal, or even that all are
of it, but that, this being the case, it becomes particularly
hard to teach. You can never, or very hardly, find any
foundation to rest on. If you talk of the Jewish Church,
they really associate no ideas with it; of the Apostles, I doubt
whether they know in the least who they are; of Jacob,
Isaac, Abraham, they are equally ignorant. They do, perhaps,
know who Adam and Eve were, and why they were driven
from Paradise; also of the Flood, but all the rest of the Old
Testament is absolutely a dead letter to them. They hardly
hear, certainly do not understand, one out of twenty lessons.
In fact, it seems as if our Protestant mode of reading huge
masses of Scripture were utterly defeating its own aim. The

poor do not for the most part know the Bible. Ask any one what the lessons were about, any Sunday you please, and you will soon find the truth of my words. So this morning I had to explain as well as I could, though I feel most imperfectly the whole matter. I began a sermon last night, but was so dissatisfied with it that I threw it bodily into the fire at past eight o'clock. It seemed so unlike what a sermon should be to be giving a bald account of the Institution of the Law; going from Adam through the whole of the Bible in twelve or fourteen pages seemed really too absurd. As it was, I contracted my account very much, merely stating that the Circumcision was the initiatory rite to the Jewish Law, which Law, I said, was given to the Jews to keep them from the heathen and to point to the Messiah. The Messiah (now I am sure they did not understand this) destroyed this Law in fulfilling it, and thereby left us an example of obedience, as well as by the course of doing so working out our salvation. This was the tenor of my sermon. The men's side, as usual, was full, but I cannot get the women to attend church in the morning. Twenty women is an average. They naturally stay at home to cook their husbands' dinners, or fancy that they do. The most of these who do come have husbands, who, I suppose, want their dinners as much as the others.

The present incumbent, the Rev. Robert Higgens, has noted down some "recollections" gleaned from old Wareside parishioners.

The last entry by Mr. Butler in the Register of Baptisms is November 10, 1846.

Walter Tween, the churchwarden, to whom Butler's "Sermons for Working Men" are dedicated, removed from the New House, Wareside, after the death of his father, soon after Mr. Butler left. He has ever since resided at Widford. Walter Tween, now upwards of eighty years of age, ever speaks of Mr. Butler in enthusiastic and affectionate terms. The other day, since the death of the Dean and Mrs. Butler, I paid Walter Tween a visit. Personal recollections came up at hazard, as, "I went on a visit to Mr. Butler at Wantage. The next day was a general fast day. 'Now, Walter, you will have nothing but bread and salt to-morrow. I don't call it a fast to have salt fish and sauce, and then other things as well.' So nothing but bread and salt we had, but they did not seem to mind it."

When the Dean visited me on the occasion of our Church Jubilee in 1891, he went to see Walter Tween. Walter told me how he seemed to be just the Mr. Butler of old times.

All the old people remember Mrs. Butler as actively sharing in her husband's labours. The old women say she was such a plain lady, not, however, at all referring to her features, or to plainness or directness of talk, but to the simplicity of her attire, silently rebuking feminine vanity. On my coming here as incumbent in 1855, I found a godson of Mrs. Butler's characteristically named "Alban" Blake. The names of most of the god-parents were set down in the baptismal register.

We had orders annually to provide a suit of clothes for Alban up to his confirmation time.

Of those who looked forward with great interest to the Dean's visit at the Church Jubilee in 1891, none was so eager as Charles K——. He had been, as a young man, scholar in the night school when Mr. Butler lived at Castlebury, in the latter part of his time. Charles seemed as though he could not enough testify his satisfaction when he saw his old clergyman again. The Dean well remembered him. A particular spelling lesson lingered in his memory: "Now, Charles, a, x, e, what does that spell?" "Surely," says Charles to himself, "I do not know justly, but it must be some tool that I use; a, x, e—bill!"

Then we have, living now in her 90th year, the original caretaker and factotum of the church, Mrs. S——. She held office from 1841 to 1882—a woman not without her good qualities, being honest and trustworthy, but somewhat tart in speech. She remembers how Mr. Butler would come down from Castlebury, for very early service, with his lantern, lighting along the little flock he had gathered on the way.

The beginning of a correspondence with Mr. Keble dates from this period.

Rev. J. Keble to W. J. B.

Hursley Vicarage, July 28, 1845.

My dear Mr. Butler,—I return you Mr. ——'s letters, and also the queries of the *pseudo* Catholic, for both which, specimens of very different sorts, I am much obliged. As to the querist, I felt a strong inclination to help him to one question more against the next edition: viz. (see queries 7 and 14), "Do you not perceive what a security liberal principles are against ill tempers, since those who hold them may use words which sound like sneering (*e.g.* Mr. Deacon Palmer's polemics), of course without any 'sourness' at all."

I sent the other papers to Pusey as you kindly permitted me, and he seems, as you may suppose, greatly pleased with them, especially with the notion in one of them about making a country parson's cottage the rudiments of a sort of monastery. P. expressed a little surprise that one should encourage a man of that stamp to go abroad when there is so much to be done at home. He is always very jealous on that score. I mentioned also to him your suggestion about a "Retreat," which he heartily enters into, and thinks Isaac Williams the person for it, and his neighbourhood the place. I mean shortly to start it to Isaac, but I am a little afraid of his shrinking from it for some reasons. Probably we shall go to Bisley soon, and then it may be all talked over. I love to think over the day you spent with us. God grant that all may go on as you wish; and I hope you will go among many old croakers, and do them as much good as you did me.

My wife, I think, is a little more hearty than she was then. Mr. Parker left us this morning, taking Netley on his way to London. With our very kind regards, believe me, yours ever affectionately,   J. Keble.

You left a sermon of Pusey's here. If you will get another I will pay for it through the Dysons.

Mrs. C. Dyson to W. J. B.

Dogmersfield, Nov. 18, [1845].

. . . For yourself, dear W., what more can your friends wish for you than that you should feel, as you now do, the fear of clinging too much to domestic happiness, and the benefit of being sometimes deprived of it? . . . It is a great comfort in the fierce storm we are passing through to know what you say of yourself. Every one who weathers a point seems to be now a great help to others, in spite of all the subdivisions of opinion amongst them. . . .

W. J. B. TO REV. J. KEBLE.

CASTLE BURY, NEAR WARE,
December 16, 1845.

MY DEAR SIR,—I have been very anxious to write to you for some months past, almost ever since our visit to Hursley in the summer. But chiefly, I believe, because I did not like to trouble you at this particular time, both on account of the time of sorrow and doubtfulness, and especially when we heard so poor an account of dear Mrs. Keble, I have always put it off.

Now, however, I am driven to write by a pressing note from Burns for the enclosed sermons which have been some time in type. In the summer you kindly promised to look at them, and advise me of any serious blunder, of which I do not feel at all secure. They are written to supply the wants of my own parish, who are perhaps more than usually uneducated. And yet, when I came to examine others, servants, small shopkeepers, and the like, I found so dense an ignorance on all religious subjects, and so much misapprehension and distortion of important truths, words seeming to have literally no meaning in their mouths, that I hope they may be useful to others. I have rather endeavoured to place pictures before them, and to make them realise what I talked about, so that they might talk about it among themselves when they get home. If you think that they are likely to do harm, or even not to do good, I am sure I should not wish to add to the great floating capital of sermons in print. Recent matters certainly, in a degree, alter the interest one takes in a work of the kind, making one write with less certainty, and entirely doing away with the *esprit de corps* feeling, yet as I do not know why I am not what I have always supposed I was, a Minister of the English Church, I suppose I ought to try to do the best I can as such. Connected with this is the other matter, about which I meant very much to ask you, the "Retreat." I am certain that hardly a day has passed on which it has not come forcibly before me. If we are to be a Church, surely our clergy must become holy. And I know personally a very large number who, partly from defective superintendence, partly from natural badness, passed the whole time of school and college in a most reckless and unholy way. Then perhaps in a year, without any sort of ἄσκησις, but merely the repentance of a heart not knowing its own sinfulness and yet not wholly devilish, they were ordained. Many of these, my own personal friends, are now repenting most bitterly ; their sins are lying like a heavy load upon them, and torturing them indescribably. They long to confess and go through some prescribed penance. . . . And of course, the same feeling of the weight of unrepented sin hinders them very much in their daily work. Sinful recollections are not cleared away. They seem to recur in the most holy seasons. Prayers are deadened. And it seems gross hypocrisy to be talking to others, and trying to raise them to a high standard of religious feeling. And independently of all this, I can only say for myself that I am in the greatest fear of having all my work secularised. The constant dealing with holy things without any intermission of prayer and watchfulness and fasting and self-examination I find most hardening. Mr. Butterfield said to me the other day that it startled him to see how little reverence for holy places was in men who profess High Church principles, and who certainly started with it.

I am sure that the requisite money would be provided at once, if only some one who could be relied upon would take the thing up. If Mr. Isaac Williams or Mr. Marriott would but take a house and let men come to it for five or six or eight weeks every year, I suppose in different parties, according as it suited, the whole seems provided for. And really one does not see how our priests are to be made holy in any other way.

Pray forgive me for troubling you with all this. But it is very near my heart, and I feel almost hopeless of myself unless I can tear myself from the routine of work and get under some rule of life from time to time. And I know that it is the case with so many others. Of the men of my standing at Cambridge I think very few escaped, and I should think it was much the same at Oxford. And how is it possible for the work of such not to be inherently rotten? I feel very much ashamed of sending all this to you.

My wife and myself are very anxious to hear of Mrs. Keble. As Dogmersfield has not said anything lately, we concluded that she was better. Pray remember us both most kindly to her, although this does not half express what we should like to say. A. is growing a fat, strong boy.

I need not say that the more faults found the more thankful I shall be.

REV. J. KEBLE TO W. J. B.

Ash Wednesday, 1846.

As I hear you have been in Oxford, I daresay you have long ago obtained an answer to the inquiry which you sent me, far more satisfactory than I can send. Why I have been so tardy I can scarce say; except that it is *I*. Marriott wrote me word that he thought something in the nature of a Retreat might be managed at Leeds, under the clergy of St. Saviour's. But failing that he seemed to say it was not impossible that he might be able to do something towards such a plan, especially if a negotiation succeeded which he was then engaged in with Newman for the loan of the house at Littlemore. You probably saw him, and know all this better than I do; and know also that our dear Isaac Williams is in such a state as to make it impossible to look to him; though his decline is very gradual, and the last accounts have seemed as if he were a little better: but the doctors think the same as before of the case.

If you attend the meetings of the C.C.S.,[1] or are in correspondence with them, I should be glad of a *private* answer to this question: Whether a church built of rough granite had better have its quoins of Caen stone or of granite ashlar, the windows being Caen stone?

---

[1] Cambridge Camden Society.

W. J. B. to Rev. J. Keble.

CASTLE BURY, WARE, March 5, 1846.

I am sure you need not apologise for not writing a reply to such as me. But I hope you will be so good on a future occasion when you should have cause to do so, as to say how you yourself are, for I only heard by accident from one whom I saw on Sunday, that you had been confined to your room for some time. I enclose you two opinions on the question you propose, which you will see coincide both in argument and conclusion. One is from Butterfield (1), the other (2) from Webb, acting *pro* C.C.S., on an official sheet. Neither of them knows for whom I ask the question. So that I hope you will be satisfied on this point. I was in Oxford for but one day, and that was spent entirely in one place. Indeed, I went there merely to see Dr. Pusey, and to be away from every one; I don't know why I should hesitate to mention it to you; to make a general confession to him. Of course my thoughts were on this one subject, and though I had said something to him some days before in London about the Retreat, yet we did not recur to it. I can only say that I feel more than ever anxious to see something of the kind established. I believe it would save directly and indirectly many souls, raising the fallen, and strengthening those that stand. For now that it is beginning to be comparatively common for men to make a general confession, it becomes a very serious question, as it seems to me, what they are to do for the future. As far as I know, though many are desirous to make a confession, and to continue it as a habit through life, the thing is all but impossible. Those few who are in the habit of taking general confessions are fully occupied without the addition of having to act as constant spiritual guides. But men might go to a Retreat periodically, and there receive the advantage of regular confession, and the continual preparation for it. When the eye is not single it seems very fearful to have to guide oneself. Pray forgive me for saying all this, but I feel it so strongly that I could not help it, as you mentioned the subject. Littlemore would, I should think, be the very place. . . . I am going shortly to trouble you with a few more sermons, but I hope you will not hesitate, if you think good, to send them back unread.

We are on the point of beginning our house. My wife begs to be very affectionately remembered to Mrs. Keble and yourself. Our little ones are very hearty, and A.'s hair is as curly as ever.

June, 1846, brought the offer of Wantage, a living in the gift of the Dean and Chapter of Windsor, vacant by the death of the Hon. H. L. Hobart, D.D., Dean of Windsor, which was made by Mrs. Butler's uncle, William Canning, Canon of Windsor. The living was a good one from a pecuniary point of view, and had been held for a century and a half by non-resident vicars, who placed a curate in the vicarage on a very modest stipend. The place, an ancient little market town lying on the northern edge of the Berkshire Downs, offered few attractions except the opportunity which it gave of hard work for the Church on "Tractarian" principles. It had, however, been the birthplace of two eminent Englishmen—King Alfred and Bishop Butler. This gave the place, insignificant in itself, a certain distinction. Letters written at the time give William Butler's first impressions of the future scene of his labours, and the misgivings and anxieties with which he entered on what proved to be the chief work of his life.

W. J. B. TO HIS WIFE.

BEAR INN, WANTAGE,
Sunday Evening [June, 1846].

. . . My friend here is "Boots," a most agreeable personage, who lionised me over the town, and with whom I confer on train lists, etc. I suspect he guesses my errand, for he just informed me confidentially that he heard great praise of my performance this morning. Sexton in gallery declared he heard the words as clear as if he was close to me. I mention this because one wants rather to know what impression a most deliberate intonation produces in a new place. . . . At the station when I got my ticket a young man, hearing me ask for Faringdon Road, asked if I were going to Wantage. He was. I thought I might pick him a little, and so we joined company. But he knew very little about it. He was a banker's clerk, seemed simple-minded and good; we took a gig together from Faringdon Road to Wantage. I paid chiefly, but saved something by this arrangement. Arrived here at twelve. Took a glass of ale and went to bed, tired as many cats. This morning I got up early and indited a note to Mr. B——,[1] explaining my case. He answered me very kindly, asking me to dinner, etc. He is a very short fat little man, perhaps fifty-six years of age or less, very kind and hospitable, with a good deal of general knowledge and fun about him. I like him very much indeed. I took morning service. Really, at times, owing to the strange differences in singing, the slovenly way of conducting the services, the Communion service from reading desk, etc., I hardly knew what I was doing. It seemed so very odd to end with the Nicene Creed. B——'s sermon was drier than hay. Not a word of sense in it. I only wonder so many people can sit through such discourses. I was as fidgety as possible, and were I likely to undergo such things continually I must join one of the sects with which Wantage is rife. Lengthy, too. "This leads me to consider," and all that. Sermon over I went to his house. I wished to preach in the evening solely to escape another of these preachments. But I thought I might be caught out if I praught from type, so, after considering the pros and cons, I determined not. . . . I dined with Mr. B——. After dinner we walked to Grove, in the patronage of Wantage. The church and parsonage were built by Dr. Cotton, of Worcester. And who, think you, is the incumbent? *Mr. Simcox Bricknell*, the man who wrote circulars about the Tractarians. He was at home, and not a bad fellow after all. Now it is past eleven. To-morrow I shall leave this at a half to seven, get to Didcot, thence to

[1] The curate in charge.

Oxford, where I shall call on Dr. Pusey. Then to Reading, whence I shall to Dogmersfield. . . . There will be a terrible coil about building. There is scarcely any glebe. Garden is sunk; churchyard cramped; house stands very low; air is bracing, so you will grow fat. Wantage Downs are famous. I like the looks of the people. They speak a very rough dialect. If we have this it *will* make a strange difference in our way of living, not our household arrangements, but in all our thoughts and ways. I tremble to think of it. And yet, on the whole, I rather hope my advisers will bid me take it. If —— have it, *he will not reside*. He came here immediately after the Dean's death and saw Mr. B——. This is, of course, a consideration. I can no more. This is horrid rubbish, but my pen has been steaming along.

P.S.—I have seen Dr. Pusey. He rests on Mr. Dyson, but considers it doubtful whether I ought to leave my present charge.

W. J. B. to J. L. Butler, Esq.

[June 29, 1846.]

My dear Father,—I wished to get Mr. Dyson's letter before writing to you again. We seemed to have exhausted all arguments on both sides of the question, all that remained being the actual decision. Mr. Dyson writes thus: "So far from altering the view I took respecting your acceptance of Wantage, reconsideration only confirms me in the opinion I gave you when here, that on the balance of pros and cons it was advisable that you should accept it. It was, indeed, chiefly on the consideration of the very great usefulness to that large parish . . . that I thought it advisable for you to give up your present charge at Wareside in exchange for Wantage. It certainly gives you a noble opportunity of doing God service through His Church, and acting on essential Church principles. At the same time I must say that, unless I were confident you would act on such principles both conscientiously and judiciously, in a spirit of charity and moderation as well as zeal, I would never advise you to undertake it. Under a different spirit such a parish would be a continual source of regret and discomfort to one of your disposition. I anticipate also a most important benefit to yourself in the larger opportunity you will have for professional reading and self-communication when your time and thoughts will be less distracted by so many demands from pupils as you now have. I take it for granted, in saying this, that you will have a good staff of curates to share your labours and give you room for rest." He writes on most kindly and sensibly, but this is the gist of his letter. So that I now hesitate no longer. I wrote to Mr. Canning by this morning's post to advise him of this, and I shall expect to hear very soon from the Chapter Clerk. I saw the Bishop of Oxford on Friday at the House of Lords. He was very kind and bland, and told me distinctly that he thought I ought to accept the charge, looking on it as a sort of call. Also he perfectly agreed to my intention of remaining here for some months to come. In the course of a few weeks I shall go there again, and make various inquiries about the condition of the house, dilapidations, etc.

W. J. B. TO ——.

AMWELL, WARE, July 9, 1846.

. . . In this matter of Wantage it seems to me strange that you should not understand how very serious a thing it is for one like myself, only 28 years old, and very much off the sort of study and preparation which a country town needs, to take upon myself the care of 3000 souls, living souls, to prepare for eternity. It certainly seems strange that you should not understand that a state of doubtfulness must come over me, fear for my own soul, and consideration for others. How am I to solve my doubts? Could such considerations as position, income, and the like come for a moment into calculation? *First Death, then the Judgement.* What have position in this miserable world, income, comforts, to do with such as these? . . . And then you do not understand that we should feel grief at leaving a work in which we delight, and terror (I do not regret the word) in undertaking so fearful a work as the charge of 3000 souls, who at present are in a most unsatisfactory condition. How little can you know of the condition of these market towns. They are the very most troublesome, most painful spots of Christ's Heritage, the Church in England. Not a clergyman engaged in them but will tell you that his heart sinks within him. And who am I, to take such a labour on myself? As for "seeing difficulties" and the like, it would be worse than foolish to shut my eyes to them. I do see the difficulties, and I only pray that I may see them tenfold more strongly than I do. This does not in the least imply that I shall not work hard to overcome them. Of course I shall. But naturally the prospect makes me sad and thoughtful. . . . I own I dread the congratulations of my friends on an occasion which involves so fearful a responsibility. And if I were to appear to hug them, I should only be deceitful. Let my friends comfort me, pray for me, advise me, make allowances for me, but not congratulate me as though I had gained a great step in life. When Death and Judgement, Heaven and Hell, are the matters in consideration, both for myself and so many others, ought I not to have done as I have done—shunned to the greatest possible degree every worldly question? And now to the course of life which I look to pursue at Wantage. I shall indeed try to become far more self-denying than I have ever been before. I shall certainly spend what money I have altogether on the place, and I shall try to get two or three men with me who will thoroughly sympathise and work with me. If I am fit for such a work, it is quite clear that I ought to be able to guide myself, or rather to know where to seek for guidance. And as I have taken Mr. Dyson's advice in one point, it would be foolish and wrong not to carry it out.

W. J. B. TO REV. J. KEBLE.

AMWELL, WARE, July 22, 1846.

I thank you very much for thinking of me and mine. It is indeed a strengthening to have the good wishes of so many and such, but I am nevertheless very much oppressed with the prospect of Wantage. I thought at one time that I should like work of this kind, but now that it has come to me I dread it very much. So many difficult points seem to arise—how much to do, how much not to do; how to encourage a Catholic $\mathring{\eta}\theta o\varsigma$ under the disadvantage of Protestant or Puritan ways, and then that whole class of questions which connect themselves with Dissenters. And then one feels so much fear as to how best to begin, whether to start strenuously and try to gain something in this way, or to wait and watch opportunities. I am not going to Wantage till Christmas, which will give me some time for reflection, and also enable me to leave this place more satisfactorily. Next Monday my wife, youngsters, and I myself go to Dogmersfield, she to remain a fortnight there, while I go to Littlemore. I shall return to Dogmersfield on Monday, August 10. We should like very much to spend a day at Hursley, if you could take us in. And we could bring or leave our little ones as would be most convenient to you and Mrs. Keble. . . . May I trouble you to look at the enclosed ?

My wife desires me to say how often she thinks of the kindness of Mrs. Keble and yourself. A. has quite outgrown babyhood.

Rev. J. Keble to W. J. B.

Hursley, Aug. 3, 1846.

Forgive my not answering you sooner. I cannot say that I have much excuse, for I have had a sort of sore throat which has kept me from duty, and pretty much at home, so that I had not much to do besides answering letters. But somehow it has crept on from day to day. I don't wonder at your many musings about Wantage, but I feel so sure that you are right in going there, that I cannot doubt your being guided, from day to day, and from week to week, to the right course of proceeding. It is a good omen, *Butler* of *Wantage*. And Littlemore, I trust, will be a good preparation for it. We shall be very glad to see you here next week, if you can manage it; but, unfortunately, we are unable to give you much choice of time. I am going, I believe, to Leamington on Monday, the 10th, for one day only, and on the 13th we rather expect some of the Irish Lefroys, who will fill our house; so that you seem put up between the 11th and 12th, if it must be that week. If those days, or any part of them, will suit you, we shall be very glad to see you, *all four*.

I have read your sermons[1] twice over, with much interest,

---

[1] *Sermons for Working Men*. Masters. 1847.

and have made a few corrections which I hope will not puzzle
you or the printer. I should say that some of the sentences
would be the better for shortening. I will just ask you in
reference to what you say in p. 92 as to the mystical interpretation—Should you not suppose it in the present rather a
matter of tradition from the Apostles, however the details of
it are the reward of holy lives and persevering study ?

I am very desirous of finding someone who will undertake
the Curacy of Shoreditch under an old friend of mine, an
excellent but a very nervous fellow—the stipend £100 a
year with a house said to be worth £50—only it is very
uncomfortable, as I daresay you know, from the *Ware*-ishness
of the people, as well as the hard work. If someone would
have the same mind with which you go to Wantage, that
would be just the thing. How glad I should be if you did
happen to know of any one. Will it be giving you too much
trouble to inquire at Cambridge for me.

W. J. B. TO REV. J. KEBLE.

LITTLEMORE, Friday [Aug., 1846].

Thank you very much for your kind words and the trouble
you have taken for my sermons. I fear that I shall not be able
to get the corrections (much as they are wanted) made in p. 86,
for that sermon is the fair proof, after the revise, merely printed
off to fill up the sheet. Not having my books about me I really
cannot find whence I got that mystical interpretation. My impression is that some outline of it struck me some time ago, but
that I feared to write it till I found it confirmed. If I mistake
not, the same view is more or less worked out in 'the Nativity.'
I do feel it the greatest comfort in this Wantage business that I
am not following my own guidance, and that so many hold one
view on the subject. If only I am strong enough for it (I don't
mean physically), it is of course important for the spread of true
Church principles that I should not decline it, being that probably
it would be passed on to some other views. I have long felt,
though I never thought myself fit but for the very smallest
approach to such a work, that farmers and shopkeepers should be
leavened with the Church. At present they are heathens in all
but one thing. Marriott's College seems the way of doing it,

giving these classes a vested interest, so to speak, in the clergy. I cannot help thinking that the domestic influence of the clergy is what really tells, or at least tells most. One may see this in the upper ranks, where a son in Holy Orders will leaven a whole 'gens.' And one should suppose that the same would tell with even greater force in the lower and less educated classes. But I cannot help thinking that a parish priest may, if he have the right way of setting to work, manage a good deal of this. I am not quite sure whether 'Butler of Wantage' is not, on a calcula-tion of chances, against me. One should suppose that *he* would exhaust the powers of Wantage to produce Butlers, and that future B.'s would [be] the poorest of their species.

All this time I have not said that the two days which you mention are the very two that suit us best—Tuesday and Wed-nesday—and we will find our way to Hursley by an afternoon train. I must leave this to my wife to settle, as she knows the trains and I do not. She will write. I have enjoyed my time here very much.

On reading your letter again, I see I mistook your words. I thought you asked whence it came? I see now that you warn me against a 'blundering' way of putting it, which shall be cor-rected. I will write to Cambridge, but Shoreditch will frighten most men.

W. J. B. to Rev. J. Keble.

Castle Bury, Ware, Nov. 17, 1846.

May I ask you to cast your eye over the enclosed? I feel rather doubtful whether in endeavouring to make things plain and popular I am not grounding too much on illustration. I was at Cambridge a few weeks since, and I tried to get some men to work up a cheap hostelry to be connected with a College as Colleges are with the University. This seems feasible enough, for all Colleges at Cambridge admit men lodging in the town, and I do not well see how, when they license every tradesman or other who applies, they could refuse a clergyman. This is all that would be required from the authorities, and with this any one willing for the work might take a house and work his men as he pleased; of course, seeing that they attended Hall and Chapel and kept to the other duties of their College. Marriott wrote to me suggesting an old building called the

School of Pythagoras for some such purpose. But we could not get this, and on the whole I did not see much spirit at Cambridge to commence an undertaking of the kind. Cambridge is as "flat" as possible. Some of those from whom I expected most are taking up queer original views of their own, as it were to hold Church views without the odium connected with them, drawing some little difference, just enough to say, "I don't agree with so-and-so." I came away more disheartened than I ever remember myself before. Carus and his friends are active enough in their way, and no doubt keep up a certain degree of morality and piety. But then a very large body of men never can feel with them, and these are left without guide or comfort. . . . We go to Wantage after Christmas.

REV. J. KEBLE TO W. J. B.

HURSLEY, Nov. 18, 1846.

It does not seem to me that in this sheet at least you have fallen into the error which you apprehend. And I should suppose that your fear of it will be a great security against it. To a certain extent, I suppose it was intended that each person should have his own impressions from the Parables and similes of Scriptures, as in life from the very things themselves; and that those impressions, being communicated, should do good. I don't remember anything in your sermons which startles one as going beyond this.

Your notion of a Cambridge Hospitium seems a very good one. I trust it will be borne in mind. If your friends with the "queer views" will only act as such an institution requires, I think we may bear with their little distinctions, which are but too natural in these times, when hardly two Churchmen speak alike.

All good be with you, your family, your parishes, and your *successor*, the thought of whom must be a great comfort to you. Thank you for mentioning A.

MRS. C. DYSON TO W. J. B.

[Probably about Christmas, 1846.]

. . . Thank you, from my heart, for your greetings of the season, and for your gift of the Prayers, which seem to me

more suitable than any collection we have seen; and the
prefatory rules must be useful. Such a collection, I suppose,
always requires that the people should be trained beforehand
to wish for it, as your people would be. Our curate observed
that he wished the print were larger, because the persons most
likely to use the Prayers may have to use it in the dusk, and
he finds the bad print of good books is really a great hindrance
with the poor. However, in the case of daily Prayers it may
be supposed they will soon be learnt by heart. In the case
of such books as Dr. Hook's *Meditations for Every Day*, which
seems in itself so good, it is a great objection. Of course, the
answer is, the expense.

We understand your misgivings about Wantage. But those
who know you well do not misgive—certainly not the Nest.[1]
There must be much to dishearten, but still a little done, a
few good Church-people trained, is a great thing in such a
place. . . . That poor dear Wareside will always be a pleasant
spot in your memory. Perhaps it would have been too much
of a romance not to be a snare, had it gone on as hitherto;
anyhow it is pleasant to know and think of. . . .

[1] A pet name among the Dysons' friends for Dogmersfield Rectory.

CHAPTER III.

TROUBLED TIMES.

THE new vicar took up his residence in Wantage in the beginning of 1847, and was alone there for a few weeks while the old vicarage (dating, it is said, from the sixteenth century) was being made habitable for his wife and children. Wantage possesses a severe, though healthy, climate, and he suffered considerably from cold and general discomfort during those early days, while he was trying to devise the best means of solving the many problems that lay before him.

W. J. B. TO HIS WIFE.

[Jan., 1847.]

You mustn't grumble at work. I only wish you were at Wantage just now and you would see. . . . My cold changed, or rather superadded influenza, bad taste and smell, etc., but on the whole I am better to-day, though far from well. V. came, to my great joy, yesterday at dinner time and we walked about a little. Fancy the difference between a village and a town; a funeral and baptism on Friday, two funerals yesterday. The number of deaths since Dec. 16 to now is 20; this is more than the average, about one a week. Then the horrid apathy and irreverence of the whole concern, the crowd of idlers, etc., made me rather down-hearted. The churchyard is in an abominable state. It ought at once to be remedied, so noisy and unclean, with long rank grass all over it. Bury me at Wareside. Railroad will take me cheap. After two or three false starts I began and wrote a sermon which under all circumstances will do, I hope. I have not seen the churchwarden, but as I spoke pretty plainly I shall ask him if it were too plain. You shall see it. V. thought it would do very well. We began Communion service from altar. It is rather lonely work without a soul but children near one. I placed V. in the stalls. Might we see them filled one day with clergy and choir. Those stalls really are a great point. I did all the morning and shall leave V. to do all the afternoon service. I must go to Oxford this week to be appointed surrogate, which is an office worth £20 or £25 per annum—likewise to get a cassock. . . . My room smokes furiously, and I have been obliged to sit with window open all this day. . . .

This is much the coldest house I ever lived in. My study has never been as high as 'temperate,' and bedroom, in spite of a fire, is so cold that I cannot sleep.

W. J. B. TO HIS WIFE.

[Jan. 31, 1847.]

. . . This day has been spent between visiting and being visited. I drove over to Sparsholt to call on the rural dean. He wrote last night to consult me about one or two points connected with a letter from the Bishop. He, however, was out, but his wife was at home, a very ladylike sensible and kind woman, whom, I think, you will like. . . . Then, as usual, I visited (1) the Ham people, a schoolmaster with a commercial school, a respectable pedagogue who might start A., if need be, i.e. if you forget your Latin. (2) A Roman Catholic family named Hunt, builders in Wantage. I sat and chatted some time. When I went away they gave me their card, and then I thought it right distinctly to tell them that I could not employ them in church work. I explained the circumstances and left them, I believe, quite friendly. (3) An old maid named Aldworth, reminding me in a small way of Miss ———, and seemingly good and kind. (4) A 'young ladies'' academy, etc., etc. In all I mooted the

school question, and all seemed to agree with me and to be willing
to help. The congregation of yesterday seems to have been the
talk of the place, so we must try to strike while the iron is hot.
. . . Two more funerals this morning. I do wish we had some
parish books. It is slow work copying and copying, as we do
now, all the rough notes of our visiting, without the satisfaction of
seeing them in some form. V. works like a horse. . . .

REV. J. KEBLE TO W. J. B.

HURSLEY, Jan. 28, 1847.

By this time I imagine you settled at Wantage and deep
in your work; wherein, such as I am, I would desire most
heartily to bid you God-speed. I know you have enough and
too much to do; yet I am about to ask two favours of you,
which may give you more or less trouble. They both relate
more or less to our dear friend Dr. Pusey. First, do you by
any chance know of a person whom you can recommend as a
fit and likely successor to Mr. Ward at St. Saviour's, now made
vacant in such a heart-breaking way? You know, of course,
the nature of the place, that it was meant to be a sort of College
of Curates, and in a humble way an effort at Anglican asceticism.
Now, whoever goes must go with a consciousness that the place
is under a sort of cloud, and that whatever sympathies he has
with Pusey must be kept under jealous control, else he will
never be able to go on with the vicar of Leeds. Indeed, I
shall tell Pusey that if the choice lies between an ascetic who
will be suspected and an ordinary hard-working curate such as
Hook would approve of, I should recommend the latter, under
present circumstances. The whole affair is a severe stab to
Pusey; only he is the sort of person whom nothing really hurts.
The other matter is a plan which P. and Marriott are
starting for a popular commentary on the whole Scriptures, on
patristic principles, to supersede Scott and Henry's, and other
such ordinary uncatholic performances. Do you think you could
find time for a portion of it? It might very well serve first in
the way of catechetical or pulpit exposition; and it will, of
course, be a long time about, so that you might take your time.

We have this day begun our work about the Church, but it
will be very slow for a long time.

W. J. B. TO REV. J. KEBLE.

WANTAGE VICARAGE, BERKS,
4th S. aft. Ep., 1846 [7].

I was not at Wantage when your letter arrived. It journeyed after me to London, and reached me on the very day on which I set out to fix myself here. This is my reason for the delay in answering it. Thank you most deeply for all your kindness. Indeed one wants wishes and more than wishes in such a work as this at Wantage. The whole population is ignorant and apathetic, and some of their ways, after dear Wareside, quite startle me. Yet there seems some sort of good old-fashioned feeling too, and so far I have met with great kindness from all. V. is with me, and this is our first Sunday. There are some very good remains in the church, among other points eighteen beautifully carved stalls in the chancel. Would that I could fill them with clergy and choir. However, I must not run on about Wantage, but answer your two questions. . . . Touching the commentary, I should be very glad to take a part, provided my work were carefully revised by an abler hand than myself, and that I had time. Whatever I do must be in the New Testament, for my knowledge of Hebrew is very imperfect indeed, the very least possible.

I am so very glad to hear of your church beginning. Slow work is, I suppose, the right work. At least, I am working myself into that belief. I hope that you will be able to receive us in the summer, and that we shall have the chance of seeing it.

. . . I have directed a small compilation of *Working Men's Prayers*, which I made out as a parting present to Wareside, to be sent to you.

REV. C. DYSON TO W. J. B.

DOGMERSFIELD RECTORY,
HARTFORD BRIDGE, May 12, 1847.

You will see I have worked myself up to answer your note with my own hand, which take as a proof that I set some value on your communication. Had you sent your question about teaching or suppressing the Church Catechism before you had the Bishop's reply, I should have said decidedly, Do not

D

give up the Catechism. If yours is to be a *Church* school that is one of the distinctive marks of it. Nor do I think you would find much (if any) difficulty with Dissenting parents of children who come to the school. In all the parishes I have been charged with I do not remember any objection being made by Dissenters to teaching their children the Catechism, except by your old acquaintance, John Burrows, the blacksmith here; and he gave way immediately. But since you asked the Bishop's advice and received his answer, your question is entangled with more difficulty. Yet after considering his answers, which seem at first to advise the suppression of the Church Catechism *quoad* Dissenters' children, as well as the respect and deference due to him after consulting him, I think I see a way by which you may follow your own convictions without offence. The first answer seems to me to be so qualified, and limited by the two following (for if "the Dissenters have nothing to do with the school"; and "the tone and management of the school are to be *essentially* Church," what need to make any break in the school teaching for a supposed possible objection on their part?) that you may reasonably take the Bishop's advice as *permissive* and not *injunctive*; *e.g.* he sanctions your conceding the point if advanced by the Dissenters, and the school cannot be accomplished without it; but does not recommend the concession without such necessity. I should suppose, indeed, that he would be really glad if you could go on with the school without it. That at least is the way in which you may quite respectfully take his advice. . . .

The Ven. Alfred Pott, Archdeacon of Berks, gives his recollections of William Butler's work in the Diocese of Oxford, which in 1847 had recently come under the vigorous rule of Bishop Samuel Wilberforce.

I am asked to put on paper some of my recollections of the work of Dean Butler in the Diocese of Oxford, with which we were both associated for so many years. From the time that he came to Wantage until the time of his leaving it we were fellow-workers in almost every important Diocesan movement.

My own intimacy with Bishop Wilberforce dated from the period of my ordination as priest at Christmas, 1846, and Butler took the vicarage of Wantage, I think, in January, 1847. I well remember his coming to Cuddesdon to consult the Bishop as to his accepting the vicarage. I was a young curate, and he not many years my senior. Of his parochial work it is not for me to speak. Others more closely connected with him in that work will speak of the wonderful way in which his energy and devotion regenerated the dormant spiritual life of an insignificant Berkshire town, and raised it to the position which it now holds. I remember one sentence in a letter of Bishop Wilberforce, where he says, "Butler's work is amazing." No one knew better than that great Bishop how to pick his men, and to make them all work under him for the good of his Diocese. It will be remembered how in those years that Diocese needed entire new organization as much as did the parish of Wantage. Consisting, as it had done from the days of Henry the Eighth, of the one county of Oxford, and even that curtailed by large peculiars, excepted from the Bishop's jurisdiction, the See had been occupied by a succession of prelates, holding with the bishopric other dignities, ecclesiastical or academical, in *commendam*, to make up the scanty endowments of the See. Then, among the many changes of our own day, the county of Berks had been taken from the See of Salisbury, in the later years of Bishop Bagot, and added to Oxford. And similarly the county of Buckingham was taken from Lincoln and thrown into Oxford on the accession of Bishop Wilberforce. It needed the genius of a statesman to consolidate these heterogeneous elements into one organic whole—still more to make the reality of Episcopal influence felt through every part of so large an area. The Bishop was supported by a noble body of officers. His Rural Deans especially gathered round him (to use a likeness suggested by one of them) like Napoleon's marshals round the Emperor. Nearly all of that company have passed away. While they continued, Butler, who became one of the body soon after he came into the Diocese, held a very prominent place. Younger in years than many of his fellows, and in some cases, it must be allowed, looked upon with a slight measure of suspicion, his enthusiasm and energy, and, above all, his strong common-sense, soon won for him a recognised position. The Bishop himself was keenly alive to his value. Butler was

never very tolerant of carelessness or neglect of duty in those
around him, and this in itself did sometimes provoke impatient
discontent on the part of those whose slothfulness was rebuked
by his activity.   I remember one of his neighbours complaining
to the Bishop. "Mr. Butler, my Lord, seems to have acquired
an undue hold upon us.   Every one is growing to look upon him
as the one authority in the Deanery."   "Indeed," replied the
Bishop, "I am truly glad to hear it ; that is exactly as I should
wish it to be."

Among the many instrumentalities for stirring up the life of the
Diocese, Bishop Wilberforce's "missions" occupied a prominent
place.   The missions of that period were altogether different in
their organization from the movements known by that name now.
They were held usually in the Lent Ember season.   The Bishop
would gather round him a body of picked clergy of various
shades of religious opinion, some from his own Diocese, some
from a distance, but all concentrated in some one important
centre.   From that centre they radiated to every neighbouring
village ready to receive them, the Bishop himself usually remaining
at the centre, himself celebrating Communion daily and preaching
several times during the week, as a rule opening the mission with
a sermon on the first Sunday of the Ember week, and closing
it with an evening sermon on the last Sunday.   On this last
Sunday the ordination was held at the central church, thus
bringing the realities of the apostolic communion before a number
who had very probably never seen an ordination in their lives,
and were ignorant for the most part of what an ordination
was.   The first, I think, of these missions was at Wantage.
I well remember the little old dilapidated vicarage at the west
end of the church where the lime trees now grow, where
evening after evening the Bishop gathered his mission clergy
and received from them reports of their day's work.   Almost
all the important towns of the Diocese enjoyed these helps
afterwards, and there were few in which the vicar of Wantage
did not take his part.

Another most important organization, which has lasted down
to our time, was the formation of the three Diocesan societies—
Education, Church-building, Spiritual Aid ; those who know something of the great educational establishments which have sprung
up in Wantage itself, under the vicar's fostering care, will readily

believe that he was a very important factor in the working of every educational effort for the whole Diocese. At the quarterly meetings in Oxford, at the gatherings of inspectors at Cuddesdon, in the formation of such institutions as our Training College at Culham, and in the management of that College, up to the time of his leaving the Diocese, he was ever an active and a wise counsellor. In the midst of all his hard work at Wantage he held for many years the office of Bishop's Inspector for the Deanery. In his examinations of schools he was impatient of slovenliness and inaccuracy, and did sometimes provoke a measure of resentment on the part of those who were themselves slovenly or inaccurate. But any one who had been with him in his own schools knew how little he tolerated such defects among his own teachers or children. It has been well said, if he was severe upon others, he was most severe of all upon himself.

It will be remembered that in looking back upon his early days in our Diocese, we are recalling a period when the whole of the present elementary educational system was in its infancy. We had to watch a development which, little by little, has grown into an organisation which we cannot now contemplate without some anxiety. But here too his strong good sense was ready to discriminate between the good and the evil inherent in the state system of education. He, and I myself, lived through a period, at the beginning of which the Department came to us, asking us to receive almost as a matter of favour to themselves, their money grants and their inspection, into a period when that inspection has become compulsory and their money grants indispensable. From the first he readily accepted the good part of the system, and did what lay in him to eliminate the bad. While you make the faith of the Church the ground-work of all your teaching, not only of what is called the religious element,—while you do this, he would say, do not reject any help offered tending to make any part of your teaching more perfect. I recollect in those early days one of his own teachers doubting whether she ought to have anything to do with Government help, or Government certificates and examinations, as things savouring of the world and not of the Church. "Use all such helps," said the vicar; "reject none of them. If the great Cham of Tartary were to open an examination I would go in for it if it would in any way help on my school in any

branch of knowledge." But an account of the vicar's work
in Wantage itself will be more fully given by another hand.

One more recollection. In the year 1853 Bishop Wilberforce
proposed to me the building of a Theological College at
Cuddesdon. The first person of whom I thought as a counsellor
in the matter was the vicar of Wantage, and I at once went
thither to talk over the matter with him. It was by no means
the easy matter which it may now seem to carry out such a
scheme, especially within eight miles of Oxford. There were
many adversaries, even among those who were usually loyal
supporters of the Bishop. It is to the enthusiastic and steady
support of Butler, and the strong faith of the Bishop himself
and some few staunch friends in the necessity for such institutions,
that Cuddesdon owed its beginnings. And those who can call
to mind those days under myself, Canon Liddon, and the Bishop
of Lincoln, will bear witness to the help given to all of us by
the same generous friend in times of trouble and rebuke and
blasphemy.

It would be easy, associated as I was for so many years with
Butler, to speak of other parts of his labours ("amazing,"
as Bishop Wilberforce called them), but it is of his Diocesan
work that I have been asked to recall some memories. There
are few (if any) left besides myself who lived through the
whole period of his life in the Oxford Diocese; of Wantage, the
Sisterhood, Worcester, Lincoln, others will doubtless be asked
to tell. Some memories are, after all, short-lived, but the work
itself survives, and the Diocese is still reaping the harvest which
was sown by the vicar of Wantage and Bishop Wilberforce.

The parish of which William Butler had now
become vicar was one that enjoyed an evil reputation.
"Black Wantage," as it was called, was one of those
half-urban, half-rural parishes which are in many
respects most difficult to manage, combining neither
the advantages of town or country. As the birthplace
of King Alfred and Bishop Butler it is not without
historical associations, but its local importance consisted solely in being the corn market of the farmers

in the Vale of White Horse. There were no resident gentry. Rope-making had been the staple industry, but it was in its decline, and an iron foundry was taking its place. There was a stately cruciform church, but the internal arrangements were far from being decent or in order, although the general effect was imposing—"a church that would awe people into devotion," as was said by one of the great architects of the day. The "Latin school" and a dame school occupied the churchyard, the latter attended by only thirty-six children out of a population of 3282. The vicarage, an ancient, thatched, dilapidated building, stood at the west end of the church. A graphic picture of Wantage is drawn in the *Bristol Times*, under date December 1847, only a few months after the new vicar's arrival, which shows how he had already begun to make his mark on the place.

Wantage, says the anonymous writer, though it has two inns, three tailors and drapers, one policeman, a brace of watchmen, and gas lamps, is little better than streets of farm-houses confronting each other, with flocks and herds feeding out in the rear. . . . While strolling about on Saturday evening I found the church door open, and entered. There were some men at work repairing and restoring the chancel. . . . The new clergyman is of the new school—zealous, anxious, ever in his work. He is evidently one of the race of clergymen who have of late years sprung up to replace the old high-and-dry denomination, and compete in energy and zeal with the evangelical order—one of a class who emerged from their Colleges at Oxford and Cambridge with ideas already formed of pastoral duty, with plans prepared and purposes fixed to carry them out with a kind of Christian chivalry. If some of them have lacked discretion, none of them have been deficient in devotedness, and many have

awakened a new spirit in the parishes over which they were
placed, filling churches that before, morning and evening,
boasted but a cheerless few, and crowding schools that before were
neglected and in decay. This, I learnt, had been the case here.
The present incumbent came after a rector [sic] with whom he
stood strongly contrasted. Wantage has been one of those places
which have commonly been considered an appanage to some
cathedral stall, or a fat gift for some favoured pluralist, who
thought it no sin, as Lord Eldon said, "to shear the sheep he did
not feed." The Dean of St. George's Chapel, at Windsor, was
the last of the favoured few to whom Wantage fell. Twice a year
he arrived with a carpet bag at the Bear Inn, received his tithes,
and returned, without leaving either his carpet bag or his blessing behind him. After such a pastor, any ordinary conscientious
clergyman must have been a change for the better; and the
present being more than commonly painstaking, the consequences
of increased zeal began to be gradually seen in increased congregations; pew doors, the latches of which had rusted in their
staples, were gradually opened; seats, from which the moths had
not been disturbed for years, began to fill; the dry-rot that
extended from pews to pulpit, and pulpit to pews, was stayed;
and on the Sunday I was there the edifice was completely filled
with smock-frocks and broadcloth. I liked the sermon, because I
thought it an original one; none of those firstly, secondly, and
thirdly compilations one hears too often, in nine cases out of ten,
and which all appear to be cut out of the same pattern.

The vicar began at once to cope with the many
difficulties that faced him in his new parish. One
was in the shape of the small hamlet of Charlton,
about a mile from the parish church, and inhabited
only by two farmers and their labourers, with the few
tradesmen who supplied their simple wants. The little
place had been utterly neglected—by Dissent as well
as by the Church—but the awakening of spiritual life
in Wantage roused the nonconformists to action, and
it seemed probable that a meeting house would be

built in the village which would certainly have been thenceforward lost to the Church. The vicar, however, forestalled them. He secured a suitable site, applied to his friend Mr. Butterfield for plans for a simple brick church to be built at a cost of £200, and on 27th April, 1848, the first stone was laid by his mother. The church was dedicated to the Holy Trinity, and was opened in August of the same year. A school soon followed. The plan for Charlton church, together with other parochial matters, is mentioned in a letter to Bishop Wilberforce.

W. J. B. TO BISHOP OF OXFORD.

WANTAGE VICARAGE, November 18, 1847.

MY LORD,—The result of our confirmation has been most satisfactory, so far, at least, as one can judge, both as regards the confirmed and the rest of the congregation present. Several of the latter said that it was to them like being confirmed over again themselves. One of our lawyers told me that he had forgotten all about his own confirmation, but this he never should forget as long as he lived. About 70 of the confirmed have become communicants, and on Oct. 31, when I administered the Sacrament, 180 were present. This seems to give an opening for a better state of things, and to justify a weekly Communion, which I for one, and the rest of our cleric party, most earnestly desire. On the Sunday which I mentioned we were in church till near half-past two, which alone seems to make a change of some kind needful. I should propose a weekly Communion at some early hour, as eight o'clock, except on the first Sunday in each month, when I would keep to the former time, *viz.* after the morning service. Will you kindly write me a word in reply to this?

Butterfield has given me drawings for a church, or rather a piece of a church, with room for about 90 people, which can be built for £120, and which will have an ecclesiastical character.

I think also that I can get a morsel of land off a little green
on which to build it. The building is contrived so as to receive
more wall, a chancel, tower, and good windows whenever money
comes to pay for them.

I shall have to trouble your Lordship again with the result
of the deliberations of the School Committee. I thought we
might resolve on some memorial to the Government, requesting
assistance, but declining it under the present arrangements
on account, firstly, of the indefiniteness of the words spiritual
and secular as used of a school, and, secondly, of the advantage
of an arbiter in all cases, than whom none can be so fitting for
the members of the Church as their Bishop, and expressing also,
if it can be done without offence, the danger which we see of
the management passing from Church hands under the clauses
of the Privy Council.

BISHOP OF OXFORD TO W. J. B.

CUDDESDON PALACE, Nov. 20.

MY DEAR SIR,—I have no objection to your proposal of a
monthly Communion at the morning service, and an early
Communion on the other Sundays;[1] but shall thank God if I
hear from you that the attendance justifies fully the attempt. It
is my own practice in my chapel here.

Your temporary church plan seems a very good one; and
the deliberations of your School Committee appear to me to
be wise, saving only that I think you should first ask assistance
simply; then, if the objectionable management clauses come,
object. Most likely they will yield; if not, present a memorial
to Government, and the National Society on the final refusal;
and *perhaps* a petition to Parliament. Lord John seems
determined to break by simple insults his truce with the Church.

---

[1] In the "Parish Journal" for May 7, 1848, appears this entry:

"Early Communion (13). I am not sure whether this will answer
or do harm, upsetting the regular course which was so prosperous
by the blessing of God. I trust that as we undertook this for the
benefit of some of our parishioners who certainly had a right to claim
it, that He will rule it for the best. It is a very serious step, more
serious than perhaps at first sight appears. It seems like the beginning
of a great work."

The next letters show how readily he accepted new responsibilities rather than forego a principle or miss an opportunity. The Rev. T. Archer Houblon had offered £1000 to build a chapel for the workhouse, on condition of its being consecrated. After much opposition this was effected, and St. Michael's on the Downs, designed by Mr. Butterfield, became a permanent chapel of ease to Wantage.

Rev. T. A. Houblon to W. J. B.

August 11 [1848].

I trust you will excuse my troubling you with this note on the subject of a chapel we are desirous of building for the benefit of the poor in the Wantage workhouse, and which is very much needed. But the Bishop will not consent to consecrate without we secure the permanency of the performance of the duty in it, and this we can only do by making it a chapel of ease to Wantage, though there is little doubt but that the Board of Guardians will continue their present salary to a chaplain. We have already obtained the consent of the Dean and Chapter to this, but do not like to take any steps in the good work till we have yours. Should you really have no objection to our placing the chapel on this footing, would you let me know at your earliest convenience, as, though we cannot commence the building this year, we might [be] collecting and preparing the materials, and fixing on the plan, so as to be ready to commence early in the Spring.

Peasemore, Newbury, Berks.

Rev. T. A. Houblon to W. J. B.

[Undated.]

——seemed determined on building a room, to be licensed as a chapel, by public subscriptions, wanting me to head them with one of a hundred pounds. I am, however, resolved to abide by the original agreement, and not to give anything unless for a consecrated building.

He was then and always in close touch with the
Bishop whom he consulted at every important point
in his work. The Bishop from the first perceived
that in William Butler he had a man of no common
gifts ; and he strengthened his hands by every means
in his power. Extracts from Bishop Wilberforce's
letters will illustrate this.

BISHOP OF OXFORD TO W. J. B.

CUDDESDON PALACE, Feb. 10, 1848.

It has occurred to me that it might aid your work if I could
come and ordain your deacon at Wantage on the Ember Sunday.
I cannot absolutely promise this, but tell me whether you would
like it.

61 EATON PLACE, March 10 [1848].

I approve entirely of your proposed missionary scheme *except*
that I think collecting only through the offertory will not
answer. I think the *habit* of subscribing good, and our people
will not be ready to give *besides* their offertory offering to this at
the offertory. Either, therefore, your common alms or these will
suffer. I have no objection to your receiving any extra gifts
as you propose; but I do not think that you will effect your
purpose if you *limit* your gifts to that.

The next letter alludes to the arrangements for the
ordination to be held in Wantage church, and to
difficulties connected with the National schools.

BISHOP OF OXFORD TO W. J. B.

5 WHITEHALL PLACE, March 4 [1848].

I do not think it will be well to alter the service. A sermon is
ordered and the litany; the *morning prayer* thus shortened is not
long.

I think, especially after last night's debate, you had better get
your committee to agree to a short letter (as he has said, "propose
your arrangements," etc.) to this effect. Propose any clause, A,

B, C, D, as you please, *changing as little as possible*, and merely adding, "and that the Bishop of the Diocese be the visitor of the said school."

Of course, I cannot but be glad to see any friends you may like to invite; specially such an one as Keble.

I will settle with the Archdeacon about a sermon. I shall be glad if well to preach once at least myself.

Do not let the Union Chapel *sleep*. C. Buller said to me, "I do not know what you want done, but *I will do it*." It is a pity to lose such an humour. . . .

The ordination held at Wantage, March 1848, is thus described in the *Life of Bishop Wilberforce*, vol. ii., p. 8 (1881).

You ask about Wantage; it was quite a pleasant visit. I got there about 4 P.M. We had a large gathering of neighbours, clergy. Tea and then to a meeting of Church of England missions. Next morning service at ten. It is a noble red [sic? old] cruciform church, and the chancel all nicely restored by the present vicar. It was crowded by a most attentive people. I preached to them on "The sufficiency of God," and I never saw a congregation more hushed into earnest and devout attention. All through the ordination there was the deepest attention. I administered the Holy Communion to 160, amongst them a large number of young people whom I confirmed here last year. We went home to dinner at three—a party of clergy, some from Oxford, some from the neighbourhood. At four we went to afternoon service, and Archdeacon Clerke preached. At seven we went to an evening litany and sermon, and I preached to them. We had some talk in the evening, an eight o'clock prayers next morning, and after breakfast I came away. Butler is working his parish with admirable diligence and, at present, success. He seems to me more to combine the good of the Evangelical party with the devotion of the High Church than almost any young man I know. His only danger is on the latter side.

Another work undertaken at this time was the closing of the churchyard, which was overcrowded,

and in the heart of the town. With the consent
of the Dean and Chapter of Windsor half an acre
of glebe was allotted for a cemetery, on which a
chapel was built. A new vicarage also had become
a necessity. The old dilapidated structure was
taken down, traces of Elizabethan building being
found in the timbers of the roof; and a new
vicarage, designed by Mr. G. E. Street, was built
on the north-west side of the church. The same
year saw the building of a girls' school, of which
Mr. Woodyer was the architect. This was opened
on the 29th July, 1850.

The two letters which follow describe the opening
of St. Augustine's Missionary College at Canterbury,
a great event in the Church history of the time.
The rest of the correspondence speaks for itself.

W. J. B. TO HIS WIFE.

[July 4, 1848.]

I have been at work this morning, positive external work ever
since half-past six, and now it is nine. This, therefore, will be
two pennyworth for you, for I am anxious, if possible, to give
you some idea of the doings of the last few days. In the first
place then, on Wednesday night at eight o'clock, V. and I left
Faringdon Road; at Slough got in three men, apparently Eton
masters, bound on the same errand as ourselves. We did not
however socialise, though one turned out next day to be Abraham
or Abram, to whom I was introduced by friendly Woodard.
Then I went to Clifton Place, and thence after some consideration
to the Adelaide Hotel, London Bridge, where I slept for exactly
three hours, rising at four. I was rejoiced, by the way, to find
that I can wake without being called. I slept just over the short
passage to old London Bridge, near a great church clock where a
church was once, and a church still standing of the respectable

C. Wren date. Under the same roof were Vincent, Mozley, Woodard, and lots more. I was off first in the morning with W., and
arriving at station just at five, found it thronged with acquaint-
ances and friends, new and old, some cassockt[1] and capt as
Chamberlain and Patterson, some great-coated and plaided as
myself and Marriott, all with little bags in their hands containing
their 'robes.' Hope looking about through his spectacles, Lady
Mildred and a select few females all in high spirits, Bishops like
blackbirds, Archbishop with suite of rosy low church chaplains
and purple flunkies, S. Oxon in full and fat fig, H. Wilberforce, Trench (by the way it is very curious how the Bishop and
he have communicated to each other expression of voice, look,
and language), with crowds more of all kinds. I was in a carriage with Henry Wilberforce, Patterson, C. Marriott, and
Crawley of Littlemore, and the conversation was very agreeable.
I taxed H. W. with his familiarity with K. Shuttleworth. He
looked a little, I thought, ashamed, but got off somehow. There
was something on the line, the removal of which caused delay,
and we did not go over fast. Arrived in Canterbury, more faces
presented themselves, for we had stopped at Ashford and Tun-
bridge to take men in. Masters, Balston, Tritton, J. M. Heath,
Flint, etc. It was raining hard, and we had a somewhat muddy
run to the College, a mile and a half distant. I was very near
missing the consecration, for fancying that all the men in the
train were invited thereto, I stayed chatting with them at the
station. Luckily I lighted on some gent in a fly, who conveyed
me part of the way; and at last I found myself in the College
Hall, this, too, filled with men—Webb, Scott, Vaughan, Blakesley,
Mr. Keble, Geo. Williams, Thompson of Trinity, Lord Powis,
Mr. Puller, Monro, D. Coleridge, Pollen, etc. I was too much
excited to see much. Things just lay on the retina of my eyes
without making an impression, just as words will fall on the ear
sometimes and you cannot bring the mind to realise them. I
heard people talking, how this was the old oak roof preserved,
and I could feel the general effect, but this was all. After a long
delay we were summoned by name, *Mr. Keble to my intense joy
first of all*, before Deans, Archdeacons, Schoolmasters, 'Apostles,'

---

[1] This form of the past tense was much used by Cambridge men of
that date, under the influence of the Hares.

Poets, Lords temporal, Ecclesiologists, or College tutors (there were no Heads of houses!). Then all in turn. With eleven others I was placed in the little Sacrarium facing the Archbishop's Throne. All the stalls were filled by men and the Antechapel by Lady Mildred Hope and her party. Then came up Archbishop and six or seven Bishops, Bishop of Brechin among them, the Archbishop and Gloucester alone remaining in the Sacrarium; and consecration service began by the procession up and down the chapel of the Archbishop, Bishops, and officiating clergymen. The service was very poor, and in some respects jarring. . . . However, I don't want to talk of this, but merely to give you my entire feelings. Then it was very slow to have no chanting, no organ, and to see all the black gowns on so joyous an occasion. One or two other things put me out a little, as you know tightly strung feelings are very apt to be easily jarred. The collection was noble, £3000; £2000 sent by one unknown contributor, £500 by another. Service concluded at a quarter to eleven, and then I went to —— and got a very minute portion of food, though in a fainting state. . . . After a time H. W. and Mary W. came in, and Mrs. Manning and Miss Byles afterwards, so that we went forth a large party to the Cathedral. By this time the close was teeming with people, and when the doors of the Cathedral opened a very disgraceful rush and scramble took place, some literally racing up the nave to get seats in the choir. There was a great squeeze at the entrance and up the steps of the choir. (Do you understand that the choir screen of Canterbury is raised on a noble flight of steps?) Those present in the morning had reserved seats, so that I was fairly placed in the stalls. The choir presented a most striking appearance, from numbers and variety of costume; but there was no separation of clergy and laity, all were in a dense mass mingled together. Women in the Stalls, laity in the Sacrarium, etc. There was a fine sound of many voices in the Psalms, etc.; and the anthem was a favourite of mine, Handel's "How beautiful are the feet," etc. . . .

WANTAGE VICARAGE, July 5, 1848.

I think I left off at the Cathedral after the rush. It was a very fine sight, only one wished to have the Archbishop on the steps outside the choir, haranguing the multitude in the nave. The sermon was slow but harmless; I could catch nothing of it but a

few texts here and there, and certain technicalities of expression.
Still, he uttered the word Church several times, and the text told
its own tale—"Make known by the Church." The singing
was good and hearty from the mass of voice. But the whole
tone of the Cathedral is very unsatisfactory, and confirms my
Chartist views. I slept out most of the sermon, and I believe
many others were nodding also. A collection, not in the
offertory, but by gents at the door, ludicrous enough it seemed
to see men with plates at the Cathedral door. E. Hawkins
was one, and I think Fagan, and others. . . . Then came
luncheon in the Cloisters and Museum of the College, preceded by wandering about the rooms. Everyone was there.
Bishop of Oxford, with Trench on one and Allies on the other
arm, Henry and Mary Wilberforce, Cyril Page, Pollen and sister,
Patterson and ditto, Puller, with whom I had some talk, old
Randolph, the Dean of Hereford, with whom I fraternized.
Everyone save Hope and Butterfield, neither of whom I saw.
The clergy were in various costumes, some with cassocks, some
without. Women folk plainly drest as became them. I made an
attempt, but failed, to catch the four o'clock train, but I didn't
care, for I thereby caught afternoon service in Cathedral. . . .
No preachment in the afternoon, which was slow. One longed
for a few good earnest words spoken from the heart. But they
didn't come. After service, V., B., sisters and I went to see St.
Martin's, a most interesting relic as you know, lately restored in
good style, admirably placed on a rising knoll. By this time we
had to run for it to catch the half-past-seven train, which however we did catch, and I found myself in a coupé with
Humphry, Lord Nelson, and J. Mozley. This gave a pleasant
journey to London, where we arrived at eleven. Even then I
saw one more, even Mrs. Keble in her cab, and had a kind
greeting from her. . . . The streets of Canterbury won't forget
the gathering in a hurry. They say that 1000 clergy were
present. I should have said that about 500 was nearer the
truth, but it is difficult to be accurate. I heard one rough-
looking fellow say to another, "I wonder what all these parsons
costs to keep." This was an obvious though not very kind
remark. But it made me ponder a little, not exactly how much
they cost to keep, but a few other points connected with it.

E

W. J. B. TO VEN. ARCHDEACON MANNING.

WANTAGE VICARAGE, August 29, 1848.

MY DEAR ARCHDEACON,—I too have been purposing to write to you to express, or try to express, the deep thankfulness with which I look back on your short abode with us, and the support which your words gave to opinions (or I should rather say a belief), which have long been growing up in my mind.

It has seemed to me that our Church, having weathered the difficulties attending the statement of the true Faith in regard to the two great means of Grace, has been enjoying a kind of ovation, and if I may say so, running riot in the glorious views which open themselves as consequences. So then that we have been neglecting, as a body, the sterner and more practical, and that we (of course especially the clergy) are greatly needing a higher standard of religious aiming, deeper spirituality, stricter ἄσκησις, a life more regulated by definite calculation of the worth of acts. Really, often I think that in this the " High Church " school is left behind by the " Evangelical." The evangelical party seem more saturated with spirituality. In order then to give this higher tone we are mercifully led on to that which will put the Church as much before itself in practice as the true doctrine of the sacraments, etc., has advanced her in the faith, *viz.* confession and absolution. We seem to be gradually drifting on to this, and so, as the channel of perfection, Satan has guarded this with especial care.

I feel so very deeply the peculiar nature of the difficulties which beset this subject, and yet on the other hand, the absolute necessity of bringing it forward, that I am more perplexed than I can say ; I am terrified when urging my parishioners to more frequent communion and the like without adding this as a preliminary, and yet I feel very fearful lest by clumsiness, lack of οἰκονομία, misuse of words, or what in effect is the same, the use of words, in themselves right enough, but misunderstood and so conveying a false impression, I should be the means of scandal. Of one thing I seem certain, that it cannot properly be urged but by a *confessing* clergy, and here I think we shall find no small difficulty. The pain and trouble will make men recoil from this in practice, who will gladly admit the theory as well as other Church views. . . .

How one longs that the halo of romance, so to say, were removed from confession, and it became a regular common-place part of Christian life. This would save what now causes so much needless pain, that, I mean, connected with self-consciousness.

This difficulty has occurred to me, and I should be glad to have it solved. Is it not somewhat unnatural, if not wrong, that any one, even a confessor, should know more of a married woman than her husband knows, and might not the neglect of this fact have been in some measure the cause of the laxity which has obtained abroad in the matter of marriage?

I assure you, with many thanks for your great kindness in thinking about me, that I do take care of my health, and (at least since Lent) I have generally made out about six hours of sleep. And I have lately been enjoying a most reposeful ten days of reading and writing at Glympton,[1] than which never was schemed a more fitting hospital for decayed parsons. . . . Charlton Chapel is working well.

Rev. J. Keble to W. J. B.

H. V., August 3, 1848.

At last Harrison has sent the sketch of the font which he proposes, and I forward it for your consideration. To our *idiotical* eyes it looks as if it would do very well. Will you kindly return it to him with any remarks upon itself or the manner in which you would wish it wrought, by whom, in what material, etc., as soon as convenient to 11 Chancery Lane? [Now, before I say the next thing, I put you upon your honour—if the subject were a fit one, as perhaps it is, I would put you upon something more sacred—not to go one farthing beyond what you had before intended to apply to this purpose; and I say the same to kind Mr. Freeman, to whom I ought rather to give something costly for the use he has been of to ——. Now if you promise me this in your heart, you may read on; if not, it will be like breaking one's seal.] The cost will be about thirty pounds. I really grudge taking it from Wantage, especially as I see no immediate prospect of being able to make an offering there. But you were so kindly

---

[1] His father-in-law's country house.

earnest I could not but thankfully say yes, only it is very possible that things may have arisen since which might draw your gift, if it were free, elsewhere; and, in one word, I trust you will consider it free.

We hope to be ready by St. Matthew's Day, but are as yet scarcely able to propose it to the Bishop. Pray come if you can, and bring Mrs. Butler. I daresay you will have to put up with some strange extempore accommodations, but that you will not mind. We mean to invite as few as we can from a distance, that our own people may have room. But it will be a loss not to have our especial benefactors, and there will be plenty of room for *them*.

I feel as I write that it ought to make one very thoughtful having to do with such a work. One may hope that one's friends are thoughtful for one. . . .

Judge Coleridge tells me of a long talk which he has had with your Bishop about this bill for people marrying two sisters. It seems to me very shocking, and that his taking part in it, which he seems inclined to do, will be especially sad and scandalous. I mention it in case you should be able and willing to influence him in any way. . . .

W. J. B. to Rev. J. Keble.

GLYMPTON PARK, WOODSTOCK,
August 21, 1848.

I ought long ago to have answered your very kind letter, especially as I do trust to be able to be with you on St. Matthew's Day. We admired Mr. Harrison's design very much, and returned [it] to him immediately, that it might be taken in hand. It is not worth while now to explain to you certain points connected with the donorship of it, but perhaps I ought to say this (and I hope you will not object to the change), that having sounded ——, and finding that he did not, as I expected, spring to meet me, from poverty not will consenting, I made another arrangement, *viz.* to offer it from the Wantage clerics, male and female. . . . I thought of a few words underneath the plinth or shaft (*i.e.* on the side of the font which touches the ground), and consequently entirely hidden, to express that the font was a gift from the Priests, Deacon, and Religious of Wantage to the Hursley church, just for the purpose of fixing the feeling. But I do not care at all about this, if, as is very probable, you may think it objectionable. I thought of this—

✛

Ecclesiæ Parochiali
S
In agro Hursliensi?
Hunc Fontem, Lavacrum Regenerationis
In honorem D.N. J.C.
Gratis animis
D. D. D.
Presbyteri, Diaconus, Lectores? Sorores?
Ecclesiæ S.S. Petri et Pauli
Indigna familia?
Apud Wantagiam.

✛

I think that I see you smiling at this. Pray correct it, if you like the idea. It is not easy to express in ecclesiastical Latin some of our present relations. Or perhaps I ought to say I am too ignorant of terms to find it easy. We had the Archdeacon M[anning] with us for a few days in the week before last. He was celebrant for us at the opening of a little £200 chapel which we have just built in an outlying hamlet.

I believe, though I dread to say it, that all things at Wantage by God's blessing are prospering, and gradually moving forward in the right direction. But how keenly one begins to feel the absolute necessity, if we are to get on farther, of a regular and so to speak common-place system of confession. Between that and anything else, *e.g.* parochial visiting, friendly relations between clergy and farmers, and all the rest, which some Bishops and all 'safe and practical' people incessantly urge as the perfection of parish management, it seems to me that there is all the difference between playing at things and real earnest work; that the one is a mere evasion, the other the true Church system, whose pain, like children dreading to have their teeth pulled out, men urge every excuse to escape. I feel this more strongly every day, while communicants are increasing with us, as everywhere else, to an almost startling extent. . . . I have got the evidence before the Marriage Committee, and I will endeavour to study it sufficiently to write to our Bishop, who has invited all his clergy to communicate with him on the subject. I declined before, for I had no means of supporting by argument my natural feelings, and I saw a danger in expressing them without this.

Rev. J. Keble to W. J. B.

Our consecration is fixed for the 24th instead of the 18th on account of the Chancellor's visitation. I trust this will make no difference to your coming. The Bishop has kindly permitted us to have the Holy Communion. The clergy to bring their gowns; service at eleven o'clock.

I have as yet, I am sorry to say, but very faint notions of the 'preaching' for which I proposed to retain you and others in that week. My difficulties are chiefly these two: the dark nights through which the people will have to tramp to the church, and my being myself engaged on somewhat of a similar task in Leeds on the Eve of All Saints and on All Saints Day. If we do manage it, I thought the subjects ought to be such as would come under this head, viz. :—'The Church and her Services as a Preparation for Eternity.' Could you without much trouble distribute this into eight or nine heads, for the day and following days till the 31st inclusive, the 31st being All Saints Eve? (I say eight or nine because of the Sunday.) And you might take any one you pleased.

I am quite delighted at the thought of your *both* coming.

W. J. B. to Rev. J. Keble.

I am very stupid, and though I have been considering your thesis for some time, I cannot satisfy myself with any result of my thoughts. Would you take such a line as that of making the (1) *penitential*, (2) *joyous*, (3) *peaceful*, (4) *praiseful*, (5) *constant*, (6) *satisfying*, character of the Church services, and then connect each with the church fabric?

I would try either (1) or (5). But I hope that you would not think of such a weak arrangement, and that if you want me at all, you will *order me* to what you like.

We are in the midst of a huge town fair, fortunately only annual, but it troubles us a good deal, tempting communicants and upsetting our schools.

Up to this point the course of the vicar's life at Wantage had been fairly smooth. It would be impossible indeed that such radical changes as he sought to make in the church and parish should not provoke some opposition, but, all things considered, his parishioners accepted them with much greater quietness than could have been expected. This was owing to various causes. In the first place, he found a genuine Church-feeling and tradition in the people, although it had been buried for many years in neglect and apathy. He used in after-years to cite, as an instance, the fact that on Good Friday there had always been a celebration of Holy Communion largely attended. He noticed also that the elder generation of the women used to curtsey at the *Gloria.* The daily services he established were at once attended by some old men and women with regularity. In fact, although the Church had been idle, Dissent had not stepped into the breach, and there was a general feeling that the parson should be supported. Then, although he came full of energy and enthusiasm to the work, he did nothing rashly or violently. He did not suddenly change the hours of service or force startling novelties of ritual on a congregation incapable of understanding them. What he found good he kept, and was content to wait until he had trained the young generation up to a higher standard. The services he introduced were supplementary to those already in use, and he was careful to draw the distinction between what was essential and what was not.

Thus, as late as June 1865, he wrote in the " Parish Journal."

A long conversation with —— makes me very doubtful as to the propriety of continuing the choral Sunday morning service after Sunday next. He is a good, sensible man, and disposed to Church feeling. He assures me that most of his class in the congregation [*i.e.* the class just above the tradespeople] are disquieted by it. They do not object to choral service once in a month, but it is the constancy of it which worries them. I do not think that it would be right to force an arrangement through which, however *in itself* more perfect and desirable, is yet against the feeling of such people as these. All that can be done is to work steadily forward towards educating their minds, and giving them a love and taste for better things. When this is done, the other will follow. Until it is done, any such advance in ritual will defeat its own object.

This wise moderation and caution bore fruit in the general acceptance of his system. Meanwhile he was working hard to influence the younger members of his flock.

He did not confine himself to collective teaching. Over and over again notices occur in his " Parish Journal " of personal interviews with individuals, both old and young, whom he sought to bring to a better way. His attention was not devoted to purely ecclesiastical objects, but he threw himself into business relating to the town. In his first year he began to make proposals for a better drainage system, for sanitary matters had been sadly

neglected at Wantage, with the result that outbreaks of typhoid fever were frequent. He also took
an active part in getting the town lighted by gas.
He was most regular in attending all meetings of
the town governors and commissioners. But a
time was at hand when he would meet with violent
opposition and bitter hostility; and this was due
to causes for which he was not responsible.

The history of the Wantage Sisterhood is told in
another place in this book, so it will be sufficient to
say that at this time, 1850, although it was already a
most valuable auxiliary to the vicar in the parish,
he was not its spiritual director. His friend, Archdeacon Manning, whom he thoroughly trusted, filled
that post.

The year was an eventful one for the Church of
England. The Gorham judgement had shaken the
faith of many of her children, and numerous secessions to Rome followed. The Mother Superior, Miss
Lockhart, was one of those who forsook the Church
at this crisis, accompanied by one of the Sisters;
and their secession was followed by that of Archdeacon Manning.

This was a heavy blow to the vicar. Apart from
the probability of his being held responsible for
the secession of the Sisters, which the outer world
would consider as the practical outcome of his
teaching, the defection of Archdeacon Manning, an
older man than himself, and one to whom he had
turned for counsel and advice, would be a grievous
shock to his confidence. The Gorham judgement

itself gave him intense pain. If ever he wavered
and felt doubtful as to his position as a member
of the Church of England, it was then. Not that
he for one moment contemplated joining the Church
of Rome; but he was shaken in his faith in his
own Communion.

His correspondence with Mr. Keble reveals his
own perplexities and fears, which, however, never
caused him to slacken for an hour in his strenuous
efforts to carry on the work for souls to which he
had been called.

Rev. J. Keble to W. J. B.

H. V., 3 Th. in Lent, 1850.

There is thought of trying a sort of Brotherhood in Plymouth
or Devonport, and some persons have agreed to act for a time
in that way, under parochial authority of course; but two
material things are as yet unprovided—a Rule and a Superior.
Can you help us at all towards either? I mean, could you
send us any written rules which you have tried yourself, or
know to have been tried, in cases at all similar; and do you
know of any one who either now or after Easter could and
would go down to take the lead in the matter—and whom you
would recommend? A person who is in many respects very
unfit has promised to go for a month after Easter if no better
can be found, but he is most desirous to find a good
substitute.

I trust you have had much help and comfort in what I see
has been going on in your parts.[1]

W. J. B. to Rev. J. Keble.

Wantage Vicarage, March 2 [1850].

I rejoice much in the hearing of that Devonport move.
From my own experience I fear that I can say little likely

[1] *I.e.* one of Bishop Wilberforce's Diocesan Missions.

to help. But if I might suggest one *danger*—I should fear, and think it most needful to guard against, a certain scornfulness and superciliousness which I seem to trace not unfrequently among those engaged in high and holy works. Might not some rule be drawn out in regard to dealing and conversing with those who are *without?* Also I would, though you probably know them much better than I, mention the Hours, translated by Albany Christie. I have found, as I think, great advantage for *myself* in using the Latin Hours, and I cannot imagine anything which can take their place.

The sisters at St. Mary's Home use the Hours in English. Our Bishop, I *believe*, saw them and made no objection. Indeed, why should he? There is, as you know, *very* little to alter, for the simple reason that they are catholic. The only other thing that strikes me is that a sort of "Fundamentum" should be laid, after the manner of St. Ignatius, so that the brethren might fairly grasp the "quid nocet" and "quid prodest" argument. This would reconcile them to inferior places, etc.

I should like very much to have a word from you in reply to this query. Will not the institution of Gorham (convicted of heresy), in accordance with a decree of the Privy Council, vitiate the whole position of the English Church? Is it enough to say this is an unjust law and must be altered? And might not the men of old, who were bidden sacrifice to idols, have said just the same and so sacrificed? Ought not the Church to be in a position to refuse, and, if she be not, is she not forfeiting her office as a teacher of the Truth, and so has she not her candlestick removed? I own that I feel a good deal frightened lest we should be sophizing. I am not at all unhappy at present, nor shall I be till the decree is distinctly pronounced and acted on. And this ought to be enough for the present. Yet having my pen directed Hursley-wards, it seems natural to "speer one question at" the vicar.

The work of the Mission was most heart-filling. We gathered strength and confidence as we went on; and at Banbury, so far as one can judge, the effect was very deeply felt. On Wednesday, *e.g.* the last day, two hundred communicants were present at eight, and at the eleven o'clock service, when the Bishop preacht on Perseverance, between two thousand and three thousand. It was a thrilling sight. We struck out in the evenings into the neighbouring villages, and preacht on Conversion, etc. The churches were everywhere filled. It was worth observing how readily and gladly the people answered the call, and however the direct object of the work might have succeeded, the following points are certainly gained :—

1. The orderly array of clergy in procession, duly vested in surplice, stole, and hood.

2. The possibility of unity of action among men holding different shades of opinion, yet in the Church.

3. The assertion of a Bishop's right to deal with the souls in his Diocese, and not merely with the clergy.

4. The sight of a clergy calling loudly to repentance.

5. The invitation to individuals to draw near for confession, counsel, absolution, and comfort.

Rev. J. Keble to W. J. B.

H. V., 4th Friday in Lent, 1850.

Thank you over and over for your note on the Brotherhood. I hope they have got their Rule from a better and more experienced hand. You were not aware how very simple the information which I meant to ask for : such as a time table, a copy of external rules, etc. I am such an entire novice in such things. It has, however, as I hope, begun. God grant it may go on and prosper.

I have been full of care about that Gorham case on the ground that you suggest, and was for instituting a suit in the Arches Court immediately against Mr. G. for heresy only, without reference to Institution or anything else, which I hoped would prevent the Archbishop from giving him mission immediately. But it seems that for several reasons this cannot be done. The next thing will be to know exactly how far any Prelate giving him mission or publicly owning his doctrine taints himself with heresy. To this end one ought to know : (1) The exact articles brought against him ; (2) the exact words of Sir Herbert Jenner Fust's sentence ; (3) those of the sentence now pronounced, not as being of any force, but as possibly containing what may taint one acting upon it with heresy. For these documents I have applied to Badeley. If it appear that there is really contradiction of the Nicene Creed, I suppose Bishops in their Diocesan Synods, and Archdeacons and Rural Deans in their fractional gatherings, are competent to state publicly the true doctrine, to draw attention to the contradiction of it, and to ask all other Dioceses to concur in demanding a Synod to put the thing to rights. I know not how else the truth is to be ecclesiastically vindicated. It is a great risk, but what else can be done? I have had half a mind to write to your Bishop about it. All honour to him for what he has just been doing for us—for the work itself and for the time of doing it. How mercifully we seem to be both punished and relieved. . . .

W. J. B. TO REV. J. KEBLE.

WANTAGE VICARAGE, March 11 [1850].

Now that the decision is fairly (or rather unfairly) promulgated, I confess that my heart trembles for the results. And after weighing the matter in such poor way as I am able, I can bring myself to contemplate two alternatives only, and it seems to me that it is my duty either to leave the Establisht Church or to give up life and everything else if needful, to work towards her Restoration. I cannot help feeling that any course short of one of these must be to the soul's peril. Naturally one clings to the latter. The former seems most awful to me, and I shrink from any condition which it implies, i.e. from 'nonjuring' Scotch Episcopal or Roman Communion. In regard to the first I feel a dread of splitting, *Babelising* the Church.

My immediate object for troubling you is to ask whether you could conveniently take me in for a night, if I can find a chance to leave Wantage for a day or two. It seems presumptuous to attempt to suggest, when heads so much wiser and hearts so much purer are set upon remedying this awful grievance. But I might *privately and to you* open a plan for action which occurs to me. My idea is that a regular organization of parishes ought at once to be formed, working under the Bishop wherever this is possible, as I think that it would be in the Diocese of Oxford; that a central committee, with as little demonstration or noise as possible, so as not to excite jealousy and talk, might act as an accumulator of facts and a provider of deputations, and that a few men might be sent about for this purpose, who would speak earnestly, *lovingly*, clearly, and *truly*, to the various parishes, at meetings to which the clergyman should admit by *ticket* such of his parishioners as would attend for the purpose of *good*, not to jeer or argue. This to be started at once, and not to cease till all England is [illegible]. My parishioners are hearty in the cause.

W. J. B. TO REV. J. KEBLE.

[? March, 1850.]

I left Hursley yesterday a happier and I hope a wiser and patienter man than when I entered it. I feel peace and confidence in the result of our struggle. Thank you very much for all your kindness. I write now (1) to enclose a line from our dear Bishop, (2) to ask you to print and let me have a copy of your Hursley petition—an audacious request—and a few copies of the Sarum Breviary prayers.

I hear from Carter as follows: "The Bishop of O., whom I saw yesterday after his return from London, where he had seen the Bishop of L., reports that *Convocation at present* is hopeless, but that there is good hope of getting the Archbishop to convene the Episcopal Bench to make a decision not on the whole subject of Baptismal Regeneration, but on the definite point of *remission of original sin* in Baptism and *its being no hindrance to grace*, to which point Keble narrows the ground. . . . The Bishop also reports that the Bishop of L. will bring in a Bill to constitute the Upper House of Convocation. The Court of Final Appeal, with some judges as assessors, to be summoned by Royal writ for the express cases."

In the Chichester archdeaconry ninety-two out of one hundred are prepared to support the move. The Archdeacon [1] therefore is in better heart. I found three more signatures at Wantage on my arrival to a requisition to the Archdeacon of Berks to convene his clergy. Every single one whom I have yet seen or heard of in this neighbourhood, a singularly dull one, has willingly come in to such a proposal. I think that we must be on our guard lest we get hoodwinked by some of our Right Rev. friends. I infer this from some touches in Carter's letter. Would it be well to print the "whethers" of yesterday morning?

[1] Ven. H. E. Manning.

Rev. J. Keble to W. J. B.

H. V., Monday in Holy Week, 1850.

I hope I have not put you out by not writing sooner. I rather waited for the good Doctor to be here, hoping to answer more satisfactorily. He says, with regard to the Convocation move, "All very well, if you can trust it when met." He quite concurs in the misgivings about our Rt. Revd. friends. For which reason I should think it very desirable that clerical movements in the sense of our resolutions, and parochial movements in the sense of this "petition," should be got up as widely and as quickly as possible. As far as I can make out, our people here are quite prepared to adopt this "petition," only there is some confusion in their honest minds about the Supremacy. . . . I think I am, on the whole, for printing the "whethers,"[1] especially if the Low Church, or any considerable number of them, are inclined to go with us on that point. I am not sure that in saying this I am not more or less influenced by the idea that Convocation cannot be got, but that a strong call made for it would have a wholesome *tonic* effect upon the Bishops.

Your letter was a great comfort to me. I do trust, for all counter-appearances, there is an immense deal of soundness in the heart of the English Church.

W. J. B. to Rev. J. Keble.

Wantage Vicarage, Sept. 2, 1850.

I have read carefully the B. C. U.[2] paper, and your alterations (proposed). I feel very strongly with you that (II.) is most objectionable, (III.) I could sign as it stands, (I.) as altered to "as a Branch," etc. I do not feel any objection to the resolutions —perhaps I should like to see the expression 'repudiation of Romanism' modified. I suppose that we must meet somewhere,

---

[1] "Probably a series of questions drawn up by Mr. Keble concerning the right of the Privy Council to legislate for the Church, the grounds of their decision about Holy Baptism, and the duty of Churchmen at this crisis."—Rev. W. Lock, D.D.

[2] Bristol Church Union—*vide Life of Dr. Pusey*, vol. iii., p. 274, etc.

and February is fairly distant. . . . I think that it would be a pity to stop agitation, unless any better plan is likely to be set on foot immediately. I am more afraid of sleep and lotus-eater lethargy than of anything else. We are in a frozen atmosphere, and to sleep is to perish—at least so it seems to me. I should like very much to ask you about Church Unions. They do not approve themselves to my mind, but so many better judges uphold them, that I think I must be wrong. I want to see Archidiaconal Unions, which would be a legitimate Church Synod, especially when, as would sometimes happen, the Archdeacon would head it. But I suppose that it is too late to talk of such an arrangement now that the Church Unions are in full action.

We have been abroad—to Germany—to take charge of Ph. Pusey. . . . I saw a good deal (for a short visit) of the Catholic clergy of the towns, and I am much struck by their friendliness and freedom from assumption. It felt like talking to a brother priest. Their tone was very different from that of some of their new men. One of them askt me if I used the 'Pusey ritus.'[1]

The four letters which follow were written to a young lady whose confidence in the Church of England had been shaken by the Gorham judgement, and by its consequences in the secession to Rome of several of her friends. She, however, remained steadfast to the Church of her baptism.

W. J. B. TO ——.

[February 10, 1850.]

. . . I think that I ought to say that I am not frightened about the Gorham case unless the decision is against the Bishop. I look on the committee of Privy Council as merely the arbiters appointed by the State to see that the Church keeps to the terms of the concordat between Church and State embodied in her formularies, as dealing, that is, merely with the establishment, not necessarily touching the Church. If they reverse the

---

[1] Many years afterwards, in 1880, a Tyrolese parson asked him, "*Sind Sie Posuit?*" He was puzzled, but I guessed the meaning and answered, "*Ja, gewiss.*"—A. J. B.

Bishop's decision, even then they are, supposing them to be *honest* men, only doing their duty, and we have no right to find fault with them, though we may find fault with our formularies as being deficient in precision, and though we may and must refuse to accept the decision for the Church. It will be the decision for the Establishment unless Parliament agrees to allow the Church to alter her formularies and still to remain the Establishment. Have I made myself comprehensible?

W. J. B. TO ——.

[March 10, 1850.]

. . . In the first place our duty is, manifestly, to wait till Mr. Gorham is inducted. Arius was triumphant till—he died. And even then it must be months before we can possibly judge of our real condition. I am inclined, though I own not very much, to the side of hope. But one thing is also clear—that we must be content to live in a struggle to our lives' end, to be "men of strife." That, if no worse, is sure to be our portion. We must fight for the truth by prayer and fasting, self-denial in everything, stern unflinching resolution to look at nothing else, be content to bear disappointment and coldness, to be misunderstood and hated. "The sword" has come, and we must not cling to "peace." . . . What a marvellous comfort to be drawn from Epistle, Gospel, Lessons, and Psalms of this day.

W. J. B. TO ——.

WANTAGE VICARAGE, June 12, 1850.

. . . Next, what is the difficulty? It lies in this that the true notion of the Church is that she is the keeper of the Faith, and its promulgator; that it lies with her to lay down, to rearrange, to define, to judge all that relates to it. Whereas now she is, it would seem, likely to admit a heretic to the Cure of souls, and to submit her decision to the revision of an extraneous and worldly court. Miserable truly. Yet against this set the fact that these evil doings are not tamely acquiesced in; that a power is rising through the Church which, one may reasonably believe, will and must, working only in faith, prevail; that such doctrines and demands as were never heard of here before, have been boldly

F

brought out in high places, that the stir is not over, but rather on the increase, and, if one may appeal to human authority, men like Mr. Keble and Dr. Pusey, holy, learned, clear-sighted, endowed with the spirit of martyrs, are far from disheartened. I will say nothing of the distinctive errors of Rome, nor of the evil dispositions which have shown themselves in those who have left us, apparently proving that God has not been with them, but one cannot help gathering from this more courage and determination to fight the great and good fight of faith, seeing that our retreat is well-nigh cut off. . . . Our work is to *pray for the Church of England without misgiving.* "Believe that ye shall have it." To doubt is to lose our power, to bring about the very crisis which we deprecate. To forsake the Church of England now, is, in my view, to destroy that chance of unity which the Romanizers so stickle for. It may be the result of the faithlessness of ―― and others that these difficulties encompass us now. Surely the book of Job may teach us somewhat not merely of patience but of a *misunderstood position.* He "had well-nigh said even as they," *i.e.* the talk and folly of his friends had nearly made him what they thought him at first, a hypocrite and sinner. Just as men would now make the Church of England a sham and an engine of Satan.

W. J. B. to ――.

[26th Sunday after Trinity, 1850.]

. . . I must in honesty say that I think our position a very painful one, though not the less on that account to be retained. I mean that since that fearful Gorham decision we are reduced to a negative argument. We cannot defend ourselves. We can only find fault with others. I am more comforted by the present mobbing of Puseyites than by anything else. It looks like reality. It is pleasant to find R.C., Low Church, No Church, rabble, etc., all banding together to destroy that one thing which oneself is. . . . You will be glad to hear that by God's mercy the good work is prospering, and that I see my way to that favourite idea of mine in former days, the double Sisterhood for Penitents and Schools.

An address of sympathy was sent from Wantage to Bishop Phillpotts which he briefly acknowledged.

BISHOP PHILLPOTTS OF EXETER TO W. J. B.

Bishopstowe, Torquay,
Easter Eve, 1850.

Rev. Sir,—Accept my sincere, however tardy, thanks for the address which you, and the other Clergy of Wantage, have had the goodness to make to me. Be assured that I feel it strongly to be not merely a gratification, but a support.

I have nothing to suggest. Such men will best act, when opportunity shall be presented, on their own principles and judgement. . . .

P.S.—Your name, connected with Wantage, cannot but excite stirring associations.

In talking of this troubled time, long afterwards, William Butler was wont to say that the rise of decided opposition in the parish might be dated from it. But secessions to Rome were not the only evil fruit of that disastrous year. On September 24, 1850, what has ever since been called " Papal Aggression " took place, and the Protestant feeling of the country was kindled into a flame by the news of the Pope having mapped out England into bishoprics.

This coming close upon the secession of the Sisters ripened the seeds of suspicion and discontent which the vicar's strongly pronounced Churchmanship and fearless attack of abuses had sown. Those who had come under his rebuke for sin, as well as those who disagreed with his religious opinions, were glad to seize the opportunity which these unhappy circumstances had given, to denounce him and his system. What made this the harder for him to bear was the fact that many who now went into opposition had been up to this time good Church people and his supporters. In the year 1852 the storm broke at a Vestry meeting, held to consider the question of the restoration of the parish church. The story may be told in his own words taken from the "Parish Journal."

Thursday, April 1. I must here record the first distinct disaster, humanly speaking, which has befallen my ministrations in this town. A Vestry meeting had been called after much consultation, to consider the restoration of the church according to plans prepared by Mr. Street. I felt the awkwardness of such a meeting when Dissenters could take a part, and more especially because I knew well their exceeding hostility to me. But —— prest the Vestry as the only means of getting at the Parish, and I think somewhat foolishly I agreed to hold it. I say foolishly, for since I did not ask a rate, the whole work might have been, and probably will be, carried through without their permission. However, I was very anxious not to appear to act in an arbitrary manner, the more as I am so continually accused of doing so. Still I was not prepared for the fierce opposition I encountered. On the previous day handbills had been printed and circulated, and the Crier sent round with his bell, and a proclamation inviting the people (Protestants) to come and oppose Popery, etc. Then the Wesleyan Preacher stimulated all within his reach, and —— gave his men half a day to come and vote at the Vestry. By these unscrupulous measures, for which I ought to have been prepared, a strong party of Dissenters of the worst kind were brought to the Vestry, and in a very short time it was packt with enemies, ready for anything. I stated my views and explained the plans, and was heard not unfavourably. Then Mr. Wasbrough proposed as a resolution, and Cooper seconded, that it is desirable to restore and reseat the church without a rate, etc. W. Dixon opposed it,[1] and then the clamour partially began with vociferous cheering of anything said against the restoration. Then —— of Fawley opposed it, not on any grounds except that he wisht to have a

[1] Tradition has handed down his opening words: "People say as how I be the pa'son's man; but I bean't the pa'son's man in this here job." He gave £25 before the business was over.

door to his pew. . . . So —— of Lockinge opposed it because of his pew. Then —— got up and said a great deal
about intoning the service, etc. —— of Charlton spoke of the
mummeries, flummeries, tomfooleries, and other savoury
expressions by which he chose to designate our services.
This brought up Trinder who, amid much interruption, took
occasion to speak of the doings of yesterday, the Crier, the
Rabble, etc. The word Rabble set the whole meeting by the
ears, and he ended his speech with much difficulty. Trinder
spoke nicely on the subject of the restoration and convincingly,
if argument could convince such a set. After a great deal of
noise, lasting for three hours, the proposition was put and
negatived by a large majority. So ended this unfortunate
Vestry. *Have we prayed* enough that the good work of the
restoration be accomplisht? All seems to me to rest on this.

Writes an old friend :

I happened to be staying at the Vicarage at the time,
and remember how he came in broken down and dejected
for the moment, and blaming himself for having made
the attempt too soon. He had originally given himself a
longer time, and then had not waited. I heard that at the
meeting he was perfectly self-controlled and equal to the
occasion. You may have heard of one famous retort at this
meeting—"Sir," said one of his opponents in a rage, "I am
at a loss to know whether you are more knave or fool."
"Time will show, sir, time will show," was the instant reply.
For perhaps two or three years after, this unpopularity
continued. I remember a rather grim joke which he was
fond of in those days,—an allusion to the cry of the French
Revolution, *à la lanterne.* He used to declare that he expected
to be hung up to one of the lamp-posts in the town, and I
think there was a spice of earnest underlying the joke, and
that he really was persuaded that he might meet with
personal violence. Insulting inscriptions were chalked upon the
walls, and Sister Harriet told me that she and another from
the Home used to go out late at night to wash them off.

It was a strange and troubled time, but he was not a man
to flinch before violence. I always think the text, "I have
set my face as a flint," fitted him, and he gained the reputation

of being (as I have heard it said) "hard as nails,"—though
there was sensitiveness and tenderness enough underneath the
surface, as those nearest to him knew very well. . . . I have
said more than once that it was remarkably your father's lot
to have one after another come to Wantage, begin divers
works (which he himself would not have originated), and then
go and leave the deserted work on his hands. This was the
case with Miss Lockhart and Miss ——, and I want to ask
whether it was not also so with Mrs ——? She built St.
Michael's and set up an Industrial School there, but I have
never known why or how she left the work she had begun.
At least we know that in every case he took up the deserted
work—though not of his own originating—and built it up again.

In addition to these parochial troubles he was not
without his share of domestic sorrow. On March 14,
1851, his eldest daughter Frances Charlotte, had died
at the age of five, only ten days after the birth of
another child. This was a deep and lasting grief.[1]

His Bishop's sympathy was not wanting.

BISHOP OF OXFORD TO W. J. B. ——.

THE CARRIAGE,
NEAR BUCKLAND, March 17, 1851.

MY DEAR BUTLER,—Thank you for your note by Balleine.
I was truly grieved to hear its sad announcement, and feel
deeply for you. This time of year comes to me so fully
charged with sorrows that I can enter into the griefs of all
others. This day ten years I walked out of our sweet
Lavington Churchyard a desolated man. I thank God for
the firm faith and meek resignation which He has given you
and your wife. It is a great thing to be so upheld. May He
never leave you nor forsake you. . . .

---

[1] More than thirty years later he wrote to one who had been similarly
bereaved : "The death of one's child is like nothing else. Even
when, after many years, the wound is more or less healed, the
feeling always remains with one, of something being gone from
one's life—a sort of blank like the loss of a limb."

CHAPTER IV.

THE PARISH.

DURING the early fifties, William Butler was much occupied in fighting the battle of definite Church teaching in parochial schools. This was involved in the use of the Church Catechism, for which he vigorously contended. It was an anxious time, for the National Society had shown a disposition to compromise, *i.e.* not to insist on the Catechism being used in Church schools, and he regarded this as fatal to true Church teaching. Many letters passed between him and some of the leading clergy of the day, Mr. Keble, Canon Carter, and others, who warmly supported his views. The following, however, will be sufficient to illustrate his position.

W. J. B. TO REV. J. KEBLE.

WANTAGE VICARAGE, Feb. 25, 1853.

I have written to the Bishop and this is his answer: "I believe you know that it had been, after a division, resolved by the Nat. S. to offer to the Bishops a common form of enquiry into the late teaching in schools ; but that on a ground of technical correctness this decision was afterwards set aside.

Still queries have been sent by many in consequence of the
promised communication from the N. S., and are being sent
by others.   The answers, I understand, so far as they have
been sent, are very satisfactory.   My advice, therefore, in the
matter would be that at present we await the replies that
are coming in, and that we resist all agitation until we see
from those replies what the real state of the case is.   That
agitation has already led to the formation of an additional
(so-called) Church Education Society in opposition to the
N. S., one of the most threatening instruments, I think, of
our further divisions."   Were you aware of this 'setting aside'
of which the Bishop speaks?   I for one was not, nor do I
think that any public notification has been made thereof.   This,
if it be so, is scarcely fair and honest, and ought to be lookt
into.   Then, one desiderates some more definite knowledge
than that 'queries have been sent by many.'   By whom?
The Bishop of Exeter, I think.   They have not been sent in
this Diocese, but possibly this may be attributed to the fact
that we are fairly mapt out among inspectors, who, at the
annual meeting at Cuddesdon, can bring forward, if desired,
the very minutest details.   I hope that we may escape another
N. S. disturbance.   Denison is a difficult dog to chain up, and
the worst of it is if he sets to work the others will do the
same, and we must go, to prevent the N. S. falling into their
hands.   I am inclined to think, or rather I feel convinced,
that our Bishop will 'shew fight' when once he is convinced
that the *nodus* is *vindice dignus*.   And moreover, from much
acquaintance with him, I feel sure that he is quite reasonable,
I mean that he is quite ready to *be* convinced, even against
his own first impressions.   But he is rather like the Athenians
at Sphacteria, afraid that all is going wrong except when he
is personally present.   And, it must be owned, Denison is not
very adroit.   The only plan, or part of a plan, therefore, which
occurs to me, is that *he* should be worked—in all the steps
which may suggest themselves as desirable to others.   I shall
write again to him soon and get, if I can, a more definite
explanation of the Committee of N. S.—their doings.   I ought
to say that he heads his letter to me 'Confidential,' though
really I cannot see what there is of 'Confidential' in it.   He
knows that you wrote to me, and that I wanted an answer

partly for you, and therefore, of course, he does not object to my passing his answer on. . . .

A compromise was the result of many meetings and much anxious correspondence, but on the whole the definite Church party had the best of it.

About this time the office of Rural Dean was added to his labours.

BISHOP OF OXFORD TO W. J. B.

26 PALL MALL, April 15, 1853.

MY DEAR BUTLER,—Will you undertake the charge of the Rural Deanery vacated by Dr. Nelson? You know me so well that I need not say one word to you as to any particulars about the office. Except that if in anything concerning it I can aid you, it will ever be a pleasure to me to do so. I am ever affectionately yours   S. OXON.

My affectionate remembrances to Mrs. Butler.

With all his external work and interests the internal affairs of his parish occupied the larger share of his thoughts, and indeed grew more absorbing year by year. In spite of the check he had received in 1852 in his attempt to get the parish church restored, he had by no means lost heart or confidence. He was content to go quietly on with his work, while the money gradually accumulated for the purpose which he felt sure he should eventually accomplish.

In an epitome of the year 1854 in the "Parish Journal" he wrote:

This year has seen one great difficulty removed, removed as I believe securely, and nothing now remains to prevent the restoration of our church to a Christian condition except the obtaining of the sum needed for the purpose. Of this we have in hand £1,050; with £500 more we may, without imprudence, begin our operations. For this much prayer is needed, as well as that no unkind feeling may remain, and so mar the work when done.

By 1st October, 1855, he had so far won over his antagonists as to be able to preside at the vicarage, at a meeting of influential parishioners, called to deliberate on the restoration of the church. By July 1857 this was an accomplished fact.

July 30. A day much to be remembered, as, by God's mercy, an end and a beginning—an end of the old degraded ungodly state of God's House, which could not but act for evil on the hearts of our folk, and the beginning of comeliness, fitness, and beauty. This day is indeed an ample recompense for much disappointment and weariness of heart, and it is, perhaps for the very reason of all this, the more cheering and sustaining. Five years ago we were all out of spirits. The hope of restoring our church to the beauty of holiness seemed almost a dream. We had no means, and the parish had set itself fiercely against it. Now all has been done, so far as it is done, well, and there is scarcely one in the parish who has not in some way contributed to the work. All have been roused to enthusiasm, and a restoration of a specially pronounced kind is so popular, that I cannot but feel and hope that it will in a degree affect all the churches in the neighbourhood.

We had endeavoured to persuade the Bishop to have no late Celebration, but as he objected to this, of course we gave way at once, and arranged accordingly. We had, however, our usual Celebration at eight o'clock, at which some 75 attended. All were hard at work till eleven, when the numbers of the clergy began to increase. Mackonochie[1] had the charge of marshalling the clergy, and of giving those who were to assist their respective commissions. The arrangement of the church within fell to Sawyer, and Harvey had the choir. Purdue continued in the

[1] Rev. A. H. Mackonochie, afterwards of St. Alban's, Holborn.

THE CHURCH RESTORED 91

barn where the feast was prepared. Porter kept the decorations
in order. Mr. —— of Charlton kindly lent his carriage to
convey the Bishop, and I went in it to meet him. We had
sent an omnibus to Wantage Road, and a van to Faringdon
Road, and they both returned loaded with friends. A Dutch
barn belonging to Mrs. Stroud was prepared on the vicarage
lawn in order that the clergy might vest in it, and when the
Bishop drove up to the vicarage nearly 100, and very soon after
upwards of 100, were collected in order. The procession of
clergy and choristers amounted to 160, and they advanced
slowly to the church round the north and east sides under an
arch of green (which had been prepared by the Kents[1] voluntarily)
singing the 68th psalm, to the church. The day was propitious,
and a little rain that had fallen served to make everything
brighter and fresher. The church was quite full; I suppose
that upwards of 1000 were collected in it, all orderly and
reverent. There was no bustle or confusion. The Bishop said
the first part of the service at the Litany desk, and then
attended by Archdeacons Randall and Clerke and by myself,
he proceeded into the sanctuary. Nothing could be more
beautiful than the decorations, which consisted of heavy green
wreaths fitted into all the arches and members of the tower
arches with festoons wherever it was desirable to cover a bare
space. A pastoral staff was lent by Radley, and a chair and
lectern for the Bishop by Mr. Margetts, of Oxford, from whom
the Eagle, the gift of the curates of the parish, had been
purchased. The "Home" provided the Litany desk. The
service was sung by the united choirs of Lambourne and
Wantage. All were vested in surplices. The service began
shortly after twelve, and was fairly sung, well in parts, sometimes but poorly, and some careless mistakes were made. The
Bishop of course preached a very noble sermon, and the
collection was made by ten men. It amounted to £167, which,
with £35 in the morning and £10 in the evening, gave us
£220, a great help towards clearing off our debt. . . . The
service was not over till four o'clock, when, after a short interval,
the whole party adjourned to the barn in Newbury Street, in
which accommodation and food had been provided for 700
people. Nothing could have been more admirable than the

[1] Local builders.

arrangements. At the high table, which was raised considerably
above the ground, sat Mr. Wasbrough (chairman), the Bishop,
the Archdeacons, the Vicar, Mr. Atkins, H. Barnett, Popham,
T. Bowles, and several ladies, while the other tables were
stretched out before it, each under the superintendence of some
one deputed for the purpose. All were very orderly and
attentive, and evidently taken and even carried away with the
event of the day. At about half-past seven we again gathered
upon the vicarage lawn and went in procession to church. The
Archdeacon preached, Trinder and Popham read the lessons,
Harvey said the service as in the morning. The church was
filled, though, from the absence of a great many of our morning
visitors, not so fully as in the morning, but with the people
whom one most wisht to see, our labouring people; and £10, of
which much was in copper, was collected. . . . The day was
kept quite as a holiday, and many of the shops were closed.

   Thus past such a day as I cannot bring myself to imagine
that I shall ever see again. Thanks again and again forever
be to Him who has bountifully heard our prayer and granted
our desire. May He now but give us strength and grace to
carry on this work to the end, to view it but as a stepping-stone
to higher things, to rest not till we make our parish such a
spiritual temple as our church now is.

One of those associated with him in the years
immediately preceding and following the restoration
of the parish church, the Rev. W. G. Sawyer, now
vicar of Taplow, has given a sketch of the Vicar's
relations with his "brethren," as he was fond of
calling his assistant curates.

   In the summer of 1854, after having been disabled for a
year, I happened to be in the neighbourhood of Wantage;
for some reason or other they were in want of help, and I
was asked to go over for a Sunday. I went for one day,
and stayed five and a half years. Butler was going that
Sunday evening to preach for Milman at Lambourne; he asked
me to go with him, and I well remember how up on the

Berkshire Downs, he offered me the curacy vacant by the appointment of H. P. Liddon to Cuddesdon. Up to that time my acquaintance with Butler had been very slight; but in this way a friendship arose which has been very precious to me. Whatever little work I may have been able to do in the Church of God has mainly been the result of the training I received at Wantage. Important as has been the place which Butler occupied in the work of the English Church at large, he must always remain in the minds of us of the older generation, as the Vicar of Wantage. He showed perhaps above any man of the period, what the Church could do among the mixed population of a small country town. I often think that it is impossible for the younger men among us to realize what was the condition of the Church in a place like Wantage fifty or sixty years ago. Butler's difficulties were immense, but the force of his will overcame them all; and the intense earnestness of his work won the respect of those of his parishioners who disagreed with him. When I first went to Wantage the church was still unrestored, and not very long before Butler had received the rebuff, which it must have been very hard for him to bear—the refusal of a faculty for the restoration of the church in consequence of the opposition of some of the parishioners. As time went on he was thankful that the restoration had been postponed, because, as he often said, the work would not have been so satisfactorily done as it ultimately was. In looking back to these days, what strikes me perhaps more than anything else, is the patience with which the Vicar waited, and the patient way in which he dealt, not only with the people generally, but with his opponents in particular. Never keeping back the truth, letting every one know what he believed, in matters which he considered non-essentials it is wonderful how forbearing he was, in consideration for the feelings and prejudices of the people, and how gentle he was in word and deed. His curates were often impatient, and would have hurried things on, but we had always before our eyes his example, the example of one who would "quietly wait." And he had his reward. When the time came for the re-opening of the church by Bishop Wilberforce, the whole parish, with only one or two exceptions, rejoiced with him in the completion of a great work. I well remember the enthusiasm with which the parish generally provided at their own cost the great luncheon which followed the re-opening services. He was friendly with the nonconformists of the town, and, as time went on, I do not suppose that a more united and friendly parish could be found throughout the country. And this without the slightest compromise of principle, but from kindness of heart, and that earnestness of purpose which always, sooner or later, wins its way.

In his dealings with his curates he was a model Vicar. Very plain spoken, and somewhat stern at times when things were done which he did not like, and still more so when things were left undone which ought to have been done, it was impossible not to recognize the loving heart which lay beneath. However hard we worked, we always had before us the example of one who worked a great deal harder. His work was essentially the work of common sense, and he hated fads. I know that I was at times a trial to him, but when I fancied myself put upon, and perhaps grumbled a little bit, the way in which the Vicar always put himself in the wrong and humbled himself before me sent me away utterly ashamed of myself and humiliated to the dust. Wantage was essentially a place of work, and in the same way as Bishop Wilberforce raised the whole tone of Episcopal work, so did Butler raise the tone of the work of the parochial clergy. And the spirit of work learned at Wantage was never, I believe, lost by the Wantage curates when they went to parishes of their own. Wantage did for the south of England what Leeds did for the north.

The impressions of Canon Carter of Clewer, one of William Butler's few surviving contemporaries, who was much associated with him in diocesan work in the early years of Bishop Wilberforce's administration, may fitly be inserted here.

I will gladly endeavour to give the impressions made on me by your dear father, and by the great part he played in the Church's life and work. We were contemporaries in the Oxford Diocese as it was being formed into a new Diocese by Bishop

Wilberforce, your father commencing his work at Wantage in 1846, myself at Clewer in 1844. We were, locally, rather far apart, and alike constantly occupied, and only touched one another on certain occasions, though having common aims and common objects at heart. It was part of Bishop Wilberforce's plan in moulding the Diocese into one whole, to gather together in his hospitable home at Cuddesdon from time to time those who worked under him. Those gatherings were of the happiest kind; and there, together with the Bishop, we planned the Oxford Lent Sermons, and the missions which the Bishop held at different centres in the Diocese,—missions, not, as now, organized scientifically, so to say, under two or three priest-missioners, but under himself, aided by several of the clergy. At Cuddesdon and in these missions was my chief opportunity of intercourse with your father.

But this is to anticipate. My first acquaintance with him was after the Gorham judgement, when, together with two earnest sympathizers, now with him at rest in God, Milman, afterwards Bishop of Calcutta, and Robert Gordon, then Rector of Avington, we joined in pressing forward the protest made under Archdeacon Berens in his Synod. By that time your father had established his fame as a parish priest. It was owing to his having thus shown his power in a true Church line of work, that Manning, then Archdeacon, having trained four sisters to be the nucleus of a religious Community, fixed on Wantage as their home. This, in its after consequences, served to bring out great points of high value in your father's character. Manning's secession from the Church of England broke up this little band of Religious, the Sister-Superior and one of the other three following him to Rome. I remember well the anxiety of the crisis, and the agitating question of the possibility of reconstituting the work, and perpetuating it through those who remained faithful to their dedication. One cannot now adequately conceive the pressing nature of such an anxiety at a time when all around was filled with distrust, and Sisterhoods among us were but in their infancy. We all feared that there could be little hope of pursuing what had been so earnestly begun. But then your father's endurance and trust, his moral energy and courage and practical wisdom, were seen; and one rejoiced with him in being able to re-establish the Community out of the apparent wreck, so as to become, under his care, so prosperous and valuable a Society as it has long been growing with its widely extended works. It was a crowning instance of what seems to have been one of your father's prominent characteristics, that what he set his mind to accomplish he could not fail to carry through.

Our Church life at that period, and for many years afterwards, was a scene of constant progress among those who were bent on sustaining what had been gained, or reviving what had been lost and was still wanting. I suppose it was the variety of mind, each with its own plans and prepossessions, acting in different ways and under different circumstances, yet with common desires at heart, to which is due, under God's mercy, the amount of success which has attended the manifold efforts of past years. Much depended on the view taken of what was due to authority—a true note of Catholic life—much on individual tendencies, and partly also on local circumstances, the issue being, whether or no to join societies then forming and work in common with others, or to do one's best alone with one's own separate opportunities. Your father's strong personality and trust in his power and energies, with a great unwillingness to be hampered by other minds or to be dependent on other agencies, led him to take the latter course. There was a further influence evidently telling upon him in the same direction. He seems to have always kept true to what are known as Tractarian principles, under which he had grown up, and a sense of what is due to authority was an important element among the lessons taught us by the great leaders of that movement. Your father, whose mind was always resting on great principles, was influenced by this feeling far more than many among us. This evidently governed his conduct in the course of the struggles which went on during his time year after year.

This sense of authority, as a habit of mind, and a sufficient law of life, appeared constantly in matters of greater or less importance. He was once asked to attend a temperance meeting and to speak. The tenor of his words was, "What can one need more than what the Church Catechism teaches as to temperance and soberness?" The promoters of the cause who desired to press total abstinence as the means of furthering temperance said he had spoilt the meeting. He could only recognise the one straight course, sufficiently, as he thought, laid down for us all.

I was at Wantage in early days at some of the great gatherings held in order to celebrate your father's parochial achievements. I often since heard details of his work which have been full of lessons to others. It was, as we supposed, Mr. Gladstone's appreciation of his faithfulness, his thoroughness, his powerful energy in the Church's work, which led to his being raised to other spheres and higher dignities. I have of late years been able only to follow him in thought with thankfulness for what he has been enabled to do in his ceaseless activities. We have rarely met, each being very fully occupied in our separate ways. I remember your father as one of my earliest friends and fellow-workers during an eventful period, and the remembrance of what he was and what he has done remains as the witness of the greatness of his aims, and of the truth and reality which have always marked his course, and must for ever embalm his memory.

Most of the correspondence of this period relates to 'burning questions,' the ashes of which are still warm. The letters here given are on more general subjects.

W. J. B. TO HIS SISTER.

WANTAGE VICARAGE, Feb. 14, 1855.

. . . How strange it is to find life gradually ebbing away, and yet to feel no older, weaker, or less full of interests, than when some seventeen years ago, our dear F. and you and I used to interchange our 'cracks' between Southgate and Trinity. Of course I don't mean that plenty of events have not occurred to alter the channel of thoughts and interests, but that the power of being interested and engrossed in these old and new objects exists with the same force as ever, and makes it still as difficult as ever to realise that death is stalking after us, and gaining daily upon our footsteps. And still it seems as hard as ever not to struggle after a sense of present security from future possibilities and contingencies, and not to long after that state of worldly prosperity which enables its possessor to say to his soul, "Soul, thou hast much goods laid up for many days." I suppose nothing but a real effort to feel and believe in that exactly counter command of our Lord, "Sufficient for the day," etc., can bring us out of that most dangerous error, which *will* go along with unabated strength and vigour of body and mind. The peculiarity of the poor worn out Crimean soldiers is that they don't care to move, to eat, or to live, but when they are once in the hospital, they only ask for present rest. . . .

W. J. B. TO HIS SISTER.

WANTAGE VICARAGE, Feb. 13, 1857.

. . . Do you know that in the old Kalendar *St. Scholastica*, sister of the great St. Benedict, stands as the patron of Feb. 10? The name seems well adapted to my especial line of work.

As you say, birthdays have a different meaning as one passes on in life from infancy to youth, from youth to mid-age, from mid-age—whither? And it seems very awful to be touching on shores which once appeared so very, very distant, and to feel that each little promontory round which the ship of one's life has past has its own tale to tell of omissions and commissions, forgetfulness of the guiding Presence, slothfulness and selfishness. Each seems markt, as it were, by some gipsy camp-fire, black yet still smoking up to heaven, where one has listlessly spent that precious awful gift of time and which now bears its solemn witness. My heart often sinks within me when I think of thirty-nine years past and gone with their summer and winter, seed time and harvest, and so little laid up to God. Only there is the trust that that precious Blood cleanseth from all sin, and that He Who knows our weakness will accept the short and imperfect snatches of prayer which one is able to utter.

Now I have said a great deal about myself, and very little about you. It is and has ever been my special blessing to have known and loved my sisters. I always think that sister's love is the mainstay, after mother's love, to English lads at school and college. I am sure that I found it so. . . .

W. J. B. TO HIS WIFE.

Yesterday was a most busy day. Before twelve I had taken part in a celebration of H. C., two Churchings (for the tiresome folk would come in separately), one Baptism, and the wedding of ——. This quite independently of P.T. classes and other work. . . . —— implored me to dine with them and I consented.

Scene I. A room upstairs. Table covered with *wal*nuts and *smal*nuts, oranges, figs, and a *huge* bridecake, raisin, ginger, orange, and currant wine. Enter —— and wife, ——, Mr. ——, a friend with huge Crimean beard, a married young lady intimate with bride, and the three Miss ——, —— and wife. The bride's small brother and big mother. Vicar. Wine and cake as Vorschmack. Conversation flagging but facetious, "little and good." Ladies rustling in silk. Gentlemen in white waistcoats and do. gloves.

Scene II. The small room below with a large table on which stand beef, mutton, turkey, ham, vegetables à discrétion, to be removed for P. puddings, mince pies, rhubarb, blackcurrant, gooseberry, "Damascene," raspberry, tarts and, lastly, cheese. The former company enter (Mrs. and —— who have very red faces having been hard at work till the present moment). Mrs. —— retains a white apron over her bridal costume as the insignia of her late office as cook. Every one does justice, ample justice, to viands, bride, next to whom I sit, has two vigorous goes of turkey and ham. I squeeze in a few jokes of a mild kind, but conversation is decidedly scanty. Crimean hero is apparently connected with the Stock Exchange, for some allusion to the Bank makes him for the first and only time open his mouth to *speak*. After cheese and grace we adjourn to

Scene III. Room as in Scene I. Company the same save —— and Crimean, who stay below to smoke a pipe of hospitality and peace. Mrs. —— joins the party upstairs and from time to time utters some highly edifying remarks, pious and suggestive. A few more jokes, but conversation still very slight. All however seem very happy, and at 4.30 I summon —— and Crimean from their tobacco, propose ——'s health and his bride's, and depart like a rocket in a shower of friendly words. . . .

In the early part of 1854, the Rev. Henry Parry Liddon came to be curate at Wantage. His powers of preaching were at once recognised and appreciated by Mrs. Butler, a keen critic. In after years, her husband was fond of quoting her remark on hearing his first sermon: "That young man preaches better than the Archdeacon" (Manning).

This was the beginning of a warm and lasting friendship—one that was only severed by death—between the Vicar and Liddon. The latter was at Wantage only about a year, and then went as Vice-Principal to the newly-founded Cuddesdon College. From that time dates a close and intimate correspondence which only ended at the death of Dr. Liddon in 1890.

W. J. B. TO REV. H. P. LIDDON.

WANTAGE VICARAGE, Dec. 11, 1858.

. . . We have had two very happy days. The little Charlton school was opened by a service therein, followed by a service in church, and a great supper to farmers, clergy, and *labourers*, provided by the farmers. Yesterday we had our second Confirmation of this year, and a Confirmation at the Home. Mackonochie was with us on Thursday; remarkably well and cheery, and apparently prudent and anxious to work *simply* for souls.

W. J. B. TO REV. H. P. LIDDON.

RED HILL, Aug. 12, 1861.

I have read your sermon carefully, and though I think the first part too elaborate and reasoned for the reading of most people, yet for the sake of the second I should be very sorry were it not printed. I have therefore sent it to Parker, requesting him to forward it to St. Edmund Hall. I do not know your address, though that seems safest. I have not received the Episcopal discourse—and now that he is fairly launched on his travels, with his six Cathedrals to preach in, I cannot imagine when it will come to hand. We left Wantage on Thursday, after getting through various parochial and Diocesan Board engagements, and to-morrow we hope to cross the Channel. May the S.W. wind subside a little! . . . I was much interested on Saturday in the consecration of Woodyer's new church, built by his exertions and mainly at his expense. He has bought (some years since) a very pretty little estate, called Graffham, near Guildford—and since his wife's death, his great desire has been to build a church to her memory. He has spared no expense nor effort of mind upon it, and the whole effect is most religious and touching; the glass is Hardman's, and it makes me more confident even than before of his enormous superiority to any of his fellows. . . . I am staying here with my old school-fellow and college friend ——. It is most delightful to be in such a house. He is a lawyer, and married early to the sister of another old school-fellow. They are both thoroughly right-minded and religious (of the right sort). He has built himself this house, and in it a little oratory for family prayer purposes. Close to him is his brother-in-law, Mr.——, another layman, of exactly the same mind. His boys are at Bradfield. Depend upon it, nothing ever came near the 'Oxford Movement' for influencing and turning heavenwards the minds of this class of men. Alas, alas! the new lights, with their religion of doubt and scepticism, little know what they throw away. Such households as this make one feel it bitterly. And yet men like —— are what they are because of their generation. How wonderful it seems. We enjoyed your visit very much. It did us all good.

W. J. B. TO REV. H. P. LIDDON.

CALDICOT HOUSE, WATFORD,
Sept. 10, 1861.

You will see from this that we are at home again, after something more than three weeks of touring. We went the old route

of Folkestone and Boulogne to Paris. Thence through Burgundy
to Lyons, stopping at Sens and Dijon—spent a couple of days
in intense heat at Lyons—thence down the Rhone to Valence—
and then in various voitures to Aubenas in Ardèche—hunting up
volcanoes and churches, and sleeping in little village inns. Le
Puy in Velay, a most wonderful city of the tenth century; Cler-
mont (it seems still to echo with Diex le volt), from both of
which we made excursions; and so home by Bourges, Orleans,
and Amiens—the last for the sake of the clean and sweet hotel,
which saves one the stench and expense of sleeping in Paris.
Riddell[1] is a charming 'compagnon de voyage,' most gentle,
unselfish, bright, and accomplisht—vigorous, too, and up to any
amount of bodily exercise, and thoroughly right minded and
sympathetic in all greater things. The tremendous heat (thermo-
meter at 96° Fahr. in the shade on a north wall one day) was
the only drawback. We had not a drop of rain the whole time.
I suppose that the south of France is one of the hottest places
in the world, and this year it was agreed by all that the heat was
more than the oldest inhabitant could remember. We have
come back very geologically inclined, and one picks up the stones
and flint of the London clay, looking instinctively for lava and
basalt. The general effect of Auvergne, looking down upon it
from the Puy de Dôme, or the Pic de Sancy, at Mont Dore les
Bains, is as if a collection of dust holes and cinder bins had been
poured out upon it in little heaps. The whole soil is cinereous,
pustulated with volcanoes, from which immense masses of lava
and basalt have been belched forth on the original granite—
filling up valleys, altering the course of rivers and damming
them up into lakes, leaving here and there huge waves, where
the lava has cooled quickly, just like breakers foaming upon the
shore. In course of time the water and the atmospheric influences acting on the weaker parts have worn them down and
made deep valleys, very fertile and lovely, mostly covered with
huge chestnuts, and permeated with springs of the most delicious
water—very often highly chalybeate and effervescent—flowing
right under the volcanic strata. The sides of the rivers and
gorges are fluted as it were with regular pillars or prisms of
basalt and, if the top soil be worn away, you see them in as
regular a pavement as Minton's tiles would make—octagonal or

[1] Rev. James Riddell, Fellow of Balliol.

some other mathematical form. Then sometimes, as at Le Puy, crags of basalt or lava having a little more iron in them than the masses round, have resisted the forces round them, and stand up in the strangest way like huge craggy teeth in the middle of the valleys, covered with churches (of course S. Michel) or castles.

Well, you will be tired with geology, and I am sorry to say, I have little else. The churches of Auvergne are very striking, mostly of the ninth, tenth, and eleventh centuries; Byzantine in structure and detail, with a series of domes, or rather quasi-domes, in lieu of internal vaulting. From what little I saw, I should imagine that the Auvergne folk are not very strong, like the Breton, in the matter of religion. On the weekdays one could run over the churches before twelve, which rarely happens elsewhere, on account of the continual Masses, which one cannot disturb. We heard a sermon at Lyons, for men only, to which we were admitted by ticket. It was in the cathedral, and about 500 were present. The preacher was very eloquent and earnest. He said that he should break through his usual course, because of the Octave of the Assumption, and took for his theme the "culte" of Mary. Nothing could be more illogical than the discourse; it was full of assertions and even misquotations from Scripture, yet telling—to the folk addressed; neither Riddell nor I felt at all more inclined to accept the views which the preacher held. It is very sad to see how the worship of Mary is obscuring that of the One Mediator. By the way, Ars is not far from Lyons, and I picked up some histories of that good *curé's* life and death. They are most interesting, and if only I had the pen of a ready writer I would certainly cook up something for the 'Ecclesiastic' which alone would enter into the thing heartily. It is very instructive to our parochial clergy to have such things brought before them. Men little know what earnest hearts and holy lives can do. It seems that to the very last he was full of apprehension for the future. "Dreadful thought," he said, "to appear before the judgement seat of God with my poor life of a *curé*."

I hope to return on Saturday to work. There is a good deal to think about, when I do begin to take things in hand. . . . Then there is all the Home and St. Michael's, with their many branches of difficulty, and finally the P. Council under Lowe have entirely reorganised the whole system of grants, making it very difficult to see our way, in the matter of £ s. d., to keep the schools going. I have glanced over their Code, and at first sight I am inclined to think that all will be right in the end. You know that I am going out as a deputation for S. P. G. in Cornwall from Oct. 6–20.

I have received the Bishop's MS. sermon, and the proof of yours. . . . The expression, "incarnate in language," is, I think, hardly accurate, considering the exact meaning of "incarnate." Would it not be well to head the pages with the subject—as Newman's are; you know what I mean. Those little things help the reader very much.

Max Müller's lectures are in this house. I shall hope to read them if I can get an hour or two amidst the chatter and interests of family re-union.

W. J. B. TO REV. H. P. LIDDON.

WANTAGE VICARAGE, July 16, 1862.

. . . Did you read the *Times* article on the Congress. It handled it according to its unbelieving cynical wont, but I must own that—bating the sarcasms, etc.—I incline to agree with its tenor. I was startled to find that Church matters were to be dealt with like geological, social science, etc., by papers and sections, and I own to an increasing feeling of discomfort at the terrible physical activity of our brethren. They really remind me of the description of the adversary in the Book of Job—"going to and fro in the earth," etc. I firmly believe that parishes are suffering greatly from the continual absence and the desultory habits of the clergy. Men find out that it is much better fun to meet their friends and talk at these gatherings than "to tend the homely, slighted Shepherd's trade" of visiting cottages and working at schools. I had intended nevertheless to enter an appearance! but a letter from —— made me so anxious about —— that instead of turning off at Didcot to Oxford, I took the express train up to London. . . . On Tuesday is our Commemoration at St. Mary's Home. You will think of us as we of you.

The Warden of All Souls' will preach. We purpose an early Celebration at the Home, and 11 o'clock matins with sermon and second Celebration in church. Luncheon at the Home. Evensong at the Home at 4. All goes on there very happily, and a few more Sisters slowly join us. . . . I agree with your argument on the subject of vows, in the main. But, of course, admitting that the *principle* of vows is accepted by the Church by the instances of ordination and marriage, it is quite another question whether it is advisable to apply it to Sisterhoods. We must not, I think, press the question at present. Once let the institution grow strong and important, and it may dictate its own terms. I was not much pleased to find that Sisterhoods were one of the subjects for the Congress to discuss. (The word *Deaconess* seems to me detestable, and the natural correlative is *Priestess*. There is an *animus* in the use of it.) There are always a host of folk ready to rush in and make talk-capital of what others have been *doing*, and I dreaded, not as it seems without some justice, what such folk would say. O what a wonderful book is the book of Proverbs—and how like men are one to another everywhere and always. . . .

REV. H. P. LIDDON TO W. J. B.

THE PRINCIPAL'S, ST. ED. H., OXFORD,
Dec. 6, 1862.

. . . Cartwright tells me that the question of your election as Coadjutor Bishop with the right of succession is very openly discussed in Toronto. Of course I did not tell him that I had heard anything of the matter. He says that there has been a "caucus" or informal meeting to deal with the subject, and that the only difficulty is the want of a fund which is to be raised. It appears that the present Bishop of Toronto is paid by the Home Government, but that his successors must throw themselves upon the local Church. But he (C.) anticipates no difficulty on this score. There is much speculation, he adds, as to whether or no you are likely to accept the post. Probably all this or more is no news to you—or you have heard something from Riddell. But Badgeley, a Queen's man from Canada, tells me the same story. . . .

W. J. B. TO REV. H. P. LIDDON.

WANTAGE VICARAGE, Dec. 19, 1864.

Do not think me a pest. I cannot help pressing once more the extreme importance, as it seems to me, of a counter-move to the Destructives. It is quite true that the religious party may not be able to agree upon a scheme, but they are not, as I think, called upon at present to do this. What is required is to show a good face to the world, to make it understood that there is at least a fair number of not unknown names who think very differently from the first memorialists. Surely this could be done.

I have great faith in *protests*. Their value comes out wonderfully in *after* times. The Sicilian Vespers came of a protest. It is like rowing a losing race. Chances occur when they are least looked for. And after all they are acts of honesty. It is something to say *liberavi animam meam*. I am going to write to Luard to this effect. The *Times*, somehow, evidently does not go heartily with the Destructives, and I cannot help thinking that they would be glad of a counter-demonstration. Even Gladstone hinted that it would be well for the memorialists to neutralise opposition by reasonable compromise. But if there is no opposition, they will have it all their own way. I think that I would rather have a compulsory than a permissive bill. Do you not think that the increase of personal holiness is some set off against other and adverse things? . . .

At this point it may not be out of place to give a brief *résumé* of the Vicar's methods of parish work, principally related by himself in the "Parish Journals" and elsewhere.

His custom of working out details upon a broad foundation of principle may be fitly illustrated from the records of his parochial work at Wantage, kept with scrupulous minuteness in what he called "the White Books," as they were bound in parchment. This parish diary begins on

August 4, 1847, and is preceded by details of the
census of 1821 in Wantage, by a list of "un-
baptized persons in the parish of Wantage being
more than three months old," and of persons living
in flagrant sin ; and a description of the "objects"
of the journal as "facts concerning the spiritual
and bodily welfare of the parishioners of Wantage,
observations on the cottages, wages, rents, marks
of progression, marks of retrogression, and the
like." Notes on the services occur frequently ;
and after a few years another series of books was
opened, with entries of every sermon preached in
the parish, with the text and the subject, each
entry being made by the preacher.

As early as January, 1848, we find that the
"communicant classes," on which the Vicar laid
such stress all through his parochial life, were already
organised. "Wednesday—Young women to prepare
for H. C. ; Thursday—Young men, and married
women ; Friday—Young women ; Evening service ;
Married men." From that time forward, till he
left Wantage, he never omitted to take these classes
himself, except in the rare case of incapacitating
illness, and once a year when he was taking a
holiday. The numbers attending the classes grew
steadily, as the newly confirmed were drafted into
them, till, at the close of his ministry at Wantage,
he could write (in an article in the *Literary Churchman*, afterwards reprinted as a small pamphlet):

I have found it necessary in a country town to form no
less than twelve classes—which are *invariably* in the week

which precedes the first Sunday of every month, and before
the greater festivals. These classes vary greatly in size. The
smallest has eight names only, the largest forty-five. On the
whole the numbers, which at first were under thirty, have now
passed three hundred. A careful list is kept of absentees, who
are always specially visited and invited not to pass over the
next time. A few, as might be expected, slip through as years
flow on, sometimes from old age, or other reasonable causes;
sometimes from idleness; but the leakage is more than made up
for by those whom each Confirmation and close and continuous
parish sifting adds.

He continues with "a few words of caution,"
which describe, in fact, his own practice for thirty
years.

(1) On no account should these classes be held in school-rooms,
parish-rooms, or aisles of the church, but in the parsonage itself.
It is of all importance to give them a friendly aspect, to take
away stiffness, and to make those who come feel themselves,
so to say, thoroughly at home. Chairs, *not forms*, should be
arranged comfortably and hospitably round the room, which
should also be well warmed and brightly lighted. (2) The
members of the classes, as each monthly week recurs, should
be *re*-visited and *re*-invited. General notices given in church
are of less than no value. Nor is it advisable to leave messages
with neighbours, for this too often gives opportunity for a
sneering remark, and breaks down the delicacy which should
characterise all that has, however remotely, to do with com-
munications on spiritual subjects. (3) The classes must on
no account be omitted. No call of pleasure or of family convenience, save perhaps once a year when a holiday is needed
for health, should be preferred to them. If once it is perceived
that the clergyman can put them aside for his own purposes,
the lesson will soon be learned by those who ought to attend.
In my opinion, all the success of communicant classes depends
simply on really hard work, which moreover will increase in
hardness as the thing takes root and grows. Much prayer,
much patience, much tact, and much perseverance are here
absolutely necessary. If a man is not prepared for this he had

better not attempt to gather them together. If, however, he is not afraid of "spending and being spent," he will, unless in very exceptional circumstances, find after a time that he has established without show or fuss, in this bit of parochial machinery, a most potent auxiliary in his campaign against evil.

A few more details may be given, for no idea can be formed of his parochial life without realising what an important place these classes took in it. 'Class-week,' as it was always called, was a time in which every fibre of his energetic nature was strained almost beyond endurance, as those knew who saw him at his hastily-snatched meal taken in the short interval between two classes. But the hardest week of the year, perhaps, was that in which the Confirmation classes, which he always took himself, coincided with the Communicant class-week, so that nearly every hour of the afternoon and evening was spent in his study, one class succeeding another with hardly any interval, till at some time after nine o'clock he would appear, saying, "I *am* tired." But he rose at six the next day as usual, ready for that work which was really his life.

He divided his Communicant classes into—

(1) Young ladies, including the daughters of the upper trades-people and the pupils of a young ladies' school; (2) young men (*a*) clerks and the better educated, (*b*) mechanics; (3) young married women and others, in two similar classes; (4) two classes of elder married women, each at a different time, so as to meet their convenience; (5) a class of lads of the choir, pupil teacher boys, and their compeers; (6) labourers; and (7) pupil teacher girls and others connected with the girls' and infant schools. Each of these classes has its own fixed hour, which is seldom or never changed, so that they may arrange

their occupations of the week in accordance with it.   According
to my experience the clergyman should always be ready to
receive the comers as his *visitors*, and to greet them as they
enter with a few kindly words to each—which will not, I am
very sure, diminish the effect of the more serious work which
follows.   The address—which he should deliver, as I think,
standing, as they sit round his table—would last generally from
thirty to forty minutes, and be rather of the conversational
than sermonising kind; given in homely yet earnest language,
brightened up sometimes with an appropriate anecdote or
mention of public events, or of something which has happened
lately in the parish, or which touches on the well-being of the
Church. . . . The whole should be concluded with prayer, that
of 'humble access' slightly altered, or some words arising
from the special subject which has been handled.   After the
class is ended, I frequently ask any who require some individual help to stay, and call them in separately; generally,
indeed, several of their own accord ask to be allowed to speak
to me.   I need not point out of how great value this is.

After he left Wantage he still continued to hold
these classes which had formed part of his life for
so many years; and at Worcester he enjoyed
gathering some of his poorer neighbours and his
servants into his study once a month to prepare
them for Communion; while at Lincoln he held
classes for his own servants and those of some of
the adjoining families, as well as for the Cathedral
bell-ringers and workmen.   His last classes were
held just three weeks before his death, in preparation for Christmas.

Another matter which from the first he regarded
as of primary importance, was the efficiency of the
schools, both as to teaching and fabric.   Thus,
under January 31, 1848, we find entered : " Worked
at school all the morning.   The first class (new)

very promising. Great want of arrangement. The lesser boys learn next to nothing." His invariable custom was to visit the schools daily, and he or one of the clerical staff always opened school with the form of prayer which he compiled. In this connexion may be mentioned the class which he held for the girl pupil teachers every day immediately after breakfast. All the school staff also assembled in the study at 12.45 on Saturday, to report on the week's work, so that he was in constant touch with every detail of elementary education in the parish.

He was able also to compare the state of the Wantage schools with that of the others in the neighbourhood, when, in 1849, he became Inspector under the Diocesan Board of Education, not only of religious knowledge, but of the general instruction, as well as of the fabric and arrangements. This post he retained as long as he was Vicar of Wantage. He enjoyed his round of inspections, and would bring back additions to his stock of amusing stories, such as : *Scene*—A village school on "the Downs." *Question*—" Now, children, tell me the name of an animal ? " (*Chorus*)—" Please, sir, a cow." " Very good ; now tell me some fish." Long pause—at last a hand timidly lifted—"Well?" " Please, sir, a *red herring*." He also gained a valuable insight into the conditions of Church work in these lonely villages, and his desire to found an educational Sisterhood must have been much stimulated by what he saw of the school teachers during his early years as Inspector.

One of his first efforts was to build suitable schools, and on August 6, 1849, the corner-stone of a school designed by Mr. Woodyer was laid by Bishop Wilberforce. As the number of children in the schools grew, other buildings were erected, but so much care had been taken with the plans for the first schools, that no structural improvement or alteration was required by the Government Inspectors till the famous "cloak-room and hat-peg" order of 1894.

We find that as early as 1848 he had perceived the unsatisfactory results of the ordinary Sunday school system :

Hitherto, he writes, the Sunday and Day schools have been on entirely different principles, our Day school learners and boys not attending any school, being all mingled together on Sunday. This was of necessity at first. For there was no school at all but the Sunday school, including among its scholars most of those who now form our Day school. The Day school then gradually attained its present size, viz. 120 on the books, with an average attendance of 106 or 7. These numbers are perfectly manageable on week days by Mr. Hyde the schoolmaster and three monitors. But on Sundays, being mixt up with all the others, the numbers (about 180 or 90) cannot be controlled by twelve or fourteen teachers. It seemed then advisable to take out of the Sunday school the Day scholars, and leave the rest for the Sunday school teachers to manage and instruct, collecting them in the English school. And this was accordingly done with very little difficulty. In church in the afternoon the numbers were 174, besides some 18 who came to the Vicarage, making 202 in all, boys under Church instruction. The two schools were divided and under much better control.

The class of boys who came to the Vicarage consisted of choir boys and tradesmen's sons; and the

Vicar never relinquished it till he left the parish. The boys used to arrive about two, and remained till the hour of afternoon service. They repeated the Catechism, and some verses of Scripture (one boy learnt all, or nearly all, St. John's Gospel by heart), and after a little teaching, the Vicar told them a story which he continued Sunday by Sunday for months on end; very often bringing in some of his foreign experiences, and not infrequently losing the thread of the tale during the week, which, however, did not matter, as his pupils were always ready to remind him of the exact point at which it had been broken off.

He considered foreign missions to be an integral part of the Church's work, and accordingly the first missionary meeting was held at Wantage on July 16, 1848, and thenceforward it became a yearly event. He always tried to secure for these meetings speakers who had had personal experience in the mission field. Bishop Selwyn, Bishop Hills, Rev. T. V. French, afterwards Bishop of Lahore; Bishop Gray of Capetown; a black clergyman, Rev. J. Duport, from the Pongas Mission; a native of Honolulu; missionaries from India, Australia, Africa visited Wantage year by year, and addressed crowded audiences. A parochial association in connection with S. P. G. was formed in 1862, under the auspices of the late Bishop Christopher Wordsworth, at that time vicar of Stanford in the Vale, and a dear friend and neighbour.

Nor did William Butler's zeal for missions confine

H

itself to his parish. He travelled as "deputation" for S. P. G. two or three times; and when he was living in Lincolnshire during the last years of his life he often came across reminiscences of his visit many years before.

He was instrumental in forming the "Special Agency for Foreign Missions," of which he was chairman during the whole time of its existence, and he acted as Commissary to Bishop Macrorie of Maritzburg from 1868 to 1890.

To return to the parish. He laid great stress on the ministry of preaching, and especially insisted on method and order in this important work. In Holy Week, 1849, a scheme of sermons was arranged, followed a few years later by one for the Lent services. His own practice was invariably to choose his Sunday morning text from the Epistle or Gospel for the week. On Sunday evenings in the Trinity season he preached a kind of commentary on various books of the Bible; and in this manner he expounded to his people, verse by verse, Isaiah, Hosea, the Pastoral Epistles, the Revelation, etc.; not attempting to enter into critical questions, but endeavouring to bring out the practical teaching of Holy Writ. On Tuesday and Friday evenings after service he gave what he called "lectures": ten minutes of exposition and application of a passage usually taken from the first lesson just read. Thus he instructed his congregation from the Bible, while he observed the order prescribed by the Church. His sermons were all carefully prepared, and often written out fully, as were also the "meditations" which he gave in the afternoon twice a week in Lent.

On one summer Sunday a wasp stung him in the throat soon after he had entered the pulpit. He continued his sermon with no outward sign of discomfort, but after service mentioned the occurrence in the vestry. "Please, sir, we saw it crawling up you, and we thought it would sting you," observed a chorister. No doubt the rustic mind which loves anything of the nature of a practical joke had hoped for a "scene" when the crisis came.

The "Parish Journal," under the date of Ascension Day, 1871, records an informal preaching. It should be remembered that this was the preacher's fourth sermon that day, the first having been delivered at the 4 A.M. Celebration.

Coming home at night I found the iron bridge filled with young men. This is a great evil. They make unpleasant remarks, etc., to girls and others passing by. I spoke to them about this; and as they did not seem inclined to move I took out my Prayer-book, read the Gospel for Ascension Day, and preached them a short sermon. This answered well. I wished them good night, and as I entered my garden they all walked away, responding to me in a very friendly tone.

In the matter of hours of service he tried as far as possible to meet the needs and convenience of all the parishioners. An intimate friend writes of his first years at Wantage:

He laid down as a principle for himself in beginning his work there, that he would not in any way alter the services which he found in use then, *viz.* the Sunday Matins, and afternoon (three o'clock) Evensong, and the monthly late Celebrations. He was ready to *add on* as many other services as he pleased as time went on, but for many years those two Sunday services went on unaltered, his object being to conciliate and satisfy the "old inhabitants" who had got used to these services, and would regard any other as innovations.

Seeing that it was practically impossible for the labourers to come to church on Ascension Day and New Year's Day at the ordinary hours, he began, in 1849, a Celebration on Ascension Day at 4.45 A.M., and finding after a few years' experience that even this hour was too late, he fixed the service at 4, and on New Year's Day at 4.30; and he was rewarded by the large attendance of those on whose behalf the effort had been made. He found, too, that the practice of early Celebrations satisfied an instinct of reverence. "I always likes to come *leer*" (*i.e.* empty, fasting), said a sturdy yeoman farmer, at one time an opponent, but afterwards a firm supporter of the Vicar.

He did not consider reading the Lessons as a matter of secondary importance. In a paper on "Utterance" published in the *Literary Churchman* for Nov. 15, 1889, he gave his matured views on this subject.

As to the reading of the Lessons, let it be remembered that as the prayers are the action of man speaking to God, so these, looked at rightly, are nothing less than God speaking to man, and the reader cannot be too strongly impressed with the great seriousness and solemnity of that which he has in hand. The book itself should be reverently handled as that in which is contained the Word of God, the very name by which St. John describes the Only Begotten Son. When the Lessons are concluded it should be closed, in order to prevent dust or injury happening to it, after the pattern of Him Who, after reading in the synagogue at Nazareth from the Prophet Isaiah, "closed the book and gave it again to the minister." The Lessons should be read not mumblingly or hesitatingly, not noisily or roughly, not emphatically or dramatically, not what is called impressively, but quietly, thoughtfully, restrainedly, with just so much, and no more, of emphasis as will enable the hearers readily to grasp its meaning. . . . Again, it is very desirable that the clergyman, before reading any portion of Holy Scripture, should study it in its original language—Greek or Hebrew. In this way not only will he appreciate far more thoroughly the meaning of the passage, but he will be secured against mistakes sometimes of a very serious nature.

"His reading," writes the friend previously quoted, "of the Bible was very impressive, though exceedingly quiet. He had a way of throwing up some word or sentence into a strong relief, so that it impressed itself on one's mind and brought out new meanings. I have often and often thought of one evening in the Home chapel when the Lesson for the day was the one about David's sin. I thought at the moment while he was reading it that it was rather a distressing chapter to read to those girls. He read it through quite evenly and quietly till he came to the last verse. Then there was a little pause, and then slowly, and with tremendous force of expression, he said, 'But the thing that David had done *displeased the Lord.*' I have never forgotten the impression he made—it was worth a whole volume of sermons.'

He gained a thorough knowledge of the people committed to his charge by assiduous visiting at their houses, not omitting such Dissenters as were willing to receive his visits. Thus he notes in May, 1862:

Visited the ——. They are strong Baptists. They received me in a very kind and friendly manner. I am sure that it is quite worth while to cultivate people of this kind, for friendliness, if it does not win them to the Church, yet disarms them for open hostility; and it is impossible to say when the good seed may be sown.

On visiting in general, he writes in October, 1851:

Our only hope, humanly speaking, and considering the un-popularity of the side which we advocate, is in gentleness, resolution, demonstrative self-denial, *and hard work in visiting.* This last, I think, we need to have imprest on us. To go out at four o'clock, stay half-an-hour or longer pleasing ourselves in some way, will not do. We must honestly and conscien-tiously devote at least three and a half or four hours daily to visiting work. Now is the time when harvest and fairs are over and people are sick. Sickness too should be taken in a business-like way. We should think what effect we intend to produce on the person, and work to that. We should visit always at the same time, so that the sick man may learn to look for the visit. We should always pray with him. It is very easy to lounge time away, which, if we were in Mr. Hart's Foundry working as mechanics, we should not dare to do.

Another paper in the *Literary Churchman* sums up his many years' experience :

Parochial visiting should be seriously accepted and taken in hand as an integral portion of the duties of the parish priest, and a definite portion of the week's hours should be allotted to the carrying of it out. I cannot agree with those superior beings who deliberately decline to visit, on the ground that their parishioners ought to come to them. Rather it seems to me that this is essentially one of the cases when Mahomet should go to the mountain, and be thankful that he has the chance of doing so. Nor, again, do I think those wise who allege as a reason for not visiting their flock that they have no "gift" for such as this, that they do not know what to say, and the like. I am quite sure that they are throwing away a very important chance, and that with a little effort against their natural difficulties, such as most of us have to make in regard to other things, and after a little experience and a few mistakes, they will find that the "gift" will come. The time given to such visiting is in no sense of the word wasted time. Most true is the old saying, "A house-going parson makes a church-going people." Nothing at all—no fine preaching, nor overflowing soup-kettle, nor system of assiduous "district visitors," brings the people to church like the regular loving visit of the parson. What, moreover, like this enables the minister to gain a real knowledge of his people's minds and natures, their weaknesses and their strong points—their needs both of body and soul? Surely everything of this kind that he can learn respecting them is helpful—not least even their language, varying as it does so much in different parts of England, and, as all know, so closely interwoven with their mode of thought. . . . Parochial visiting to be really effective must be carried out with a definite purpose and object—that object in few words being, like all the rest of a minister's life and duties—the winning of souls to Christ, and the maintaining them in the right course. . . . The winning of souls much resembles the taking of a city. Trenches must be laid down, often far from the walls, gradually to approach nearer and nearer, till the opportunity is found for entering. Thus the minister—never having lost sight of his real object, *viz.* to do the work of Christ and "preach His gospel to every creature," at least of those committed to his charge—must be contented often, it may be for many years, to talk on general subjects—as the health of the family; their worldly condition and prospects; events which have occurred in the neighbourhood, whether public or private; the garden, if there be one; but, above all, as the topic most unfailing of interest and most legitimate, the children—their characters, their progress at school, their present and their future. Such subjects as these, kindly and sympathetically handled, will break down barriers of shyness and reserve, and open the door for more directly spiritual work. Confidence once thus kindled, there will follow in the right time counsel as to private or household prayer, encouragement to regular attendance at the House of God, the importance of Holy Communion, the best method of maintaining the Christian battle against the world, the flesh, and the devil; possibly also the meaning of true Repentance for past or present sin, in its threefold division of Contrition, Confession, and Satisfaction. . . . As to the time of visiting—the afternoon hours are, on the whole, the most convenient for all classes, especially for the poor, whose cottage or lodgements necessarily require the morning's ordering, before a visitor can be welcome. . . .

It has sometimes been found a good plan—where *the clergyman is sufficiently well known and on thoroughly intimate terms*—to visit in the early evening, that is, after the day's work is ended, and before the elder portion of the family has retired to rest. In this way, and often in no other, acquaintance may be made with the *men*, who are necessarily for the most part absent from their homes, and invisible or at least unapproachable during the day. The writer of this paper, taking the idea from the busy parochial life of Bishop Stanley of Norwich, used occasionally, as it seemed to him with much advantage, thus to visit some of his flock. At such times, in houses where such a practice would be acceptable, it might be proposed to read and explain some short passage of Holy Scripture, and to say a few Collects taken from the Book of Common Prayer. . . . As much respect should be shown to the poorest cottager as to the greatest peer. The head should always be uncovered on entering the house, and a chair should not be taken till offered. These may seem trifles, but they may materially affect the position of the visitor in the estimation of the visited. . . . Then, too, let the clergyman be careful not to confine his visits to the poor, as though they were a marked-off class, or as if he had no place in the houses of others. All should be visited, rich, poor, tradesmen, farmers, gentry, professional men, Dissenters, Church-people, friends, and even—if he have any—foes. Is he not the minister of the whole parish? If he have any doubt as to his welcome, if the very touch of the latch fill his mind as with the anxiety of some difficult problem, at the thought of what to say and do, let him offer a word of momentary prayer, and he will never find this to fail.

It is astonishing what solid and definite work may thus be done, far more than by sermons or by any merely general teaching, how many difficulties may be explained, how many stumbling-blocks removed, how much the tone of a parish may be lifted, how much interest excited in the Church, how the clergyman himself may win love and legitimate influence. To this it may be added that nothing is more refreshing to one who has the slightest love for souls than an afternoon thus spent. The sense of being kindly welcomed and greeted, the sense of knowledge gained of his people, the sense of duty accomplished, the sense of having distilled some good and abiding teaching, the sense of having gained warm and attached friends,—all these combine to "reward sevenfold into his own bosom" the man who, instead of wasting his hours in lingering over a novel or newspaper by his fireside, or flirting at lawn tennis, or seeking what is called society, or even following out congenial studies, visits steadily, prayerfully, and laboriously that flock over which "the Holy Ghost has made him overseer."

The deep interest in his people which these extracts illustrate, caused him not to confine his labours for them to spiritual concerns. As in most old places, many of the cottages in Wantage were hardly fit for human habitation, and those who lived in them led lives not far above "the beasts that perish." As early as 1849, the Vicar purchased a batch of these cottages, pulled them down, replaced them with properly built houses, and tenanted them with respectable families. This he did on several occasions, and some of the other Wantage residents followed his example. Another matter which he had much at heart was the health of the town. He soon discovered that the systems of drainage and of the water supply were highly unsatisfactory, as was proved by frequent visitations of typhoid fever ; and he went about with the town surveyor personally investigating nuisances, and never resting till the arm of the law was brought to bear upon them.

He did not overlook the value of thrift, and at the beginning of 1859 he set on foot a penny bank, which for many years he attended every Saturday evening. He was astonished at the power of saving

out of their small earnings shown by the labouring
class as soon as the opportunity was put within
their reach.

He took part in such social festivities as the
annual dinners of the "clubs" or benefit societies;
and from the beginning of the Volunteer movement
he attached himself to it, partly from his strong
sense of patriotism, and partly from his feeling of
responsibility as the representative of the Church
in the parish.   Thus he writes on Oct. 16, 1873:

> The prizes of the Volunteers given away to-day.   I was
> asked to give them, and to join them afterwards at supper.
> This I gladly did, because I am convinced that at this present
> time it is of all importance for the clergy to assert and accept
> their position as the ministers of the great national Church,
> and therefore interested in all the concerns of the people
> among whom they are.

Colonel Lord Wantage, V.C., with whom the
Vicar was closely associated as Chaplain to the
Berks Volunteers, has recorded his recollections of
him in his military capacity.

> Among the Vicar of Wantage's many great qualities, were
> some characteristic ones which especially endeared him to his
> country neighbours and friends, outside his own parochial
> domain.   He had a spirit of uncompromising partisanship
> which led him to throw himself heartily into the ranks of
> those who were carrying out projects or movements which
> coincided with his own convictions of what was good, right,
> or patriotic.
> Patriotism was indeed a marked feature of his singularly
> manly character.   He was an Englishman and a patriot to his
> heart's core.   The military instinct was strong within him, and
> soldiers and everything connected with them appeared strongly
> to his imagination and his sympathy.   He saw clearly, and in

his addresses to soldiers brought out strongly the great qualities requisite alike to make a good soldier and a good Christian.

The early stages and subsequent more complete development of the Volunteer movement very precisely fell in with the combative elements in his character.

The notion that England was to be left at the mercy of a possible invading foe would put him into a state of hot indignation, during which he would pour forth floods of patriotic sentiments, sometimes almost unmeasured as coming from a minister of peace. On these occasions he would give expression to his confident opinion as to the necessity of every Englishman being trained to arms for the defence of his country, and of every child being taught the discipline of drill.

It was not unnatural, taking into account these sentiments, that he should throw himself heart and soul into active support of the Volunteer movement, especially in his own county, and he found a congenial spirit in his neighbour and attached friend, Colonel Loyd Lindsay, who commanded the Regiment raised in the County of Berks.

The Vicar took great delight in being present in his capacity of Regimental Chaplain during the week annually spent by the Regiment in camp in various parts of the county. For many years he continued to fill the duties of Chaplain, associating freely with his military comrades, and exercising among them an influence for good which must have left a deep mark on many. He was always punctual to hold a short open-air service at the close of the early morning drill. On Sundays an early Celebration in a small tent specially arranged for the purpose was followed by a full parade of the troops and an open-air service. The spirit-stirring sermons he preached on these occasions, sometimes standing on the ancient Tumuli of Churn Down, or under the spreading oak trees of Berkshire Forests, and once on the slopes of the Saxon burial hill at Lockinge, with the troops drawn up in line, and the villagers of Ardington and Lockinge grouped on the grass terraces of the steep hill side—are still vividly present to the minds of his old comrades.

The special excellence of the "Wantage" Company, which he regarded as peculiarly his own—their prowess at the rifle butts and their success in the "tug-of-war"—were frequent matters of exultation to him.

On Low Sunday it was, and is still, the custom of the Wantage parishioners to give up the body of their church to the Volunteers and Yeomanry of the district, while neighbouring families interested in them found seats which the good people of Wantage readily accorded them. On these occasions, after a hearty service and an eloquent sermon from the Vicar, a military parade was formed around the statue of King Alfred in the market place, and the troops marched round the town—the band playing, and the Vicar in his Chaplain's uniform marching in the forefront, his keen face lighted up with martial ardour.

When the Vicar left the corps on taking up his duties at Lincoln, his comrades of the Berkshire Regiment presented him with a piece of plate, having words of respect and affection engraved on it, which ever afterwards found an honoured place on the sideboard at the Lincoln Deanery—reminding him doubtless of happy days and warm friendships.

This sketch of his methods in his parochial work may be summed up by some extracts from the "Parish Journal," written at the close of the years 1864, 1867, and 1876.

Summary, 1864.—Lukewarmness is a great evil, which of course brings with it inconsistency and carelessness. How can they be met? Only, as I believe, by self-sacrifice, earnest watchfulness, and readiness to take advantage of every opening and opportunity. There is great danger lest we be satisfied with interesting and drawing people to us without spiritualising and Christianising them, lest we suffer them to rest satisfied with mere decency and the minimum of service. We are set among people naturally unholy, careless, unbelieving (in the deeper sense of the word), that is, having no natural leanings towards the unseen and the heavenly. Should not all our thoughts be bent towards raising them? ἡμῶν τὸ πολίτευμα ἐν οὐρανοῖς ὑπάρχει? Our visits should be regular, and with this end before us, however far off we may seem to be from attaining

it. What is needed is a gentle pressure, the carefully considering of each soul's needs, and the moving it on gently in
that direction. Some need the very simplest elements, prayer,
decently regular attendance at church, and the like; others
should be stirred towards Holy Communion; others again to
daily service, or at least occasional but *regular* attendance on
week days; others again to higher things. Wherever there
is difficulty—and where is there not in dealing with souls?—
we should bring the case at evening before God, and pray
for help before entering into the house. The work should
be recognised as the real object of our lives, the reason why
God has made us, and not as a πάρεργον to be taken up and
laid down at our pleasure. It should occupy our thoughts
and our hearts.

Summary, 1867.—To rush forward would simply be to alienate
our best. We have to teach, give *them* a desire, and *then* to
act. Meanwhile, there is plenty of work to be done of the
more solid kind; the poor to visit and lead onwards, the
children to teach to pray and to love the Church. *Evening*
visits, children called in and questioned and examined, regular
house-to-house work, the watching for a gleam of desire in
the hard and ungodly, earnest prayer for our people, pleading
for them with God, thinking over them individually and
collectively, daily attendance on the sick; there is in all these
enough, and more than enough, to occupy and satisfy one.
Nothing but this kind of *solid service* will keep this parish
up to the mark. Our people are not enthusiastic, but they
have, nevertheless, certain principles, admitted truths, on which
we may build, and for which we should carefully and discrim-
inately look. May God grant us all a true spirit of love of
souls, and that readiness to *give up all* for the sake of those
souls for whom Jesus died, without which no ministry can ever
be otherwise than "as sounding brass or as a tinkling cymbal."

Summary, 1876.—Our work then lies before us: steady,
persistent visiting, gaining a thorough knowledge of our people,
and bringing *them* to know *us* and our motives and ends;
earnest thought-out sermons and instructions in Church of every
variety; inculcation of Christian duties, especially of private
prayer and Holy Communion; watchfulness over our children, to
see that they are taught why they are (1) Christians, (2) Church-

men; trying by all legitimate means to win Dissenters and the careless, of whom, alas! we have very many among us; preparing bright attractive services; readiness at all times and at all costs to devote and sacrifice our time, our means, and all that we have for the sake of those to whom we are sent. Nothing short of all this will be strong enough to resist the atmosphere of evil and indifferentism, of ignorance and perverseness. May God grant to us all the strength and grace which we need!

CHAPTER V.

THE SISTERHOOD.

A BREAK must now be made in the narrative of the parochial work at Wantage to tell the story of the Sisterhood, which, starting from small beginnings and under great discouragement, was destined to claim a large share of William Butler's life and interests. His indomitable energy and perseverance which refused to acknowledge defeat so long as something remained worth fighting for, carried him through difficulties and opposition which would have cowed a weaker man. The history of his forty-five years connexion with the Community is closely interwoven with his life and work as a parish priest.

As early as 1839 Newman, Keble, Pusey, and Hook were corresponding on the possibility of establishing societies of *Sœurs de Charité*. It was not, however, till 1845 that the first trial was made by the establishment of Dr. Pusey's Sisterhood in Park Village, Regent's Park.[1] About three years

---

[1] See *Life of Dr. Pusey*, vol. iii., p. 23, *et seq.*

later Miss Sellon's response to the Bishop of Exeter's appeal for workers amongst the poor in Plymouth resulted in the establishment of a Sisterhood to carry on the works of mercy in that town.

The events which led to an attempt at founding a Sisterhood at Wantage were nearly coincident with those which led to the founding of Miss Sellon's Community.

When William Butler entered upon his parochial work in Wantage early in 1847, he had already conceived in his mind a plan for organising a Sisterhood, which should not only be a handmaid to him in the work of female education in his parish, and in visiting the sick and poor, but should ultimately train Sisters to go out two and two into the villages as school teachers, and so provide for the better education of the poor in rural districts. He foresaw that the battle of the Church would be fought in the schools, and having been struck by the isolated condition of the village teachers, and by their lack of a high standard, he desired to set on foot a scheme to raise their tone, brighten their lives, and increase their usefulness as Church workers.

Ere long he thought he saw a realisation of his hopes. Archdeacon Manning was anxious to find work for a friend of his, Elizabeth Crawford Lockhart,[1] who had sustained the great grief and shock of seeing her brother and step-mother join the Church of Rome, but who, under the influence of

---

[1] Cousin to John Gibson Lockhart.

Manning, was at that time kept loyal herself to the Church of England.

Miss Lockhart was a woman of no ordinary character, and her cultivated mind and holy life endeared her to her friends, among whom she reckoned the Kebles and Dysons. This led Manning to speak of her to Mr. Butler, who sent her an invitation to Wantage early in 1848. She spent the Lent of that year at the Vicarage, and soon became a loved and trusted friend of the Vicar and his family.

The Vicar and Miss Lockhart, both being eager to set the work on foot without loss of time, allowed no difficulties to stand in their way. As no house was available, two cottages were taken, and soon after Easter the nucleus of the present Sisterhood was formed. The household at first consisted of Miss Lockhart, who was the Mother Superior, and Miss Mary Reid, who had been for some years connected with the Lockharts as mistress of a small school established by them at Chichester, and besides these, two young girls who were to make themselves useful in the house, and to be trained to take part in the work with the possibility of some day becoming Sisters. The arrangements of the little household were of the simplest and most inexpensive kind. The help of friends on visits was gladly welcomed, and one who in those early days was frequently there gives details of their life:

One of the cottages had been inhabited before by a working shoemaker, and my bedroom was the room in which the cobbler sat and worked; it was on the ground floor, very little above the street, and I could hear the passers-by and the old watch-man who used then to patrol the streets crying the hour of the night.   The oratory was upstairs, a little blue-washed place with sloping roof and roughly-boarded floor; the only furniture consisted of two long desks with sloping sides made of bare deal, at which we stood to say the Offices.   There was room for three or four at the outside to stand on either side. Here sometimes the Vicar would come to join in one Office or another, or occasionally to give us a few words of exhortation.

Such notices as "Lauds with the Sisterhood ¼ to 6,"—"Lauds and Terce with the Sisterhood, and addressed them on their first beginning.   May He ever help them and prosper their work,"—"With Mr. Keble to Prime at the Sisterhood," are of frequent occurrence in the "Parish Journal" during his first years at Wantage.   Here also came Arch-deacon Manning from time to time.

The National schools were not then built, and the girls' school was carried on in two cottages which were adapted for the purpose.   Here Miss Lockhart and her staff taught daily.   School began at nine A.M., then all went to church for matins at ten, and back to school till twelve, and again in the afternoon from two to four.   Some visiting was also done by the Sisters among the sick poor. Towards the end of 1848 the little household moved into a larger and more commodious cottage.   In February 1849 they were joined by Harriet Day : she was sent by Mr. Henry Wilberforce to make trial of the life and work in the newly formed Community.   Later on came Charlotte Gilbert, a servant maid, the daughter of a labourer.   These two only among the earliest members of the Society ended their days as Sisters of the Community.

In an address delivered to the Sisters in 1873 the Vicar referred to these early beginnings.

It is now twenty-five years since I was first consulted, young as I was, and unworthy as I was and have been ever since, as to the practicability of forming a Sisterhood to work among the poor of the parish of Wantage. There was then but one other Sisterhood in existence in the Church of England, and I differed from others, much more worthy than myself, who feared the effect of such an experiment in the unprepared state of the minds of the people in general for such a step, and with the help of the noble and gifted woman who determined to devote her life and her means to the work, this Community was begun. How from that time it has been carried on, and at the cost of what anxiety, with what earnest prayer, with what hopes and fears, only myself and one other know.

It is with deep thankfulness that I look at what we are now and think of the trembling beginning of that work which I cannot doubt God has indeed blessed. The distinguishing characteristic of this Society from the first has been simplicity. Our object at the beginning was to gather together those who would be content with a frugal life, patient toil, quiet appearance,—content with yielding themselves in simple-hearted devotion to spend and be spent for their Master and their Lord,—I repeat, great simplicity in dress, and, if I may use the word, in ritual: hard work and little show has ever been the mark of this Community. Does this seem a poor and unsatisfactory sort of aim? Surely not! if we consider Him Who was "the lowly" as well as the "undefiled One." Is not the Hidden Life the ideal of the true Sister, and where can she find it sooner than in extreme simplicity, a quiet exterior, and in deep humility.

But though the first beginnings were so happy and peaceful it was not long before the hope of founding an Educational Order was destined to receive its first rude shock.

In order to understand how penitentiary came to take the place of educational work in the early days of the Community it will be necessary to recall the state of the English Church fifty years ago.

As the standard of holy living was raised by the inculcation of sound doctrine, and the note of penitence was emphasised as one of the essential marks of a sanctified life, the desire was awakened in the hearts of many to extend a helping hand to that class of sinners, who, often more sinned against than sinning, are looked upon as the outcasts of society. The Church of Rome and the Protestant bodies on the Continent had long established homes for the reception of fallen women, and these had been valued as a means whereby many weary and heavy laden souls had been reclaimed from a course of sin and misery and led into paths of peace; but until 1848 the Church of England had not borne witness against the sin of impurity or extended the hand of compassion to those desirous to return from their evil ways by raising up for their reception homes in which the work undertaken should bear a distinctly spiritual stamp. The Rev. John Armstrong (afterwards Bishop of Grahamstown) is justly regarded as the originator of the Church Penitentiary movement, and he was instrumental in arousing the conscience of a large number of Churchmen to the duty of caring for these poor neglected outcasts. But apart from any direct connexion with Mr. Armstrong, two Church Penitentiaries came into existence about the same time. The first of these was opened by Mrs. Tennant at Clewer on St. Peter's Day, 1849, the other a few months later at Wantage. Miss Lockhart had been only a short time at work in the parish schools, when probably influenced by Manning, she conceived herself called to the work of rescuing the fallen. This change of purpose, involving as it apparently did, failure of his carefully thought-out scheme for an educational Order, naturally was the cause of no small disappointment to William Butler. He expressed his feelings in letters to Archdeacon Manning, who rejoined:

LAVINGTON, Sept. 25, 1848.

I have been most sincerely grieved at the thought of having grieved you. And I hardly know what to write. It was thought right towards you that such an idea should not be entertained without your knowledge. And the effect of this communication is no more than to prevent a sudden misunderstanding hereafter, if the day should ever come. I say this, because clearly as I seem to see the work and the way, of which Miss Lockhart has spoken to you, as falling within the will of God, yet I have so deep a sense of the duty not to change any work without overbearing reasons, and of the singular awfulness of the work she referred to, that I think my life (no certain one) may probably drop before it becomes a practical question: and if I live, so long a time may elapse before it could be attempted, that I think Miss Lockhart's stay at Wantage as permanent as your incumbency. I don't say that it might not end during your incumbency, but your incumbency may end during her stay. Therefore I do not see that you need be disquieted.

He wrote a little later:

I have been called away to London, and got home only last night, or your letter should have been answered sooner.

I thank you for it very sincerely. It takes from me a fear and a pain I could not but feel. Though I never for a moment doubted the perfect right and fitness, by the rule of nature and of the spirit of our correspondence, yet I felt that nothing short of a high submission of will, an *abnegatio sui tertii gradûs* would suffice to keep from between us a feeling [of] grief arising from contrariety of will. But your letter sets me at rest for ever: and I feel sure that with such a discipline of self, even such a loss as I trust you may not incur, would turn into blessing to your flock and to your own soul.

While the diversion of Miss Lockhart's energy to penitentiary work was still pending, the Vicar, writing to Mr. Keble, refers to the Sisters' work during the first year of their residence in Wantage.

I wanted also to talk to you about our Sisterhood here, which has, by the blessing of God, sped so fairly. It is exercising daily more influence on our people; and as a washer-woman said to me the other day, "It makes one ashamed of oneself to see Miss L." All classes take to it. But as I think you know, I shall lose a great mainstay, Miss L., for the Penitentiary, and with her at least two will swarm off, leaving, in fact, Miss A. alone. Two or three will, however, I expect, join us; but it is most needful to preserve continuity, and I am very anxious to keep Miss A. as head of a future Home.

On July 22, 1849 (St. Mary Magdalene's Day), the Vicar thus addressed the Sisters:

Dear Sisters, a year has now passed since first we met to set apart, as far as in us lay, this house, and you who were about to dwell here, to the service of Almighty God.

It seems but yesterday since we knelt here together, and
yet these twelve months have been able strangely to change
the whole current of your lives. You feel yourselves distinctly
set apart—I who address you feel it. Others little used to
look with a discerning or even friendly eye on the higher
aimings of the Christian life, feel it and own it also. Your
life has now assumed, so to say, a permanent mould. The
Religious Life, to use a technical phrase, has become your
natural life. The ways of the world:—secular arrangements,
times, studies, society, things not out of place, nor wrong,
would now seem strange and jarring to you. Religious order,
regular hours of devotion, the weekly Celebration, involving
a daily preparation of a more or less formal kind, seasons
of silence, penitence; sorrowing, rejoicing, as the Church
appoints, with Christ; have now wound themselves round
your very being, edifying and sustaining your souls.

This feeling of sanctification is exactly that which was
needed to enable us to strike root downwards for the present,
and by God's blessing hereafter to bear fruit upwards.

After some months of consideration, it was decided, with the approval and concurrence of the
Vicar, that a Home for penitents, with Miss Lockhart as its head, should be opened at Wantage,
under the direction of Archdeacon Manning, and
with the Rev. T. Vincent, who was working as
curate in the parish, as chaplain.

On a bright winter's morning, Feb. 2, 1850,
four priests, four Sisters, and a few friends met
together to dedicate the first penitentiary work
undertaken by Sisters in the Church of England
since the Reformation. The event is briefly recorded
in the "Parish Journal."

Feb. 2, Purification of the B. V. M.

The house in Newbury Street was opened with a Celebration.
Vincent arranged the chapel. Three sisters, two assistant

friends, two penitents were present at the Celebration, together
with the Archdeacon, H. W.,[1] Vincent, and myself. Before
the Celebration I said the benediction from the Rituale for
the house.

The service was most thrilling, and one could not but rest
in faith that God's blessing is on the work. In the evening
the Archdeacon addressed the "Familia."

Miss Lockhart wrote a fuller account of the
ceremony to a friend.

PENITENTS' HOME, Feb. 6, 1850.

You will have heard from Mrs. Pretyman of the safe arrival
of her beautiful scrolls, and the actual beginning of our
work. I should like you to have been with us on that morning,
nothing could have looked more solemn and bright withal
than our little chapel. The altar, with its pure white frontal,
ornamented only with five gold crosses, candlesticks and altar-
plate really befitting an altar, and between the candlesticks and
a three-branched light in the centre four vases, very beautiful
in themselves, filled with white camellias, and a wreath of
flowers resting upon the window-sill above.

We had four priests, the Father Director, Vicar, Chaplain,
and H. Wilberforce. The Vicar said the Office for Blessing
the House, and then the Archdeacon celebrated, the women
being allowed to be present on this occasion. They are not
to be so generally, as the Archdeacon does not think it safe
for them until they are better prepared. In the evening he
preached as nobody but he can, to the whole household,
dear ——, who has permission to come to our Offices, being
also present.

On Sunday he celebrated again at eight o'clock, and
preached for the Vicar's schools at church in the morning,
H. Wilberforce officiating for us, and before evening service
he spoke to the Penitents alone in the chapel, and after it
to us. I was sorry there were but two yet come, E. G., and
M., the workhouse girl; two others have come since and we
are keeping the remaining places for E. Ryle's pupils who
are now in hospital, and are to come as soon as they are

---

[1] Rev. Henry Wilberforce, vicar of East Farleigh.

well enough. We are still in much confusion, but hope by next week to be quite settled; the two houses make it much more difficult to arrange things in a regular orderly way. Charlotte Gilbert, the probationary lay Sister,[1] is very useful. I like her much, and hope she may like the life well enough to stay with us. . . . I have always forgotten to say to you that we are by no means in a condition as you seemed to think not to want help. The resources our Father Director counts so touchingly upon are neither more nor less than the alms of the faithful, which he feels sure will never fail us if God indeed prospers our work. We have enough to support ourselves and six penitents, but about £200 a year will be wanted for rent, chaplain's salary, etc., so if you know any one who would like to help us either by giving or collecting, we shall receive it thankfully, so that it be not given by constraint, but for the love of God and of His lost sheep, and of course the larger our funds the greater will be our power of enlarging our limits.

Hardly however had this new work been fairly started when the attractive power of Rome proved too much for the Superior, and before three months had elapsed the following entry appears in the " Parish Journal."

April 17. Archdeacon Manning came. Much interesting though sad talk with him. I fear much trouble here from one quarter. May God in His mercy avert it and soften the blow.

The tidings of this great trouble, after the blow had fallen, were sent to Mr. Keble.

[1] Charlotte Gilbert was the only lay Sister of the Community. As time went on Mr. Butler found the problems which presented themselves in classifying the members drawn from various social grades, into Choir and Lay Sisters, to be so great that he resolved after much careful consideration and consultation with those who had practical experience of the difficulty, to have only one social grade within the Order which he founded. This is one of the distinguishing notes of the Order of St. Mary the Virgin of Wantage.

[July, 1850.]

I am ashamed to trouble you, but you will, I know, be
interested in the sad news that Miss L. has finally determined
on leaving us, and that this day she will join her brother. We
have done what we could in some ways for her, but the strong
draw towards Rome, together with the undermining support
of her spiritual counsellors, shivered all my attempts to pieces.
Now we are in much trouble to keep the work up; we have
no one on whom we can rest, indeed, the household is a body
without a backbone, just standing up and no more. The Bishop
kindly offers to do all he can for us. But he is overwrought
with so many things. And my hands are indeed so over-
loaded that I can [hardly] keep what is on them already.
Vincent holds up nobly. Can you find anyone for us? We
are not at present in want of money, for the heaviest and
main expenses are frankt to the end of the year. But the
anxiety is boundless.

What is doing in the Church? Are men failing, or why is
the great meeting put off?[1] It is very depressing to us at a
distance.

The calamity which had befallen the infant
Community did not stop here. Sister Mary quickly
followed her friend and Superior. Henry Wilberforce,
too, had seceded to Rome. Would the step he had
taken affect the two—Sister Harriet and Sister
Charlotte—who remained, and who had been sent
to Wantage by him? This was naturally the thought
uppermost in the mind of the Vicar, and he resolved
to throw himself into the breach and try to hold
the position.

Sister Harriet was a woman of a remarkably shy
and retiring character, and up to this time had
come little into personal contact with the Vicar,

[1] To protest against the Gorham judgement. *Life of Dr. Pusey*,
vol. iii., chap. x.

and indeed stood so much in awe of him, that
when he came to the house she used to contrive
some errand amongst her poor people to take her
out. But now, if the work was to be carried
through, it was to her that he must look at least
for temporary help in this crisis. She had been
converted from Socinianism by Henry Wilberforce,
and felt she owed to him her very soul. Surely
the step he had taken must be right, and she
would follow him and her friend Miss Lockhart,
to whom she had deeply attached herself, into the
Church of Rome. Thus she argued, but the Vicar
would not let her go without seeking to convince
her in calmer moments of her error, and to retain
her in the English Church. He invited her to stay
at the vicarage; while there he not only instructed
her daily as to the position of the Church of her
baptism, but gradually gained the deep affection
of her nature, and the visit was the beginning of a
friendship which strengthened as the years went on.

Bishop Wilberforce, to whose fatherly advice
William Butler had looked from the earliest beginnings of the Community, at this juncture proved a
most kind and helpful friend. He took an early opportunity of visiting the house, and at his suggestion
various modifications were effected.

From this time till 1854 the Sisters worked on
under the superintendence of the Vicar without
formally appointing a Superior. With William
Butler as their spiritual guide, the little band of
Sisters caught the spirit of singleness of purpose

which he strove to instil into them. In spite of
all difficulties and disappointments the Vicar was
able to look even hopefully forward, and to write
cheerfully to Mr. Keble at the beginning of the
New Year:

WANTAGE VICARAGE, Jan. 9, 1851.

Many happy New Years to you and yours and all at Hursley.
It seems strange to write so blithely in this day of sorrow,
but I think in spite of all there was no harm in wishing
and even hoping. . . . Miss Hedger (Sister Catherine) deserves
great consideration, for she came here in the hour of our need
without having any kind of acquaintance with us or our work,
merely invited by a mutual friend. She has now given up
home and sisters, after a bitter struggle, to uphold our Home,
and is moreover able and discreet. Things have prospered
under her care beyond our hopes. . . . It would be an exceeding
pleasure to us to show you "the Home." You know that
Miss Ashington is likely to come here again as a permanent
sister; she talks of coming on the 20th or 21st.

Philip Pusey is staying with us, as merry and funny as a
kitten. . . .

A few months later he wrote:

We are all very strong and hearty. In the Home are eleven
penitents and five Sisters, and we just keep about £120
between us and jail.

Slowly, and yet always steadily, the work grew
and developed under exceptionally difficult circumstances. As more applications were made for
admission to the Penitentiary, increased accommodation was obtained by turning lofts into garrets, and
out-houses into laundry and work-rooms, and finally,
by building a temporary chapel. So short-handed
were the Sisters at times that on two occasions
they turned to the Clewer Sisterhood for help, and

their appeal was generously responded to by that
Community.

There was much which gave encouragement to
the workers. Some of those gathered into the
Home caught the fire of love for souls and sought
to reclaim others. In 1851 a penitent was dying
of consumption. Her constant prayer for nearly a
year was that a sister, whom she knew to be living
a life of sin, might be led to repentance. As each
new-comer was admitted, she eagerly inquired her
name. After many disappointments the poor sufferer
had at length the happiness of welcoming the sister
for whose salvation she had so earnestly supplicated.
The other had heard of her dying condition and
had walked all the way from Bristol to see her.
When she knocked at the door she had neither
knowledge of, or desire for, repentance. Her visit
ended in her remaining and attending on her sister
during the last weeks of her life, and the one
who had learned penitent love taught with failing
breath the love of the Saviour who had died for
sinners.

One other incident bears testimony to the same
earnest zeal on the part of the penitents. One of
their number was unsettled and resolved on leaving
the Home. Three others banded together to win
her by their prayers to remain. They asked permission to be allowed to spend a day in fasting
and prayer in behalf of their companion. This was
not allowed them, but the chaplain, having spoken
to them collectively and ascertained that all desired

to help her, consented to their giving up their breakfast and spending their time in devotion which he himself conducted. Before the day closed they had the joy of having their companion among them, willing and anxious to remain.

As the work developed the fact became more and more apparent that a duly appointed head was needed for the well-being of the Community, and William Butler's clear judgement and discernment of character led him to see in Sister Harriet, whose retiring and shy nature made her known to few, the one to whom under his care and guidance he could trust the ruling of the Sisterhood. In the "Parish Journal," February 21, 1854, he notes:

> The Bishop went in the morning to the Home and there instituted Sister Harriet. This seems a most important step, and probably she is the first ecclesiastically appointed Superior in an English house of this kind since the Reformation.

After her death in Jan. 1892, he thus described her character to the Sisters:

> Hers was indeed a life of faith. It was no light thing in those early days to go forth like Abraham "not knowing whither he went," trusting to the call of God, certain that where He called it would be right to follow; so it was she came to Wantage. She was always the same—timid, diffident, yet full of simple faith. Humility, simplicity, faith, love, were the characteristics of her whole being. . . . Her singularly truthful and quick nature made her thoroughly grasp and rejoice in the teaching of the Sacramental doctrines of the Church, and she remained, in spite of all temptations and difficulties, firm and faithful to the Branch of Christ's Church established in our land.
>
> So diffident was she and retiring, that for a long time it seemed impossible that she should hold a position of respon-

sibility and direction of others, but in answer to many prayers
she was pointed out as the future Mother of the Community.
. . . It was indeed mainly owing to her singleness of mind,
combined with much firmness of purpose, that the Community
was enabled to face the difficulties of its earlier years. . . .
Scarcely ever did her judgement fail, whether of persons or of
things. It was quite impossible to know her intimately without
loving and admiring her. And certainly nothing has done
more than her loyalty to the teaching of the Church to
impress upon the Community that character of sober obedience
which I trust it will never abandon.

And now the work to which he had so faithfully
clung when those who were its originators had
failed seemed fairly to have taken root. Before
the close of 1854 William Butler was eager in his
desire that the Community should have a permanent home; this could only be suitably effected
by building. By July 25 of the following year
matters were sufficiently in train for the foundation stone of the present St. Mary's Home to
be laid.

The day began with a storm of rain which, however, cleared
off by one, when the Bishop, accompanied by the Archdeacon
of Berks, Dr. Wordsworth, Milman, Barff, Thirlwell, Trinder,
Du Pré, Houblon, Cranmer, G. Sawyer, Smith, and the clergy
of the parish, proceeded to lay the corner stone of the new
St. Mary's Home, on the ground purchased from W. Dixon,
at the top of Mill Street. The service was adapted from
that used on a similar occasion at Clewer, and the choir sang
it extremely well. Many of the farmers and others were
present from the market, and a goodly attendance of our
Church folk. Altogether the whole service was very satisfactory and cheering. May God prosper the work. . . . The
Bishop addrest the workmen especially, and very much to
the purpose, on the duties and blessedness of labouring in
such a work.

September 15th, 1856. The new St. Mary's Home entered.

September 19th, 1856. Service at the Home on entering and using the (temporary) chapel for the first time.

An address to the Sisters given about this time reviews the work of the first eight years, and shows the spirit in which the foundations of the Order were laid.

We have now, by the mercy of God, all but completed the eighth year of our existence as a society. The history of our fortunes and trials, the hopes and fears, the difficulties and the marvellous reliefs, the encouragements and mercies, of that octave of years, would indeed take long to tell.

When I look back to our small beginning, when I think of the fearful shock which, in its tender growth, our society received; when I consider the just suspicion which then lighted upon us; the difficulty, nay, as it seemed almost impossibility of supporting even the three or four penitents and the three Sisters engaged in their education; our fruitless endeavours to find any one to whom we could fitly confide the charge of the household, and our total inexperience in this kind of work, I do indeed bless God for the bountifulness with which He has heard our prayers, and supplied us with exactly the help we needed, and granted us so much absolute success. Especially, my Sisters, I would thank Him that while He has given us what we needed, He has never given us more. . . . Very wholesome then for us is this our simple unadorned and formless household. We may indeed be thankful that we see not our reward. It must be good for us, it is like our Lord Jesus Himself. And, believe me, we need not fear—"Fear not, little flock," it is His own gracious word. The "little one" in God's good time shall become a thousand! . . . Let us indeed see that it is no lower motive than the love of Jesus which constrains us. . . . Thus shall you have that peace which He alone can give. . . . The Lord Himself shall be your inheritance and your lot. He shall dwell with you and make His blessed presence in all its warmth and light, its grace and truth, its perfection of holiness felt and recognised. And in his own good time perfecting, establishing, strengthening, settling you. He shall give you the consolation of a manifold blessing. Yea! the Lord shall increase you more and more, you and your children.[1]

But while the Vicar was thus guiding the Penitentiary work under the Sisters' care, his original wish of establishing an educational Order had lost none of its fervour. When the Sisters in 1850 moved into a larger house, the cottage was retained for the teaching staff of the girls' school; and before long a lady was introduced to him who seemed likely to be a valuable helper in this work. About the same time a family of five sisters, ardent and instructed Churchwomen, settled in the parish. They lived together for some years, helping the Vicar in every way, and especially by forwarding the various educational works which were now springing up in Wantage. At the end of 1851 he wrote in the "Parish Journal": "Our school staff promises better than it has ever done. The great accession to the parish of the Miss W.'s is indeed a subject of greatest thankfulness."

But in spite of all this, the next few years brought much disappointment and failure.

The girls' schools were, from one reason or another, a source of much anxiety to the Vicar. Still his constancy and perseverance in work to

---

[1] In a letter, dated Florence, May 12, 1890, he wrote: "One thing I feel pretty sure about, the danger of having too much beauty, and too many valuable things in religious houses or even in churches. In the one case they tempt the spoiler, in the other they make God's house into a mere show-place for casual visitors. I am thankful that our Community goes in for simplicity and plainness."

K

- which he had once put his hand never failed, and
he was rewarded by seeing his desire realised, though
not quite on the lines he had first laid down.
The story of success gradually growing up out of
disappointment and apparent failure is to be found
in the " Parish Journal ":

1852. Miss —— began a work school for the girls of the
parish who have past school days. They are to receive one
shilling weekly and their work sold. This will be a great
thing for them, enabling the mothers to spare them from that
demoralising habit of carrying babies about at sixpence a week.
We are working up a small middle school in connection with
the day school, under the superintendence of Miss ——.

The year 1853 saw the beginning of a fresh
educational work, combining under one roof a
training school for girls going to service with one
for pupil teachers in National schools. A lady
who had begun at Littlemore a school for the
training of girls for domestic service wished to
remove it to Wantage, and to complete her project
by building a suitable home.

The Vicar, overweighted with the financial anxieties
of his various schools, was not desirous for the introduction of another into his parish, and said: "One
more school would fairly ruin him"; nevertheless,
the house was built and the work began.

In the entry at the close of the year he expresses
grave concern about his schools.

There is constant anxiety about those in charge of them.
Miss ——, from her delicate health and other anxieties, is
scarcely to be depended upon for long, while Miss ——, by
whose exertions the middle school is sustained, is absolutely

engaged to the St. Saviour's Sisterhood as soon as her place can be supplied. We need much prayer for our work. I feel daily more and more how little is needed to break it rudely to pieces, and how helpless we ourselves are. Such as it is, God alone has brought it to pass, and He alone can uphold it. Are we sufficiently convinced of this ?

The offer of some voluntary workers in 1854 cast a ray of brightness on what would otherwise have been a very depressing year with regard to the schools. The draft of a letter to one of these ladies shows the plan of operation the Vicar had in view. In writing of the female department of his parochial work, he says :

It consists—(1) of a large National school; (2) of an infant school; (3) of a middle school for tradesmen's and farmers' daughters; (4) of a small training establishment for mistresses; and (5) of an industrial school for girls who have passed through the curriculum of the girls' school.[1] . . . Our present desire is to extend our operations through the deanery of Wantage, of which I am Rural Dean, and endeavour to supply the various schools and poor parishes of which it is composed with school mistresses of a more truly religious character than are, as I find from long experience, at present to be obtained.

1855 opened with fresh hope, and on St. James's Day, on which day the foundation stone of St. Mary's Home was also laid, the Vicar was gladdened by what seemed to be the accomplishment of his long-cherished plan, the beginning of a School Sisterhood.

At eight o'clock the Bishop instituted ——, ——, and —— as Superior and Sisters of the new School Sisterhood, whose charge should be the training of young children, servants, and governesses.

But before twelve months had run their course

[1] To these was shortly added a ladies' school.

the scheme which William Butler had with so much patience and prayerfulness sought to carry out, had come to an end.

Oct. 1. Visit from Superior of School Sisters full of troubles. There is need of help for the Middle school which is in danger of falling to pieces. Sister Mary is overworkt and I fear will not pass her Government examination.

A mistress must be provided for the Girls' school, provision must be made for pupil teachers. . . . My fears last year about the School Sisterhood have been sadly realised, and now after much demonstration and talk, after the solemn service and the Bishop's address on St. James's Day, it seems that Miss —— is a person far too self-willed and unpractical to leave in command . . . but besides all this, the poverty of the household renders it absolutely necessary to make a complete change. I cannot but believe that with proper management and greater openness all might have gone well, but as it is we must be content if we are not buried or damaged in her ruin. . . . There are of course, thanks be to God, subjects of joy and hope. Mrs. —— and her new buildings in Tanner Street seem likely to afford a good prospect of carrying on an educational work.

Feb. 17, 1856. Much anxiety about Miss —— and her Sisterhood. After willingly leaving all things in my hands, she now writes very dictatorially arranging them in her own way. This of course cannot be permitted, and I see nothing but a separation in prospect. May God guide us all in this matter and suffer no human feeling to stand in the way of His holy service.

April 12. It is very grievous to have been forced to give up a plan which promised so well as that inaugurated on St. James's Day, but the extreme irregularity of the Superior and her impatience of control made it hopeless to go on with her aid, and I must now carry on the work in a different fashion. I trust and pray that we may yet gain the assistance we need, and work through the ladies of the Home an educational system.

But at present with the very small numbers and invalided condition of those who are there, it would be quite wrong to build castles. We must just struggle on from hand to mouth and pray for help. Everything is for the present provided, yet I feel that all is uncertain and that everything may in an hour be thrown on my hands. It is a most anxious and critical time and only God's help will carry us through.

St. James's Day. One cannot help recalling St. James's Day of last year and mourning over the failure of what seemed then so fairly hopeful. God grant that such failures may make us more careful and prayerful.

The anxiety shown in these extracts was but too well founded. By the end of 1856 the Superior and another member of the School Sisterhood had joined the Church of Rome, and the third died a few months later.

Whilst William Butler had thus been experiencing disappointment in the work which was so dear to his heart, he was also at the same time full of anxiety for the Penitentiary, the support of which had been left upon his hands. When he received it into his parish, its originators had undertaken to provide funds for its maintenance, but with the secessions to Rome the channels through which the funds would have flowed were cut off, and there was no alternative for him but to accept the additional burden. Not only the material responsibilities, but the spiritual duties also at times fell to his charge when ill-health compelled the chaplain to be away from his post. Extracts from letters to Sister Harriet[1] and from the "Parish Journal" show how continuous and unflagging his work for the Penitentiary was:

[1] Appointed Superior, Feb. 21, 1854.

1852. I keep thinking of you all, and when I find a chance of advocating your cause. . . . I cannot tell you with what pleasure I think of our common work. Difficult and discouraging as it is, there is quite enough result, and more than enough promise, to cheer us on, and to me the feeling of definiteness which is given is well worth almost everything.

1853. We visited Wells on our journey, and there I saw our old friend, Ellen. . . . She was very glad, as you may suppose, to see me, and I thought her manner and appearance very much improved.

1857. Some more money is really needful, only about £3 in the last fortnight. I must try some other plan.

1862. I should like to do more at the Home; the little I see of the girls makes me long to look after them.

1862, Feb. 2. Anniversary of the opening of St. Mary's Home. This gives one many thoughts of great thankfulness to Him who has so mercifully supported and blessed our work.

And in 1863, in his deep anxiety to further the work, and to strengthen the hands of the Sisters, he asked his beloved and revered friend, Mr. Keble, to preach the sermon at their anniversary festival.

W. J. B. TO REV. J. KEBLE.

WANTAGE VICARAGE, Monday in Whitsun Week, 1863.

I hope that you will not think me very troublesome or impertinent in the matter of this letter.

July 22, St. Mary Magdalene's day, is the Anniversary of the Dedication of the Chapel of St. Mary's Home, and we keep it every year as the Sisters' Festival. The exterior Sisters for the most part contrive to be there, and a few friends in the town and neighbourhood "assist" on the occasion. It would be a very great help to us, and the Sisters would consider it as an exceeding kindness to them, if you could preach the sermon. They merely want a few words of encouragement from friendly lips—written or unwritten, as the lips prefer. Theirs is an anxious life, and they value most highly anything which speaks of sympathy and recollection of them. I know that I am asking a great deal; but, as I said at first, I hope that you will forgive me for the work's sake. We are all very happy here, with four of our children together keeping ——'s sixteenth birthday. A. has come from Oxford, where he is sojourning and reading till he joins Trinity College, Cambridge, in October.

W. J. B. TO REV. J. KEBLE.

WANTAGE VICARAGE, May 31, 1863.

We are most thankful to be able to think of your coming amongst us, and if, *quod absit*, anything should hinder you, we will do the best we can to rig out a spar.

I take it for granted that you and others know the real mind of the Chancellor of the Exchequer,[1] and certainly nothing that he has done is irreconcilable with true, though perhaps rather stern, filial holding to the Church. I suppose that minds cast, like his, in a very logical mould, find an especial difficulty in not "sticking to their texts." The Bishop defends him heartily. The word of his which I least like, though I can explain it, is that in his speech in the Qualification for Offices Bill, to which, by the way, I would gladly have agreed, when he said that the Church had nothing to fear from the attacks of Dissenters, but only from her own internal differences. Of course taken rigidly this is quite true, but it looked as though in his opinion Churchmen were to do nothing to meet the fierce efforts of the enemy, as if they were to hold the trowel only and not also the sword. . . . I have sent you a couple of sermons, preached at the Dedication of the chapel. Surely of all practical revivals none is more useful than that of Sisterhoods.

Also, I venture to send you an *Oratio Procuratoria*, written by a very great friend of ours, which some of us persuaded him to print. We think it a very pretty bit of Latin.

W. J. B. TO REV. J. KEBLE.

WANTAGE VICARAGE, July 11, 1863.

The special point is, I think, to encourage and strengthen the Sisters, as Sisters, rather than as connected with this particular work of a Penitentiary, though of course the latter

<hr>

[1] Right Hon. W. E. Gladstone.

would come in. It seems to me that in these days of "lower Empire" luxury, it is no slight matter to have ladies living together and "enduring hardness." It is a witness to the Cross, when the doctrine of the Cross is all but dying out. Could it not be shown that the Church has recognised the spirit of such associations from very early times, and that Martha and Mary have both their place? Then would it be possible to touch upon the dangers—so opposite—which beset each, and to show how in each line—whether in the living in the "world," or in the Sisterhood, singleness of purpose and the thought implied in the Collect for VI. Sunday after Trinity would keep people right? Would such a text as Eccles. iv. 9-12 do? This is merely what occurs to me in answer to your question, and I hardly venture to send it. Pray do not think it at all necessary to use it. We shall be only too thankful for whatever you may kindly say. . . .

We must now trace the lines laid down for the guidance of the infant Community. There is no doubt that an active Order was that which had commended itself to William Butler's mind; but an address given in 1849 shows clearly how, in those early days, he was not only desirous of training souls for the Religious life, but that he was willing, should it be the leading of Divine Providence, that the contemplative life should have freedom of development.

To serve is Martha's special work, to contemplate is Mary's. Martha provides that Mary may have leisure to gaze. Mary could not contemplate did not Martha serve. Mary's eye must be for internal things if Martha cared most for external. Martha purchases, arranges, helps; yet had she that in her heart which she rather loves; for she serves, works, buys, holds, dispenses for the love of Christ. Hence she will serve, and from morning to evening, that others may enjoy His Beloved Presence. The two characters form a perfect whole. Each may, neither need fail.

Martha may be cumbered about much serving, Mary may sit at His feet and despise her sister. Yet while Martha serves for the love of Christ, gladly aiding Mary, whilst Mary sits for the love of Christ, gladly praying for Martha, His blessing is on each, each has a portion of the blessing of the other. Mary has chosen that good part which shall not be taken away from her. Martha has served Christ, and shall follow Him where He is, "For where I am, there shall also My servant be."

Moreover in this present time surely Martha's work must be the fittest preparation for Mary's. Surely it is hard to leave this world after many years spent therein, suddenly to renounce that increasing activity of mind and body, so common in this generation; the heart languishes for want of that to which it has been used, the sudden revulsion is too great, there is danger of formalism; it is unnatural to take up a life of entire prayer and contemplation without some preparation, some gradual step-by-step beginning. Martha's part seems well fitted for this. Martha loves Christ, is in His Presence, sits not at table, but serves. What next, but that she shall partake of the fulness of joy at His right hand? She is doing the very part of Christ, of Him Who is among men as he that serveth. Has He not said of such, "He shall gird Himself, and make them to sit down at meat, and will come forth and serve them."

But one thing surely is needed by each; the idea of constant service . . . the Cross of Christ is grievous to those only who endure it not. . . . Seek Martha's work, seek Mary's work if you will, go on from strength to strength, but look upon yourselves as for ever set apart, and the world as crucified unto you, and you to the world.

Rules for the conduct of the Community, regulating hours of prayer, work, recreation, etc., were drawn up and received the sanction of the Bishop of Oxford in the early days of its existence; and William Butler's own words, written at no great length of time before his death, show the solid basis on which he sought to build it up.

It may be well once more to state the principle on which the Community of St. Mary the Virgin is based. It is this— simple, honest loyalty to the Church to which it belongs, that is the Church of England, the Church of our native land. We believe that the Church of England is a true branch of Christ's Catholic Church, and that she has a right to lay down for her children what they are to believe and to do. We believe that in her Prayer Book her teaching and will are found. We are not desirous to follow our own fancies, or to set forth doctrines and ritual which belong to the Church of Rome. We are satisfied with giving dignity and beauty to that which we have of our own. We wish to follow in the steps of those great men who heralded the great Catholic Revival in the Church of England, and who never "left their first love," as Dr. Pusey, Mr. Keble, Charles Marriott, Hugh James Rose, and others of their kind—men who combined the highest saintlinesss of character with deep knowledge of theology, keen appreciation of the standpoint of the Church, and amplest learning and scholarship.

No one can read the "Oxford Tracts" without finding himself in an atmosphere of honest Anglican teaching as different as possible from some of the wild talk of the present day. In this, by God's mercy, although it may not fall in with some modern popular notions, we hope to abide.

But everything which brought out great principles and added beauty and dignity to the worship of God he allowed in the chapels of the Community. Nothing slovenly or tawdry could for a moment be tolerated by him. His keen eye was sure to detect the least flaw in the minutest detail. Everything connected with the service of the altar, or with any service or portion of the House of God must have the most scrupulous and reverent care.

The thoroughness which he looked for in all that was connected with the chapel and its services was to be carried into every detail of the daily routine. The care, the orderliness, the love, the devotion of the Home of Nazareth were to be the Sister's pattern in her daily duties. Truly he could have said with St. Paul that the foundation he had sought to lay was Jesus Christ. The theme of the Retreat addresses, which in the early days of the Community he used annually to give, bore most frequently on the life of our Holy Redeemer, and in these meditations he would emphasise the first principles of the Religious Life, Poverty, Chastity, and Obedience, which on one occasion he said " ought to be engraved on the threshold of the convent door as they were the very conditions of a Religious Community."

He was ever careful himself, and impressed on those who co-operated with him in the training of souls to respect the individuality of each one. On one occasion he wrote : " We must enclose all kinds of fishes and bring them into God's service, toning down yet without destroying the savour of the individuality." No one knew better than he how to allow scope for the enthusiasm of the young and ardent, while he controlled and directed it. And in all that he counselled and ordered he himself set an example. The intense reality which the spiritual life was to him, and the training and discipline of the character required for a close following in the footsteps of our Divine Master, was that which made his teaching ring so true, and consequently carry with it such weight. The lines

written under a picture of our Lord bearing His
Cross, which hung over the mantelpiece in his study,

> "Lord, my life's sole object be
> With pure heart to follow Thee,"

were not only the aim of his own life, but that
to which he sought to lead those under his
training.

Among the thirty-four works[1] in the hands of the
Community at the time of his death, nine were of
the nature of Penitentiary work, thirteen were
schools, and eight were in connection with parochial
work. His interest in the various works of the Community was keen. For many years he never failed
to pay annual visits to his foundations, but with
the increasing demands which work of all kinds
made upon him, he was not able in latter years to
observe this with regularity. It was his rule for
some years to write to all the heads of Branch
Houses at Christmas and Easter; and he was
able to continue his Christmas letters to the end
of his life.

[1] These were: at Wantage, the Penitentiary at St. Mary's
Home, St. Michael's Schools for Teachers and Industrial Girls, St.
Mary's and St. Katharine's Schools; at Paddington, St. Anne's
House, St. Mary Magdalene's Home, and St. Mary's College; the
House of St. Mary and St. John, Kennington; St. James's Home,
Fulham; St. Matthias', Earl's Court; a Home for Inebriates at
Spelthorne; St. Helena's Home for discharged female prisoners, at
Ealing; in the Peterborough Diocese, St. Mary's, Ketton, St.
Mary Magdalene's and St. Anne's, Leicester, St. Mary's, Narborough;
the Cornish House of Mercy at Lostwithiel; St. Peter's Mission
House, Plymouth; St. Mark's Mission House, New Swindon; the
House of the Holy Rood for Incurables, at Worthing; All Saints'
Mission House, Wigan; various schools and orphanages at Poona,
where also the Sisters have charge of the Sassoon Hospital.

With regard to the other side of the work, the development of elementary schools under the government system necessitated the employment of properly certificated teachers, and the chief educational work of the Community henceforward lay in the charge of St. Michael's Industrial school, into which also the mistresses, pupil teachers, and monitors moved in 1858, and in carrying on the "Middle school," which provided what is now called Secondary Education. At the end of 1862 the Vicar writes :

> The Middle school has thriven under the care of the ladies of the Home. I have some anxiety about St. Michael's, which has never quite satisfied me. I had good hopes, but now illness and death seem to shatter all plans, and it is difficult to see one step ahead.

But in spite of many difficulties and anxiety caused by several outbreaks of typhoid fever, the work steadily advanced, and the pupil teachers for many years entered as head girls into Salisbury Training College, one in 1860 appearing as first in all England.

It became, however, a very grave question whether the house which seemed so admirably suited for educational purposes would not have to be abandoned. During the fifth visitation of typhoid, the subjoined entry was made by the Vicar.

> Feb. 4. Illness still at St. Michael's. Miss Osborne, after nursing most carefully those who were ill, is now attacked herself. This house is a matter of great anxiety, and it is very difficult to see what is right to be done. It seems pitiful to give it up, after all the expense it has cost, and all the

benefits it seems calculated to give, and yet these outbursts of fever thoroughly paralyse everything.

Happily with improved sanitary arrangements in the town and school this was the last outbreak of fever, and the entries of the final twelve years of the Vicar's incumbency tell a tale of success crowning the faithful persevering and prayerful efforts of his earlier years at Wantage. Among the terse and pithy sayings which might be called his axioms, one which he constantly repeated as an encouragement to others and which was certainly the result of his own experience, was: "Prayer, faith, and grind will carry most things through."

So the work was prospered; and when he resigned the charge of Wantage, the schools which thirty-four years earlier had contained thirty-six children—twenty-four boys and twelve girls—had increased to over 750 scholars, varying in age from three to nineteen or twenty.

Not content with merely supervising the labours of others, he took his own part in the work of education; and as early as 1850 he instituted a daily arithmetic class in his study, from eight to nine A.M., for the girl pupil teachers. After a few years he changed this to religious instruction, choosing a subject not included in their year's curriculum. In these classes he went most minutely and carefully through a large portion of the Prayer Book and some of the Epistles, spending a year or more in the study of the shorter Epistles, and two or three years over the longer ones. One day in the

week the religious instruction was set aside for a
perusal of the Saturday examination papers, an
awe-inspiring time to both pupils and teachers, and
much to be feared by any one who had been idle
over her week's lessons. Sometimes he would vary
the usual lesson with mental arithmetic or the
study of words, drawing out the reasoning
powers of his pupils, and making them answer
intelligently, accurately, and briskly. The stroke
of nine was a signal for the class to come to an
end, and all might be seen hurrying to school with
the Vicar in time for school prayers, which began
punctually at five minutes past nine.

His educational power was shown by his methods
of training those under his care. He considered
that a somewhat dry though open and kind manner
best marked the relation between teacher and
taught, and he greatly deprecated any approach
to petting or the like as dangerous in lifting individuals out of their class, and affording a stimulus
to vanity. He always aimed at combining strictness
and an almost stern manner with kindliness and
geniality, which led those with whom he dealt to
perceive his fatherly heart, and to turn to him in
difficulties and trials with confidence and trust.
The teachers trained in his schools always addressed
him as " sir," a title of respect which he deemed due
to the Vicar of the parish. He considered equality
and familiarity in manner to be opposed to the
spirit of the Fifth Commandment.

In his visits to the schools his keen eye instantly

perceived want of method or care in any department, and he was as quick in speaking of it as in seeing it. He commented as fully upon the needlework of the girls and of the pupil teachers as on their history and arithmetic papers, and under his vigilant rule there was no possibility of any continuance of slovenly work. His own enthusiasm and devotion to duty inspired his teachers, so that an *esprit de corps* was created among them which, even when they had left Wantage, enabled them to retain the high standard which he had set before them. "Mak' sikker" [1]—make sure—were words very frequently on the Vicar's lips, and he impressed upon his teachers never to believe that their pupils knew anything unless they had proved for themselves that they did.

The high standard he set before his young people, and to which he expected them to rise, made them afraid of him until they learnt that he was anxious to encourage all honest effort, and was ready to be their friend; then a deep reverential love grew out of the fear he first inspired. His resourcefulness never failed him in finding endless ways of making his teaching attractive and of encouraging his pupils; punishment was not often resorted to,[2] and he con-

---

[1] See *Tales of a Grandfather*, vol. i., chap. viii.

[2] Once when he was showing the schools to a friend on her first visit to Wantage and some children came in after prayers had been read, he said "You see those silly things, they have come late and will get a pat, unless you beg them off as an act of clemency on your first visit." She said "May I," and he replied, "Yes, you may,"—and it was promptly done.

stantly impressed upon his teachers that it was some defect in their management if their children required punishment. "The children get punished, but the teachers deserve it; the children get the prizes, but the teachers earn them," he would say.

But it was in dealing with the really troublesome that his power was most felt. He never would let them pass out of his ken, and he often succeeded in making them good in spite of themselves. He believed in their best, and made them believe in it also. He used to say, "If people will not do right, you must make it more unpleasant for them to do wrong than to do right"; and thus the difficult and troublesome girl found it the happiest and best plan to follow the path of right.

He insisted that all whom he taught should look him straight in the face. One week-day evening when he was preaching, the pupils of St. Mary's school failed to look up at him. Before leaving the pulpit steps he called the Sister in charge to him, and said he would not preach to "tops of pates."

The following extract from a letter written to one in charge of an educational work, is characteristic of his thoroughly practical mind :

I cannot too earnestly impress on those who have the charge of bodies the importance of having everything super-eminently clean, bright, graceful. I am quite sure that the more you have together the more important all this becomes. Food, clothes, bedding, tubbing, light, air, recreation, work, all need careful thinking out and must be perfect; well looked after as well as well arranged at the first. Evil creeps in

L.

insensibly, unless the greatest care is employed. No one can be trusted by the head of the house—what is everyone's work needs constant looking after and testing.

His love went out to the children in all the schools, but pre-eminently to the young teachers who came in a special way under his care and training. It was one of his keenest pleasures to keep up a knowledge of them when their apprenticeship was completed, to hear from them and write to them.

In his journeyings he would take opportunities of seeing one and another, if his work took him into their neighbourhood. The children in the first class of the National schools were taught to write to him as Vicar of the parish on his birthday, and as the pupil teachers left Wantage for work elsewhere they, too, would carry on the practice, and letters flowed in to him from many parts of the world, to which answers were always promptly written. He greatly valued these tokens of grateful affection. "No one," he wrote on one of his latter birthdays, "who is not like me, growing old, can appreciate how the heart clings to the love of loving hearts. Love is the one thing which remains when all earthly work and hope are ended." And not only his former pupil teachers, but many others who had been trained in the various schools in Wantage were wont to write to him on his birthday.

In answer to some of these he wrote:

Thank you heartily for remembering my birthday. It is

very delightful to me now that I have withdrawn myself from parish work, and from the close connexion with lads and lasses, to find so many still looking upon me as a friend and pastor. You would have been amused to see the barrow loads of letters, etc., which greeted me on the morning of Feb. 10th.

Time is rapidly passing with me, and I shall soon pass with it, and the wide waters of Eternity will be before me. I trust that I may be ready when the time comes for that call, "Put thy house in order, for thou must die and not live." It is the only real and certain thing. If that goes right, then all goes right. At the same time the thought of it need not make one morbid or morose or dull or cheerless. While one lives one loves, and love is the best preparation for *Heaven*.

LOWER HOUSE OF CONVOCATION, 1885.

I am writing in the midst of talk and bustle, but I must somehow try and send you a word in reply to your very kind memory of my birthday. . . . Each of the first class girls wrote me their greetings, all well written, spelt, and expressed, and full of Wantage news. . . .

Little gifts, too, from any of his former pupils were valued and referred to years after by word or letter. "I often think of you," he wrote to one of the old pupils of the Middle school, "when I put on my best coat which always carries in its pocket the Prayer Book and little cloth case you gave me." It was no wonder that with the consciousness of the love that went out to him in response to his pastoral love and care that he could write, "I always feel when I leave you all at Wantage that I have left my heart behind. . . . Wantage, like Calais on Queen Mary's heart, is written on mine."

A former pupil of St. Mary's school writes:

I had heard a good deal of the Vicar of Wantage even in

the far north, but not until February, 1876, did I see him. My friend and I called at the vicarage, and after some conversation the Vicar proposed taking us over the National schools. . . .

I spent most of the next two and a half years at St. Mary's school, where I often passed the vacation too, and words would fail to tell of the home and happy atmosphere of that wonderful place, all emanating from the Vicar, for his influence told in every department, and no detail of the work or character of each pupil was too small to interest him, and he cared the same about what we should do or be on leaving school. At that time there was a weekly privilege for the older girls, viz. to go to the vicarage on Wednesday afternoons for a class on St. Matthew's Gospel. His notes were so exhaustive that they branched out in every direction, and were given in his characteristic bright fashion. With all the extensive duties of his daily life, the Vicar only allowed absence from home to interfere with this class. Still more to us were the monthly Communicants' classes. . . . It was certainly our own fault if in a year we did not see twelve distinct steps in the ascending ladder.

If we passed public examinations, the first thing was to go and tell the Vicar. And then what interest he took in our games! I can see him now in the playground watching our favourite "French and English," helping us to put our whole hearts into it by his cheering interest and laughter. . . . What high praise it was to hear from his lips, "*She*'ll do," or *She*'s no goose," or "There's some fun in *her*." And when school days were over he never forgot his pupils. The list of their names which always stood on his study mantelpiece, was graven on his heart, and he even seemed to remember the circumstances of each one, and often asked us about one another years after he had seen some of us. . . .

You know how the constant wandering incident to my life made many gaps and long intervals in my seeing the Dean. But his welcome and interest were always the same. As time went on the long intervals made it more possible to see a change in him: physically, the greyer hair, the slight stoop, and if it is not presumptuous to say it, the ever-deepening beauty of the expression of his wonderful face, and the ever-nearing closeness of his "walk with God"—so near that when the end came there was not far to go. It was one of his favourite expressions, "To walk with God."

On his seventieth birthday the teachers trained and training at St. Michael's gave him a revolving bookcase, which delighted him greatly. He alluded to the gift in a letter to the Sister in charge :

I need not say how deeply and gratefully I value your kind words and those of many others which greeted me to-day. I begin to think that the best and brightest examples of good women, simple, affectionate, true, pure-minded, devoted to their duties, are to be found in the class of school mistresses—certainly taken one with another I know of nothing better than our girls. I do not mean that they are faultless, but they show what honest living is, and what true women's work is. . . . The circulating library stand is delightful. It is what I have longed for and never hoped to have. It will be useful too to others when my short span is ended. I mean to have a brass plate on the top with all the names engraved upon it which you have sent me. I must try and write a line of thanks to them all.

He sent to each donor a copy of a sonnet :

GRATIARUM ACTIO.

Much loved and loving Friends, in joy I greet
　　Your kindly gift, with precious memories fraught
Of long past hours, wherein in converse sweet
　　We sought with ardent effort—teacher, taught,—
To search the depths of that great Book, whose lore
　　Is the great joy of souls, which to have known
Is wealth far richer than the golden store
　　Or all the treasures that in earth are sown:
Gird you then well with this—"fight Faith's good fight—
　　Quit you like men—be strong"—in faithless days

Hold fast the Truth; in darkness be the light;
  Defend Christ's Bride, the Church; Christ's Standard raise
Howe'er the world may scoff; and in His might
  Guide on His little Flock to love and praise.

Like other founders of Religious Orders, William Butler recognised the importance of associating with the Sisters earnest-minded people, both men and women, who, while living in the world, should yet be glad to undertake some portion of the burden of maintaining the charitable works in which the Community was engaged. The first name on the list of exterior Sisters, a roll which now numbers several hundreds, is that of Mrs. Butler, who all her life not only took a keen interest in the welfare of the Community, but for many years acted as treasurer of the Penitentiary funds. Not only were the original infirmary wing and the embroidery room the gifts of an exterior Sister, but the embroidery work itself was started by exterior Sisters living in the world who desired to add to the funds for the support of the Penitentiary work :

"It is impossible to say," wrote Dean Butler in one of his annual letters to the associates of the Community, "how much you and others have given us of comfort and support. Without your ready help we should indeed feel weak and lonely. As it is we have the happiness of being surrounded by a very atmosphere of prayer and affection, rising up from many hearts and lips in nearly all parts of the world. We can only in return assure you that your efforts are not wasted. They are expended on Christ's little ones, Christ's poor lost sheep, those heathen for whom as well as for us Christ died; and you will receive, it cannot be doubted, the reward in the resurrection of the just."

He naturally made acquaintance with any who were staying at the Home, and such acquaintance often ripened into friendship. In the early days of the Community a lady travelling on the G.W.R. on her first journey to St. Mary's Home met a fellow-traveller who, finding out her destination, talked much of Mr. Butler, and warned her to beware of him and his religious opinions, for " he was a very dangerous man." Afterwards, when the lady became well acquainted with the Vicar, he heard the story, and when she left the Home he presented her with a copy of his *Sermons for Working Men,* having written below her name, " from a dangerous man."

His advice and sympathy were always ready for those who sought them, and in latter years he helped many associates by annually conducting a Retreat for them, which work he continued till the last year of his life.

One who attended several of these says:

There were one or two special marks of his teaching in Retreats.

1. It was so bracing, and it made one return to one's duties in the world with a steady determination to go out and carry on bravely the Christian warfare.

2. It was essentially practical. It was to be the *doing* the will of God, feelings were nothing; the text was, " If ye love Me, keep My commandments."

Fresh resolutions were to be put in practice at once—they were to be something very simple, something one could set up in one's heart, which would stand firm, strong, untouched, and which one could bear with one to the grave.

3. Always, but especially in his three last Retreats, there

was strong teaching on the Church, and loyalty to the Prayer Book. Religion was set up before us as a strong stern thing, and what we had to do was to strive after honest simple obedience to rule—not self-pleasing, but endeavouring in all things to do what pleased God.

4. His high ideal of woman's work, viz. the calming, purifying, and elevating of society. He impressed upon his hearers, that to woman belongs the formation of the character of all around her, her children, her servants, etc. On woman also depends in a very great degree the whole happiness of the circle in which she lives, and on her far more than on the man depends the spiritual life of the family. He unhesitatingly asserted that if society is corrupt, then it is the woman's fault. Man may tempt, but it is for the woman to be faithful and firm, and by her faithfulness she will help man to mend his ways, and lead him on in all that is holy and pure and good.

5. The Bible knowledge gained. This was a very distinct feature, and one always went forth from his Retreats with a sense that one had made several strides forward in the knowledge of the Bible.

Lastly, cheerfulness, hopefulness, faithfulness, was the last word to us as we were about to go out of Retreat.

Another associate writes :

The notice of what proved to be his last Retreat for the associates at the Home reached me in Florence. I had never before been free to attend one, so I arranged my journey at once and set off, arriving in time for one of the most helpful few days of my life. The depth and yet the simplicity of the addresses, and the wonderfully beautiful prayers at the end of each, can be known only to those who heard them, for it was always the way he said things as much as what he said that was so impressive. Busy as he was up to literally the last moment, he found time for a few minutes conversation at the end of the Retreat. He was standing—one foot on a chair—all ready to go away, quite worn out, but bright and interested as usual. I told him my special trouble, and it was indeed perplexing. His answer was, "My dear ——, *pray* about it!" And these, his last words, will suit every time, every place, every circumstance.

His training, writes another, was bracing, and I think I might venture to say that the distinctive notes of most of those who were formed under his guidance are cheerfulness and common sense. He always set himself against any kind of morbid melancholy, or even any that was not morbid. He would not have people ever brood over grief, or go on sorrowing for what was irremediable. "It is no use crying over spilt milk" was one of his oft-repeated sayings; another, "Je pleure mon Albert gaiement," the words of Alexandrine de la Ferronays.[1] He could sympathise most tenderly with sorrow in the first instance, but he could say something sharp if the sorrow was prolonged beyond what he thought right and reasonable. He set himself against moodiness or depression, or the sort of melancholy in which young women sometimes indulge about not being understood, not being sympathised with, and so forth. Indeed he gave no quarter to any sort of sentimentality whatever. He was very encouraging to those who were willing to do their best, but were discouraged by failures. His sense of humour came into his training, and he did not hesitate to use a grotesque word or ludicrous illustration where it expressed his meaning, or was likely to impress it on the mind of his hearer.

His continual teaching was the acceptance of God's will in all things, and at all times. "Let 'Thy will be done' be your moral tonic." When he received a telegram summoning him home on account of sudden and serious illness, he said, "There is nothing for it but what I am always saying to you all, 'Fiat voluntas Tua.'" . . . Those who did not know him intimately could have no idea of his great tenderness of heart. In real trouble, real difficulty, real sorrow, he was ever ready, and one never went away empty.

The understanding he had about illness or weak health was sometimes almost unexpectedly striking, and especially so the last three years before his death. He was so hard upon himself that one was surprised at the way in which he entered into the difficulties of bodily weakness, but he did so to a very marvellous extent. And when he advised laxity for a time, one felt one could trust him because he was so hard and self-denying himself. In one of his last conversations he deplored the laxity

---

[1] *Récit d'une Sœur*, par Mme Augustus Craven, vol. ii., p. 385.

of the present age as compared with the times of Keble, Pusey, Marriott, etc., and quoted the texts, " Endure hardness, as a good soldier of Jesus Christ," " When Jeshurun waxed fat he kicked." . . . He always tried to develop individual tastes in those under his training by suggesting books and employments suited to them. His whole life was full of thought and care for others; such little matters as a careful and prompt answer to every letter were never overlooked by him.

Another writes :

I think it was the combination of holiness and love in the character of the late Dean of Lincoln which attracted people to him. When I first knew him, more than twenty years ago, I was more struck by his brilliant gifts of conversation, his acute eager concentration of mind on argument, and the sense of *controlled power*, which was evident to any one who was in his society; but the better I came to understand him, the deeper became the impression of his great personal holiness. He was quite unconscious of the effect it produced, he never seemed to think at all about himself in his intercourse with others, his sole desire was to make them good and happy servants of God. His own life had been devoted to his Creator from early manhood, and he was able " with a heart at leisure from itself" to throw his whole energy into setting forth the glory of his Master, and exhibiting as fully as possible the method of the English Church for winning souls. His standard for himself and others was a high one—to attain it meant giving up a good deal, but then he was so certain of ultimate peace and consolation, that it gave courage and hope; he always braced, never depressed the heart. The Presence of God ruled his life, and especially his intercourse with others; this prevented all 'sentiment,' or dwelling upon his personal sympathy (tender and deep as it was), and raised the soul nearer to the source of all love and pity.

I was going through a great spiritual crisis during part of the time we were friends, and was led to consult him, not in the way that many persons did, in confession, but as an adviser. As soon as he realised that my doubts were real and not affected, he took me in hand, and with the most touching patience and unfailing kindness helped me; he wrote constantly, entered into every difficulty, and guided me till, after some years, the light came.

The only rule he gave was "Persevere, live exactly as if you believed." The clearness and strength of his faith of course steadied mine. I will copy here a prayer he sent me, which probably he used in the case of others. "Almighty God, in Whom our fathers hoped and were delivered, and put their trust and were not confounded, have mercy upon me Thy much tried and troubled child and servant, and help me to find peace and rest. Remove from me (if it seem good to Thee) the cloud of doubt and distrust which oppresses me; open my heart to faith and hope and love; teach me to know Thee Who and as Thou art; and if it seem good to Thee that even through my whole earthly pilgrimage I should never pass from darkness and sorrow into light and joy, do Thou Thyself hold me fast to Thee, and bring me at last to the glorious vision of Thy brightness and glory, where Faith and Hope can no longer totter, nor Love fail; through Jesus Christ our Lord. Amen."

It is quite impossible to describe his sympathy. He always prayed for his friends, and I recollect his saying once of some one who had died, "Forget! how could I forget? When one prayed twice a day for him for years. *Now*, I shall only put him the other side of my prayers." This habit kept his interest warm and keen, and to the end of his life he never omitted writing in every crisis of joy or sorrow that came to me or mine. We talked a great deal—of many things, his and my work—but he never dwelt upon the former, except in connection with the Sisters, or those who carried on the many branches he had originated at Wantage and elsewhere. One letter mentioned his thankful joy at having been spared to communicate in the church of his baptism (St. Marylebone). I fancy he had not been in it for seventy years. His joyous nature, the ceaseless activity of his life, his tender compassionate sympathy, his strong will subdued by God, have ended as far as this world is concerned; but he is nearer than ever to the everlasting Love and Purity of his Lord.

The increased distance from Wantage of his home, first at Worcester and then at Lincoln, together with his advancing years, made him consider the question of laying down some portion of his charge;

but happily he was never called upon to decide which of those many interests, so dear to him, he should let go. It was his desire to retain his relations to the Community which he said was dearer to him than his own life, as long as his life was spared; but it was this work which specially taxed his strength during his latter years, and made him consider seriously during the last few months of his life whether he could continue the burden of it, and the very frequent and long journeys which it involved; for, except at the time of his annual holiday, he seldom let more than three weeks pass without being at Wantage. While he was there in November, 1893, the Archbishop of Canterbury (Dr. Benson), who was staying in the neighbourhood, came to see St. Mary's Home. It occasioned deep joy to the founder that the work he had so lovingly reared to the glory of God should receive the blessing of the head of the English Church, and it was, as it were, the placing of the last stone on the edifice he had been instrumental in rearing. The Archbishop alluded to his own pleasure in a note he wrote to the Dean shortly after: "What a welcome at Wantage, and what a gift to light on *you* there."

One more visit in Advent which, at the time, impressed some with a feeling as of a farewell, and Christmas letters interchanged—(loving words to the Sisters in India were among the last he wrote)—brought his earthly work for the Community to a close. In the words of the Bishop of Lincoln:

"At his Lord's command he had worked, at his Lord's command he was ready to die. He had not striven to win souls to himself but to Christ, and to Him, without one single word of fear or anxiety, he resigned all that mysterious spiritual work in which for so many years he had been ceaselessly engaged."

CHAPTER VI.

REMINISCENCES BY REV. V. S. S. COLES.[1]

My first sight of my future Vicar was at Eton in 1858 or 1859. He used to visit his son, who was older, and three divisions higher in school, than I was. I remember well the first time I saw him walking quickly along past Williams' shop. I think I must have been told already that "Butler at Balston's" was the son of the Vicar of Wantage, but I am not sure that I knew even as much as that. At any rate his appearance struck me as different from that of any of the High Church clergy I had seen before, such as Archdeacon Denison and Mr. Carter. He was much more like the ideal I had formed of a mediaeval or foreign ecclesiastic, and seemed to embody those vague possibilities of what was hidden in the English Prayer Book, which were so attractive to many young people at that time. I had a good look at him soon after, during some lecture at which he was present in the Mathematical School, and then, as I watched the eager, active play of his face and lips, and the restless (not to say dangerous) swing of his foot, a certain fear

[1] Various illustrative letters, etc., have been inserted in this narrative. These interpolations are marked by brackets.

began to be mixed with the unique attractiveness which he inspired.

Both feelings remain still, the sense that there never was any one quite like him, and the conviction that his displeasure was a serious thing to reckon with; though from a date not much later than 1858 they have been united with grateful affection.

When I went up to Oxford in 1864, my friend, Montague Noel, was just moving to Wantage from his first curacy.[1] The Vicar encouraged him to ask his undergraduate friends to Wantage, and he was the more disposed to take a kindly interest in me, because I was a pupil of James Riddell, who had prepared him to see a "clumsy Christian." A third link with Wantage was found for me in Father S. W. O'Neill. I had been "up to" him in school at a time when, as a deacon, he was still in the Windsor rifle corps, and before his title at Clewer had brought him into contact with the Catholic teaching which he at once assimilated. Part of the time between his resignation of his Mathematical Mastership at Eton and his admission to the Cowley Society, was spent by him as Curate of Wantage, and surely it is not the least

[1 Extract from a letter to Rev. M. H. Noel, from Rev. H. P. Liddon, dated 16th Sunday after Trinity, 1865:—"What you say about the Vicar delights me. It is precisely my own feeling; after a lapse of eleven years I look back to my curate life at Wantage with the most genuine pleasure, as to a time when, in the best sense of the term, the sun was shining. You will gather up a great deal of spiritual and practical experience to make use of in after life. . . . But much of the benefit of contact with a good man cannot be reduced to writing: it is the insensible though real action of spirit and character of which we can only measure the drift and power after some considerable lapse of time."]

of the blessings which came to Wantage with the Vicar that it should have a share in the memories, experiences, and prayers of so simple and devoted a saint as Simeon Wilberforce O'Neill.

What struck me most in the parish when I was at last able to see it? I am bound to say that I was much more ready than I ought to have been to criticise as well as admire what I saw. It was Noel's mission to "bring things on," and my sympathies were entirely with him. Even then (and much more now), the Vicar's power of using an enthusiasm which he controlled while he used it, seemed to me very remarkable. He always appreciated Noel's character; and indeed the special work which St. Barnabas has done in Oxford owes very much to his Wantage training. In return, it may be noted, that in later days, when the Dean was far from pleased with the Ritualists, he was always willing to preach at St. Barnabas, and always remained a warm friend and helper to Noel.[1]

[1 On Sept. 22nd, 1877, the Vicar wrote to Rev. M. H. Noel recommending the avoiding of things " needlessly irritating," and added : " We do not enough realise the tremendous task which we have set ourselves, viz. to deprotestantise a nation—practically unbelieving, which instinctively feels that Protestantism is like itself, and therefore makes it its religion." On April 26th, 1892, he wrote : " I am delighted to hear how well things go with you. But you really deserve that they *should* go well, and you take the right way of making them go well. My three rules of Faith, Prayer, and Grind, are yours also, and they always, so far as I have seen, succeed. . . . I have marked October 23rd to preach." And on August 18th, 1893, in answer to a request for a sermon at the Dedication Festival : " Alas! I have not got a single day in October which is not filled with some tormenting engagement. I quite dread the thought of it, and wish that it were well over. I am always thinking of *solve senescentem*

It was then partly as a critic that I arrived at Wantage, and my contribution to the facts which will give a picture of the Vicar's life is that in spite of my undisciplined desires for what Wantage did not give, it was simply impossible to resist the fascination of the Vicar's strength and thoroughness. Moreover, though desires for coloured stoles and other luxuries were repressed, we knew well enough that the Vicar was taking pains not to give scandal to the Wantage people, and that at the Home he was always on the side of development.

His thoroughness went into everything. He could pass by things which he felt did not concern his work and duty, when weaker men would have felt constrained to touch them ineffectually, but what he did touch he dealt with thoroughly. Though there was little show of ritual, the changes and improvements all pointed straight to great principles. The chalices, patens, and altar-linen were all accurately and fully cared for. After Holy Communion, a Thanksgiving was always said in the vestry, which included the great prayer of St. Thomas Aquinas, *Gratias Tibi ago*. While other people were introducing lights and vestments, the Vicar of Wantage bore an almost more striking witness to the Real Presence, by the provision of the white houselling-cloth laid along the

equum; but no one else seems to think of it, and I have to keep trudging on, with everybody's packs on my back. I always enjoy a visit to Oxford and St. Barnabas, though the thought of dear Freeling being no more with us makes me sad. No one has done better for the Church than you. I cannot say how much I admire your steady, unflinching work."]

altar-step at all large Communions. The Daily
Service was sung with severe adherence to Plain-song,
not only for the psalms, but on week-days for the
hymns also, which were taken invariably from the
Hymnal Noted.

I need hardly add that the moral severity, the
appeal to the gospel pattern of life, which Dean
Church tells us had so much to do with the motive of
the Oxford Movement, had laid its sacred mark upon
William Butler and his home. Early rising never
laid aside, is always impressive to lads, to whom it is
always difficult, and the wonderful arrangements of
the first hours of the Vicar's day were more than
surprising. Before ten o'clock matins he had said
his prayers, often been at the altar either of the
Home or the parish church, taken a class of pupil
teachers, said Terce with his own household, and done
a good deal towards dealing with the day's letters.
I can hardly explain how it was, but he was the only
man whom I remember to have said the Offices as
quickly as he did without irreverence. I suppose it
was that you felt he was not hurrying for any reason
except to get more time for other things done unques-
tionably for the glory of God. Other good men have
given an example of reverence, but his example of it
was special in that he was so truly human in all his
talk and ways. His stories, even when they were
almost avowedly repeated again and again, convulsed
us all, with the best possible conscience; he could
turn from business, discussion, playfulness, to say
prayers without any loss of dignity to himself or the

supreme cause which he always represented. Prayer,
though his utterance was alert, quick, bracing, to
those whom he led, always entailed a real sacrifice of
time and energy. Matins and evensong could never,
I think, have been omitted, though sometimes the
pauses between the departure of one penitent and the
entrance of another, when he was hearing confessions,
were thus utilised. His well-worn Bible and his
Latin *Paradisus* were always at hand, and yielded
up their treasures to the intent eye, and firm grasp,
which showed how even a few moments during the
reading of a Lesson, or the short pauses in the
Eucharist, were used to the best effect.

It was characteristic of the Vicar to disapprove of
Total Abstinence, and of a too rigorous devotion to fish
on Fridays, but every meal, hearty as he was, was
touched by habitual discipline, and no one could
have doubted the fitness and reality of the grace
which he always said in Lent—a humble deprecation
of severe judgement on our unworthy following of
our Lord and His saints.[1]

Two things you certainly soon heard of, whoever
you were, if you spent any time at Wantage, the
schools and the communicant classes. These were

[1 This grace was : " Blessed Lord, Who for our sake didst fast
forty days and forty nights, and hast given grace to many of Thy
saints to follow Thee in watchings often, in fastings often : Grant to
us whose faith is imperfect and bodies less subdued, grace to follow
Thee more distantly in a contrite and humble spirit, and grant that
the sense of this our weakness which we meekly confess before Thee,
may in the end add strength to our faith and seriousness to our
repentance ; Who livest and reignest with the Father and the Holy
Ghost ever one God world without end. Amen."]

the Vicar's delight, and he told you about them and let you see his methods, with almost boyish pleasure. The school prayers, modelled on Prime, as the family prayers were on Terce, and carefully sung morning by morning, lay at the root of his system. His daily teaching of the pupil teachers, the constant reports brought to him week by week, and often day by day, of attendance and other matters, by the head teachers, his frequent visits to the schools, secured his influence on the whole work. It has often been remarked that he succeeded with girls, perhaps with women, better than with men, though this latter statement can only be made with very real qualifications. I have heard him say many times that in the upper classes the women were better than the men, and in the lower the men were better than the women, because among the poor the money was in the hands of the wife, and among the rich in the hands of the husband. I think this saying of his points to facts in his own experience; he succeeded pre-eminently with educated women; he did more with working-men than with rich men.

Others will have spoken of the foundation of the Community of St. Mary. But the Sisters themselves cannot look at this great work from outside, and I may be allowed to bear my testimony to the impression which the Dean's tender and manly guidance of the Sisters left upon those outside the Community.

It is, I suppose, one of the great Christian para-doxes that good men must always feel debts of infinite obligation to the example and influence of

holy women, and yet recognise that the man's relation
to the woman is that of a ruler and guide. "The
head of the woman is the man." If I am not mistaken, the Dean has left a pattern, almost ideal, to
all who are called to discharge the delicate and important work of the pastor of a religious female
Community. He built up the Community of St.
Mary because he never allowed his self-depreciating
reverence to degenerate into weakness.

If the great work of his life was the foundation of
the Community of St. Mary, I believe that his encouragement largely helped Father Benson's venture
upon the similar undertaking for men at Cowley St.
John. The educated men whom he did influence
certainly found that his help was as unique as it was
excellent. But it was on women that his best
strength and most constant pains were spent, and
probably no man was ever more entirely the true
pastor in all his strong, fatherly, reverent dealings
with them.

Every priest who has found himself responsible for
a genuine parochial charge, after having formed his
convictions on the principles of the Anglo-Catholic
revival, has been compelled to consider what place
the doctrine and practice of confession ought to hold
in his work. To such a man the value of it will
probably be, as it was to the Vicar of Wantage, a
matter of happy experience, and the desire to offer
to others what has been a great blessing to himself,
must be very strong. At the same time, the prejudice against confession, still strong in the English

mind, must have seemed, when William Butler began
his ministry, almost impregnable. This being so,
many clergy who practised it for their own good,
never mentioned it in their public teaching. Others,
determined to escape the questionings and self-
reproaches which silence seemed to entail, taught
confession with hardly any hope that their teaching
would be accepted. But to hold back a means of
grace from his flock, and to relieve his own responsibility by a profitless and harmful defiance of popular
opinion, were alike alien to the Vicar's mind. He did
what some few other men of like character did also. He
abstained from speaking of confession in his Sunday
sermons, or hearing confessions in church. Those
most closely connected with his work, Sisters and
clergy, he drew to his own practice, and upheld them
in it. In the system of penitence arranged for those
who were the first charge of the Sisters, and occasionally, in special cases amongst his parishioners, he used
confession, and when he did use it, his mode of
ministration was most thorough and definite, but he
never expected that it would become familiar to the
mass of his people. What seems to me characteristic
of him is that he believed that some of the advantages
of the universal recognition of confession, as part of
Church discipline, could be obtained by his communicant classes. The connexion may not seem obvious,
as it must be clearly understood that no questions
were asked at the classes; they were not on the
Methodist plan, but rather partook of the nature of
what are now called Meditations and Instructions.

Yet the fact remains that when he was asked what he hoped to do about confession, he often referred at once to the classes, no doubt partly because he hoped that some of those who attended them would take the opportunity of remaining for confession, but also because he felt that the really pastoral relation, which as distinct from the forgiveness of deadly sin, is one of the chief advantages of systematic confession, might thus be obtained.

It may be doubted whether his solution of a very difficult problem is beyond criticism, but that he should have sought to secure as much of the essential advantage as he could, when the complete attainment of his aim was impossible, seems to me characteristic of one of the most prominent and admirable principles of his life.

[His matured views on this subject may be gathered from a letter to Canon Carter, and the printed declaration which he signed in company with others of the same school of thought.

W. J. B. TO CANON T. T. CARTER.

TENBY, Sept. 10, 1873.

I most willingly authorise you to append my name to those who sign the paper on Confession. Having said this, I will add that I think that it lacks the terseness and neatness of that which we sent out some six years ago on the subject of the Real Presence. *That* declaration fairly cauterised the wound. Nothing serious has been done since. Even the Archbishop (Longley) admitted that it had compelled him to revise his opinion as to what the Church of England permits, "though," he added, "I am an old gentleman, and I cannot change my own private views." Could not then *this* declaration be reduced into a few balanced and well-guarded sentences? People will read what is short—but not what is long. . . .

DECLARATION ON CONFESSION AND ABSOLUTION, AS SET
FORTH BY THE CHURCH OF ENGLAND.

We, the undersigned, Priests of the Church of England, considering that serious misapprehensions as to the teaching of the Church of England on the subject of Confession and Absolution are widely prevalent, and that these misapprehensions lead to serious evils, hereby declare, for the truth's sake, and in the fear of God, what we hold and teach on the subject, with special reference to the points which have been brought under discussion.

1. We believe and profess, that Almighty God has promised forgiveness of sins, through the Precious Blood of Jesus Christ, to all who turn to Him, with true sorrow for sin, out of unfeigned and sincere love to Him, with lively faith in Jesus Christ, and with full purpose of amendment of life.

2. We also believe and profess, that our Lord Jesus Christ has instituted in His Church a special means for the remission of sin after Baptism, and for the relief of consciences, which special means the Church of England retains and administers as part of her Catholic heritage.

3. We affirm that—to use the language of the Homily— "Absolution has the promise of forgiveness of sin,"[1] although, the Homily adds, "by the express word of the New Testament it hath not this promise annexed and tied to the visible sign, which is imposition of hands," and "therefore," it says, "Absolution is no such Sacrament as Baptism and the Communion are."[2] We hold it to be clearly impossible, that the Church of England in Art. xxv. can have meant to disparage the ministry of Absolution any more than she can have meant to disparage the Rites of Confirmation and Ordination, which she solemnly administers. We believe that God through Absolution confers an inward spiritual grace and the authoritative assurance of His forgiveness on those who receive it with faith and repentance, as in Confirmation and Ordination He confers grace on those who rightly receive the same.

4. In our Ordination, as Priests of the Church of England, the words of our Lord to His Apostles—"Receive ye the Holy Ghost; whosesoever sins ye remit, they are remitted unto

[1] Homily "of Common Prayer and Sacraments."   [2] *Ibid.*

them, and whosesoever sins ye retain, they are retained"—were applied to us individually. Thus it appears, that the Church of England considers this Commission to be not a temporary endowment of the Apostles, but a gift lasting to the end of time. It was said to each of us, "Receive the Holy Ghost for the office and work of a Priest in the Church of God, now committed unto thee by the imposition of our hands"; and then followed the words, "Whose sins thou dost forgive, they are forgiven, and whose sins thou dost retain, they are retained." [1]

5. We are not here concerned with the two forms of Absolution which the Priest is directed to pronounce after the general confession of sins in the Morning and Evening Prayer, and in the Communion Service. The only form of words provided for us in the Book of Common Prayer for applying the absolving power to individual souls runs thus: "Our Lord Jesus Christ, Who hath left power to His Church to absolve all sinners who truly repent and believe in Him, of His great Mercy forgive thee thine offences; and by His authority committed to me I absolve thee from all thy sins, in the Name of the Father, and of the Son, and of the Holy Ghost. Amen." [2] Upon this we remark, first, that in these words forgiveness of sins is ascribed to our Lord Jesus Christ; yet that the Priest, acting by a delegated authority, and as an instrument, does through these words convey the absolving grace; and, secondly, that the absolution from *sins* cannot be understood to be the removal of any censures of the Church, because (a) the sins from which the penitent is absolved are presupposed to be sins known previously to himself and God only; (b) the words of the Latin form relating to those censures are omitted in our English form; and (c) the release from excommunication is in Art. xxxiii. reserved to "a Judge that hath authority thereunto."

6. This provision, moreover, shows that the Church of England, when speaking of "the benefit of absolution," and empowering her Priests to absolve, means them to use a definite form of absolution, and does not merely contemplate a general reference to the promises of the Gospel.

7. In the Service for "the Visitation of the Sick" the Church of England orders that the sick man shall even "*be moved* to

[1] "The Form and Manner of Ordering of Priests."
[2] "The Order for the Visitation of the Sick."

make a special Confession of his sins, if he feel his conscience troubled with any weighty matter." When the Church requires that the sick man should, in such case, be moved to make a special Confession of his sins, we cannot suppose her thereby to rule that her members are bound to defer to a death-bed (which they may never see) what they know to be good for their souls. We observe that the words, "be moved to," were added in 1661, and that therefore at the last revision of the Book of Common Prayer the Church of England affirmed the duty of exhorting to Confession in certain cases more strongly than at the date of the Reformation, probably because the practice had fallen into abeyance during the Great Rebellion.

8. The Church of England also, holding it "requisite that no man should come to the Holy Communion, but with a full trust in God's mercy, and with a quiet conscience," commands the Minister to bid "any" one who "cannot quiet his own conscience herein," to come to him, or "to some other discreet and learned Minister of God's Word, and open his grief; that by the ministry of God's Holy Word he may receive the benefit of absolution, together with," and therefore as distinct from, "ghostly counsel and advice";[1] and since she directs that this invitation should be repeated in giving warning of Holy Communion, and Holy Communion is constantly offered to all, it follows that the use of Confession may be, at least in some cases, of not unfrequent occurrence.

9. We believe that the Church left it to the consciences of individuals, according to their sense of their needs, to decide whether they would confess or not, as expressed in that charitable exhortation of the First English Prayer Book, "requiring such as shall be satisfied with a general Confession, not to be offended with them that do use, to their further satisfying, the auricular and secret Confession to the Priest; nor those also, which think needful or convenient, for the quietness of their own consciences, particularly to open their sins to the Priest, to be offended with them that are satisfied with their humble Confession to God, and the general Confession to the Church: but in all things to follow and keep the rule of Charity; and every man to be satisfied with his own conscience, not judging other men's minds or consciences; whereas he hath no warrant

[1] Exhortation in the Service for Holy Communion.

of God's Word to the same." And although this passage was omitted in the second Prayer Book, yet that its principle was not repudiated, may be gathered from the "Act for the Uniformity of Service" (1552), which, while authorizing the second Prayer Book, asserts the former book to be "agreeable to the Word of God and the primitive Church."

10. We would further observe, that the Church of England has nowhere limited the occasions upon which her Priests should exercise the office which she commits to them at their ordination; and that to command her Priests in two of her Offices to hear confessions if made, cannot be construed negatively into a command not to receive confessions on any other occasions. But, in fact (see above No. 7, 8), the two occasions specified do practically comprise the whole of the adult life. A succession of Divines of great repute in the Church of England, from the very time when the English Prayer Book was framed, speak highly of Confession, without limiting the occasions upon which, or the frequency with which, it should be used; and the 113th Canon, framed in the Convocation of 1603, recognized Confession as a then existing practice, in that it decreed under the severest penalties, that "if any man confess his secret and hidden sins to the Minister for the unburdening of his conscience, and to receive spiritual consolation and ease of mind from him; . . . the said Minister . . . do not at any time reveal and make known to any person whatsoever any crime or offence so committed to his trust and secrecy, (except they be such crimes as by the laws of this realm his own life may be called into question for concealing the same)."

11. While then we hold that the formularies of the Church of England do not authorize any Priest to teach that private Confession is a condition indispensable to the forgiveness of sin after Baptism, and that the Church of England does not justify any Parish Priest in requiring private Confession as a condition of receiving Holy Communion, we also hold that all who, under the circumstances above stated, claim the privileges of private Confession, are entitled to it, and that the Clergy are directed under certain circumstances to 'move' persons to such Confession. In insisting on this, as the plain meaning of the authorized language of the Church of England, we believe ourselves to be discharging our duty as her faithful Ministers.

Ashwell, A. R., Canon of Chichester.
Baker, Henry W., Vicar of Monkland.
Bartholomew, Ch. Ch., Vicar of Cornwood, and Rural Dean of Plymton.
Benson, R. M., Incumbent of Cowley S. John, Oxford.
Butler, William J., Vicar of Wantage, and Rural Dean.
Carter, T. T., Rector of Clewer.
Chambers, J. C., Vicar of S. Mary's, Soho.
Churton, Edw., Rector of Crayke, and Archdeacon of Cleveland.
Denison, George A., Vicar of East Brent, and Archdeacon of Taunton.
Galton, J. L., Rector of S. Sidwell's, Exeter.
Gilbertson, Lewis, Rector of Braunston.
Grey, Francis R., Rector of Morpeth.
Grueber, C. L., Vicar of S. James', Hambridge.
Keble, Thos., jun., Bisley.
King, Edward, D.D., Canon of Christ Church, Oxford.
Liddell, Robert, Incumbent of S. Paul's, Knightsbridge.
Liddon, H. P., D.D., Canon of S. Paul's, London.
MacColl, M., Rector of S. Botolph, Billingsgate, London.
Mackonochie, A. H., Perpetual Curate of S. Alban's, Holborn.
Mayow, M. W., Rector of Southam, and Rural Dean.
Medd, P. G., Senior Fellow of University College, Oxford.
Murray, F. H., Rector of Chislehurst.
Pusey, E. B., D.D., Canon of Christ Church, Oxford.
Randall, R. W., Incumbent of All Saints, Clifton.
Sharp, John, Vicar of Horbury.
Skinner, James, Vicar of Newlands, Great Malvern.
White, G. C., Vicar of S. Barnabas, Pimlico.
Williams, G., Vicar of Ringwood.
Wilson, R. F., Vicar of Rownhams, Southampton.]

I have mentioned that the Vicar was one of the earliest friends of the Society of St. John the Evangelist. He himself became an associate of the Society, and the American Father Grafton, now Bishop of Fond-du-lac, one of its earliest members, took a Retreat at the Home soon after his arrival in England. Thus, in the case of one of the highest and most single-minded efforts springing out of the Oxford Movement, the help which it would be natural to expect from so powerful a personality as that of the Vicar of Wantage, being, as he was, in full sympathy with the movement, was not wanting. This leads to the consideration of his relation in general to the University and the Diocese. He used to say that he could imagine no lot more happy than that of a man who was a member of the University of Cambridge, and lived fourteen miles from Oxford. Others have contributed their knowledge of his Cambridge life and associations. He often spoke of his first acquaintance with the Tractarian teaching having been due to his friend Philip Freeman, afterwards Archdeacon of Exeter. They went together on a reading party to the Lakes. Each was to take one book for recreation, and when it occurred to Butler to exchange with his friend, it was the *Christian Year* that fell into his hands.

The late Dr. Luard's[1] was the name I remember associating most closely with his visits to Cambridge, and I well remember his interest in a course of University sermons which he preached there, while I was curate at Wantage. They were, I think, to have been on some subjects connected with the Person of our Lord; but finally the Vicar took the Trials of our Lord, a subject which his habitual treatment of the Gospel narratives in Passion-tide had made familiar to him.

I believe his sermons at Cambridge did their work, as certainly did some which he preached in Oxford; but with all his great interest in literature and his love for the Universities, his was not an academical mind. No man was ever more relentlessly bent on testing theory by practice, and Common Rooms, patient of many theories, pause when a rapid and decisive

[1] Registrary of the University.

transition from the abstract to the concrete is pressed upon them.   Perhaps, too, some of the epigrammatic attacks, which were among the Dean's most effective weapons,—" Are you a sacerdotalist or a Plymouth Brother ? "—would be least effective in academic society.   But the witness of Wantage to the possibility of carrying Church principles into practice was not lost upon Oxford.   It was his way to make much of special friends, and his relations with a place or a group would be through the friends who linked him to it.   His special and dearest friend in the University, James Riddell, was taken from him and from Oxford when his brilliant career was only approaching its fulness.   Those who remember will not doubt that any man who had his usual resting-place in Oxford in Riddell's rooms in Balliol, was worthy of the best that Oxford had to give.[1]

This may be the place to say a word as to William Butler's relations with Bishop Wilberforce.   The two

[1 The publication of a poem on "Balliol Scholars," by Principal Shairp, of St. Andrews, gave great pleasure to the Vicar by the terms in which James Riddell was spoken of.   He wrote to express his gratification to the Professor, who thus replied : " I have heard of you often from dear C. E. Prichard.   The way he used to speak of Wantage and the life lived there remains ineffaceably on my memory. I think it was at an earlier time that he used to go there than those visits of James Riddell to which you allude.   Thank you for giving me those strangely touching words with which you say that James Riddell closed his last sermon in your church.   They are so very like himself.   I had two years ago, from C. W. Furse, notes of another sermon he preached on a Good Friday in his church, which contained much of his beautiful spirit.   My visits to England are now few and at wide intervals.   I don't see much chance of my being able to get to Wantage, greatly as I should wish to do so.   But, as you say, community of friends makes friends, and for the sake of those whom we have loved and lost, I shall always think of you as of an unseen friend."]

men understood each other as only men of action can.
Their bright amusing conversation was that of those
who shared the relaxation earned by the toil which
both knew well.   Nevertheless, the Vicar of Wantage
was not simply one of Bishop Wilberforce's men.   He
loved his Bishop and served him loyally, but it was
not on the Bishop's teaching that his convictions
were formed.   To many who did not look below the
surface, it may have seemed that Samuel Wilberforce
was a genuine disciple of the Revival.   I remember
the spot in Oxford where in 1868 a man just taking
his degree, who has since had a foremost place in our
Church life, said, " I have been brought up to look
upon the Bishop of Oxford and Dr. Pusey as being
the same thing : I am just beginning to see that their
line is different."   Where that difference becomes
defined, William Butler stands on the side of Dr.
Pusey and not of Bishop Wilberforce.   Apart from
the truth, as I believe it to be, of the stronger
position, the Dean's adherence to it exhibits the true
greatness of his character.   As I have said already,
no man ever gave closer heed to the probabilities of
success in restoration and development of Church
life.   His hand always touched the pulse of his
parish.   No fear of seeming weak ever forced his
hand.   But it was just because his mind was entirely
made up on the central doctrines of the Revival that
he could afford to be patient.   He did not need to
prove the strength of an immature conviction by
forcing it into rash action.   At the bottom he ever
held those sacerdotal doctrines, which, distinct as

they are from the tendencies which really make for
the Roman theory, are, and were still more, forty
years ago, thoroughly unpopular in England.

The two things for the sake of which High
Churchmen have been forced to sacrifice opportunities of reaching their fellow-countrymen, are the
claim of an integral place in the pastoral system for
voluntary confession, and the belief in the reality of
the inward part of the Holy Sacrament, apart from
reception. On both these points it was the advantage, as regards success, the weakness, as regards
consistency, of Bishop Wilberforce, to be, perhaps
at the verge of it, but still undoubtedly on the
popular side, and he was well aware that this advantage or defect was not shared by Butler. Something
has already been said about his views as to confession. Roughly they came to this, that it was
desirable for all who could believe in it, almost
indispensable for the perfection of the clerical and
the religious life, so desirable for some who had
fallen deeply, as to make it necessary to be bold in
propounding it. It was only his intensely practical
habit of mind which hindered the Vicar from pressing
it where he knew it was impossible to carry it, and
where he trusted that the fact of such impossibility
pointed to the guidance of the Divine Will.

No doubt this position far exceeds the limits
allowed by Bishop Wilberforce, in his published
utterances, to the use of confession. Far more did
his position fall short of that to which the Vicar's
deliberate conviction had led him on the matter of

the Real Presence. The Bishop was, no doubt, in this matter a genuine follower of Hooker, or, to be accurate, of Hooker's teaching in the fifth book of his *Ecclesiastical Polity*. The belief in the Real Presence as held by Dr. Pusey rested on the force of the words of our Lord as interpreted by the teachings of the Fathers. Hooker's method was rather to consider what is the true purpose of the Sacrament, and then to inquire what manner of Presence is necessary to that end. This method would commend itself to a mind like that of the great organising prelate, who may be pardoned if in so busy and hard-pressed a life he sacrificed something of the abstract completeness of truth to the concrete necessities of his flock. But it was a sacrifice which, in this matter at any rate, the Vicar could never have endured, because the complete truth of the Real Presence had made good an appeal to the needs and instincts of his own heart, and he had been led to see its astonishing power for good in the spiritual life of foreign Churches, and especially of their religious communities. I think it was about the year 1867 that he made a study, during his holiday, of some of the Jesuit houses in France. I can never forget his account of this tour on his return. He had done the thing thoroughly, like everything else. He had gone prepared for controversy, humbly secure that he was doing God's work at home, and that it was impossible that he could be called to sever his connexion with those whom God had taught with and through him, but at the same time, with an open mind, ready to learn all that the sight of principles just reviving at home, but here in France habitually accepted, could teach him. Thus when his hosts, stimulated to their most eager and demonstrative efforts by the value of one who seemed a possible convert of the first rank, pressed him with *a priori* arguments for the Papal monarchy, he felt an almost amused pleasure in reminding them that the English were never logical, and strong in his conviction that their theoretical structures would not bear the test of historical fact, bade them grateful farewell, while they stretched after him eager hands, and kept repeating, "Soyez conséquent, monsieur."

[Some letters written to Mrs. Butler at this period describe these visits to the Jesuit Fathers, and also show his remarkable power of throwing his mind into the subject before him, undistracted by preoccupations. For it was during 1867 that, as the following chapter will relate, for several months he was awaiting the decision of the Archbishop of Canterbury on his acceptance or refusal of the See of Natal.

W. J. B. TO HIS WIFE.

PARIS, August 16, 1867.

. . . Well, I am quite converted, and could spend weeks in Paris. It is really a wonderful place, and I see no special reason to suppose that the devil built it. It was a goodly sight last night to see the immense masses of people, perfectly sober and orderly, traversing the Place de la Concorde in all directions. And the loveliness of the scene was beyond description. There was a vast network of lamps festooned from the Tuileries right away to the Arc de l'Etoile—all round those waterworks and the huge obelisk, and the Rue de Rivoli had two long straight lines of light on each side to the very end. The British Embassy was very cleverly illuminated, and as for the Prince Napoleon, his house was a great blaze of light. Then of course there were 'feux d'artifice,' etc. We wandered up and down till we were tired, more astonished at the behaviour of the people than anything else.

I slept like a dormouse—dreaming however greatly of Colenso, whose pupil —— had been. He told me a good deal about him. He was kind and painstaking, but always broaching strange ideas. . . . I breakfasted at ten or thereabouts (the room was full of compatriots), indulging only in coffee and bread and butter; and then I mooned forth to S. Sulpice, to one of whose professors, M. Hogan, I had an introduction. He was described to me as a French Liddon. Unfortunately he was 'en vacances' till Oct. 1. I therefore put a bold face on the matter and walked straightway to M. le Curé de S. Sulpice, by name Hamon, with my card and letter. He was at home, and we had a deal of talk. Of course he drove at me right and left to convert me, and this wasted a deal of time. It was useless to say, "Monsieur, j'ai pris mon parti—j'ai lu tout ce qu'il y a à lire," etc. He would return to the great question. His point was simply iteration of 'pasce oves meas.' Without the Pope no unity—no faith. Greeks are schismatics. You are mere women-ridden slaves—governed by the Court of Admiralty. Alas! you poor Anglicans, we pity you with all our hearts (and, suiting the action to the word, he threw his arms round me), we love and would fain make you right. You are brought up in the midst of prejudice, etc., etc. His arguing was very weak, and when I said, "If the Pope is all that you say he is, why should there ever have been the General Councils?" he answered, there *never* was any real need of General Councils— the Pope only called them together out of complaisance. Well, but, said I, the Council of Constance deposed the Pope. He simply denied it. As for S. Cyprian, he tried to make out that he gave in to the Pope. Have the goodness, said I, strong in my S. Cyprian, to show me the epistle. Surely, in the Council of Carthage, he distinctly, with his bishops—wrongly, I grant— decided against the Pope in the matter of heretical baptism. He said that he would do so, but did not fulfil his promise. I looked on all this as so much lost time, being very anxious to talk to him about Confession and various other matters. He told me that he had 60,000 people in his parish and 25 curates.

I am to call to-morrow at 12.30 and be introduced to some school Sisterhood. From him I went (with a note from him) to les Petites Sœurs des Pauvres, in the Rue de N. D. des Champs, and stayed an endless time—two or three hours, I think. A dear young Irish lady, a nun, took me in tow. I could have cried with delight at what I heard and saw. If I were to be converted it would be by such sights as that, not by the good Father's argument or eloquence.

The buildings form three sides of a quadrangle—the entrance being the fourth with a very pretty garden in the middle. I observe that a *cloister* is everywhere 'de rigueur.' They have 250 old men and women under their roof, all happy and apparently good. Wonderful are their arrangements for victuals and clothing. I saw a drawer full of crusts, etc. The kitchen was a model of neatness. The beds—in long rooms—as clean and comfortable as possible. Each bed had a bolster and two pillows with the whitest of counterpanes. The old men were playing cards—the old women needling. Some were sitting in the cloisters, others sunning themselves in the garden. I asked heaps of questions which were all answered simply and naturally. There are about 1500 Sisters occupying 100 houses. They have no money. It is all spent in building. They are recruited from the bourgeoisie, with a few Dames de qualité. They are all *alike*, and have to perform two years of novitiate at the Mother house. No one is admitted who is older than 35, because there is so much hard work to be done. They take vows for three years only, and are admitted by the Supérieur Général, a Priest deputed by the Bishop. Next to the Sisters of S. Vincent de Paul they are the most flourishing order in France. My conductress had been in London originally, but had been sent to Paris some four years ago—time enough for her to talk English in the funniest French fashion—and French, as she said, well enough to amuse all the rest.

I saw all the old people in their various rooms, and contrasted them mentally with our grumpy old wretches under the benign influence of —— and the Board of Guardians. I am sure that we shall never do anything decently till the English Government works on very different principles and accepts religion as a *happyfying* thing. The good Sister told me that the deaths of these old folk were often most edifying, almost miraculous sometimes. The Sisters never interfere with them in matters of religion. They may be Mahometans, if they like. All this is left to the Vicaire of S. Sulpice, deputed by the Curé to look after them.

I lingered on, till I could in decency stay no more, left a 'pièce de dix francs,' and by a circuitous railway route at the cost of 4d. and an hour, made for the Exposition, at which I had but a little time to spend. It closes at six. I saw however a few more interesting things, and then fell in with the enormous crowd as they 'débouched' into the Parc which surrounds it. I began to be very hungry, and though the whole of the huge oval is surrounded with eating places, I could not make up my mind to settle down anywhere. The waiters seemed pert, and the prices high. At last I espied 'le grand Restaurant de Suffren'—dinner 3$^{fr.}$ 50$^{c.}$ with a bottle of wine. I entered, had a ticket handed to me by a tall gentleman ('décoré'), and asked for a dinner 'en maigre,' which they had some difficulty in supplying. By dint, however, of fish and 'légumes,' I made it out pretty fairly, and sat wondering at the good temper and unwearied waiting of the 'garçons,' and also at the splendour of the room. Although merely run up for the nonce it is lofty, beautifully painted, capable of holding 400 or 500 people. The arrangements were perfect, and everything of the very best. Notwithstanding the vast number of guests, each was thoroughly cared for. Then I wandered about the Parc looking at the quaint buildings, all huddled together— Japanese, Tunisian, Swiss cottages, models of catacombs, an Egyptian temple. It is enough to turn one into a little Alice,[1] and as the evening began to set in, I walked homewards along the Seine for about a couple of miles. En route I asked a man for the Pont de la Concorde, who answered, beating his breast simultaneously, "English, English." He turned out to be a master bricklayer from the Potteries, with his wife. We had a deal of talk. He expressed great astonishment at Paris, thought the French far ahead of us, and was especially struck with their behaviour last night. "Why, sir, if it had been in England, half of them would have been drunk, and they would certainly have smashed those lamps for mischief's sake." He was a Churchman, and I directed him where to go on Sunday. He had met no

[1] *Alice's Adventures in Wonderland.*

English, and was very pleased to have an opportunity of venti-
lating his mother tongue. . . . I quite regret to leave Paris. . . .
I shall try to get an introduction from my friend M. le Curé de
S. Sulpice to some of the clergy on my line of march.

I could go on prosing for ever on the wonderful lift that
France has gained in all respects during the last twenty years;
but, like an honest man, I must add that the lady the concierge
(English) at the Hôtel Vouillemont, who is 'catholique,' declares
that the English people are much better, and that the French
are selfish and wicked. There is some comfort in that for a
wounded spirit. . . . I forgot to say that I went into N. D.
des Champs, a very pretty *wooden* church capable of holding
500 or 600 people—a far better instrument than iron.

W. J. B. TO HIS WIFE.

SOISSONS, IX S. after Trinity, 9.30 P.M. [1867].

So here I am in this world-old city of Soissons, after a most
interesting day, quietly sitting down to write you an account of
my adventures. I thought this morning of Goldsmith's line,

"Remote, unfriended, solitary, slow,"

and find myself neither one nor the other. But to continue my
history since Friday evening. Saturday I invested in pen and
ink, and have enjoyed peace ever since. Had a long talk with
Madame la Concierge of the Vouillemont, who, though herself a
'Catholic,' has no faith in the French, declares that they are
wicked and selfish, and hate us although they make their fortune
by us, as she tells Monsieur of the hotel whenever he makes his
many unkind remarks, as he did only to-day when she went to
post *my* letter to you. She is married to a Belgian, whose ways
are English, else she would not have had him, and she goes to
Bath, her native city, in January to place her daughter as a
pupil in a convent there. Then I started for S. Sulpice to find
M. le Curé, was hindered for a minute, and arrived just too late.
'Il est sorti il y a cinq minutes.' I was much aggravated, but I
turned my misfortune to account by hunting up Hachette's Library
and getting a guide-book for the part of France which I was about
to visit, and looking at the Hôtel Cluny, which is close at hand.
. . . Soissons contains some 12,000 inhabitants, and is
crammed with curiosities and relics, as you may easily imagine.
One seems to breathe a Merovingian air. Chilperics and Clotaires,

and Louis le Débonnaire, and folk of that sort, rise up round one.
Well, after 'du café,' and after fulfilling my own duties and
Services, I started for the Cathedral and High Mass at 9.30,
soon stumbled on the sous-sacristain, inserted a franc into his
willing paw, and asked him for a 'siège' whence I should not
be 'dérangé,' and asked a few questions as to how to get a
guide-book for Soissons. He put me in the part which surrounds
the choir, and I saw and heard to advantage. When service was
over at 11.30, a very pleasing young ecclesiastic accosted me,
and requesting me to follow him 'chez lui,' offered not only to
lend me books but himself to have the honour of showing me the
lions of the place. It was exactly what I wanted. I carried home
his books, got an hour's study of them, and from one till seven
he acted as my guide. He was extremely intelligent, and besides
giving me all information about Soissons, I learnt much from him
about the state of ecclesiastical concerns. He lives in a pleasant
little room, well filled with books and prints. His name and
title is "l'Abbé Ply, Vicaire et Maître de Chapelle de la Cathé-
drale." We went first to the Abbey of S. Médard, formerly
Benedictine, a regular S. Denis of the olden days. There are a
good many remains—chapel, crypt, etc.—and it is now turned
into a Hospital for Sourds-Muets et Aveugles, under the charge
of Sisters 'de la Sagesse.' A very bright pretty young woman,
the Superioress, showed us over the establishment, and I literally
heard the deaf and dumb *talk*, and the blind read and play. I
made my small offering, thankful for the chance, and then we
marched off to S. Jean des Vignes, which must have been a
magnificent church; now only the face remains, *i.e.* two huge
towers and spires, with a triple doorway deeply recessed. We
climbed up to the top and had a good view of the country. My
friend told me that it is the current tale that Fénelon described
the island of Calypso from this *riant* valley. It seems that he
lived somewhere hard by while he wrote *Télémaque.* Thence to
the 'petit Séminaire,' where there is a very interesting Roman-
esque church, and so up and down, seeing everything, and having
much talk as we passed along. My friend spoke very differently
from M. Hamon of S. Sulpice, whom he called 'un homme très
distingué.' He told me that the power of the bishops was
'énorme,' also that the congregations of regulars did much harm.
There is always an appeal to Rome from the bishops, but the

Government always takes part with the bishops, declining to know anything about Rome, and the result is constant acts of tyranny and injustice.   There was a good deal of truth, he said, though mingled with mischievous intention, in *Le Maudit*. Gallicanism is extinct.   Two bishops were actually deposed for not accepting the new dogma.   Also one of the professors in the seminary was expunged for holding Gallican views.   The fact is that the bishops find that nothing but Ultramontanism will hold against the Erastianism of the day.   At the present time there is not a potentate who favours the Church.   He gave a sad picture of the religious condition of France.   The lawyers are unbelievers (Voltairiens), the doctors materialists, the bourgeoisie careless, the majority never confessing from the day of their confirmation, except a mere show of it at marriage, seldom sufficient for absolution, till they die, when they make a perfunctory confession in order to be respectably buried.   If the clergy visit they are told, "We are delighted to see you as *friends*, but we do not want you as *priests*," etc.   There is great difficulty in recruiting the priesthood.   The mass are sons of artisans and labourers, the best are sons of farmers.   In the seminary here are 70 or 80, not sufficient for the wants of the diocese, which contains 670 parishes.   Things are better in the country, but the pay is very little, often only 900 francs per annum, scarcely enough to buy food and raiment.   A man must be very gentle, complaisant, self-denying, and devoted.   I longed to ask him whence he sprang.   His tastes, talk, and intelligence and manners were thoroughly of the best.   He was fond of heraldry, architecture—had a keen eye for stained glass and good pictures.   Finally he gave me a letter of introduction to M. l'Abbé Parizet, Chanoine aumônier de l'Hôpital général de Laon, and we separated, swearing eternal friendship. . . .

W. J. B. TO HIS WIFE.

RHEIMS, HÔTEL DU LION D'OR, Aug. 20, 1867.

. . . I want to give you my impressions of Laon before something else drives them out of my head. . . . You have no idea of the magnificence of Laon.   There it stands in the midst of the sandy plain, something like Windsor Castle.   It is a most picturesque walled town, and reminded me of Aubenas.   Formerly it was 'la Laon Sainte,' from the heaps

of churches and religious Orders which filled it. You will
remember it as the battleground of Hugh Capet and the
Charlemagne race, then the endless quarrels between the
Communes, who seem to have had special privileges, and the
bishops who also had special privileges, and wished to 'parson
'em up too tight,' especially one Gaudry, whom the people
finally murdered, etc., etc. . . . My friend M. l'Abbé Ply at
Soissons had given me an introduction to the Aumônier of
the Hospital. I went to his abode, but he had gone to some
sort of reunion in the country. I then resolved to betake
myself and my letter to the Pères Jésuites who inhabit the
ancient Abbaye de S. Vincent, a fine bold *spur* once strongly
fortified, directly opposite Laon, and connected by a most
exquisitely beautiful walk along the old fortifications. The
heat was tremendous, and I could find no response to my
knocks. At last I heard voices, and stumbled upon a whole
regiment of 'frères convers' solacing themselves in a roughly
built summer-house. I gave my card, and was ushered into
the building. After a quarter of an hour, an intelligent and
kindly man of about forty years old appeared, accosted me
very pleasantly, and conducted me over the place. I was
there for two hours and more. Of course we went at the old
story. He showed me a rubbishy account of the conversion
of a certain Mr. Pittar from the Church of England, written
in very bad taste, and as weak as possible. If these good
people knew how little impression that sort of thing produces
on the mind of those who have fought the thing through,
they would go to work in a different way. His great point
was 'One Faith,' 'One Church,' 'One Pastor,' 'On this
rock will I build My Church,' etc. A Retreat was to begin
that very day. About forty were expected of the neighbouring
clergy, and my friend had the arranging of the beds, etc. It
amused me much to see them troop in—much as we do at
Cuddesdon—looking for their rooms. There was a salutation
consisting of an approach of the two faces, first on one side,
then on the other—then followed the pointing out of the
room, and a kindly " Vous voilà, monsieur," as each was suited,
or " Voulez-vous prendre quelque chose ? " " Voulez-vous dîner ? "
I asked if I might join myself to the Retreat for two or three
days (it lasted a week). My friend in the kindest way

promised to inquire of the Father who gave the Retreat, but
evidently was doubtful as to the result; and finally, though
he said they would gladly receive me for a 'Retraite par-
ticulière,' which of course was not what I wanted, it came out
that the Curés and Vicaires present at the Retreat would
have thought it not quite the thing to be associated with a
'ministre protestant.' He wrote a very kind letter in my
behalf to l'Abbé Modeste at Rheims, whom I shall visit by-
and-bye. . . .

W. J. B. TO HIS WIFE.

HÔTEL DE LA VILLE DE PARIS,
STRASBOURG, Aug. 27, 1867.

. . . I have now got a regular line of work before me, from
which I do not intend to swerve. Before I say more of this,
I must tell you how much Rheims Cathedral satisfied me.
There is really nothing like it, according to my idea. It rises
in perfect proportion, like a growth from the earth. Every
bit of it is *thought* out and *carried* out—the west porches,
the sides, the buttresses, east end, and general ornamentation.
. . . I went up to the top with a very agreeable old gentleman,
the concièrge, whose son is a coiffeur in Edimbourg. He left
France, said my friend, because he could not bear to work on
Sundays. It is very delightful to me to get to the top of
these places because the eye ranges over all those old historical
battlegrounds, and you can picture to yourself a little of the
past. Of course I had the good Joan of Arc before me. It
seems to me that there are some pages of history for which
one would freely give one's life to prevent their having existed.
How those brutes of English *could* burn Joan of Arc, I cannot
imagine, and when one says English, of course it was quite as
much the French. . . . Well—I must pass on. At 8 A.M. I
had a 'rendezvous' with my friend, the Père Modeste, who
in the kindest way selected one of his party to take me over
the ecclesiastical institutions of Rheims. The Père who went
with me was evidently a very clever man, a little perhaps over
thirty. He could talk English, French, and German, and was
full of feeling and humour. We went first to 'le Bon Pasteur'
whose mother-house is, as you remember, at Angers. There was
some little ceremony but no real difficulty in obtaining per-

mission from 'le Vicaire Général,' a very pleasing old gentleman,
from whom I learnt a good deal as to their *modus operandi*.
He said that at first they took every applicant, but the row
of 1848 for the time broke up their house, and they began
again on better principles, refusing the worst, and confining
themselves to those who had not gone so far wrong. The bad
ones, he said, were "diables incarnés" when they became
furious, and did the others harm. Then we went to the house
itself—a good spacious building, with an excellent garden.
The Mother-Superior, a lady of high family, was in bad health,
but her deputy took us over the place, and every now and
then a nun or two joined us, and chatted. The system seems
much freer than ours. The rooms are filled with beds, and a
couple of 'consacrées' penitents who have given themselves to
the house sleep with them, while a Sister has a room at the
end. They are engaged much as ours are, in washing, sewing,
cooking, etc. One was sullen, and wanted to go, and I was
struck by the exact similarity of her looks and manner to ours
under like circumstances—looking on the ground, picking at
her clothes, etc. Among the younger ones was a poor little
thing of nine years old who had run away with a lad from
her parents. The good Père said a few words in each room,
and then all, Sisters and penitents, knelt for his blessing. We
saw another institution—educational—kept by the Frères
Chrétiens, and then I went home and had my déjeuner along
with the Pères Jésuites. Of course all this was intermingled
with hot and interminable discussions which amuse them,
improve my French, and do no harm. I told them that 'l'esprit
anglais est très inconséquent.' "Mais soyez conséquent—soyez
conséquent," shouted my good friends, and we all laughed
heartily. . . .

In the carriage was a chatty man, who told me that he
was inspector of all the schools in that part of the country,
Catholic, Protestant, etc., etc., an 'Israélite.' Pleasant—would
it not be—to have our schools inspected by an Israelite?
Unfortunately he got out at Bar-le-Duc, and I missed what I
much desired, a conversation with one of the other side. . . .
I went out to find the Strasbourg Pères Jésuites, and thence—
only think of this—I was actually taken to 'Monseigneur
l'Evêque,' whom I had first seen figuring in one of the Emperor's

carriages, and I was honoured by half an hour of 'causerie'
with him. He is a regular 'jolly old brick,' as you will see
when you have seen the photograph which I have purchased
in honour of the visit. He was very affable—was beginning
his tour of Confirmations, thirty leagues off, to-morrow, else
would have, etc. Gave me free permission to circulate through
all the works of piety in the Diocese. Explained to me the
condition of Alsace where are 1,000,000 of inhabitants of whom
200,000 are Protestants—told me how he chaffed the Protestant
'Surintendant,' one Braun, on the subject of mixed marriages,
and begged me to call again if ever I came to Strasbourg.
'Voilà!' . . .]

But all the while he felt a power among these disappointed Fathers, to the attraction of which his
conscience offered no opposition. He saw no reason
why he should join them in making the Pope the
centre of their system, but he felt that principles he
had long accepted would justify him in seeking to
imitate the devotion which made the Blessed Sacrament the centre of their life. On his return to
England this thought, if I am not mistaken, was very
prominent in his mind and conversation. He did
not hesitate to regret the law of the English Church
which made reservation impossible, except by what
seemed to him to be a sophistical disobedience. It
was however at this time that he taught the Sisters
to value a pause of some minutes after the Consecration and before Communion, during which special
adoration might be offered to our Lord, present in
His glorified humanity under the Sacramental veils.

It was his convictions on such points as these,
which, in his case, as in that of Dr. Liddon, did not
allow of a perfect sympathy and co-operation with

the great Bishop of Oxford. No doubt in both cases
they also retarded the promotion which would else
have been so natural at a much earlier time than that
at which, to some degree, it came.

I cannot leave the mention of Oxford without
giving myself the pleasure of noting that in later
years Butler's habitual host in the University was
the one man who so eminently carried on the traditions of refinement and uncompromising faith, which
marked the early Tractarians, George Noel Freeling.
I am not sure whether the Dean ever stayed in
Oxford after his beautiful presence had been withdrawn;[1] they were not very long parted, and their
rest is one.

But, if William Butler's thoroughness kept him in
the ranks of the unpopular, it must be plainly stated
that this does not mean that he threw in his lot with
the Ritualists. On the contrary, as soon as they
became a well-defined party, he stood aloof from
them. His action in this respect turns principally on,
or may be illustrated by, his relations to Alexander
Mackonochie. The future Vicar of St. Alban's, Holborn, came, I think as his second curacy, to Wantage,
and remained there until he was chosen by Mr.
Hubbard to lead the mission of which he was about to
provide the external apparatus, into the slums of
Holborn. The Vicar used to say that if Mackonochie
had gone straight to St. Alban's from Wantage,
instead of spending an interval at St. George's
Mission—where the pea-shooters and profanity of the

[1 He was Canon Bright's guest at Christ Church in Oct., 1892.]

Protestant mob tended to drive him into whatever was most opposed to them—the result would have been other than it has been. During the early years of St. Alban's the Vicar of Wantage preached there from time to time. On one occasion bouquets were provided not only for the choir-boys, but for the clergy, possibly as a step to the wreaths of roses with which the Canons of St. Paul's were anciently decked on Corpus Christi Day. The Vicar related to us when he came back to Wantage how he had furtively laid down his nosegay on a seat during the procession, and how it had been gravely restored to him by the Ceremoniarius. 'Tantum religio potuit.' Before long the developments at St. Alban's went beyond the lines which Butler could conscientiously accept, but his friendship for Mackonochie was never shaken. He regretted the introduction of the mid-day Choral Eucharist. To him, as to Mr. Bennett of Frome, it seemed fitting that the Divine Mysteries should not be exposed to the possible irreverence and almost certain unpreparedness of an eleven o'clock congregation. At Wantage, as at Frome, the Choral Celebration was early, and that which followed matins was plain Celebration, intended for aged and infirm communicants. It may be questioned whether the missionary power of the mid-day High Service, the experience of which is perhaps the best argument in its favour, ever came under the notice of the Vicar. Certainly there were other matters connected with the ritualistic development which would have made him disinclined to look favourably upon

it, though as to the privilege and benefit of assistance
at the altar when not actually receiving, he had
no doubt whatever.[1]

It was, I think, in the summer of 1870 that the
Vicar spent Trinity Sunday in London, and went
with a friend, for whose opinion he had a great
respect, and who was strongly opposed to the new
departure, to see some ritualistic churches. I think
they chose St. Michael's, Shoreditch, in the morning; certainly they went in the evening to St.
Paul's, Lorrimore Square. Here notice was given
of the observance of the Feast of Corpus Christi
on the following Thursday, and the preacher explained that, although it was not a feast marked
in the Prayer Book, the origin of festivals had
been their spontaneous local observance, and it was
fitting that the desire for a festival of the Holy
Sacrament should give rise to a development of this
kind from local centres. I have been accustomed
to connect the Vicar's dislike of Ritualism with that
Sunday.

It would have been difficult for him, in the
midst of his unceasing work, to have entered upon
a thorough study of ritual, and impossible for him
to have taken the matter up without thoroughly
studying it. Now and then the fitness of some

[1 He wrote in the "Parish Journal," on April 2nd, 1869 : "I should,
indeed, be grieved if 'non-communicating attendance' were to be
substituted for regular and frequent participation of the Bread from
heaven. We should gain little if the sacrifice were offered, and
the partaking of the sacrifice ignored or set aside." But see
Appendix II.]

isolated point of ritual, from its connexion with doctrine, struck his imagination and his devotion. I remember, for instance, that when during his illness after an accident in 1872 I had the privilege of giving him Holy Communion, he received vested in a stole, having learned, as he said, that every Communion of a priest had something of a sacrificial character. But, on the whole, he did not take to the ritual movement. I think he never felt as much at home in a chasuble as in a surplice and stole, and the elaboration of details of ritual was thoroughly distasteful to him.

On one point connected with this matter I feel at a loss to describe his position : indeed, I am inclined to think that he never quite defined it himself ; I mean I do not know what to say as to his sympathies during the ritual prosecutions. It is quite certain that he looked upon that interpretation of the royal supremacy which justifies the ecclesiastical jurisdiction of the Sovereign exercised through the Judicial Committee of the Privy Council, as impossible, and irreconcileable with a belief in the spiritual authority of the Church. He had known long before I knew him the strain of the Gorham decision, which cost him the loss of H. E. Manning, and with him of Miss Lockhart, who was first Mother Superior of the Home. His reason for not following them did not lie in any acquiescence in the decision of the Privy Council, but in his heartfelt repudiation of the moral authority of that decision. He delighted to quote Mr. Keble's strong statement, that if the

Church of England did not destroy the Privy Council the Privy Council would destroy it; he did not hesitate to describe the Church of England as a bleeding heart from which the life was flowing through the wounds inflicted by the Erastian action of the State.

So far as the Church has now been relieved in any degree of the evils arising from the Privy Council's jurisdiction, it has been in consequence of the resistance to the ritual judgements, and their final discrediting in the case of the Bishop of Lincoln. It is, however, the fact that, during the anxieties of the Purchas and Ridsdale cases, the Vicar of Wantage was far less keen as to these particular instances than he had been on the general principle brought into prominence by the Gorham judgement, and later by the prosecution of Mr. Bennett. What I believe he felt was that while the claim of spiritual jurisdiction by the Crown was as disastrous as he had always maintained it to be, dignity and the proportion of truth suffered through the emphasis laid on points of ceremonial. It was no point of conscience with him to resist these decisions, though it was not a point of conscience to accept them. At some moments I think it must be allowed that he tended to the opinion that on matters not essential, even though belonging to the spiritual domain, the decision of the State should be treated with respect.

[His views on the relations of Church and State, especially as bearing on the subject of Ritualism, were expressed at various times to Canon Liddon and

others, and near the end of his life, to the Very Rev.
Randall T. Davidson, Dean of Windsor, now Bishop
of Winchester.

W. J. B. TO REV. CANON LIDDON.

WANTAGE VICARAGE, Dec. 5, 1870.

While candidates for Confirmation are coming and going, I
must try to sandwich in a few lines suggested by your letter
of this morning. I quite agree with you that the judgement
on A. H. M., viewed from a legal point, is harsh and unfair.
And you know how for years the Court of Final Appeal has
been in my opinion the great σκάνδαλον in the way of the
Church—I may say even also of the State—for what can be
more [*illegible*] than for the State to incite her people to accept
and believe in a man-made religion—and to this *practically* the
decisions come. But my quarrel, so to call it, with our dear
old friend, is quite apart from the P. C. I complain (and I
think that people like Lord ——, a type of a class not the worst,
complain also with justice) that he is trying to force into
the use of the Church of England that which the Church in
no way authorises, that he is making his own private fancy
the rule of public ministrations. In other words, he is acting
in the very most Protestant fashion. Of course he would say
that he went by the rule of the Catholic Church, etc., but
unless he is prepared to assert that Rome, and nothing but
Rome, teaches that rule, I cannot see where he finds it. I
maintain that no work can stand which abjures obedience. If
I cannot obey where I am, I should think it my duty to go
where I *could* obey. *Individuals* are far too weak and ignorant to
be permitted to take lines of their own, except within certain
specified limits. And it seems to me that this determination
to make out a new religion—which this really is—*e.g.* the en-
forcement of fasting Communion, the making confession a
matter of salvation, or at least a duty for every soul—besides
a heap of ritualistic practices, some of the queerest kind,
which he introduces into the services, must naturally kindle a
correlative antagonism which will not stop till it has caused
great damage far and wide. And I own that I find myself in
a trying dilemma.

I sympathise with all my heart in the demonstration of
Catholic and Sacramental teaching which A. H. M.'s line, as I
think, only simulates. I cannot express my opinion without the
certainty of being misunderstood, yet I feel it untrue to throw
myself heartily into the ranks of the defenders, as I gladly
would have done if only I could believe his method to be loyal
and true. I am writing, as you will perceive, somewhat
hurriedly and dishevelledly—please remember in strict privacy
to you.

W. J. B. TO ——

March 7, 1871.

I have thought very carefully, and I trust without any sort of
personal feeling, on the serious issue which lies before us. I
come to the conclusion that I have only two alternatives between
which to choose. I must either be ready to resign my work,
or ready, if compelled, to obey. It seems to me almost immoral to *chance* what may come—to say if we hold together
'they' will never venture to attack so large a party, and the
like—and to comfort oneself with this. It is at least possible
that 'they' may do so; and I am bound to express to those who
ask me, and to settle moreover for myself, what I should do
if I *am* attacked. This is why I state distinctly now, before
the crisis arises, that I should not consider myself as acting
rightly in the sight of God if I were deliberately to say, "I
shall stand firm," supposing that by firmness is meant the giving
up of that to which I believe God has sent me, rather than that
I should consent to celebrate at the N. end of the altar. I
ask myself which will most damage the work of God—the
separating myself from those precious souls among whom I
have ministered for so many years, and leaving them to the
sort of teaching which in all probability, under the circumstances of the case, would follow mine—or the yielding to what
in fact, when you come to analyse it, is brute force, in a matter
which only indirectly affects the truth—I say the former. If
the doctrine were directly impugned, the case would be very
different. But I can teach it, even though at some disadvantage,
in many other ways, even supposing my position at the altar to
be interfered with. Of course if I were bidden not to teach it
at all, I could have but one answer to give—and to teach it
all the more.

I am very sorry to differ from you and others as to the wisest and best course. But I cannot set aside what my conscience dictates; and you will, I know, give me credit for dulness and ignorance if you will, but at least for honesty of purpose. For the present I shall certainly go on as I have gone on for the last twenty-four years, and the arrangement of the Church is such that it is very unlikely that any one would be idiotic enough to wish me to celebrate at the N. end, where I could not possibly be seen. But I do not choose to shelter myself under this, and therefore I speak my mind.

W. J. B. TO CANON T. T. CARTER.

WANTAGE VICARAGE, March 19, 1877.

I do not feel that my opinion is worth anything, but as you wish for it, I will try to state shortly what occurs to me. Certainly in olden days those who professed High Church principles paid great deference to bishops. Witness the giving up of the 'British Critic'—so very able and useful as it was—at the desire of Bishop Bagot; and I remember well how, at the Consecration of Hursley Church (1848), Mr. Keble made all kinds of arrangements which were distasteful to himself, to meet the wishes of Bishop Sumner.

It is quite true that the bishops have for the most part acted, as we think, in a cowardly and one-sided manner; but I do not agree that even this exonerates us from certain duties which we owe to them. Is there not a certain Sacramental strength given to *order*, which may be called the promise of the Fifth Commandment?

I am greatly in favour of Liddon's suggestion—not his however only—of endeavouring to get at least points of doctrine ruled by the collective Episcopate. I believe that they would be 'guided into truth.' In regard to individual bishops, for my own part I have always accepted the directions of *our* bishops. Certainly it may be said that men like Bishops Wilberforce and Mackarness are exceptions. But I am quite sure that if *any* bishop, in whose Diocese I was, had bidden me take down the pictures of the Stations from the walls of my church, I should have obeyed him without demur, and I should have believed that in doing so—somehow or other—

the work would have been more prospered than if I had retained them against his will.   I cannot help thinking that if some of our friends had yielded in such matters as this, the graver questions of the position of the celebrant, etc., would never have been raised.   The P.W.R. Act no doubt puts the bishop in a false position.   It makes him the instrument of an Act of Parliament officer, instead of a father in the Church.   But it seems to me that *that* is *his* affair. *We* have nothing to do with the action of the State law, but with the bishop.   In his inner consciousness he may be Lord Penzance's servant, but outwardly he speaks to us as a bishop.

I do not wish to speak positively, or to tie myself down to an opinion, but I incline to think that I should obey the bishop in all but questions of doctrine.   There my own conscience *must* be master.

W. J. B. to Very Rev. Randall T. Davidson,
Dean of Windsor.

The Deanery, Lincoln, April 3, 1889.

I have read your letter to the *Times*, and I heartily recognise the fair and kindly spirit in which it is written.   It seems however strange to me that a man so clear-sighted as you are should not perceive that in the sort of challenge which you throw out to the High Church leaders to formulate their conception of a satisfactory final court, you effectually cut the ground from under their feet by requiring that the proposed court shall be such as will satisfy and pass through Parliament. It is, I fear, quite beyond all hope that Parliament will ever consent to the kind of court which could possibly content those who look upon the Church as a divine institution. Abstractedly there is no reason why in England as well as in Scotland an Established Church should not manage its own concerns.   But in England the State has got the Church in a vice, and will not release it, except by the action of disestablishment.   All the influences of the country would oppose any step towards rendering real liberty to the Church ; not least of all a very large proportion of her own laity and clergy.   The High Church party is in a most pitiful minority, and always must be so. Its teaching goes directly against the idea which the great majority of people form respecting religion. It is, in a word, *sacerdotalism*, the one thing that they hate, because it opposes itself to human pride and human sensuality. It is useless to assert—as may be asserted truly—that the Prayer Book and Catechism are on our side. *Plymouth Brethrenism* is practically the religion of the land, of all except the Roman Catholics, not of course actually professed, but the fair logical outcome of the principles which men hold. As things are, the Prayer Book and Catechism give to such as myself a fair chance of holding one's own, and personally I should be quite content to avoid all litigious matters, except perhaps what is called the Eastward position, and work on, as I have worked for many years, teaching through *them* that which I believe to be true. I wish with all my heart that others had done or would do the same. I believe that these great results would have followed. We could have done the work, so far as it is possible to do it, and kept the persecutors at bay. But the party called Ritualist would not be patient, in fact in many cases have no real love for the Church, rather like chaos and anarchy, always crave for καινότερόν τι, and have dragged *us* into the mess. It is they who have brought into discussion this question of the court, and forced the Church to face it. I remember too well the Gorham decision of 1850. It was very startling. But while it upheld in his preferment a man of unsound doctrine, it did not go so far as 'quemlibet occidere populariter'—to give wrong judgement *against* any one in order to please the people. It certainly watered down the plain teaching of the Baptismal office, but it did not punish clergy for following the direct orders of the Rubrics and the previous decisions of the Council itself. It is this burning sense of injustice which has stirred up many hearts, and I see no way out of the difficulty so long as this court continues to give such judgements.

I dread Disestablishment with all my heart, because I know pretty well what the result of it would be. It would throw all power into the hands of a laity who, although no such ignoramuses or such tyrants as the Irish laity, would nevertheless very materially narrow the liberty which is now enjoyed or maintained. The Ritualist party would at once find their position intolerable, and so would many who are not Ritualists but *are* High Churchmen ; and as a choice between two evils, the supremacy of ignorant Protestant laity and that of the Pope, many would prefer Rome. People had better realise the *fact*, viz. that Rome would be the real gainer. The Church of England, so far as one can judge, would sink to the level where it stands in the Colonies, *i.e.* a secondrate or thirdrate sect. Her ministers badly paid and hardly dealt with would no longer count as gentlemen, enthusiasm would die out, and although it might drag on a somewhat unhonoured existence, it would no longer be the Church of the people.

The best solution of the difficulty, so far as I can see, is that such a judgement may be given as shall quell these efforts of the Church Association to bully and destroy that with which they disagree. I believe that if these attacks were once for all firmly checked the present stress and tension would be relieved. I am confident that the clergy who would grievously transgress would be so few as to be outside of consideration. The vast majority would be content to be guided by the Prayer Book, their conscience, and the wish of their congregations.

The Church Association folk are not candid. They pretend zeal for the Prayer Book now, because it suits their turn. Formerly they mobbed Mr. Courtenay of Exeter to death, and drove Mr. Bennett from Knightsbridge, because they obeyed the Rubrics and the Bishops of London and Exeter who wished to maintain the Rubrics. What these men really want is to stamp out what they call *Sacerdotalism*, which has as fair a claim as their own to find a place among us. Keep these men from mischief, and all will, I believe, be well ; bating of course the differences and anomalies which cannot fail to arise where some 15,000 men are concerned.

I have written nearly as long a letter as your own. I trust that as I felt constrained to read yours, you will not call me by evil names for asking you to read my reply.

THE VERY REV. RANDALL T. DAVIDSON TO W. J. B.

Private.   4th April, 1889, DEANERY, WINDSOR CASTLE.

I am grateful to you for your most interesting and important letter. I only wish you would say publicly, either in a letter to the *Times* or otherwise, what you have said privately. I cannot see that the position you take up corresponds in the least to the position of those whom I have tried to get an answer from. You feel, as indeed I do myself, that the present final court is unsatisfactory. Our difference as to its unsatisfactoriness would be a matter of degree. But, unless I misunderstand you, you are so far prepared to make the best of a difficult position that you do not desire in the meantime to fly in the face of the existing authority, such as it is, and to flout it and jeer at it before the eyes of the public. You feel as I do, that it is possible to teach all true doctrine about the Church's rights and authority without defying unnecessarily the powers that be. My 'challenge,' since you call it so, though I did not use the word, was certainly not directed to any one who holds that position. If I seemed to include all such, I must have expressed myself awkwardly. I believe incalculable good might come from such an one as yourself speaking out about the impracticableness of the extreme men; but it would be an unpopular thing to do, and it is perhaps not fair to ask you for such an utterance, not that you would mind the unpopularity, but it might lessen your good influence with some of your friends.

I am, as you may imagine, half buried in the letters I have received upon the subject. I wish most of my correspondents expressed their meaning as clearly as you do.]

These disconnected remarks have started from the time when I came to Wantage before my Ordination, and record impressions which, though matured later, have their roots in that time. I ought to ask myself what can be contributed from my memories of my two years service at Wantage, from Advent 1869 to the beginning of 1872?

The Vicar's invitation came with most welcome kindness, when I had disappointed his hopes for me of a good class in the final schools. He knew well that I had not worked as I ought, and no one appreciated better the value of a good degree. I had dreaded his displeasure, and his generous offer of work at Wantage, without a word of blame, was one of the most comforting things I have ever experienced. So I went to Cuddesdon already accepted for Wantage, and had the good fortune while there to have some hand in persuading Herbert Woodward[1] to give up the idea of another curacy he was thinking of, and to look forward to joining the Wantage staff. For my share in this at any rate, the Vicar would not have repented of his kindness.

As to my own relations with the Vicar, I think I can sum up my experiences in the two words, strictness and confidence. It was a strict standard of life that he set before us; he expected it to be strictly observed; where he felt that it helped us, he even required a somewhat strict account. But along with this, he trusted us in a way that could not but win trust in return. We were left free to conduct our school classes, to preach our sermons, even to arrange (in my case) for Charlton Confirmation classes as we thought best. This combination of strictness and confidence had the effect of making us feel that, while we were still very young, and needing a hand over us, we had received an office which he respected, and to which he gave its due. As soon as we were ordained priests, he was careful to give us our turns in celebrating, reserving however the right to take the place of the celebrant if he was at all late. He took me himself to many of the houses in Grove

[1] Now Precentor of Worcester Cathedral.

Street which were to be in my district, and pointed out I think, one or two which I was to make a new start with, as they were more or less offended with him.

In Lent the Vicar came down and started some mission services in the Grove Street chapel. His sermon remains in my mind more distinctly than any other I ever heard him preach. (I was seldom in the parish church on Sundays.) It was very characteristic; a powerful translation into easy form of the beginning of the Ignatian exercises, on the purpose of God for each man's life. "You could not be in a better place for your salvation than you find yourself in, by God's appointment."

We met every day in the Vicar's study at one o'clock, and sometimes waited for him, as his work at the Home was growing, and kept him longer than he wished. He would rush in, talk to us while he washed his hands, arrange a number of details, lay his finger on some of our weak points, make a joke or two, tell us news (which he always seemed to find time to get at), and finally, as I have already said, pass with unfeigned reverence, but unabated energy, into the Oratory for Sext. After dinner there was another conference and Nones. In 1870 the Franco-German War was going on, and the Vicar always had the morning's facts ready to talk about at dinner. Like every great human interest the shock of the two nations moved him deeply, and he delighted later to spend what time he could give in the service of the

Hospital Corps in Germany. His days were always full, but he would find time to entertain a guest, his own, or ours; a lad from Oxford, or a priest, or any one who turned up. Now and then there were special people, whom it was a great memory to have seen, Archdeacon Freeman, Miss Yonge; above all, Bishop Forbes.[1]

Comparing the Vicar's work with that of other men in similar positions, I have been struck by the freedom of his life from those half-secular employments which so often intrude upon time due to the highest ends.[2] He never seemed oppressed by business; now and then there would be a meeting of the Governors of the Wantage Charities; I think once a year they came to dinner: an occasional morning would be given to a sanitary committee. But such things were never to the front, though evidently they were not neglected. Excellent business habits made their execution light; very much was done quietly and effectively by Mrs. Butler. It seemed always possible for the head of the parish to seek first the kingdom of God.

He was far too much in earnest to be distracted. When his going to Maritzburg as Bishop was not improbable, he thought out all that would have to be done; Sister Eliza, the successful and devoted mistress of the Middle school, was ready to go with him; he had thought of plans for raising

[1] The Right Reverend A. P. Forbes, Bishop of Brechin.

[2] He always declined to become a magistrate, saying that "preachee—preachee," and "floggee—floggee," were incompatible occupations.]

necessary funds; but all was to go on at Wantage as if he were not going to the last half-hour.

After I left Wantage, I had the privilege of often seeing the Vicar there, and afterwards at Worcester, and once, I think, at Lincoln. But I can hardly add anything of special interest as to this time. It only remains to note some miscellaneous facts or thoughts which recur.

He was a severe critic of methods which seemed to be fussy or unduly valued, apart from the spirit which should inspire them. "I shall not believe in Retreats till the clergy leave off smoking, nor in missions till all the Penitentiaries are filled," was a characteristic saying.

It seemed to me very characteristic of him that he conceived a great love for the manly simple character of General Gordon. There were certain persons in the parish at Wantage to whom he was very closely drawn, such as William Dixon, the good old farmer, who trusted him at first and supported him through opposition[1] (he was dead before I knew Wantage); Sister Eliza, certain Sisters and teachers still living, and amongst his curates, William Newbolt, Montague Noel, and Henry Houblon, his successor at Wantage. Outside the parish he had an unbounded delight in the work of James and Tom Pollock at Birmingham, in Reginald Porter's dutiful and deep work at Kenn, more than all in the successive works by which his great friend Albert Barff

[1 He opposed him however at first in the matter of the Church Restoration.]

has served the Church. For him at North Moreton the Vicar of Wantage preached a Mission, the only one he ever took,[1] and up to the last he stood in the closest relation to this dear and trusted friend.

My last interview with him, and my last letter, remain in my mind. I met him at the Wantage Road station in the Lent of 1893, and he drove me up to the Home in his fly. His ceaseless talk never flagged the whole time : amongst other things he spoke with great satisfaction of his grand-daughter's coming marriage. Miss ―― kindly asked me to come to the Mead[2] later, and the Dean was quite himself, as I had known him for about thirty years, eager, combative, generous, full of sympathy, knowledge, criticism, bent always and above all upon the only aim of his strenuous life, his untiring duty, his deep undemonstrative love―bent upon the single-hearted service of God.

In the following summer it occurred to my mind during a Retreat for the Sisters that, as the number of those who are departed increases, it would be well to commemorate them at one Eucharist during the Retreat. I wrote therefore to the Dean, and asked if he approved of our using a special office, that for Easter Eve. He wrote back very warmly, thanking me for consulting him, agreeing with the appropriate opportunity for such a commemoration, saying that he had intended to have provided for the inscription of the names of the departed on diptychs.

[1 He preached at St. Paul's during the London Mission in Feb., 1874.]
[2 The house at which he was staying.]

Thus my last communication with him referred to that interchange of good offices between the living and departed, which satisfies one of our holiest instincts. Some day, perhaps, it may be permitted me to celebrate the Holy Eucharist at the altar which is his fitting memorial (I can well remember how he devised its erection about the time when I was his curate) at Wantage.[1] If I am so privileged, I know that along with the sacred words, once so familiar in the dignified utterance of his sonorous voice, there will come to my mind the text which I have long associated with him, "I have set my face like a flint, and I know that I shall not be ashamed."

[1 Extract from "Parish Journal," June 7, 1871 : "We have said matins in the S. Aisle, partly to avoid the dust and dirt, partly to try the effect of a service said there. It will not, I think, do for matins, still less for evensong, but it is quite desirable at some future time to have the week-day Celebrations there. The only question is how far we can safely venture on erecting another altar. It is a matter requiring very serious consideration, and earnest prayers for guidance. Altars are too solemn to be stuck up here and there like tables, according to the fancy of this or that person." This South Chancel Aisle now forms the Memorial Chapel, restored and fitted up for Divine Service in memory of his life and work at Wantage.]

CHAPTER VII.

THE NATAL DIFFICULTY, AND MR. KEBLE'S DEATH.

THE year 1865 marked the beginning of a crisis in William Butler's life. For the first time since he had entered upon his work at Wantage he was within measurable distance of leaving it.

The troubles that arose in the matter of Bishop Colenso are told at length in the *Life of Bishop Gray*, of Capetown. Here it will be sufficient to say that on account of writings which the Bishop of Natal published throwing doubts on the authenticity of parts of the Pentateuch, and also, later on, impugning the Divinity of our Lord, Bishop Gray, as Metropolitan of the Ecclesiastical Province of South Africa, took steps to depose Bishop Colenso from his See, with the concurrence of the other Bishops of the Province. The next point was to find a successor, and William Butler's name was brought forward on the strength of a letter from Dr. Pusey to the Bishop of Capetown, in which he stated that "Butler of Wantage" was ready and willing to step at once into the breach. This statement was founded on a conversation with Mr. Liddon, in which he had repeated some general expressions used by the

Vicar ; but, as Mr. Liddon wrote subsequently, "not making anything approaching to a formal offer to go to Natal . . . and I repeated your words to Dr. Pusey in the way of conversation, and, if my memory does not deceive me, in order to meet some expression of sorrow which fell from him as to the lack of devotion among the English clergy."   But, as it will subsequently be shown, not only had he no intention of putting himself forward for the anxious post of Bishop of Natal, but after his nomination he never swerved from the three conditions he laid down, namely, (1) That his election should be proved to be valid ; (2) that he should be *sent* by his own Metropolitan and Diocesan, as representing the Mother Church ; and (3) that a sufficient income should be guaranteed to enable him to leave his wife and family at home for a time, and to carry on the work at Wantage till he should resign the living, as well as to meet the wants of the Diocese, which was deprived of its endowments and churches by the decision of the secular courts, which did not recognise Bishop Gray's acts as legal.

His sympathies were altogether with Bishop Gray, as his letters show.

W. J. B. TO REV. J. KEBLE.

WANTAGE VICARAGE, April 8, 1865.

. . . Touching Bishop Gray, it seems to me that the formal excommunication of Colenso, however in itself proper and desirable, might lead to very serious complications. *E.g.* How would it affect clergy who without acknowledging him as their Bishop, admitted him to Communion ?   I suppose, at least in

England, there would be a difficulty in refusing him—at all events many estimable people would feel it to be so. Unless the excommunication were taken up and endorsed by the bishops of the Church in England, it would put Bishop Gray in a position of isolation. Would it not be better to stick to the Act of Deposition—gather the bishops of the African Church—make arrangements for Natal—and call upon the English bishops to declare themselves in the matter?

Almost on the same date Bishop Gray wrote to William Butler expressing his thankfulness that he should be willing to come out as chief pastor to the afflicted flock in Natal. But at that time he did not entertain the idea, and another clergyman, the Rev. F. H. Cox, then at Hobart Town in Tasmania, was recommended by the Archbishop of Canterbury for election. He accepted the nomination, but subsequently withdrew, and on October 25th, 1866, the Vicar of Wantage was elected Bishop by the Diocese of Natal, but with seven dissentient clergy. Thus the crisis began. A trying time followed. One of the chief obstacles that lay between him and his acceptance of the See was the question whether his election was canonical. He also firmly held to his original stipulation that an income of £600 a year should be secured to the See.

Feeling doubts as to the validity of the election, he put the decision into the hands of his Diocesan, Bishop Wilberforce, and the Archbishop of Canterbury, Dr. Longley. They wrote on January 12, 1867: "We advise you to suspend your decision until these important questions concerning your election shall have been completely answered." The

Bishop of Oxford was all along in favour of his acceptance. After the decision had been made he wrote to Bishop Gray, " No doubt, so far as we can see, if our dear Archbishop had seen his way to stand firm, Butler would wonderfully have restored all things."

On receipt of the news of his election, Butler wrote to the Bishop of Capetown :

WANTAGE VICARAGE, Dec. 28, 1866.

MY DEAR LORD,—I received your letter with a mass of others from Natal upon Christmas Eve, just when all our preparations for Christmas were completed. You may easily imagine the anxious consideration which I have tried to give to a subject so all-important. My ties to England are strong and numerous. Yet I dread from my inmost soul the responsibility of withdrawing myself from what may be a call from God, however stern the sacrifice it may demand. I have therefore resolved to leave myself unreservedly in the hands of the Archbishop of Canterbury and the Bishop of Oxford, my natural ecclesiastical superiors, feeling sure that you and the Natal clergy will be satisfied with this decision, and also believing that I shall in this way most legitimately find out the Will of God for myself. If they say 'go,' I shall feel myself bound—utterly unequal as I am to accept such a post, pressing and imperative as are my home duties—to go. For the present I will add no more. The Bishop of Oxford is now at Addington with the Archbishop, and I have little doubt that by the next mail they will have settled the question. Meanwhile I am always with deep respect and sympathy, yours most faithfully.

On learning the Archbishop's and Bishop's opinion, he wrote to the Dean of Pietermaritzburg :

WANTAGE VICARAGE, January 24, 1867.

I enclose a copy of the joint opinions of the Archbishop of Canterbury and the Bishop of Oxford. This opinion has been drawn up with very great care, and the advice of several, both lay and clerical, of the best and most influential Churchmen has, I know, aided them in their conclusion. It leaves the case in a condition not, I hope, altogether unsatisfactory to you and the other brave and good men who have so long borne the brunt of the conflict. It seems to be agreed that the condition of the Church in Natal is such that you are perfectly justified in electing a Bishop. But at the same time the soundest men here are of opinion that the late election requires rectifying or revising. Among others, the Bishop of Grahamstown doubts its validity. . . . As far as I am concerned, I am simply passive. I dare not act for myself. The balance of duties seems too even. You could not have called any one with more ties to his native land, engagements of every kind—domestic, parochial, public. I have children growing up, boys just budding into manhood, daughters educating, a father-in-law and a mother, both of course aged, yet both strong and well, and keenly alive to the pain of such a separation. A flourishing body of Sisters established here and elsewhere, looking to me as their founder and guide. Then schools and parochial institutions of every kind rest on me. All this, I feel, involves me in much entanglement. Yet after much deliberation I have resolved that if the way is clear I must make a sacrifice which will cost so much pain not to myself only but to so many others; and weak and unfit as I am for such a post, I must place myself at your service.

Pray however do not consider yourself pledged to me by your late vote, but if you can find anyone who seems to you better suited for your wants, or whose name would create more unanimity of feeling among the clergy, do not hesitate to set me aside.

His most confidential correspondent during the trying time that followed his election was his friend H. P. Liddon.

W. J. B. TO REV. H. P. LIDDON.

CALDICOT HOUSE, WATFORD, Jan. 18, 1867.

I have received from the Archbishop and Bishop, together with two private letters—the enclosed[1]—which I send to you in *confidence*, for I do not as yet know what use I am permitted to make of it. It seems to me very full and helpful. I am going

[1] See *Life of Robert Gray, D.D.*, vol. ii., p. 299 (1876).

to Cuddesdon on Saturday, and I suppose that after a talk with the Bishop, I shall know more exactly what to say and what to do. I hope that you will think that I have done rightly in this very difficult case, and I should like also to think that Dr. Pusey was satisfied that I am not a 'malingerer.' I had, I think I may honestly say, quite made up my own mind on the subject. I mean that I was and am ready to do *whatever* it seems right that I should call my duty, and I had gone so far as to arrange my plans in case the opinion went in favour of my starting at once. I really know not what I could have done more, but of course there is in everything so much room for self-deceit that I almost fear that I have said too much.

I have spent nearly a fortnight in great rest under my mother's roof, and hope to return to Wantage on Monday. I went on Sunday to St. Mary Magdalene's, and heard a most wonderful sermon from Stuart. I should like to tell you of it at length, but I must repeat one passage.

"The Wise Men were wise, my brethren, because they perceived the meaning of the star. They were wise because, etc., etc., etc., and they were wise because they offered incense to Christ. The new wise men (*we* think them very foolish men) say that we must not offer incense to Christ, but we don't intend to mind them, my brethren," and so on, all said with the quaintest accent and manner. I had a chat with A. H. M. on Tuesday. He looks, I think, worn, but is, as ever, very cheery and genial. How very good is his exposition of Faith. It is worthy of some old Eastern bishop. . . . Philip Freeman [1] is very desirous to publish an annotated copy [of the *Christian Year*] with parallel passages. He would, I think, undertake the classical parallels, for which no man is better fitted. He also wishes to give the 'motif,' so to say, of each poem, which would I think be very useful. In fact, just as Dante was edited immediately after his death—so to bring out the meanings and allusions of the *Christian Year* by the efforts of various minds. . . .

After many months of uncertainty at length the decision came. It was founded on what may be

[1] Ven. Philip Freeman, Archdeacon of Exeter, author of *Principles of Divine Service.*

called a bye-issue, and it came at a time when William Butler's consecration as Bishop seemed to be only postponed till the last legal difficulties were overcome. But in the course of 1867 a Declaration was put forth on the subject of the Holy Eucharist by some of the leaders of the High Church clergy, and William Butler's name, as the list was alphabetical, headed it. The Archbishop took alarm at this, and thought that a man of less pronounced opinions would find more favour with the clergy of Natal. This practically decided the question. His own words, in a letter written to *The Guardian*, under date 21 November, 1867, are sufficient :

Will you have the kindness to publish the accompanying extract from a letter received by me from the Archbishop of Canterbury.

When, at the end of last year, the news of my election to the See of Pietermaritzburg first reached me, the circumstances of the case appeared to me so novel and so important that I felt myself bound in common prudence to look to those for counsel who from their position of authority, were most able both to give it, and also to assist in meeting the difficulties which could not fail to surround an effort made in the face of keen and intelligent opposition, to win for the Church in the Colonies her true and rightful privilege of unfettered religious action. I therefore placed myself unreservedly at the disposal of His Grace the Archbishop of Canterbury. He has come to the conclusion, after—it cannot be doubted—much careful consideration, that some other than I will best satisfy the requirements of the Diocese, and it would be both ungrateful and unbecoming in me to dispute his decision. It will be seen therefore that whatever regret or pain this somewhat unexpected result has caused, I have no course left but to decline the honourable, if anxious post of Bishop over the orthodox members of the Church of Natal.

                                          WILLIAM BUTLER.

ADDINGTON PARK, Oct. 29th, 1867.

I have come to the conclusion that I ought to dissuade you from availing yourself of your election to the See of Pieter-maritzburg. To my mind the appointment of any one of very marked opinions to the See would be open to serious objections, and it would be better to select some one more calculated to meet the various shades of religious opinion that exist among faithful members of the Church of England in the Colony of Natal.

He wrote privately to the Archbishop of Canter-bury :

WANTAGE VICARAGE, Oct. 30, 1867.

MY LORD ARCHBISHOP,—You have been good enough to permit me to seek your counsel in this anxious matter, and I am bound to follow it.

Pardon me, however, for saying that I receive it with mixed feelings. I had so long endeavoured to look at the difficult work in Natal and the painful separation from home ties and duties as almost certain to be my future lot, that I can scarcely now bear to give it up. I have however no doubt that others can be found far more worthy than I am, to help on the great work of freeing the Church of England from her present embarrassments in the Colonies, and that your Grace's decision is an indication to me that such is the Will of God. I have only to ask your permission to publish the letter which I received this morning, and to remain

Your humble and dutiful servant.

That the final decision came as something of a blow is evident from Mr. Liddon's reply to a letter which has not come to light.

THE REV. H. P. LIDDON TO W. J. B.

CHRISTCHURCH, Thursday, Nov. 7, 1867.

I was truly sorry to miss you so yesterday. The fact is I had quite given you up, thinking that you had come to view the matter as settled, however painfully in some respects, and so had taken leave of it. I do not think that you need deem all the anxieties and discomforts of the last two years as lost. On the contrary, your 'zeal,' as the Archbishop quaintly calls it, has really given a bodily shape and active impetus to what else might never have passed beyond the region of aspirations. The Archbishop now is pledged to do something towards providing an 'orthodox' bishop for Natal, and that he is so pledged is practically your doing. I am not sorry, for higher motives than the strong selfish reason which enters into my view of the matter, that you are kept by God's providence in England. You never could be replaced at Wantage, and your departure would have snapped or loosened more sympathies and supports in many directions than, of course, it would occur to you to think of.

It may be just as well that the struggle with Colenso should not be complicated by a Sacramental controversy, such as a much less shrewd opponent than he is, would be sure to raise on your arrival. . . .

It was characteristic of William Butler that he did not permit himself, during this long period of suspense and anxiety, to relax his efforts for the welfare of his parishioners. The "Parish Journal" contains the usual close inspection and criticism of services, schools, and the rest of the parochial machinery, the constant anxiety for the spiritual condition of his people, the same expressions of humble sense of failure. In the summer of 1867 when the decision seemed to be suspended, like the sword of Damocles, by a single hair, he went abroad for his holiday, and, as has been seen in the previous chapter, made a study of certain aspects of French religious life. His correspondence reveals some of the workings of his mind on the Church difficulties of the day.

W. J. B. TO REV. H. P. LIDDON.

WANTAGE VICARAGE, Feb. 8, 1868.

Thank you for your kind letter. I should have been delighted to have caught you for a few minutes. As your scout comfortingly told me, you had scarcely left your rooms when I called, from which, as I told him, I concluded that it would be some time before you returned.

The course of events moves on so rapidly—alas, almost always in one direction, that of ἀτοπία and anxiety,—that it is a great comfort to compare reckonings, and to feel that those who are like-minded are within hail. Have you seen the admirable answers of the Bishop of Capetown to Archbishop Thomson and Bishop Tait?[1] For dignity, argument, and gentle but unmistakeable suggestion of consequences, they are, I think unrivalled. In a letter which I have received from him to-day he tells me that the Bishop of London writes to him plainly that he *is* in communion with Colenso! It is right—nay, our bounden duty to act very cautiously, with all charity and all hope. But there is a limit beyond which I, for one, dare not pass, and if this coming session of Convocation do not in some way firmly and distinctly deal with this question, I conceive that action of some kind on *our* part will become a vital necessity. The time is rapidly nearing, when the Bishops *must* be made to see the real state of things, and fairly to face the consequences, *i.e.* the possibility of a large body of the most devoted of the English clergy being forced to accept *at least* inaction, from the absolute impossibility of co-operating with those who trample or allow others to trample on the 'vivendi causae.'

A very cheerful letter came from Miss Milman to Mrs. Butler a day or two ago. He seems to be making good progress; but India, she says, is as England was twenty years ago.[2]

How severe an ordeal William Butler passed through during the many months of suspense would

[1] See *Life of Robert Gray*, vol. ii., p. 38, *et seq.*

[2] The Right Rev. Robert Milman, consecrated Bishop of Calcutta, Feb. 2, 1867.

be known to but few. The outside world, ignorant
of his sensitiveness and the tender fibres of his
nature, would imagine that the prospect of a battle
would be acceptable to one who appeared to many
combative rather than sensitive. But a letter written
by Mrs. Butler in October, 1867, when it seemed
almost certain that the decision would be in favour
of his going, tells a very different tale. After describing her own feelings, and saying that in her
case the worst was now over, she says:

> But all this comes new to W., and he is, alas! drinking the
> cup to the dregs—not shrinking from it, or giving way, but
> feeling its bitterness. This week of his communicant classes is
> very trying—the grief and lamentations of young and old are
> hard to bear, and, as he says, all this brings before him in
> strong contrast the exchange of hatred and reviling for love
> and respect. Depend upon it, no warm weather or variety of
> scene can ever make up to him for the loss of all he *really*
> cares for.

The hearts of the people of Wantage had been
deeply stirred by the fear of losing their Vicar, and
the churchwardens had written privately to the
Archbishop, begging him not to let him go. The
feelings of the parishioners took shape when the
final decision had been made, in an address, dated
Wantage, Nov. 20th, 1867:

> REV. SIR,—We, the undersigned parishioners of the parish
> of Wantage, having heard the plain and lucid statement made
> by you from the pulpit in reference to your nomination to the
> Bishopric of Natal, and all the subsequent proceedings, ending
> in the opinion of the Archbishop of Canterbury that some other
> person should be appointed to the vacant See, desire to express
> our gratification that you are still to be our spiritual pastor,

and our sympathy at the trials which have been brought about by the late proceedings.

We duly appreciate the many works which have been done by you in this parish during the last twenty years, and we sincerely hope that your life may be long spared to continue the good works which have emanated from your zeal and energy, and we also beg to express our feelings of love and regard for yourself personally, being satisfied that under your guidance we shall be kept from the strife and contention which have disturbed so many parishes.

This address was signed by representatives of all classes in the parish, some of whom had been his chief opponents in former years. A still more substantial proof of the people's gratification was a testimonial consisting of nearly £100, which he accepted, and expended in filling the west window of the church with stained glass.

In the course of these years of grave anxiety his most trusted adviser, Mr. Keble, was taken to his rest. To the last letters exchanged between them is added one written many years later to the Rev. Walter Lock,[1] author of a *Life of John Keble.*

W. J. B. TO REV. J. KEBLE.

WANTAGE VICARAGE, Jan. 28, 1866.

. . . I need not say to you how much we think of dear Mrs. Keble and of you. If by taking duty at Hursley, or in any other way, I can be of the least service to you, I know nothing which will give me more pleasure. I pray heartily that the God of all comfort may give you in this hour of sorrow a double portion of that comfort which He has given to so many through you. My wife joins me in deepest sympathy, and so do the 'Sisters.'

[1] Now Warden of Keble College, Oxford.

Rev. J. Keble to W. J. B.

BOURNEMOUTH, Feb. 13, 1866.

My wife has just reminded me about sending this which I inclose, with all best wishes and thanks for your good prayers and all your kindness: nor least for your friendly thought of helping me in case of need in my parish. It would be a keen necessity which would force me to have recourse to persons so much overtasked already, and I trust it will not occur; but we thank you all the same.

The messenger has not yet come, but fresh symptoms have occurred which seem meant to warn us of his approach. I wish we were all as prepared to part as (humanly speaking) she by God's mercy is to go.

The enclosed is especially, of course, for the Home.

W. J. B. to Rev. J. Keble.

WANTAGE VICARAGE, Feb. 14, 1866.

We do indeed feel very deeply the kindness of Mrs. Keble and yourself in remembering the Home and its needs at this special time. It seems almost to ensure to our work an interest in the prayers and good offices of the Blessed. Much indeed do we need them.

Thank you also very much for your account of dear Mrs. Keble. How like a sweet autumn seems her gradual fading; if indeed that be the right word! Pray do not hesitate to accept my offer, if you need help. I have at present a supernumerary curate, *i.e.* one more than my actually needful number. I saw Liddon a few days since at Oxford. It is a great piece of good fortune that he should have got the Bampton Lectures. I lent his sermons to my neighbour, Lord Overstone, a complete Whig of the old school. He was so charmed with them, that he bought them at once, and talked of taking lodgings at Oxford to hear his Bampton Lectures. I thought that you would be interested in hearing this.[1]

---

[1] The "Parish Journal" for 1866 contains these entries: "Thursday in Holy Week, March 29. Our dear friend Mr. Keble departed to his rest. April 6. Mr. Keble buried at Hursley. It was a touching and yet blessed sight to see the gathering of good and earnest people round the grave of that holy and revered friend. The day was sunny and bright, and all spoke of peace."

Rev. H. P. Liddon to W. J. B.

60 Upper Seymour St., W., Good Friday, 1866.

You will be very deeply distressed at hearing that dear Mr. Keble died at Bournemouth yesterday at one o'clock. His brother Mr. Thomas Keble was with him, and read the Commendatory prayer at 8 A.M., and again at one, as he passed away. It is only within the last four or five days that we have been alarmed about him: as probably you have heard at the beginning of last week Mrs. Keble was thought to be dying; but on Wednesday she rallied in her wonderful way. But the strain had been too much for him.

The blank which his death has made—in earth—is something terrible. But how high must be his place in heaven! I *try* to think of this. That he should thus lie down to die beneath the very Cross itself, is quite in keeping with the whole of his most beautiful and saintly life.

W. J. B. to Rev. W. Lock.

The Deanery, Lincoln, Whitsunday, 1893.

Dear Sir,—Though I have not had the pleasure of making personal acquaintance with you, yet I venture to trouble you with a few words respecting my dear friend Mr. Keble, whose life you have lately written with so great discrimination and sympathy. I believe that there are very few now alive of those who like myself were privileged to be admitted to intimate friendship with him, and therefore I desire, before I too am called away, to offer you a few reminiscences of one so altogether noble and uncommon. To do this will be a sort of relief to myself, and pray deal with what I am endeavouring to jot down exactly as seems best to yourself.

I had the great good fortune of passing the first two years of my ministerial life at Dogmersfield, where the Reverend Charles Dyson was rector. It is a very small parish, but for some time past he had been invalided by pulmonary weakness, which rendered a curate's help absolutely necessary. He was a very remarkable man—one of the famous old C. C. C. set—and in some ways looked up to more than any other both for his vast knowledge, high character, and slight seniority. Mr.

Keble was his bosom friend, and on one occasion when a
difficult question was asked, referred the questioner to "a
certain wise old man who lives at Dogmersfield." Mr. Keble
visited Dogmersfield Rectory not unfrequently, and in this
way I first became acquainted with him. He was particularly
kind to all young people, and again and again invited me to
Hursley, whither one went almost trembling with gratitude
at his intense kindness, and at the same time with a certain
sense of awe. The way of living at Hursley Vicarage was in
some ways of the same style as Dogmersfield Rectory, and
[it was] inhabited much in the same way. Mrs. Dyson and
Mrs. Keble were both childless; and in each case a most
charming sister of the husband made part of the family.
Nothing could be more simple—even homely. And yet one
felt that there was a very atmosphere of high intellect and
refined taste. There was an old-fashioned garden, fertile and
full; a fine growth of trees, mostly elms; small but cheerful
rooms; not very many books—classics and Fathers of old
editions, as Savile's *St. Chrysostom.* Mr. Keble had at that
time a very comfortable pony carriage, and a couple of rough
grey ponies.

After that first visit I felt myself at home at Hursley, and had
the pleasure of introducing Philip Freeman, the author of
Principles of Divine Service—afterwards Archdeacon of Exeter—
and of spending a day in my marriage holiday under the
Vicarage roof. Mr. Keble was one of the kindest of men,
liberal in all money matters, free of his time and knowledge, and
most encouraging to young men such as at that time I was. He
was even good enough to look through and help me greatly in
preparing for the press a volume of *Sermons for Working Men,*
which I published in 1847. With all this however he was
a man who knew well how to hold his own. In the kindest, yet
most unmistakeable manner, he could 'put down' anything that
seemed foolish or undesirable. I remember once, at a time
when Dr. Pusey's relations with Miss Sellon were much criti-
cised, . . . I ventured to say something of the kind. He
turned sharply upon me with, "You must not say that. Remember, I am a regular Puseyite." At another time, when
staying with me at Wantage, a number of us were discussing the
evils of pluralism; suddenly he looked up and exclaimed, "My

father was a pluralist, and—(with a pause) I am not ashamed of him." When I had to preach the sermon at the Anniversary Church Festival, just as the bell had stopped and we were passing his study, I asked to look at a passage in *St. Chrysostom*, which I was about to quote. He asked me whether I would have the Greek or the English translation. Having only an instant in which to glance at the passage, and knowing the difficulty of recognising the contractions without a little practice, I asked for the English, and received from him a sort of ' Et tu, Brute ' look. He was very fond of the little formula, " Don't you think ? " " Don't you think," he said to me on one occasion, " that the time is coming when we shall have to preach a great deal about the Fifth Commandment ? "

He could sometimes be even angry. On one of the famous meetings of the National Society, in 1848, when Archdeacon Manning, as he then was, had carried a somewhat trimming resolution, he was much vexed, and said, " It is not the first time that Manning has let us down." He had no confidence in him, nor in any one who acted diplomatically. He felt keenly Newman's article on the " Lyra Innocentium," in the *Dublin Review*. I was with him shortly after its publication, and he was greatly offended at certain expressions and statements contained in it. At the same time he was most considerate of anything like real feeling. Long after he had laid by the money to build the present Hursley church he waited to begin the work for the sake of one old man who had a pew in which he had worshipped for years, and to which he was much attached.

A day at Hursley was not to be forgotten. Prayers were at eight, always said by heart by Mr. Keble, covering his eyes with his hand ; then followed a meditation, one of the R.C. Bishop Challoner's, very short and simple ; then the plainest breakfast. Mattins at ten, I think ; dinner, again most plain, at one. A walk in the afternoon ; tea at six, after which he would sit in the window, putting together his sermon, or any literary work— generally on scraps of paper, backs of letters, and the like— and entering whenever there was need into the conversation of the party.

He was most particular in observing the fasts and festivals of the Church. On a fast-day he never took butter at breakfast.

And I remember how, during the 'Expectation Week' he would never leave home, but continued as it were waiting with the apostles for the 'Unspeakable Gift.' It happened that some business once called me to Hursley at that time. He asked me to preach, but I of course declined, hoping to have the opportunity of listening to him. There were perhaps a dozen people in the church. He turned to them from the reading-desk and addressed them, as was his custom at that time, quite without note. He spoke of the Apostles waiting. "Perhaps," he said, "you would not think ten days a long time. But just think for a moment. They were waiting for the great promise, the greatest Gift that even God could bestow on man. They were eager to do their Master's bidding, but till the Gift came they could not do it. They desired to preach the Gospel, but till the Gift they must remain inactive. They prayed all day and still it came not. They prayed all night and still it came not. O depend upon it, ten days was a very long time for them to wait." That was all, most simple, and yet as he said it, most impressive.

There are few things that I rejoice in more than that it was given to me to introduce H. P. Liddon to Mr. Keble. Mr. Keble had more to do with forming Liddon's mind than most people are aware. The simplicity and directness combined with the scholarship and great ability of Mr. Keble had a great effect on Liddon, steadying him, and *Anglicising* him, and helping him to guide others. Also we owe to Mr. Keble the absolute firmness of Miss Yonge. I mean her strong grasp of Church principles, in spite of many forces which might have drawn her into the 'femme forte' direction.

I could with a little effort recall much more, but I dare not inflict more upon you. As I said in the beginning of this letter, pray destroy or do anything that you like with what I have written.

CHAPTER VIII.

THE FRANCO-PRUSSIAN WAR.

THE anxious question of Natal once settled, he resumed the thread of his parochial life, which, indeed, had never been dropped. His letters to Mr. Liddon give glimpses of his work and interests:

W. J. B. TO REV. H. P. LIDDON.

WANTAGE VICARAGE, Dec. 10, 1869.

It is so long since anything has passed between us that I feel quite shy in beginning a letter—the more so as I have really nothing special to say, and write only because I want to hear of and from you.

Have you been in Oxford all the term? I suppose that you find, as I find, that local and immediate claims on one's time grow more and more absorbing, just as, if one's microscope were stronger, one might write treatises on a rose leaf or a fly's wing. It is quite inexpressible how very much more I become tied to Wantage, and simply, as I imagine, unable to leave it without injuring the work of the place. Rightly or wrongly, I keep on enunciating that work is best done for the Church by doing that which is directly given, and I shrink greatly from external calls. Our annual confirmation took place last week. The Bishop of O. kept on coquetting with it, saying that he would come, etc., then hoped that I would make the ground certain by making sure of another Bishop in case he was prevented; finally did *not* come. Fortunately I had caught Addington

Nassaviensis,[1] and he most kindly confirmed, and received or professed a Sister (I cannot get the verb right) the next day. It amuses me in the midst of the world-shaking changes which go on on all sides—politically, socially, ecclesiastically, and, above all, ritually—to find how little we move here. You might almost return as curate, and find just what you remember sixteen or seventeen years ago. I do not mean that various things have not been done, but the general $\mathring{\eta}\theta o\varsigma$ is so similar. Of course sooner or later the tide must turn here as elsewhere. I trust not in my time.

Those two meetings at Oxford and Cambridge simply fill me with amazement. That a body of men, mostly clergy, and all members of the Church of England, should almost passionately resolve on praying the legislature to do that which must, *ex hypothesi*, divorce their own religion from the education of the place, is the strangest and most inconceivable phenomenon that, I venture to say, any age in the whole history of the world can show. And the grotesque —— actually applauds and rejoices. I wish that people would realise the existence of that extremely sectarian sect—the non-believers, or rather the believers in not believing—and see how they are playing into their hands. This is the religion which they are foisting on future England.

We are all as usual—getting older, etc., gradually but surely.

.   .   .

W. J. B. TO REV. H. P. LIDDON.

WANTAGE VICARAGE, Dec. 12, 1869.

Your letters always open a whole mine of thought, and I cannot rest without giving vent to some of the things that occur to me. The first is a very earnest wish that you could come here, were it only for a night. I long to talk over some of these most serious matters with you. You see I live so very narrow a life, among my flock and with the dear good Sisters, that I have really no chance of knowing what the true workings of things are. I am tied by the leg, and Oxford near as it is—and still more London with its stir and interests— are almost 'terra incognita' to me. I shrink from societies and gatherings and the like, partly from sheer occupation, and

[1] The Right Rev. Addington R. P. Venables, Bishop of Nassau, Bahamas, 1863 to 1876.

partly because so little seems to me to come from them. So in regard to this Temple [1] business. I simply know the fact that he is designated a Bishop, of course by the Prime Minister, but the arguments for such a step I know not. I take it for granted that Gladstone has condescended to explain himself to someone, and I cherish a kind of hope that a man of his goodness and intelligence in Church questions must have some kind of plausible ἀπολογία to put forth. You probably know all that can be said on both sides. I have not taken any vigorous part in the matter, because I conceive that the evil lies far more deep than the mere appointment of a man of T.'s views. It lies, as it seems to me, in the co-existence in one community of three sets of minds, or schools, vitally differing each from the other, cohering simply by the fact that they are in a State Establishment. *If* they are there, each, I suppose, has a sort of claim on the donors of patronage, and it is only a question of time when its claims shall be allowed. If a man of T.'s opinions held office . . . of course he would be appointed to-morrow, made Archbishop of Canterbury if a vacancy occurs. Accidentally there happens to be a Prime Minister of (supposed) High Church opinions, and we are therefore astonished and scandalised by his selection of Temple. But if he had appointed (say) Bright, the principle of evil would have been there just the same, only waiting its opportunity to start into life. All our misfortunes date from and have their origin in that hideous Gorham decision. When one has lived through that, nothing seems unendurable. Until that has been dealt [with], we have nothing for it but to look for wave after wave of trouble. And what pains me most is to see how the moving spirits among us ignore and set aside this. Men like our dear friend A. H. M. and those whom the *Church Times* represents, go on perfectly at ease, until they are told to wear fewer flounces of lace, or the like, and then they shriek and scold as if life depended on it. I never could persuade A. H. M. to take up the Court of Final Appeal with a will. Now the E. C. U. is most anxious to do so. But why? Because it has given judgements adverse to Ritual, not because it is inherently evil.

[1] The Right Rev. F. Temple, then Bishop Designate of Exeter, now Archbishop of Canterbury.

Touching the Oxford meeting, is it quite impossible to organise a counter meeting? You *cannot be worse off than you are*. And even a moderate gathering would be better than none at all. Dr. Pusey, Bright, various Heads of houses, Stubbs, Medd, Wall, yourself, and others whom you know better than I, would surely constitute a meeting whose counterblast would not fall impotent. It is, I think, a rule that 'if a thing *cannot* do harm and may do it [? good], it is best to do it.' The worst that can follow is that people may consider such a meeting inferior in influence to the first. And if they do, it is possible that this may encourage the enemy to proceed. But the enemy is at your doors now; and certainly silence will not keep him away. I have great faith in those who fight losing games! It sometimes happens that a chance occurs when people least expect it. However you of course know all about this far better than I. Do try to pay us a visit.

W. J. B. TO REV. H. P. LIDDON.

WANTAGE VICARAGE, Dec. 15, 1869.

Thank you very much for your letter of yesterday. I am tempted to send you the enclosed which I have just received, as an interesting and somewhat typical statement of views. It is written by a really good fellow, in Holy Orders, a Fellow of Trin. Coll. Cam., with whom I had ventured to expostulate when I saw his name at that meeting at St. John's. Curiously enough, from different premises he and you seem to arrive at the same conclusion, viz. the desirableness of breaking up the collegiate system. . . . I try and try to put myself into these men's attitude of thought and I cannot. I cannot understand what are the motives that are at work within them. I quite understand your republican unbeliever who runs atilt at everything human and divine, except his own wild vagaries. But what thoroughly puzzles me is why men who profess to believe in something, who call themselves Churchmen, who accept our Lord's Divinity and Atonement, should lend themselves to forward the work of destruction and help to break down all those barriers by which faith has been kept alive in our own land. It is easy, of course, to say that the faith can take care of itself. But that argument, fairly worked out, would do away with the very existence of the Church. What is that but the divinely appointed Body to preserve the deposit intact?

May I say one thing, my dear friend? Do you not think that it would be well for you not so very much to inhabit the House of Mourning? You have had so very much of sorrow during the last few years that it cannot have failed to give all things a somewhat mournful aspect to you—and is this quite wholesome? Pray forgive me for saying this. . . .

W. J. B. TO REV. CANON LIDDON.

WANTAGE VICARAGE, Feb. 20, 1870.

I have been most busy for the last twelve days, preaching and talking till I was more than weary to our dear Sisters at Bedminster, Plymouth, and Lostwithiel, and to the various congregations and workers and friends connected with each of the little communities. Most interesting and most successful they are, winning souls and drawing love to themselves, and proving more and more clearly that in them we have the true 'missing link' which can bring all classes into one, and train souls to accept the 'sincere milk of the word.' You will think me very enthusiastic, but you must forgive me. My heart is greatly moved at seeing what organisation, self-sacrifice, can do, even with such minute branches as we have been able to plant out. It is fortunate for you that I am not likely to see you for some time, else you would have, I fear, a tremendous outpouring. Well, all this prelude is to explain why I have not written to you before, not to congratulate you, for I really cannot congratulate any one on receiving ecclesiastical preferment (even without cure of souls, the responsibility of a high place is, 'à mon avis,' very great), but to say how deeply I am interested in all that concerns you, and therefore not the least in this,[1] which seems to open out a new sort of life to you. Very earnestly I pray that in this, as in so much else, you may have the door opened to you to spend and be spent for Him Whom only in this world and for ever it is worth while for a reasonable being to love and to serve.

I feel unhappy at the thought of your being separated from Oxford, and I cannot think how the great cause will bear your

[1] The Rev. H. P. Liddon was appointed Canon of St. Paul's in 1870.

removal. Is it not possible that you may still retain your connexion with it ?

In the summer of 1870 he was taking his holiday in North Germany, and at Cologne came for the first time in contact with visible tokens of the Franco-Prussian War. The sight of the sick and wounded, and the accounts of the great battles, so moved him to be up and doing, and to take part in the work of the Red Cross Association, that he went to the English Chaplain at Berlin and asked if he could render any help. He was referred to the Ambassador, Lord Augustus Loftus, who replied that he had no applications. Finding he could do nothing, he dismissed the subject from his mind and continued his tour. In crossing the water on his way home, he met with a lady who had been acting as chief of the nurses at Sedan, and she said, " We want you to come out ; you will be useful among us in many ways." After due consultation, he went to Colonel Loyd Lindsay and offered his services, which were gladly accepted. He received a commission under the Red Cross Society, and went out in September to Arlon, the place selected for the English depôt. In a lecture which he afterwards gave in the Wantage Church Reading Room, he detailed his experiences. He said the collection of stores afforded evidence of the benevolence of the English people, but at the same time showed their utter ignorance of things needed. He was requested by Captain Brackenbury to proceed to Sedan to ascertain the numbers of the wounded there and in the neighbouring villages, and the requirements of the various hospitals. He found great difficulty in getting admitted into Sedan, where he became acquainted with the horrors of war in the most terrible form. There were about 2000 wounded in Sedan, and an average of 150 in each of the 20 villages he visited. Subsequently he went to Saarbrücken. It was always a great sorrow to him that he was prevented continuing this work, which, as he said, really seemed to lift one above the earth, but the dangerous illness of one of his curates from typhoid fever recalled him to Wantage.

Most of the letters written at this time have been preserved, and give a vivid picture of what he saw.

W. J. B. TO HIS WIFE.

COLOGNE, Aug. 24, 1870.

. . . I have had a great deal of talk with Harperath,[1] and the more I hear, the more wicked and wanton the whole thing appears, and the more I feel that the Prussians are justified in all that they have done—so far. They may be stiff, perky, unpleasant neighbours and the like, but there was no act of theirs to justify L. N. in declaring war at this tremendous cost. And they are quite right in resolving that, for this generation at least, the French shall know what war really means. While I write, I wait for the arrival of the daily steamer, filled with wounded, to be distributed here and at Düsseldorf. The Deutz Hotel opposite has the Cross flying to show that it is taking them in, and there is an ambulance of some kind on the quay of the steamers. The quay is covered with people, and will be more so—with lint, chairs, fruit, wine, etc. The whole of Cologne is filled with 'landwehr' steady, stalwart, soldierlike,

[1] The landlord of his hotel at Cologne, and a friend of many years' standing.

men between thirty and forty, who are going off to supply the places of the first line, the regulars. These 'landwehr' have all passed through their military course; many have fought at Sadowa, etc., as their medals and crosses show, and they leave at home in farms, etc., wives and children. Many of them are gentlemen, or at least of the better classes, as is easy to perceive: and here they are going off to-morrow to become food for powder, because the French choose to go to war. Harperath's whole body of servants, including a 'boots' who has been with him twelve or fourteen years, and who cried, he said, like a child to leave him, must be off to the war. He told me that for a day or two literally he and Madame were left alone. Fortunately there were no 'Reisende.' Can we wonder that the Prussians are stern in their justice, and that the shops are full of indignant chaff or rather, bitter satire sometimes not very refined, on L. N., Eugénie, and little 'Loulou.' All his dicta are travestied, *e.g.* 'l'Empire c'est la paix' and the 'Baptism of fire.' They never forget to give full dimensions to the 'corporation' of this 'Empereur,' and all the 'diablerie' in which the Germans delight, comes out in one form or another. 'A dream and the reality,' represents L. B., etc., greeted by Victory, about to enter Berlin. Underneath the whole French army is passing under the yoke. Then 'Vaterland's Lieder,' 'Die Wacht am Rhein,' etc., are everywhere. Harperath tells me that all business is stopped, and well it may be. Two days after war was declared Cologne was full, every one rushing home. One night the Swiss train from Basle threw 800 upon the town. People rushed up and down frantically to find beds. His house was filled with all sort of swells. A few days after *all* was gone, and the soldiers swarming into the trains. The 33rd went out 3000 strong, and returned in a fortnight with 300 survivors. They were all, he said, clean, well set up young men. All Cologne is in mourning. His wife has two cousins in the war and another is off to-morrow. . . .

Well, my next will be from Berlin. I shall know then something of my future. I could easily give a fortnight if it would be of any avail. If not, I suppose that I shall return upon my steps and find my way home. May the Calais route be open.

W. J. B. TO HIS WIFE.

STADT ROM, BERLIN, Aug. 29, 1870.

So much has happened since I wrote from Cologne that I hardly know how to begin or where to end. I will begin at the end. I told you that I had made up my mind to offer myself, if any use could be made of me, for the care of the wounded, or rather for the care of those in charge of them. I went therefore to the eleven A.M. matins at the Monbijou Palace, and spoke to the chaplain, a Mr. Belson, who has been thirty-three years here, and talks with so strong a German accent that I took him for one. He seemed to think the thing practicable. The Ambassador, Lord Augustus Loftus, was however at Potsdam, three-quarters of an hour's rail from Berlin, and as the matter was pressing he advised me to go to Potsdam and there catch him. He wrote a note of introduction. Accordingly I started at three, duly arrived at Potsdam, and of *course* found H. E. out for the day. However, I asked his dining hour—seven, said the somewhat surly Prussian, who kept the door—and meanwhile I addressed myself to dinner, of which I got an ample allowance—excellent crayfish soup, beef steak, butter, cheese, and unexceptionable beer for 18½ groschen! Then I wandered into Sans Souci, and saw the water-works—poor and stupid—and the old 'Schloss,' and the new 'Schloss,' and the purlieus of 'der alte Fritz,' and thought of the queer lots who had promenaded there; and then I went back to 22 Weinmeister Strasse, a very long walk, where is the Gesandschaft's summer residence. I believe that he *was* at dinner, though I called at 6.30, and that seven was some dodge of the porter's. However, he did see me, and told me, as I thought very probable, that there was really nothing that he knew of in which I could be utilised, and so there is an end of that. I made an offering for the wounded through the chaplain; and at all events I feel that I have done my best. You may think it Quixotic, but if you saw the carriages full of prisoners and wounded, and read and heard the accounts fresh from the battlefield, you would not, I think, be surprised that one should long to help, even if it were but scraping 'charpie.' . . . There are but few, comparatively, of the wounded here, but heaps of prisoners at Spandau, the fortress

not far off. . . . But there are no rows. Everything is
perfectly calm and quiet. · The news shops only and the print
shops are besieged. I quite marvel at the simple unelated
demeanour of the people. It is not that they are not interested,
but their self-respect restrains them. If you talk to any one you
very soon find out what lies underneath. Meanwhile the war
slays its tens of thousands, and you see people in mourning,
just enough to show that the blow cuts deep. . . .

W. J. B. to his Wife.

Köln, Sept. 4, 1870.

. . . Here I am at last, having arrived last night; as usual.
I need not tell you how the chorus from Paderborn here is
'Napoleon *ist* gefangen.' I heard it first at eight A.M., and the
whole line of railway (at least at all the stations) is decorated
with green boughs and flags, and resounds with the shouts of
boys and men in and out of the train. This seems like the
beginning of the end. It is quite clear that the French have
nothing to oppose the solid steam-engine-like movement of
the German troops. As I felt sure after the first battle, the
French are out-numbered, out-manœuvred, and out-*manned*.
The Germans are better all through. The more I see of
these Germans, the more rejoiced I am at their success. They
deserve it. They have made sacrifices of the most tremendous
kind, and they are merely obtaining that for which they have
been willing to pay the most costly price, *i.e.* security from
a very vexatious and capricious neighbour. It is absolutely
absurd to suppose that the Germans could court war. Think
what war is to them. It is not as with us, a mere risking of
the off-scouring of the nation, nor as with the French, a matter
of conscription from which the wealthier and better can escape,
but it is an affair which touches the *whole* nation. As I read
in the *Norddeutsche Zeitung* or some such name, a sort of
Government paper, yesterday, in a battle there stand side by
side the master of a manufactory and his men, professors
from the university, married men, clerks from offices, and
nothing but necessity to protect life and land, no love of
glory, no desire to add fresh territory, or the like would
induce them to go out. They are not 'enfants perdus' or

gladiators or adventurers, but solid steady men, for the loss
of whom nothing can compensate. It was a cruel and wanton
act of him who forced them into this bloody war, and now
that he is, as they say, "caught in a mouse-trap," you may
rely on it, there will not be "my brother Benhadad," but
something just and stern will be his portion. As the papers
rightly say, "The French might have been at peace with us
for centuries, we wanted no war; but we are determined to
give them a lesson now which they will recollect for at least
another century." I fully believe from all I hear and read
that they will annex Strassburg, and probably Alsace. I am
sorry for this, but I am not surprised. If you could see, as
I have seen, the wounded borne through the streets on 'Bähre'
on men's shoulders, and the lists of dead which the newspapers
give day after day, you would feel that the Germans were
right in 'scotching' this serpent of France, which has for
so many years raised its head and threatened to swallow them.
Nothing is more foolish than for the 'junker conservatif' party
in England to hanker after the French, except for the Radical
party to imagine that the German cause is the cause of liberty.
The Prussian régime is at least as despotic as the French. It
is true that one is governed by a king, the other by an emperor;
but the principle of government is exactly the same in each.
In fact, the name of emperor applies rightly only to the
Emperor of Rome. It is the equivalent secular to the Pope,
and as there can be but one Pope, so only one emperor. King,
grand duke, elector, are all in truth absolute. But the English
ignoramus does not take this in, and shudders at the word
emperor. Cologne was thoroughly alive last night. Cannons
were firing from the Caserne across the river, and the whole
city was hung with flags, and brilliantly, if not ingeniously,
illuminated. You may imagine how picturesque was the Hohe
Strasse in its narrowness and the height of the houses. I
wandered about for an hour or more. All the people were
orderly; there was no evil, as far as I could see, of any kind,
either of drunkenness or otherwise. Joy was on every face.
A regiment of boys with coloured lamps on poles, marched
in quick time singing some patriotic song, and the Caserne
on the other side of the river was very lively. Old Harperath
mounted a fine twenty years' old Prussian eagle, and tallow was

plentifully displayed in the windows facing the streets. With
him I have had much talk. The dinner to-day was at first
literally a table d'hôte, for he and I were the only diners.
Afterwards madame came, and I think five more guests. But
he is very cheerful. He invested 5000 thalers in the Prussian
loan, and besides good interest, his purchase is now worth
£150 *premium*. This makes up for other misfortunes in the
fewness of *Reisende*. I am occupying the room which you and
E. had last year, with the oleanders and view of the Rhine.
. . . Whom should I meet in the Dom this morning but
the Master of Trinity and Mrs. Thompson. He was disposed
to be very chatty, thought that the German papers have been
too bragging and exacting. He forgets to make the allowances
for a people who have suffered for years under the provocation
of France, and who have suddenly, and to their own surprise,
found themselves the strongest people in Europe. All I can
say of my own experience is that, for civility, if you treat them
rightly, I know none who surpass them. They will stand no
nonsense, and they have no grimace about them, but in all
essentials there is nothing to be complained of.

He returned to England, and started again for
the seat of war, to serve under the Red Cross
Society for aid to the sick and wounded, on
Sept. 20.

W. J. B. TO HIS WIFE.

ARLON, Sept. 23, 1870.

Here I am at headquarters, going off to-day on a job . . .
as 'éclaireur' to find out what is wanted in all the country
round Sedan. I am on a roving commission to buy myself
a horse and get on as I can, reporting diligently to headquarters ;
I hope that I shall do it all right, but am anxious, as you may
suppose. They want more men, and I mentioned ——. Capt.
Brackenbury eagerly accepted. But at dinner I heard so much
of the dysentery and typhus at Saarbrück that I told them that
I feared to send for him. . . . The weather is lovely, so
bright and calm. The country too is very charming. My
route is (1) to Libramont ; (2) Bouillon, where I have a letter to

the commandant; (3) to Sedan, where I hope to sleep, and then about the country, especially to Donchéry.

W. J. B. TO HIS WIFE.

SEDAN, Sept. 24, 1870.

Here I am in the centre of all the worst suffering that has fallen on this unfortunate land. I arrived here yesterday evening, and a young doctor who was with us distinctly perceived and pointed out to me the smell of putrefying human flesh, as we drew near the gates of the town. But I had better begin at the beginning and give you the whole of my story. I wrote last on Thursday from Arlon, having just received my instructions as 'éclaireur,' and having my journey before me. I have now, I hope, half accomplished my errand, and finished with Sedan. I left Arlon by the 10.30 train, and proceeded by train to Libramont, thence by two omnibuses to Sedan, changing 'voitures' at Bouillon. In the train I travelled with a Mr. and Mrs. Beauclerk, whom I had met the day before. They were at Sedan at the time of the bombardment, and were among the first to look after the wounded. They, with some Belgian gentlemen and ladies, had bought straw and carried the wounded on a roughly-formed ambulance, till better arrangements could be made. They described the sight of the 80,000 prisoners, guarded like sheep, with a few hundreds of Uhlans behind and before, driving them in with their lances if they straggled. Mrs. B. had her apron full of bread which she gave to the prisoners, and was threatened with death by a Prussian officer for doing so. In the omnibus I came upon an American Major-General, who had permission from Count Bismarck to join the royal headquarters. We had the coupé to ourselves and made a pleasant journey of it. He is a strong-built soldierly man, named Hazen, and had commanded a 'corps d'armée' in the American War. He knew no French nor German, but otherwise was a thoughtful and well read man, full of fun. . . . I also travelled with two doctors, one an old army surgeon who had been in the Crimean Campaign; the other, a bright young fellow, also a doctor, named Colley—late Davies—formerly scholar of Trin. Coll. Cam. We all four consorted together and made a merry time of it. The road went through the great forest

of Ardennes, and was very beautiful in parts; atmosphere as
before, charming. When we were some miles from Sedan a
spring broke, and we had to creep all the way. Thus we found
out what is a town in state of siege. We arrived at Sedan at
7.30, and found the gates shut for the night. Two poor young
mothers with their babies whom in the danger they had sent off
into Belgium, were of our party, and there seemed before us
nothing but the woods, in which to this day dead bodies are
continually found. However, by proper application and suppli-
cation, we got in with such luggage as we could carry, and then
came the question of a bed. The first hotel, de l'Europe, was
crammed, and poor madame, evidently worried to death by
applications for beds, was inclined to be savage at me for
pressing her to find us (the M.-G. and myself) somewhere to
stow our carcases. I bethought me of a garçon to conduct us,
and promised him a franc if he would find us a lodging. *This
acted*, and we were soon in the strangest house I ever saw. It
seems like nothing outside; and inside, as the landlady told me,
she found room for forty-five people. There is a spiral staircase
which saves room, and off it open a regular rabbit warren of
'chambres à deux pièces,' in one of which M.-G. and I took up
our abode. The smells are *awful* inside and outside, and I have
just soaked our room with carbolic acid, which a benevolent
doctor has bestowed upon me. (We are all—I mean the 'rouge
croix' folk—very soon hail-fellow-well-met.) I think that the
Prussians need only enclose the place for a few days to fill it
with typhoid. Everywhere the drains are most dreadful, but this
corner seems the worst of all. Everybody must be at home at
nine P.M. else he is in danger of being arrested—'nicht nach
neun Freilass,' said a Prussian soldier to me when I asked whether
it was true. We got a good meal at the hotel, and madame became very gracious when she found that she was relieved from
the difficulty of the bed. This morning I had planned to get a
'voiture' and hunt up the different places to which I was bound,
but soon found it hopeless. No one would let me have a horse,
and the various 'patrons' were disposed to be very sulky. I
caught something about 'autorisation,' and gathered that if I
could get a *command* from the Prussian authorities I could floor
them. First I got hold of a bright sort of a fellow, a hanger-on
at the hotel, and engaged him for the day; then after breakfast

started off 'pour réclamer mes effets,' which were numerous owing to my purchases at Brussels, from the omnibus bureau. I got them and the M.-G.'s portmanteau with some difficulty, and then proceeded to the Commandant's office, where my friend hoped to get tidings as to how he should proceed to head-quarters. You cannot imagine greater politeness than the Germans showed us. I stated the case, showed the permit, and finally had the pleasure of hearing that at 'zwei Uhr,' a German architect was to be sent off in a 'Wagen,' and that he might go with him. Then I thought that I would do a stroke of work for myself, and accordingly pleaded the importance of my commission; and readily obtained the order for horses. You should have seen the change it produced on the state of things. 'I might have what I liked, when I liked, how I liked.' 'Would I have one or two?' etc., etc. So I arranged to do my work here to-day and start to-morrow for the villages.

My first point was the Anglo-American Ambulance at the barracks, on the top of a hill overlooking the Meuse. . . . I found Miss Pearson, etc., and C. Wood. With them I arranged for a Celebration at eight to-morrow in her rooms. . . . She is to accompany me to-morrow.

I soon found that no one could really help me, and that I must take my own line. I went therefore next to the 'Société Française pour le secours des blessés,' and had a long conversation with M. de Martagnac, who is its head. He gave me a list of the villages where wounded are, and also told me what was chiefly required. I was particularly anxious to obtain details, and not *generally* that they would be glad of anything that we could send. I find that *trousers* are most required. The shells have torn them to pieces. On the whole the wounded are gradually being 'évacués,' by which it is meant that they are being sent away. Two thousand are at present in Sedan and its neighbourhood. Some 400 are to go off on Monday to Charleroi and the N. of France. The Belgian authorities however refuse to receive more.

I took careful notes of our conversation, and went on to the Couvent de l'Assomption, which a letter to Colonel Lindsay described as battered in and made by the Sisters into an Ambulance. Their resources, it was added, were exhausted. The Mother, an intelligent German from Munich, received me, and we went over the place together. They have now no wounded, only sick. Fever, small-pox, etc. The place was scarcely touched. The poor nuns had hidden themselves in the cellar, like wise women, and they had plenty of everything, though at one time they were badly off. Cigars would be acceptable, and I sent them 300 out of ——'s stock.

From them I proceeded to the French Military Hospital authorities, and met there the first really serious Frenchman I have seen. A boy wanted to guide me to the battlefield, and told me quite cheerfully, ' Mon père a été tué.' The women seem to feel it more. I could not persuade one of these in the omnibus that the Prussians did not use poisoned bullets. She would have it so, and the tears came into her eyes when she spoke of the frightful night which they had spent when the troops were driven into Sedan.

This officer whom I saw at the French Military Hospital interested me much. He seemed thoroughly beaten down by their troubles, yet was quite intelligent and responsive, and grateful for what little one could say or do. From him I heard the same story of lack of ' pantalons,' and he showed me the Belgian letters, which seemed to pain him a good deal. Lastly I visited the Prussian medical folk, and made them the offer of a château near Arlon, which had been placed at Capt. Brackenbury's disposal—for the Belgians do not refuse the Prussian wounded. This offer required a good deal of consideration. The question of transport is very difficult, and I am to receive an answer to-morrow. You will see that this was a good day's work, for each visit involved a good deal of talk and thought. . . . I must not forget to say that I prepared an elaborate despatch, and contrived to get it sent off by private hands to Capt. Brackenbury, to get it to-morrow, Sunday.

I walked to Balon, a little village close to Sedan, where Porter and his Sisters are. He was out. I saw a doctor with whom he lives, a pleasant fellow, quite enchanted with P., and promised, if I have time, to dine with them to-morrow. This doctor gave me the carbolic acid with directions how to use it. Balon is much knocked about by the cannon balls, and there too I fell in with the dreadful smell of putrefying human flesh. On the whole, I must confess that I am surprised to find how quickly things seem to be righting themselves. The towns will not suffer much.   The Prussians behave themselves, as almost all people of all classes tell me, very well—pay for everything, ill-use no one, do not swagger.   There are, of course, stories of this man's corn being taken, and that other losing his wine; and I see that the feeling of the nurses and swells is on the French side, but I cannot agree with them.   The country folk will certainly suffer a great deal, but in limited localities.   I have not yet seen Bazeilles, where I am told the whole place is utterly destroyed, nor the battlefield which is still covered with débris of every kind.   The peasants alone are permitted to pick them up.   A lot of tourist gents are already on the spot, trying to make capital out of everything.   The Prussian sentry was refusing admission to two regular *h*-less English snobs, when I went up with Miss Pearson to the Ambulance this afternoon.   She was quite a match for them.   They wanted to go through the Ambulance and see the wounded, and appealed to her to let them in.   She told them that they must get an order from the 'Commandant.'   The doctors appear to be a good set of men (English I mean), kind, intelligent, unaffected.

The difficulty of the situation is that a staff of workers and a great depôt of stores are gathered into one place—for a time they are wanted—then the wounded become fewer from death and other causes, and there is little or nothing left to be done. I fancy that Metz and its vicinity will soon want help; and then will come the Paris work.   We know nothing in the way of news.   .   .   .   No food of any kind, save perhaps bread, can be got between meal times, *i.e.* eleven and six.

I do not know how Capt. B. will look at my despatch; but I have really got a good insight for him into what is wanted here, and especially what is not wanted.   .   .   .   I am so far exposed to no danger whatever, except that from evil odours, which the carbolic acid neutralises, and so you may tell every one who is anxious about me.   And that I cannot write more letters, for my time is fully taken up.   .   .   .

W. J. B. TO HIS WIFE.

SEDAN, Sept. 25th.

Although I wrote you yesterday I must set to work again this evening, and give you my impressions fresh after the work of to-day. I celebrated Holy Communion this morning in Miss Pearson's room in the Croix Rouge. The congregation consisted of Miss P., a Mrs. Mason, whom I know not, and C. Wood. Then we had matins and litany. C. W. breakfasted with me at the Hôtel de l'Europe, and I was about to start at ten A.M., accompanied by Miss P., on my journey through the villages, when R. Porter came in. Of course this delayed me; we had a quarter of an hour's chat and I promised to make my way to him this afternoon, but was unable to do so. He is outside the town, and the gates are shut at seven. Now for my expedition. I made a complete tour round the town, beginning with Bazeilles, which is about three miles south, and visiting Lamoncelle, Darguy, Givonne, Olly, Floing, and one or two besides. This kept me entirely in the district where the great battle was fought, and I saw all the remains of its traces. First of all, the village of Bazeilles is utterly destroyed. It is a large village, 1800 inhabitants, a sort of country-house place of the bettermost Sedan folk, and full of woollen workers and farmers. These people had fired on the Prussians as they drove the French through the village, and every house was deliberately fired. It is simply a village of shells of houses, and the road is covered with tiles and bricks—not many of the people were killed, 20 or 30 at the most, which was exaggerated into 300. Near this we found ambulances established in a large château, under the charge of Mrs. C—— and the Mother Superior of All Saints. The former was busy cooking, and a wonderfully graceful pretty cook she looked, dressed in a large cook's apron; but not a bit less like the high-born lady. They had forty-eight wounded; had three operations, amputations, the day before, but were well supplied with everything. Pyæmia, in spite of all their care, had set in, and they had lost a good many. The château belonged to a Comte de Fiennes who lives in the south of France; but no questions are asked in these times, and everything, to use a slang expression, is 'walked into' without scruple. We then drove on to another large village, La Moncelle, and found both Prussians and French in various châteaux. There were a good many, 250 or thereabouts, gradually however being moved away to Lille and to Belgium. We distributed freely our stock of cigars and chocolate, and gave, I think, much satisfaction. Poor fellows! they were—and this applies universally—

patient and even cheerful. Only in one case, where lock-jaw had
come on, was there any moaning. Some faces had the hectic
of fever, some the pallor of death; but they showed us their
wounds and the bullets which had been extracted, and chatted
about their homes. Nothing could be better under the circumstances than the treatment they received. The rooms were
quite sweet and the beds clean. Generally they had bedsteads,
sometimes they were on the ground. We questioned the French
carefully, out of the reach of the Prussian ears, and they all
had one story—that they were well taken care of and wanted
for nothing, except perhaps sugar in their coffee or matters of
no great importance. Then, I think, some of them said they
were left too long without drink. Sometimes we were told by
our man, a handy fellow whom I have employed since we came
here, that the French had no bread, and so on; but when we
came to investigate the matter it invariably turned out to be
a thorough mistake. However, as I said, the cigars and chocolate brought many a smile of pleasure, and I think the money
was well laid out. We went through pretty nearly the same
sort of careful visitation in all the spots where wounded were
to be found. In several places they had all departed, and there
was no one but the surgeons, French for the most part, and
very gentlemanly, pleasant men. One of them told us that
the German terms had been refused. He was to go on to
Paris without delay.

The next important place we saw was Floing, close to the
great cavalry fight in which 20,000 cavalry were engaged. We
saw there 150 French and Germans, under a very gentlemanly
German doctor, who gave us coffee, and who, the first of all
we had visited, specified certain things for which he would be
very grateful. We had some difficulty in making out 'kettel-
säge,' but at last I divined it to be a surgical instrument, and
so it proved to be. I made him write all down, and promised
to send him from Arlon all that could be got. Ale and porter
were among his wants—strong English, not the light German
beer. These men are severely wounded, and not likely quickly
to be removed. We found in a cottage a wounded French
officer; his thigh was broken, and I should fear that he was in
great danger. He was engaged to a lady, to whom he begged
us to transmit a letter which he wrote in pencil while we were

there. Alas! she resides in Paris. How is it to reach her?
His host was a baker, an old man who remembered 1815. It
was nothing, he said, to this. People then behaved well—these
very Prussians—but now they pillaged everything. His two
cows, his fodder, his flour, all his stock-in-trade was carried off
in Prussian waggons. His wife had much to say on the subject,
and she brought forward triumphantly her grandson who had
gained three prizes at school, and had sold them for five francs
to help the family in their troubles. Notwithstanding all this
the old couple were cheerful and hospitable, and brought out
a bottle of wine to do us honour. We clinked glasses and
drank to better days. He told me that the peasants would
not have a republic, and spoke kindly of the Emperor; he had
been deceived by bad ministers; if he had himself commanded
things would have gone differently; and so on. The weather
has been very favourable for the wounded—bright, without
being sultry, and there has been little wind. A large proportion
are recovering, and even men who have lost limbs are rapidly
being removed. Carbolic acid is freely used.

As I said before, we passed over every portion of the huge
battlefield. It was seven and a half miles long, four and a half
broad. The natural situation most lovely as usual in battle-
fields; two long lines of hills, broken, of course, by water
courses and undulations, face one another, on which the two
armies had their cannon, and between which the actual fighting
took place. On the left of the French position is a wooded
slope, apparently almost impregnable. This it was which the
Crown Prince of Saxony carried after a desperate struggle, in
which the superior physique of the Germans told. They drove
the slight French recruits, as I was told, like sheep before them.
After this came the cavalry battle in the bottom towards the
right of the French, in which the Chasseurs d'Afrique were
borne down by Bismarck's regiment. Either before or after this
the French cavalry got into a trap. They were regularly
hemmed in while the tremendous Prussian artillery played upon
them. The scene was frightful—horses and men fell over one
another, and the poor horses shrieked piteously. All this part
of the field was trodden to pieces with horse hoofs. The horses
are buried under mounds, the men in long level pits on which
roughly-hewn crosses are placed. Even now, after all the work

of the relic-hunters and the peasants (to whom an exclusive right is given, by a decree, of picking up the remains), the ground is scattered with knapsacks and shakos, iron cuirasses, and the like. My man picked up for me the cartridge box of a mitrail-leuse, which I must try to bring home. Except in this particular spot there is not much to see. Here and there one saw something which betokened soldiers' presence, or the movements of artillery; but I am quite sure that if I had known nothing of the history of the time I should have passed by without perceiving that a bloody battle had been fought.

One of our party the day before yesterday, in bringing a fourgon from Arlon, actually picked up a man who had lain in the woods wounded since the battle. He had lost his senses, and wildly asked my friend which party had won the victory. He picked him up and brought him to Sedan.

Nothing surprises me more than the rapidity with which everything is falling into its natural condition. Except for the German soldiers and the Red Cross people, there is nothing to betoken the terrible distress of so short a while since. The hotel people seem rather distraught, but the crowd of visitors is enough to account for that, and lodgings are hard to obtain. Tourist gents of all countries are flocking in to roam over the battlefield. This will help to put some money into the people's pockets. M. de Martagnac, the son of the deputy whom I saw this morning in his dressing-gown before I started, and people of his rank, are depressed and serious; but the folk generally prefer, I really believe, the German to the French soldiers. Porter has some terrible experiences to relate of the atrocities of the Germans; but it is to be remembered that he is in the very heart of the battle-ground, where wounded fell most thickly, and where the difficulty of treating them properly was very great. I hear that all the English party are ordered to Arlon. I am naturally going there to-morrow. My Prussian order from the Commandant stands me still in stead, and I have ordered a 'voiture à deux chevaux,' which I hope that C. Wood will share with me. I go by Florenville, carrying my own despatches. . . .

Arlon, 27th Sept.—I arrived here yesterday at six, after, as I expected, a charming drive. Part of the journey was over the ground of the day before, through Bazeilles, Balon, etc.

I stopped for a few minutes to see R. P. and his party, and left them a bottle of eau de Cologne, much needed, I assure you, in these parts. I saw three ambulances under the hills, the soldiers were mostly badly-wounded Germans. They were well cared for and happy. One of the Sisters has got typhoid. The road went right through the battlefield, and I was surprised to see so few traces of what had happened; the beetroot crops were uninjured, though the men and guns went right over them. Of course there were such things as old knapsacks, a dead horse or two, and the little poplars had been cut down by the Germans to make sleeping places, a plan which they prefer to the trouble of carrying tents. One saw these little huts in lots here and there. At one house near Bazeilles when the owner, a peasant, did not understand some order, he was shot close to his own door. We passed the spot, but the dead were all buried carefully, and there were no sights of horror. The German army regularly scraped up the French from the Belgian borders and then fell upon them, as I have described. We then arrived at Douzy, where Mr. and Mrs. Beauclerk established an English ambulance, now broken up. I found there however a good many wounded, chiefly Saxons, after the great attack; they had those bright, responsive Saxon faces, mostly fair, a few, however, dark. There were two ambulances, and I took note of what they required. Mrs. Loyd-Lindsay's bottle of chloroform came usefully to hand here. They were out of it, and most thankful. Then we drove on through the Ardennes, the forest opening out into distant views of lovely atmospheric tints. We passed a wonderful pilgrimage place, where the driver assured me that miracles were constantly wrought, after confession and Communion. . . .

W. J. B. TO HIS WIFE.

SAARBRÜCKEN, Sept. 30, 1870.

Well, I am ashamed to write this letter, for in fact I have done nothing worth my salt since I wrote before. The truth is that the work which depended on Arlon is now coming to an end. The wounded are in course of speedy removal, and the headquarters of the Society are to be removed to this place. . . . The lieutenant, or storekeeper, Mr. Bushnan, is a very jolly fellow, and received me most kindly. He had Captain B.'s room made ready for me, and gave me all information but no work. I must stay here till to-morrow and then I am to start off as 'éclaireur,' taking up my quarters at Rémilly, some forty miles west of this on the road to Metz. This is to be a depôt of the Society, and I hope to make it useful for the villages round, which are more or less filled with wounded. I wrote to you last from Arlon, and gave you an account of the stores, etc. It is a strange life, as you may suppose, to find oneself in the midst of a set of people whose names for the most part I have never heard before, doctors young and old, newspaper correspondents, agents of the Society of all degrees, young and middle-aged, all very friendly, working hard when there is work to do, and at other times idling, chatting, etc. On the whole they seem to be a good sort of fellows, with plenty of work in them, not very refined, almost, I should think, without religion, though quite proper in language and far from jeering or mocking, kind and really anxious to do their best. . . . From Arlon I had a slow but not uninteresting journey. . . . At Conz, a lovely village in the valley under the hills from which the Moselle is fed, with the broad river flowing under groves of walnuts, there was a long wait, nearly four hours. The train had been taken off. I walked about therefore with my friend the doctor, and heard the same story as Porter tells, that after two or three days the bulk of the doctors and others who look after the sick grow weary of their work and neglect it. He says that it is most trying and wearying, that the only special practice which a surgeon learns is how to deal with comminuted fractures, and that a good many have been sent out who have neither heart nor skill. Of course he excepts men like the American Dr. ——, Dr. Frank, and Dr. MacCormac. He says, and I think wisely, that there should be a committee of surgeons to pronounce on a man's capabilities, and that those sent out should not be paid in advance, but by the *head* surgeon at the end of each week's work. This tallies with reason and experience. From Conz to Saarbrücken is six hours nearly. The road along the valley of the Saar is very beautiful, and the atmosphere as before was exquisite in lights, quite sparkling and effervescent. In fact, the weather has been most fortunate for the poor and wounded. Saarbrücken you remember, not however in its present stirring condition, but as a stupid sleepy German third-class country town, paved roughly, and inhabited by a rough set of folks, also a longish distance from its huge ugly station. It is not asleep now, but all alive with Johanniter and endless soldiers, an 'étappe commandant,' 'gewündete' carried through the streets, etc. The hotel at which I dined last night was crowded, no room to be had there. I had an introduction to one 'Wassenborn' next door, but a baroness had 'bestellt' the room. Madame kindly sent me with her girl to her sister named *Philippi*, whose husband keeps a restauration chiefly in beer and tobacco, and I engaged a room looking very like *bugs*. My friend here, Mr. Bushnan, relieved me of this, and sent for my luggage and established me here where I am. . . . The railway authorities have lent a large piece of land near the station, on which a builder of the town has undertaken to erect a large shed to receive the stores without delay. Fourgons are to arrive at once from Arlon, and here are to be the new headquarters, from which Rémilly, a branch depôt, and other places will be supplied. I expect to find things very rough at Rémilly, and still more in its vicinity. . . . The room in which I am writing is exactly opposite the heights on which the French guns were posted; a chassepôt bullet pierced its shutter and made a mark on a piece of furniture. There it is to tell the tale. When I have finished this I am going to walk round the French position. News came yesterday, 'affichéd' at the railway station, of the capitulation of Strassburg. I wish that Metz would do the same, but on the contrary the Prussians lost a good many from a sortie, both killed and taken prisoners, and a lot of wounded came into this town. The French took eight waggons filled with provisions. In consequence it is considered that the villages round Metz are likely to treat ill any whom they may recognise as strangers, and this makes my good friend Bushnan a little anxious about letting me go. I have no anxiety myself about it, and only, as you may suppose, grumble at being idle. It certainly was most unfortunate that I missed having the charge of the All Saints Sisters. That was *exactly* my work. Then one could have chatted with and read to the poor wounded men all day long, whereas now I have to wait for jobs. I feel as if I had no

right to be, as it were, enjoying myself and "seeing life" while
my brethren are doing the parish work. However I am quite
sure that it is not my fault, nor, as far as I can see, the fault
of any one. I am come just at the end of one set of things
and the beginning of another. I expect that Miss Goodman
will have the command of a hospital here which is to be given
over to us by the Dutch and Belgians, and then I shall be more
in my element, unless indeed, I am at Rémilly. . . I am
longing to hear from you again, especially as you may suppose
I want a full account of Sunday. Michaelmas Day was spent
by me mostly in travelling, but I find a little sermon here in
my bedroom in a picture of an angel carrying a child, a photograph set in needlework, with the inscription, "Habe Acht auf
deinen Engel und höre seine Stimme."

W. J. B. TO HIS WIFE.

HÔTEL GUÉPRATTE, Oct. 1, 1870.

. . . Things move on so rapidly that it is hard even after
only one day to remember just where I left off. Anyhow, I
had brought myself to Saarbrücken. It seemed as if there was
nothing for me to do here at present, for the 'fourgons' had
not arrived, and until then we could only sit still, or make
arrangements for their reception. They had left Arlon on
Wednesday, only sixty miles distant, and we wondered what
could have hindered them. Of this more anon. Mr. Bushnan
recommended me to hunt up the field of Saarbrücken, where
the French suffered their first defeat, and Spicheren, where
they were completely driven back. This according I did. The
river Saar, swift and deep, winds through the meadows, now
being mown, full of herbage and wild flowers; and so far as I
could find there is no ferry or bridge except here, where the two
bridges give the name to the town. The speciality of the Saar
seems to be its power of naming places. Besides Saarbrücken,
there is Saarlouis, Saarguemines, Saarables, Saarbouy, and many
more. You remember the position of Saarbrücken, in a valley
between two ranges of hills. The Prussian frontier extends
irregularly beyond the Saar. Saarbrücken itself is not more
than two miles from the French frontier. Spicheren actually
is within it. I mounted, therefore, the ridge which is W. of

the Saar, and soon found myself among the traces of a battlefield. There soldiers were wandering about, one of whom, a
"Krankenträger," joined himself to me, and lionised me everywhere for a couple of hours. From him I got hold of the whole
idea of the battle. The French posted their cannon first immediately over Saarbrücken, i.e. a quarter of a mile a top of it (you
remember that the river divides it from St. Johann), the
Prussians theirs on the heights over St. Johann. When the
French first approached and had their guns in position, there
were only 500 Prussians in the place. The French delayed
the attack for three days, in which time all the troops that
could be collected from Baden, Wurtemberg, etc., and Prussia
itself, came down by the railroad, for strange to say, though
the French bombarded the railway station, not however
damaging it, they did not do the obviously reasonable thing,
viz. to cut the line. When the Germans had strength enough
they on their part attacked the French, and drove them back
over a *riant* valley, broad and well cropped, in the midst
of heavy rain, to a tremendously strong position, half a mile
in the rear. It is on the top of a very steep hill, a grind
even for me, with one rough 'pavé' or 'chaussée,' and a couple
of watercourses. Eight horses were required for each cannon
to tug them up the hill. This hill was roughly escarped, and
all along the ridge a little ditch was cut, in which the French
riflemen were sheltered as they fired on the Prussians who
climbed up the sides. At the top is a wood, another great
advantage to the French, who found their shelter behind the
trees. Four times they drove back the Prussians but the fifth
charge settled them. Of course efforts were made, not in front
only but round the sides, and it was one of these side attacks
which at length succeeded. I suppose that it would be impossible for any army to drive out such soldiers as the French,
so strongly intrenched, with only a front attack. Then in two
hours the whole of the Prussian artillery, 300 pieces, were
dragged down and up, and the French defeat was complete.
I believe that more French than Germans were engaged, 100,000
to 180,000, but of this I am not sure. The view from the
Spicheren heights is most lovely, over the valley, the town,
and the river to the heights on the other side. The battlefield has more relics of the fight than I saw at Sedan. My friend

the soldier picked up one thing after another, and said simply "Deutsch, Französisch," and then threw it away. I have become quite learned in cartridges. The German had paper, the French cardboard boxes; also the French use long 'mêches,' the German short, etc. There were little boxes full still of grease for boots, knapsacks, innumerable cartridge boxes, leather belts, tin cooking pots, tin tubes which they stick on wooden handles when they want to roast anything, and thrust them into the fire,—braces, bits of letters, newspaper fragments, cooking places, flasks of leather, all sorts of débris. The trees were splintered and cut to pieces. Here and there a bullet was visible still sticking in the trees. It was a strange feeling to wander in the little thicket filled with such speaking relics, and think what was going on there so few weeks since—the anxiety, and the fierce passions, the disappointment, and the joy of victory. As I said, it was steep climbing even for me, unencumbered as I was, and without an enemy firing down upon me. One may imagine what it cost the Germans. The field is dotted about with burying places,—here 30, there perhaps 47, and so on. Near the town there is a large grave where 374 lie together, among them an uncle and nephew, one a general, the other in the Grenadier Guards, name Von François. This large grave has a good number of crosses upon it. Those in the fields are merely mounds hedged round with the dry bushes which the Prussians had previously cut down for their bivouac—or, as they say—*bivac*. On the descent which leads to the village about half-way down there is a pretty knoll of trees with a Crucifix not the least injured by the bullets. There was something there to make one meditate mournfully.

The poor horses were all carted together to a long grave near to the town. My friendly soldier brought me back safely into the town, after having cut out two or three bullets from the trees that I might carry them home as relics. I picked up two or three more things which I thought the children might care to have. I might have filled a waggon if I had cared to do so. . . . Now, I believe, I shall have some regular work. I am to be general store-keeper, account keeper, over-looking kitchen arrangements, etc. One of the London military commissionaires, of whom we have four, is

to be my man. Dr. ——, a German doctor of much
experience who has been for years resident in London, and
is practically an Englishman; a very pleasing, though rough
and ugly Scotch *Episcopalian* from Aberdeen; a couple more
doctors, Miss ——, and some Sisters, will form our staff. . . .
Rémilly, about forty miles hence, *is* a nasty place. There
are two Englishmen just arrived, very ill with dysentery,
from R. The account they give of the place is sickening.
It is the main depôt for the villages round, which are crammed
with sick and wounded from Metz. We are going to establish a
depôt there also. The difficulties of getting to work are really
very great. (1) There is the jealousy of the Johanniter,
which now seems fairly removed; (2) the ignorance of the
German authorities as to the nature of the English work;
(3) the difficulty of carrying the bulky stores from place to
place. The trains are uncertain. Long 'convois' of provisions,
etc., are always arriving for military objects, and the passenger
trains have to wait for them. Horses are very dear and
hard to get, and apt to break down when you have got them.
The younger Bushnan started from Arlon on Wednesday
evening with seven fourgons. I was to have gone with them,
but Mr. Capel strongly advised me to go by train. It was
most fortunate that I did so, for only this morning (Saturday)
did they come into Saarbrücken, having taken seventy hours
to haul sixty miles. One horse was paralysed—three others
came to grief—a man from whom they had hired horses stopped
in the middle of the road, refusing to go further, and demanded
to be paid for the whole journey. When they refused to
pay, he tried to take their harness, then brought a body
of peasants to attack them. They were literally forced to
fight with their fists, *i.e.* the drivers, Bushnan, an English
groom on one side, and the peasants on the other. The peasants
outnumbered them, and took various of their things. And
finally entering Saarbrücken the soldiers stopped them, would
not believe they were not French, took all their hay and
straw, wanted to steal their wine, and not without bribes
permitted them to proceed. The fact is, we are in a false
position. We are not understood. We are, as it were, forcing
our benevolences on people who return our kindness by thinking
us officious or fools or *interested*. It will be some time before

things go straight.   Meanwhile there is nothing for it but patience and good temper. . . .

W. J. B. TO HIS WIFE.

SAARBRÜCKEN, Oct. 3, 1870.

. . . I wrote a long letter on Saturday, giving you while I had it fresh in my mind the history of that first battle which practically settled the whole matter of the war.   Since then I have heard various details.   It seems that the Germans, though only 500 men appeared in Saarbrücken, had filled the woods with soldiers who were ready to pounce on the French if they had attempted to advance.   It does not appear, however, that the French knew this.   The French occupied the railway station, and did not cut the line, because they meant to use it to enter Germany.   This turned out very badly for them.

This place is full of English—a motley lot—an odd 'galère' indeed for me to find myself in.   Various newspaper correspondents, regular old hands, who have been for similar tours in the Crimea, America, etc., describers of Atlantic cables, Great Exhibitions, and opening of isthmus canals ; philanthropists, employés of the English Society of all ranks, down to four commissionaires with green uniform and medals—not the least respectable of our party—a couple of doctors, and now Sisters of mercy.   We are all good friends together. . . . Last Friday, as I told you, I had not enough to do, and had almost made up my mind to return home this week.   Now I seem to have a prospect of real usefulness and I shall of course stay longer.   It came about in a funny way.   There is a Scotch doctor—a demonstrator of anatomy at Aberdeen—a clever fellow, and, as I accidentally found out, an Episcopalian.   We soon made friends together, and he rejoiced in coming to my Celebration on Sunday morning, in spite of the much chaffing of ——.   When I told him my intention of returning, he said that I should be most helpful if I would take charge of the stores and medicines in the 'Lazareth,' which we are about to occupy in force.   It seems that there is always a prejudice against doctors taking this office. . . . While I was considering this, I found to my surprise and gratification that —— and the commissionaires would be grateful for a short service on each Sunday morning, and I believe that several of the English con-

nected with the Society as clerks and the like would also come.
This would make a tidy congregation. Then to complete all and
to my great surprise, yesterday evening at 5 P.M. the Sisters ——
with Mrs. —— arrived from Sedan, or rather Balon, where they
had been at work. That work is nearly ended. They were
delighted when we met in the thronged hotel passage, having
given themselves up as 'gone coons' when they left Balon and
the ministrations of R.P. The difficulty at present is to get them
lodged and fed, and also to set them to work in the hospital,
which is now nursed by Sisters who, though certainly not enough
in numbers, have done their work splendidly. I believe that
nothing could have been better managed than this hospital—one
of many in the town—which we are now going to take into our
hands. The two doctors there, a German from Ems and a
Dutchman under the Dutch Society for the wounded, have
shown great skill and had singular success. It will not do for
us to make any mistakes, nor could we dispense with the Sisters
who are there at work. You cannot imagine the thin-skinnedness
of the doctors and sick-helpers. I have learnt a good deal
about the Germans since I have been here—their great cere-
moniousness, their more than self-respect, their immense pride.
There is a touch of the Scotch nature in them. Go to work the
right way and they will do anything for you; but tread on their
toes, and you had better pack up and go home at once. So
that the getting into the hospital is a ticklish business.

Tuesday. Since I wrote the above I have again visited the
field of Spicheren with two of the Sisters and Mrs. ——. . . .
We had another beautiful day, and we wandered through the
woods tinged with autumn colouring, quiet and peaceful, still
filled with the remains of that deadly struggle. Some men
were removing a body or filling in a grave after its removal.
One of them took out of his pocket a handful of bullets of
all sizes and a Prussian eagle off an uniform. I gave him a
franc, and distributed them among the Sisters, who were collecting relics to show their school children in London. But
the odour of decaying flesh still hung about them, and it was
almost impossible to wash it away. We went on to the Crucifix
which overlooks the village, and knelt down together and offered
some prayers. Poor Spicheren! it is a little dirty, roughly
paved French village, with however a hostelry where I got

some good wine. How the country folk must have been surprised by the rush of those two great armies! The two nations
were afraid to accept one another's courtesy. Each thought
that the other had poisoned their food. . . . To-morrow I
shall be in the Hospital, there to live while I stay here. . . .

W. J. B. TO HIS WIFE.

UHLANEN CASERNE, Oct. 6, 1870.

. . . Here, I assure you, my work is well cut out, and unless
I am forced by your next letter to return to my proper and
natural duties, I feel that I ought not to leave my post. I
entered, yesterday, fairly into work. I have the charge of all the
eatables and drinkables, all the 'comforts,' so to call them, of this
hospital. I apply for what is wanted to Mr. Bushnan, and I
give out things on the doctor's requisition. I keep regular
debit and credit accounts, not of money but of things (*Waaren*),
and I spend my day among my stores. Beyond this I visit
the sick and wounded, chat a little with them, bring them
cigars to cheer them, etc., etc.; and further I have services for
the Sisters, and have arranged with the greater part of the
English folk here, who are tolerably numerous, to have a
service on Sundays. It took some days to put all this straight,
but now there is, I think, no more difficulty, and it seems
provoking—to use such a word—to have to leave it. You
can scarcely imagine the difficulty of getting *anything* done—
above all in *my* line. You must remember that I am in a
position entirely new to me. First of all I am a subordinate
and not a principal. Not as at home 'monarch of all I survey,'
but forced to be most particular not even to seem to assert
the very least authority of any kind whatsoever. If I were to
take up the slightest bit of ground not my own, there would
be instant confusion, and in some or other way I should be
snubbed. Then I have to deal with a very strange set of
people, quite other than any who have hitherto fallen in my
way.

. . . Then there are four commissionaires, good honest
fellows, who . . . were really unhappy because they had no
service last Sunday; then the whole throng of 'freiwillige
Kranken-pfleger' . . . some gentlemen, others clerks and couriers,

then hangers-on like —— or —— , then the correspondents of
the papers. . . . Two or three Germans hook on to us at dinner.
You may imagine what a strange life it is, and how much self-
control it requires to hold one's own and keep on good friendly
terms with them all. . . . All this, as you may suppose, is not
to my taste, though it is not bad practice for my temper and
disposition.

  . . . We breakfast at 7.30.   At 8.30 we go to the hospital,
which is only five minutes off.   There Dr. Rodger and I remain.
I have a room on the ground floor just at the entrance, formerly an officer's room, hung round with battle pictures, and
within it a smaller room, fitted up roughly with shelves.

The Dutch were here before us, and they have left us some of
their stores. *Our* stores come in by degrees, and I stow them
away with the help of one of the commissionaires, a good
fellow enough—Irish, named Connell. He thinks poorly of the
foreigners and their ways, and compares the somewhat slipshod
arrangements of this suddenly-created hospital with the order
and discipline of a regular English one.   Then all the morning
the German Sisters come in for cushions, bandages, brandy, etc.
We lost one poor fellow yesterday from secondary hæmorrhage,
after an amputation performed by the Dutch doctors before they
left the place.   At the moment we had no brandy in store.   I
rushed out and bought some in two minutes, but it was too late.
He died.

A sentry with bright steel bayonet and gun barrel marches up
and down before my window.   Nevertheless a good many stray
visitors flock in, and as I come first, it falls to my lot to entertain
them.   A Dutch *prediger* rejoicing in the name of Cohen Stuart
paid me a long visit this morning.

I got hold of a couple of strong lasses and made them dust
and wash these two rooms, and clear out the heap of useless
rubbish—furniture and old stores—which littered the floor, and
I am now fairly tidy.   But the hospital itself is in a bad
condition and the doctor is sadly afraid that pyæmia may set
in.   The people whom he employed to whitewash crawl about
and get nothing done.   The stores are very slow in coming in.
I feel, if only I had a week of command, that I could put the
whole thing into real trim—and by degrees, as far as the stores
are concerned, I am getting pretty much my own way, and

setting them to rights.   But of course my present ignorance of what is necessary stands in my way, and I find out only by degrees the need of this or that. . . . As I told you, I do not care one straw where I am posted, I want only to be of use to those who are suffering in this hideous war, with the 'arrière pensée' of helping the English folks to keep religion within their souls. . . . I found a fine well built man to-day, a French officer, who is suffering terribly from a wound in foot. He has been two months in bed.   I took him a great pot of calf's-foot jelly.   He has a German Sister to nurse him, and neither can speak a word of the other's language.   Our English Sisters all speak French, but the fear of exciting jealousy is such that we do not dare to give the work of nursing him to them.

You will be glad to hear that the best beer in Saarbrücken is sold just across the road.   I have lodged the Sisters in the Restauration where it is to be found. . . . I am surrounded by carbolic acid and chloride of lime, and the smell of them, fortunately healthy, is never out of my nose.

4.15.   I have just returned from visiting my friend the French officer.   His wife is with him, very lady-like and pleasant.   He was ten years at Saumur in the Cavalry barracks, and we had a joke about the windmills.   He knows all the Loire country and ('comme on se retrouve') our old friend, M. ——.   I took him a handful of cigars.   They both agreed that the war was causeless and unjust. . . .

W. J. B. TO HIS WIFE.

UHLANEN CASERNE, Oct. 7, 1870.

. . . Another day has nearly passed of this new and strange life of mine.   There is not much variety, yet somehow or other it is not devoid of a certain kind of interest. Very gradually I am beginning to make acquaintance with the wounded.   I was afraid to put myself forward at first, for —— is inclined to be snappish, and I do not want to be in the wrong.   Of course I have no absolute right to be anywhere but in my pantry.   The hospital is a huge barrack, full of rooms of all sizes.   Some have eight beds, others one only.

The officers are, as far as possible, placed in single rooms, and I have made acquaintance with them—one, M. le Capitaine Sacquet, of whom I spoke to you yesterday whose wife, a very pleasing woman, looks after him, and two others, one from 'les Basses Pyrénées,' the other my friend from Rennes, quite a young fellow, sous-lieutenant. The B. P. officer had three brothers in the Crimea—one lost his leg. . . . I ventured to visit them all (men) to-day, and fine fellows they were, very courteous and manly. They seem pleased to see me, and I shall now try to visit them daily. . . . Did I mention to you that we have 70 patients and probably soon 120 will be here. To-day has been a very serious day. Several operations were performed, and the doctors were very anxious.

However, D.G., so far all has gone well. And now the white-washing is going on in good earnest. Also stores are coming in. Yet no port wine has been sent, and our telegraph to England has not been responded to. The hitch is with those wretched Luxemburgers, who are a bad, selfish lot. I am very sorry that we have guaranteed their neutrality. Everything goes on well through Belgium and through Prussia. But the railway necessarily passes through Luxemburg, and they keep the goods at the custom houses, though the packages are all duly marked with Red Cross. My stores consist of linen of all sorts, beer, wine, brandy, jelly, olive oil, extracts of meat, refreshing drinks, filters, slop-pails, linseed meal, candles, soap, etc., etc. By the help of my Commissioner Connell all is in capital order. I have a note book in which I write down all that comes in and goes out. *E.g.* knock comes. "Herein." A gentle-voiced German Sister appears. "Caplan, der Doctor hat mich geschickt zu fragen ob Sie haben," this or that. To which I generally reply, "Meine Schwester, wir werden sehen." Probably Cognac is the object of her search. "Schwester, haben Sie Ihren Propfenzieher ?" She always has it ready in her pocket, and I make a joke about its being her "Breviar," at which she laughs heartily and carries off her prize. Then perhaps Mrs. —— comes in, looking worn out and pale. She wants pillows, sheets, soap, candles, red wine, also begs for a slop-pail. I produce the articles, open a bottle of beer, pull out my private stock of biscuits, and persuade her to take something. Our worst want now is candlesticks.

The town is *brosiered*, and we must wait till some can be made. A bottle with a candle stuck in it is our only resource. . . .

I cannot help smiling sometimes at myself and my work, yet really I think that there is some satisfaction in finding that I can do what I am told to do. Sometimes I have feared that my masterful nature had no humility in it. But I am nearly sure that want of humility is not my special fault.

You cannot imagine the loveliness of the weather or the beauty of the situation of Saarbrücken. Each night the bright moon shines out of the bluest of skies, and is reflected in the Saar. In the morning it is coolish, and rather dull for an hour or so. Then the sun comes out, and the day is clear and warm, not *hot*.

. . . You would be amused at our hotel dinner at seven. . . . The room which is small is crammed with Johanniter in their splendid uniform, with Maltese cross on their breast and embroidered on their coat, Prussian officers, sometimes a French officer on parole, English waifs and strays, occasionally distinguished men whom we gradually get to know, as Capt. Hozier who is sent out by Government to Prussian headquarters. There is, as you may suppose, a mighty jabber. Dr. Rodger, my Scotch friend, and I, retire in good time, but the rest of the party keep the ball going till a latish hour. . . .

I am in some difficulty about Sunday. They all profess to wish for a service, and I have made up my mind when and how to have it, *i.e.* in our sitting room for matins, when the doctor has cleared out, and H.C. in the Sisters' room at seven or eight.

. . . But whether they will come to matins—indeed whether without a real effort they *can* come—is another question. You see in what a quaint position I am. Every one is very civil—I mean of the English folk—but I feel that, with the best intentions on both sides, our lines of thought and objects are as different as possible, and I dread boring them. . . . (Enter Mrs. ——, "O Mr. Butler I am so glad that you are still here. Have you any extract of meat?" "Alas! no, none has been sent!" "What shall I do? One of my poor patients is very weak, etc., etc." Then I remember my private stock, and rush off and fetch my flesh pot. "Thank you, *doctor*," she replies, "I am much obliged.")

Until to-day I have had no chair in which to sit, simply a

four-legged backless stool. I could stand it no longer, and went
out and bought myself a cane chair for 7fr. It is to be Connell's
perquisite when I go. You would laugh to see the said Connell
with the German soldiers and other folk. He talks to them in
simple plain Hibernian English, despises them for their ignorance,
considers them all to be a pack of rogues, though I suppose
honester people could scarcely be found, and never for a moment
has his eyes off the plunder, unless I am there to guard it. He
is a capital fellow, and shrinks from no amount of work. He
lives in the Hospital and receives his 'rations.' This morning
they doled him out a basin of coffee, as he said, as if he was a
beggarman. There was some nasty stuff at bottom. I sent for
' Herr Inspector' and we soon had an [? explanation], the result of
which was such a dinner as Connell had never put into his stomach
before, finishing up, as he expressed it, with jam for dessert.

W. J. B. TO HIS WIFE.

UHLANEN CASERNE, Oct. 9, 1870.

Your letter of yesterday reached me at dinner time, and you
may suppose I had not much appetite after reading it. I carefully considered—wakeful as I am for half the night—what
must be my duty; and I trust that the telegraphic message
which I despatched will make you easy as to my speedy return.
I saw that I could not be in England for Sunday, and therefore
I thought it best to give a service here, and a Celebration to
the Sisters, and then to start to-morrow, Sunday evening. . . .
I am just becoming intimate with the French officers,—such
good pleasant men as they are! Poor Captain Sacquet and
his wife told me all their troubles to-day, how he had lost
everything, *équipement*, property, etc., how terribly expensive
his journeys had been, and what it would still cost to make
his way to Valenciennes. I prevailed on him—' en titre d'un
prêt'—to accept 100 francs, and I never felt happier than
when I put it into his hands. We had much talk about the
battle of Spicheren. His vis-à-vis told me how he happened
to be wounded. He and seven other officers, finding the
ammunition running short, and perceiving the importance of
holding a certain point for a time, took muskets and went
round for all the cartridges they could find. Then they lay

on the ground and fired at the advancing Prussians. One of his brother officers exhausted his stock of cartridges and then rested his head on his hand. This was enough for the Prussian riflemen. A ball broke his arm and ran round into his chest. My friend raised himself to pick up his wounded comrade and was hit on the thigh. He is the man from Béarn; name, Hittos. We exchanged cards, etc.[1]

To-day is our first day of rain. It is however very warm, though not sultry. We are now beginning to get things into order, and I really believe that in a few more days I should find a great deal of interesting work. As it is, I am kept hard at my stores all day, and you would be amused at my new habits of business and regularity. You must not imagine that I had the least idea of doing nothing except store-keeping. I only meant it to be a *pied-à-terre*, and, in fact, in a few days I have no doubt that I should have had the offer of some really important post. Touching ——, and the difference between him and me, the real fact is that he has had so much more detail work than I, and his accounts of the men's sufferings are likely to be right enough. I only described what I actually saw in my rapid walks through the various hospitals. Here of course it is otherwise, and here I am in a position to appreciate more closely what the results of wounds are. Nevertheless I still maintain—and the doctors corroborate my views—that there is not, *on the whole*, as much suffering as might be expected. The men are wounded when mostly in a strong and healthy condition, and better able to endure. And one of our English nurses told me that in hospitals in London the people in surgical wards are more cheerful than those in medical.

We sent off six fourgons full of food and medicine to Rémilly this morning, and we expect an immense supply immediately from Ostend. Oh dear, I shall have to cross by that way, the Calais boats have at length come to an end. People are very kind and express all sorts of regrets at my departure, especially my 'orderly' Connell, to whom I have bequeathed my chair.

[1] The friendship with Captain Sacquet was kept up by letter for many years, and in 1874 a visit was paid to Bourbonne-les-Bains, where the Captain was trying, not very successfully, to get his wound thoroughly cured.

W. J. B. to Rev. Canon Liddon.

Wantage Vicarage, Oct. 29, 1870.

. . . You heard perhaps that I had been in France and Germany lending a very feeble hand to help a little in the hospitals, etc., near Sedan and at Saarbrücken. I was called back, to my great regret, by the dangerous illness of Weaver.[1] He is, D.G., quite recovering. I saw, however, enough to realise more than otherwise would have been possible of the sorrow and suffering which spring from war, and to be converted into an upholder of peace at *almost* any price.

Mrs. Butler to her Daughter.

Wantage Vicarage, Nov 16 [1870].

. . . Imagine a telegram at 2 P.M. yesterday from Colonel Loyd Lindsay to your father with an urgent request for him to go out to Germany and look after the wants of the 300,000 French prisoners of war there, followed up this morning by a long letter with many most interesting enclosures from German people (of highest class) praying the Society to help at once to keep these unhappy men and officers from perishing by cold and want. The Government act most liberally, but they cannot get beyond what are called necessaries of life in the way of food, nor give clothes and comforts and help in sickness. The Queen of Prussia is most anxious in the matter, and one of the letters was in fact written at her desire. But it is as much as her place is worth to let Bismarck know of her asking *English* to help *French*. He hates us. So don't betray Her Majesty! Last night the thing seemed impossible, and your father wrote a line to Col. Lindsay to that effect; specially till after Confirmation this day three weeks. But the letters were fearfully constraining. Colonel Lindsay would go himself (as organiser, etc.), but that he cannot be spared from the work at home. He pitches upon your father as *the* man for the case. As he justly says, "A man may live a long life and never have such a chance again of serving his fellow creatures." . . .

However, the parochial difficulties were found to be insurmountable, and with deepest regret on the Vicar's part, he declined the post.

[1] His senior Curate.

CHAPTER IX.

CLOSE OF THE WANTAGE LIFE.

THE year 1872 witnessed the first break in his parochial life. Up to this time he had been singularly free from serious illness, and although leading a life of constant hard work and rigid self-denial, he had never as yet broken down. But there were not wanting symptoms of a change, and those who watched him knew that his constitution, however hardy and vigorous it might be, could not stand the long-continued strain with impunity. He was undoubtedly on the brink of an illness when an accident abruptly put a stop to his work. On the 24th July he was thrown out of his pony carriage in Wantage, and received a serious injury to the spine, the effects of which he felt to the end of his life. He had to lie on his back for six months, and the doctors afterwards said that this enforced rest was probably, humanly speaking, the saving of his life, or at least the means of averting a complete break-down of the nervous system. The following letter, written by him from his sick-bed, is eminently characteristic :

To the Editor of the "Reading Mercury."

Sir,—In your account of the accident which befell me on Wednesday last I am said "to have jumped, or been thrown out" of the carriage in which I was. Permit me to say I was thrown out, and on no consideration would I have jumped out; and, lying here helpless, I am glad to have the opportunity of doing good to my fellow-creatures by pointing to my own case as an advantage of the former course. At the place where I fell, a few pounds more impetus, just that which a spring would have given, would have rendered my injuries very serious, if not fatal; whereas now, by proper care, and I need not add, by the mercy of God, I trust in no very long time to be able to return to my duties with "mens sana in corpore sano."

Wantage Vicarage, July 27th, 1872.

A little later he was moved to Brighton, and thence wrote:

W. J. B. to Mrs. Wilkins.[1]

Lee House, Brighton, Oct. 16, 1872.

My dear Caroline,—If loving words could mend one's bones, I ought, after your kind and welcome letter of this morning, to be quite strong and well. It gave me great pleasure to read it, and to hear about James, and the children, and yourself, and the parish generally.

You want to know how I am and what I can do. I am very much better in my general health, but my back is not right. The doctor here has discovered that one of the joints of the spine is forced, by the violence of the blow which I received from the back of the carriage, slightly out of its place. This is the cause of my not improving; and unless it can be put right the consequences will be serious. He speaks however very confidently of curing me in about three months. Meanwhile I have to lie on a board from morning till night, and I assure you that I am becoming quite used to it. You know that I always was a lazy man, and now I can indulge myself.

[1] The daughter and wife of Wantage tradesmen, who had been brought up under the Vicar's teaching, and for whom he always felt a warm friendship.

I get up to breakfast with Mrs. Butler, take a quarter of an hour's walk in the garden, lie on my board till luncheon time, and then have a drive for a couple of hours (generally along the cliff by the seaside), then to my board again. I am never allowed to *sit*, except at meals; and thus I have to hold this paper on which I write over my head, and write *up* instead of *down*, which is rather tiring work. . . . Now, I think, I have told you all. I need not say to you how much you are all in my thoughts and prayers. I am not sorry to be obliged to [remember?] that all real good work is the work of God Himself, though He makes use in His wisdom of poor weak sinful men like me, and He can and will carry it on (now that I am disabled) by His own almighty power. I am most thankful to have such good [accounts?] of everything. . . .—Your faithful friend and pastor,   WILLIAM BUTLER.

He returned to Wantage on January 24th, 1873, and gradually resumed the full swing of work, though he felt more and more that the burden of the parish was overtaxing his strength; and he foresaw that a time was coming when it must be laid down. Yet the "Parish Journal" shows no signs of abated vigour or weakened interest. The classes, the close inspection of the school, the assiduous visiting of the parishioners, all went on as in the years before the accident; while the growth of the Sisterhood brought with it greatly increased work for its founder and guide.

W. J. B. TO REV. CANON LIDDON.

WANTAGE VICARAGE, May 17, 1873.

In the stupidity of my nature I had not perceived that the Sunday on which you kindly wish me to preach at St. Paul's is the *last* Sunday in Advent. Would it be possible to commute it? The second or third Sunday would suit me very well. But I do not like, if it can be avoided, to omit my annual shout at the people here about keeping Christmas rightly. Our folk need continued prodding to keep them up to the mark. I have read the debate in Convocation on confession, and I think that it might have been worse. The article in the *Times* is characteristically unfair, and does not honestly represent what took place. As for stopping the use of confession, that is impossible. It is now, like Christianity in the early days, in the forum and everywhere, and sooner or later, the bishops will be forced to admit this. . . . When people like —— and —— go to confession, practically the game is won. . . .

Bishop Mackarness had made him an Honorary Canon of Christ Church in 1872, a preferment which he valued very highly, and on 21st February, 1874, he received the first public token of the appreciation with which he was regarded by the clergy of the diocese. He was elected Proctor in Convocation. When asked if he would stand, he stipulated that he should not have personally to canvass any of his clerical brethren. The Rev. W. G. Sawyer, Vicar of Taplow, has given an account of the circumstances of the election :

It may be interesting to record the circumstances under which the Vicar, as we always loved to call him, was elected as Proctor to Convocation for the diocese of Oxford. His election was a cause of much pleasure to him, for two reasons, viz., because it opened out to him a new field of usefulness, and also because election to Convocation is the only public way in which the clergy of a diocese can show their regard for one of their number. It having been announced that Dr. Leighton, Warden of All Souls, did not intend to offer himself for re-election as Proctor, the Rev. Edward Elton, then vicar of Wheatley, now rector of Sherington, wrote to me as an old Wantage curate, asking what I thought about Butler being put forward as a candidate for the vacant Proctorship. "This step Mr. Elton took, not as being an intimate friend of the

Vicar of Wantage, but under a deep and pressing sense of
the work he was doing at Wantage." (These are Mr. Elton's
own words.) The idea pleased me very much, and I felt that
if we could elect Butler it would show our appreciation of
what he had done, and that it would be a great gain to the
diocese. Mr. Elton and I talked the matter over, and it was
agreed between us that I should write to a number of representative men in different parts of the diocese, asking whether
they would be disposed to support the Vicar of Wantage if
he was proposed. It was fully recognised from the first that
he would not be elected without a contest; for there still
existed at that time, what now seems to us so strange, the
idea that Butler was a man of extreme opinions, and that
notwithstanding his great work at Wantage—which those who
looked at it from the outside could not understand—he was
not to be trusted as an English Churchman. This is a very
curious fact. We soon found that if he was proposed, he
would be largely supported. Meeting Bishop Mackarness I
told him what we meant to do; his answer was, "then you
will have a fight," to which I replied, "we know that, but
we do not mind." A large committee was formed to promote
Butler's election, of which Rev. W. W. Jones, Fellow of St.
John's (now Metropolitan of Capetown), the late Canon
Freeling, Fellow of Merton (who succeeded Butler as Proctor),
and myself, were the secretaries. Our meetings were held in
Mr. Jones' rooms at St. John's, and the diocese was thoroughly
canvassed. We soon found that a storm was rising, and Mr.
Burgon, Fellow of Oriel, and Vicar of St. Mary's, Oxford (afterwards Dean of Chichester), was proposed as a candidate in
opposition to Butler. Many hard things were said, and there
was considerable excitement in the diocese. On the morning
of the election Mr. Burgon's committee made the proposal
that both candidates should be withdrawn, and that all should
unite in supporting Rev. A. P. Purey Cust, Vicar of St. Mary's,
Reading (now Dean of York). Some of us felt that hard
and unfair things had been said about Butler, and we refused
to withdraw his name. There was a very large meeting of
the clergy of the diocese in the Sheldonian Theatre at Oxford
on the day of the election. Canon Charles Lloyd was re-elected
unanimously, and Butler was proposed by Mr. Ridley, Rector of

Hambledon, and seconded by Mr. Clutterbuck, Vicar of Long Wittenham. He was elected by a very substantial majority. Mr. Burgon wrote a very strong and angry letter to the *Times*, complaining that Butler had been put forward in a hasty way, and that the diocese was taken by surprise; but the letter was written in complete ignorance of the true state of things.

It is interesting to bear in mind that Butler had been only a short time in Convocation when there was a great change in the opinions of his opponents. He very soon won their confidence, as he did of all those who really knew him; and I well remember his telling me that he had lately met one, well known to both of us, who had opposed his election more strongly than perhaps any one in the diocese, who said, "So far as I am concerned you will never be opposed again, and you may remain Proctor as long as you like."

REV. CANON LIDDON TO W. J. B.

CHRIST CHURCH, OXFORD, February 21, 1874.

I was sorry to miss you when you called at my rooms this morning. But, instead of going out for a walk, I went to the Sheldonian Theatre, and heard all the proceedings there this afternoon.[1] And the result gave me more pleasure than I can well say, alike on public and private grounds. As the schoolmen would say, it was, both positively and negatively, good. . . . And positively, because, not to add to all that was said in the theatre to-day of a more delicate character, such an independent public interest as this is what you have long seemed, without seeking, to want as the complement and crown to your work; and it will, I hope and expect, open the way to other things,—at any rate to opportunities for influencing the public action of the Church, which will be reassuring to persons like myself who watch the proceedings of Convocation with some anxiety. And it will be, I hope, not other than welcome to you.

Sometimes too, I trust, that your London duties may coincide with my times of residence, and that we may get the incidental advantage, if not of entertaining, at any rate of seeing you more frequently than has been the case in the last few years. . . .

[1] The election of the Proctors in Convocation for the diocese.

I had almost forgotten to thank you for my share of the great obligation which the D. and C. of St. Paul's has incurred by your recent mission work in the cathedral.   May God bless it to many souls !

W. J. B. TO REV. W. G. SAWYER.

WANTAGE VICARAGE, March 1, 1874.

I do not feel as if I had half thanked you for all your great kindness, and hard work on my behalf.   I can honestly say that I value your affection, and that of so many others, *far* more than the actual success which came of it.   I believe that if I had foreseen how very serious a matter it would become, I should not have ventured to allow myself to be put in nomination.   If we had been beaten, I have little doubt that we should have had leading articles on the text in more than one newspaper.   They would have represented it as a sign of the inherent soundness of the Church, shown in the spewing forth of an obnoxious and dangerous faction.   It was, beyond all comparison, the most important of the Proctorial elections.   What we have got to fight for is liberty and recognition.   The appointment of men like Liddon and King to high positions is one great step towards this, and the Oxford election for Proctors is another. . . . Now I hope to be able to be of a little service in the work of reforming Convocation and making it what it ought to be, of real value to the Church.   Strange to say, so long ago as 1841 I had set my heart to see Convocation once more in action.   I have a note in one of my books on the subject written at that time.   It seemed to me that a Church without a governing body must get into messes, and Convocation seemed the natural Church council.   I got what information I could from Vincent's father, who was Chapter clerk to Westminster.   Then came the Bishop of Oxford's vigorous and wily efforts to resuscitate it ; and now the 'sleeping beauty' is awake, and needs only to be taught how to move. I hope that the enemy will now be quiet, and leave me in peace. . . .

W. J. B. TO REV. E. ELTON.

WANTAGE VICARAGE, March 9, 1874.

MY DEAR MR. ELTON,—I have been so much occupied since Feb. 21 that I have been unable before this to write to you to

thank you for the kindness you have shown me, and the trouble
which you took in my behalf in regard to the election of Proctors.
I should certainly not have suggested my own name for such an
office, nor did I in the least expect to be elected. And this
makes me feel the more beholden to those who were good
enough to think well of me, and earnest enough to carry the
matter to a successful issue. I trust with all my heart that
I may not disappoint you. At present it seems to me that there
is little to be done until Convocation can be placed on a sounder
footing and made more really representative, and therefore more
trusted by both clergy and laity. I mean, therefore, to keep as
much as possible out of the somnolent nebulous debates with
which the columns of *The Guardian* teem, and to try to work
towards reform. . . .

Among the Dogmersfield and Hursley circle of
friends was Miss Charlotte Yonge, who soon became
a friend of their friends at Wantage. Letters passed
occasionally between her and the Vicar.

W. J. B. to Miss C. M. Yonge.

Lee House, Brighton, Aug. 16, 1870.

My dear Charlotte,—Emma some time since asked me
some question in your behalf connected with Tau in Ezekiel. I
was very busy then, and I fear did not quite grasp the point
of it. Since I have been here I have looked up all that I
believe is to be said on the subject, and it amounts to this.
The fathers almost universally accept the Tau as the sign of the
Cross, foreshadowing, as the Paschal Lamb foreshadowed the Lamb
of God, the Cross itself. The present ת or Tau is, they say, not
the original form of the letter. Before the time of Ezra the
form of it was T, *i.e.* the *Greek* Tau and the Latin also. Some
Syrian versions actually translate "Mark with the Cross." Of
course, Rev. vii. 3, etc., is the exact counterpart to Ezek. ix. It
is maintained by Cornelius à Lapide that T was marked in the
heart of the god Serapis as a sign denoting future life. Various
other explanations have been given—that it is the first letter of
תִּחְיֶה "thou shalt live," or תָּם "innocent," etc., but it seems to

me that the other is right. I am here till Thursday with my
mother and sister, *en route* to Dauphiné, i.e. I, not they. I have
never seen La Grande Chartreuse, and now that I am baulked of
Ober Ammergau, I thought that I could pick up something there.
However, this terrible war makes movements of this kind
uncertain, and I hardly know what will become of me for the
next three weeks. How strange it is to have so wonderful a
duel at one's doors, and to feel so utterly careless as to which
prevails ! Of course, abstractedly, one would wish well to
France ; but the Secret Treaty, and the insufficiency of the cause
of war, neutralise this feeling in this present instance. But the
tremendous probable issues take away one's breath. One can
but gaze and pray, as in some frightful storm. . . . Have
you read the life of Père Besson ?

Miss Yonge gives her impressions of Wantage
and its Vicar :

I had heard much about Wantage before I saw it, from the
inhabitants of Dogmersfield Rectory, where both Mr. and Mrs.
Butler had been almost like a son and daughter. There is a
sermon of Newman's on St. Ambrose and his influence on St.
Augustine, showing how many of the greatest and most active
workers have felt the influence of quiet, hidden saints ; and
what the Rev. Charles Dyson, his wife, and his sister Mary
Anne, were to many, and especially to their curates, might be
cited as an instance.

Owing to bad health, there was an air of venerable age about
Mr. Dyson even at Oxford, for it was a joke that the first time
they met, when Mr. Keble had just gained his scholarship at
Corpus at fourteen, Mr. Dyson thought, "Here are boys coming
in to spoil all our comfort"; and Mr. Keble thought, "Here
is one of the old dons I have heard of." But there was soon
an intensely warm friendship between them, and likewise with
the future judge, John Taylor Coleridge ; and the wisdom of
Mr. Dyson was always referred to, as in course of time the
brilliant appreciation, and the constant sympathy and good
sense of Mrs. and Miss Dyson.

The latter had a most remarkable mixture of enthusiastic
idealism and practical sense ; and in the early days of Dogmersfield Rectory, when all was fresh and they were just entering

on the work of a country parish, so small in population as to
be readily workable, and with a lady of the manor who was
a model landlord after the notions of those times, there was
much that was bright and helpful. The Tracts for the Times
were disseminating principles, and accounts of their influence
came in; while work in the same direction was done by zeal-
ously instructing the cottage children and by writing, among a
conclave of friends, a number of books adapted for their use,
and those of young people of the higher class. Some of the
earlier volumes of the *Magazine for the Young* thoroughly reflect
the parish treatment, and the enjoyment of it, shared by the
future Mrs. Butler and her sister. Among these friends the
translations from Fouqué were undertaken, Sintram, translated
by Mrs. Butler, being a book that has told deeply on many
minds. I think Mr. Butler wrote a review of these and of
Fouqué's life in the *British Critic*, or *Christian Remembrancer*.

Miss Dyson used to relate how the offer of Wantage was
accepted with the wish that Mr. Butler could find a wise old
curate, not to work, but to advise. Not that his vigorous nature
needed direction or stimulus. It was the time of fresh renova-
tion in the Church, and of experiments. This is not the place
to tell how they were begun. When I first knew Wantage the
principal improvements were already established, and nothing
struck me so much as the zest, life, and spirit which pervaded
everything. The early service, the merry breakfast, the schools,
the parish visiting, the mid-day dinner with the curates, the
various claims on the afternoon, the classes (for pupil teachers,
for communicants, male or female on different days), the evening visits to parishioners, so as to see the men or boys; the
evensong, with a sermon twice a week; all concluded by a
supper as lively as the former meals had been; all came in
quick succession, and there was something brilliant and sometimes quaint about all.

Once I had the pleasure of listening to a lesson to the pupil
teachers. They were numerous, and their class was a regular
preparation for Training Colleges, and, as diocesan examinations
and syllabuses had not begun, a teacher had more choice of
subjects. This lesson was on the last chapter of the Epistle
to the Philippians, and I remember especially the dwelling on
the word crown in its distinctive meaning as the crown of

achievement, not the diadem of royalty. Also the moral deduced
from the message to Euodias and Syntyche of the harm good
women do to a holy cause by disagreement. The beginning of
his teaching of these girls was the enforcing of undivided attention, and of good hand-writing. 'The Vicar' could be very
sharp where these failed—'fainéant' spirits fainted, strong ones
rose into enthusiastic affection and energetic work, and admirable
persons were the result.

Once too, as I came down stairs, the study door was open,
and I had a glimpse of the elder men's communicant class. They
were fine old country men's heads, and I told the Vicar that they
looked like Conscript Fathers, which amused him very much.

The schools were in admirable order, from the infants upwards,
and thoroughly well taught and grounded in religious subjects as
well as in secular. But Mr. Butler laid great stress on the
work upon growing lads and lasses, holding that the great matter
was to impress them and keep them in hand, at a time when
their characters were forming and their experience beginning.

The vicarage is before my mind—the mullioned windows of
the dining-room, festooned with creepers; a shady walk leading to the churchyard, bordered with limes, and skirting a lawn.
It was a place of general hospitality for gentle and for
simple, where endless deep discussions and many merry jokes
might go on among old and young, specially after supper when
the day's work was done, and its humours could be related. For
playfulness was a great element in the household, and Miss
Dyson, who loved it well, used to say that Mrs. Butler's strong
sense of the ridiculous[1] had been a great safeguard against eccen-
tricities of ritual, when so much was experimental and curates
were hot-headed and theoretical.

There certainly was an uncompromising contempt of nonsense,
and therewith of unreal sentiment; and there were some who
could not stand the ordeal of irony. The atmosphere was a
good deal like a brisk frosty morning, excellent and enjoyable
to the active and energetic, but a severe test to the weaker,
or to those who thought charity akin to indifference to evil.
Simple folly was borne with, humbug never tolerated.

Bishop Samuel Wilberforce once said (in joke) that at Wantage
there was no rest day or night. Everything was done with

---

[1] Inherited doubtless with her Canning blood.

full activity by day, and at night first there were conversations lasting into the small hours, and then the doves cooed and the clock chimed!

All was however delightful to those in high health and high spirits. One visit I remember, made memorable by an expedition to Fairford to see the marvellous windows with which Mr. Keble grew up, and his old home, with the rooks about which he wrote a poem for his little nephew (in *Miscellaneous Poems*). It was a drive, interesting and delightful in all ways. Another time we went to Dorchester, the Oxfordshire Dorchester, with the writhing Templar on his tomb, and the Jesse window in solid stone, not merely glass. Also there was a picnic to what was called Scutchamer Nob (supposed to be King Cwichelm's knoll), a round Berkshire mound surmounting other hills, near the supposed site of Alfred's battle of Ethandune. Near at hand was the White Horse, a very Saxon specimen of drawing indeed, all legs upon a slope; but whose scouring in Alfred's tenth centenary is celebrated by 'Tom Hughes,' and commemorated by the Wantage Grammar School. There too we saw Wayland Smith's cave, a disappointment, since it is only a cromlech in a copse, not at all favourable for Tressilian's adventures with Flibbertigibbet.

All these were times of most interesting conversations, I wish I could remember them minutely. One, I know, was on the Sabbatarian question, when Mr. Butler was more tolerant of selling sweets on Sunday than I expected. I remember his saying he had tried to persuade an old woman that it was not wrong, because he found that it kept her from Holy Communion, as she would not give it up, though her conscience went against it. He said he had grown up to consider a sweet or cake a legitimate Sunday treat, when at school at Westminster. I did not and cannot agree.

We were quite agreed in disliking the system of sending Sisters out on a "Quête." It is more blessed to give than to receive, but there is no blessing on begging. The Wantage Sisters have never done it, yet they have thriven. This is all that I clearly recollect. There were other meetings, and especially one when he came to us for Mr. Keble's funeral. He was full of two things—the dangers of *Ecce Homo*, and the beauty of *Gerontius*. He *would* read to us

T

the most undesirable bits of the former; my mother said on the principle of "come and smell this, it is so horrid." But he advised me not to read it for the sake of others, or any such books.

Gerontius he read us likewise, with exceeding admiration; but after we had stood at that grave, with the celandines sparkling in the sunshine on the bank, while the twenty-third Psalm was sung, "I felt," he said, "as if it were all swept away."

A few more letters exchanged with Dr. Liddon bring the correspondence of the Wantage life to an end.

REV. CANON LIDDON TO W. J. B.

CHRIST CHURCH, OXFORD, Monday, March 20, [1876].

Ever since the news of Bishop Milman's[1] death reached us, I have been thinking how very sorely it *must* press upon *you*. When I first became curate of Wantage, in Jan. 1853, I remember your saying out in the garden, "There *is* one man of genius in this neighbourhood, Milman of Lambourne; we must go over and see him." We did go, and drove back at night by moonlight; and those first impressions, deepened and enriched as they were by subsequent contact with him, have been a mental treasure of mine ever since. I owe them really, as so much else, to you; and my own feeling at his removal from this earthly scene must be a sort of faint reflection, I know, of yours. And yet what an event it really is! And how quietly the world takes it—except a friend here and there—just as if nothing very particular had happened at all!

No person now left in the high places of the Church, as it seems to me, combined so much, and combined it so well as he did. To begin at the bottom, he was a philologist and a philosopher—two minds not often found in one, and both so necessary for India! Then he was a man of steady adherence to principle, yet of immense consideration for others—even *The Record*, I see, has a respectful word for him on this score. Then while he was a thorough Ecclesiastic, or Christian in Holy Orders who believes his creed and work to be of the *first* im-

[1] Bishop of Calcutta; died March 15, 1876.

portance, he knew enough of mankind at large to do them justice.

I cannot say how much I had looked forward to the privilege of seeing him again. W. H. Milman says that they were to have arrived in England on May 24. Poor Miss Milman! what she will do out there alone! and with all the anxieties which must attend and follow *his* death, I cannot think. . . . I follow the *texts* of your Lent addresses each day : they are here in my study hanging up, and do me good, as well as the Wantage people.

W. J. B. TO REV. CANON LIDDON.

WANTAGE VICARAGE, January 2, 1877.

. . . I thought on Sunday of your kind wish that I should preach at St. Paul's that night, and grumbled in my mind at the shortness of the tether which the work of a place like this allows. But I was well rewarded and rebuked on Monday, when we had 333 communicants, of whom 230 came to church at 4.30 A.M. I am very thankful to see that the daily Sacrifice of the Church is once more offered in St. Paul's. It cannot, I think, fail to bring a blessing on all the dwellers in London, perhaps even on others to whom the Cathedral of London seems, though technically it is not, the metropolitan church.

We are all (D.G.) well and cheerful. The change from strength and vigour to old age and decrepitude, which I suppose must come in course of time, has not fallen yet on our household. . . .

REV. CANON LIDDON TO W. J. B.

KILCOMAN, July 13, 1877.

I must write one line to say how grateful I (with many others, no doubt) am to you for what you said in Convocation on the subject of confession. Even at a time of excitement like this your words cannot fail to do a great deal of good, and this notwithstanding ——'s invidious comments upon them. ——, however, is not likely to harm you much ; he is a master of popular platitudes, but not a man to move mountains whether for good or evil. How odd it is that so many sensible people, who know nothing whatever about confession from a personal experience, yet can make the strongest statements about it on purely *a priori* grounds. In any other subject-matter they would be the first to feel the absurdity of such a proceeding; but *un*-theological passion, disguised under the form of zeal for the purity and simplicity of religion, is capable of a good deal that is absurd or worse. . . .

REV. CANON LIDDON TO W. J. B.

3 AMEN COURT, E.C., August 1, 1877.

. . . I saw an account of the Wantage festivities[1] in the papers, and read them, you may be sure, with great interest. If you were an Italian, what an inscription you would put up to commemorate the Prince's visit! But, as you are an Englishman, you will probably do nothing of the kind, though these mementos have their use for those who come after us. . . .

In 1880 his parochial life ended. He had gone abroad in August for his annual holiday, and, as his custom was, left his letters to accumulate during his absence. In the heap that lay at Wantage was one that would materially change his life. It was an offer from Mr. Gladstone of a canonry in Worcester Cathedral. Some three weeks passed, and no answer being received by the Premier, the curates were communicated with; the letter was found and opened, and its contents were telegraphed to the Vicar in Tyrol. He returned at once to England, and went to Worcester to see the place and make the necessary inquiries about the canonry, which had been previously held by a personal friend of his, Richard Seymour.

There were two points which needed settling before he could make up his mind to accept the

[1] When the Prince and Princess of Wales came to Wantage to unveil a statue of King Alfred, which was set up in the market-place by Sir Robert Loyd Lindsay, now Lord Wantage.

preferment. He could not endure the thought of a severance of his connexion with the Wantage sisterhood, and he was determined not to alter what had been his practice during the whole of his clerical life in using the eastward position in celebrating the Holy Communion. Finding there was no difficulty on these points, he accepted the canonry. These letters show what his feeling had been in making the decision to leave his old home.

W. J. B. TO ———.

Sept. 3, 1880.

Mr. Gladstone has offered me the vacant canonry of Worcester. In a worldly point of view it is a 'good thing.' But I cannot accept it without first ascertaining how far it would accord with my present work. I received a telegraph message at Innsbruck, and I wrote to Mr. G. to that effect. It is very kind of him to offer me the first piece of real preferment that has fallen into his hands, considering that he cannot rank me among his supporters.

W. J. B. TO ———.

Sept. 8, 1880.

The matter is all settled. I found that I could hold the canonry without giving up the work of the Sisters and of the diocese, though eventually I must resign the parish and with it of course the vicarage, which I love so much and which so exactly meets my needs. At Worcester there is a large house, much too large, and very ugly though comfortable, needing more servants and state, etc. But all doubtless will shape itself.

W. J. B. TO REV. W. G. SAWYER.

WANTAGE VICARAGE, Sept. 14, 1880.

Thank you very heartily for all your loving words and deeds. I know well that I have no truer friend than you. Nothing

ever more surprised me than the offer of this canonry. I neither
sought it nor cared for it. When I was elected Proctor for the
diocese, owing to your kind and vigorous exertions, I felt that I
had attained an honour of the most heart-satisfying kind. To
be elected by one's fellows—fastidious and critical as the clergy
are—seemed to me enough to gratify all one's ambition. And
with that I simply hoped to hold on as long as I had power to do
justice to such a charge. I did hope eventually to resign
Wantage, and to say, ' Pauperiem sine dote quaero.' Now
however in this canonry I have what enables me to do this
'handsomely.' People will understand that it is impossible to
hold a parish which makes such a demand on one's powers,
together with an office which necessitates three months' absence
yearly. While at the same time I hope to live here—at first at
' The Mead,' then wherever I can—and watch over the Sisters,
and take such part as I have hitherto taken in the general work
of the diocese. This is what the Bishop wishes, and what falls
in with my own instincts. Enough about myself. .   .   .

W. J. B. TO MRS. WILKINS.

LEE HOUSE, BRIGHTON, Jan. 9, 1881.

.   .   . Believe me, that nothing but a clear perception that
this change will in the long run be the best for all could have
induced me to make it. It is true that I might have gone
on for some time longer, but then I might have broken down
just when it would have been of all importance to be well and
strong. .   .   . Moreover, it is to be remembered that life
does not last for ever. We must all try to look forward a little
to that blessed time when there shall be no more separation,
but all shall be one and together in the Presence of our
blessed Lord. .   .   .

Naturally the first thing that occupied his
thoughts was the appointment of his successor. He
could not have left Wantage with any happiness
had he not been assured that the vicar who came
after him would carry on his work in the same spirit
and on the same lines. Fortunately the appoint-

ment of his friend and former curate, T. H. Archer Houblon, then Rector of Peasemore, completely set his mind at rest on this subject.

He had always disliked testimonials,[1] but it was impossible for him, after such a life and work, to leave his parish without many tokens of the love and esteem of his people. He was also greatly touched and pleased by the gift of some carved oak book-cases from his former curates, made for his new study at Worcester ; and a letter from Mrs. Butler to the Rev. W. G. Sawyer tells how the idea was conceived and carried out.

WANTAGE VICARAGE, Dec. 19, 1880.

Thank you for your letter, and for the confidence reposed in me. Nothing could be better than *bookcases* for the dear kind old-Curates' offering. Especially as Henry Houblon 'takes' to those that line the study here. If the cases did not swallow up all the money (which *I* esteem a most generously large amount), then some books might be added. Of course there are difficulties in the way of selection, but I think that if you will trust to me to negotiate the affair, with the help of Lady Alwyne Compton—whose taste, cleverness, and leisure are always at her friends' disposal—and of an ingenious man in old oak, named Jeff, we might manage to have the right sort of book-cases erected and planted, unbeknown to the Vicar. The one thing I deprecate is the money being handed over bodily to him, not so much that he would lose it ! but because it would be unpoetical, and he would be hurt and pained instead of having his heart so touched and made happy by the constant loyal affection of his much loved fellow-labourers. It quite made my heart bound, when I was recalling all the old names with the Houblons, and being reminded that in that long list there was

---

[1] He once made an epitaph on himself :

"Willing, but weak and witless, one lies here
Who died without a ' teapot ' or a tear !"

not one but was doing good and acceptable service to our dear mother the Church of England. If you and the rest approve, then I will set to work by letter, and circumvent the Vicar's orders to his carpenter. We do not now expect to be at Worcester until the 12th January, but we shall turn out from here the previous week. It is very trying to break up one's home of thirty-four years standing, and there is a deal to be done.

Some years later, in March, 1885, when, owing to a fall at St. Giles's Vicarage, Reading, which renewed the old trouble in his back, he was obliged to lie quiet for a time, he refers to this gift in lines which portray the characters of his former fellow-workers. The little poem was privately printed, and sent to those old friends who formed its subject. A few extracts are given.

The motto to the poem is :

Μὴ ἀλλάξῃς φίλον ἀδιαφόρου, μηδ' ἀδελφὸν
γνήσιον ἐν χρυσίῳ Σουφείρ.
σοφία Σειράχ.
Z'. ιη.

It begins :

Dear Brothers and old Comrades, who the fight
Have fought with me of faith, in that great fray
'Twixt ill and good, death, life, the fiend and God,
Dear friends of many a year, I love to dwell
On days past by, when to the little child,
Or aged man just tottering to the grave,
Or widow in her woe, or youth, or maid,
Or suffering saint, or hardened sinner's heart,
Or those who hardly live by parish dole,
In school or church, or busy tradesman's house,
In poor man's cot, or field, or market place,
We strove, God helping us, to teach His Word.
And now I sit and muse, while each and all
Those well-remembered names, for ever stamped

On that their kindly and most welcome gift,
Holding what next I love, my store of books,
The gleanings of a life-time, bring to mind
Those well-remembered faces, voices, forms.

The verses proceed to describe in a few lines for each, the characters of those who formed the long line of Wantage curates. Among them was A. H. Mackonochie, 1852 :

Next I see one with countenance serene,
And kindly smile, and firm resolving brow,
Whose single aim has been the Church's weal,
And ever to resist man's alien law.
Dear friend! fain would I that thy lot were cast
In less perturbèd waters, where thy love
And self-forgetful zeal and earnest word
Had found free course for that thy heart's desire,
The priest's best work, the winning souls for God.

Then follows H. P. Liddon, 1853 :

Here too is he, in word, in lore unmatched,
True courtier of the Queen of Sciences,
The learned theologian, firm and strong
To hold the faith once given to the saints,
Yet gentle as a child, whose sparkling wit
And playful humour, brightening argument,
Refutes gainsayers, yet leaves no wound behind.

Next :

two brothers, one whose joy has been
The weird agaric and the hidden lines
Of rock and fossil to investigate.
The other, vigorous, hearty, truest friend ;
Of hirsute aspect, yet of gentlest heart,
Much to be cherished, worthy there to dwell
Where souls need strong, and wise, and tender guide.

The late Father O'Neill, who came to Wantage in 1864,[1] is thus described :

[1] See Chapter VI., p. 175.

> And here is one most faithful, blunt in tone,
> No smooth-tongued man-observer, knowing naught
> Save Christ and Him the crucified, and those
> For whom Christ died, offering in distant land,
> 'Mid strange and dusky faces, all he had,
> Till martyr-like at length his life he gave.

So he goes through the long list, lightly touching the characteristics of each with a loving hand, till the conclusion is reached :

> And thus, as when some noble drama done,
> The last act finished, voices hushed and still,
> They who so well have wrought, together stand
> Just for one lingering moment, side by side,
> While they who gaze are filled with gratitude
> For all they have seen and heard—and solace sweet
> Which they have tasted while the play went on ;
> So I, recalling four-and-thirty years,
> Those strangely mingled days of joy and woe,
> Of disappointment, and of good success,
> Of efforts—some rewarded, some in vain—
> Of steady growth amidst anxieties,
> Of seed oft sown in tears, then reaped in joy,
> Ever have these before me, comrades true,
> And lift up thankful heart and voice to Him
> Who made us all of one mind in one house.

In the last entries he wrote in the " Parish Journal," he said his farewell to his Wantage life.

Dec. 31, 1880.—Thus then ends the last, or thirty-fourth, year of the present vicar's incumbency of Wantage. In looking back to the days gone by, there is indeed the deepest cause for thankfulness. God has indeed prospered and blessed this work, giving " beauty for ashes, the oil of joy for mourning, the garment of praise for the spirit of heaviness"; for a miserable unedifying service the sweet singing of the choir ; for a church, dirty, disfigured, unchristian, our present beautiful House of God ; for communicants, scarcely one in 150, 600 ; for schools not worthy of the name, where some 24 boys and 12 girls were educated, the only *general* school of the parish—build-ings, and teachers watching over 600 children, besides the Grammar school revived in better character than ever before, and St. Mary's school where other classes than the poorest are admirably taught and trained ; and then lastly, the Community of Sisters, whose very presence brings blessings with it. Nor must we pass by St. Michael's on the Downs, nor our little chapel at Charlton, nor our mission room in Grove Street, all of which are exercising the happiest and most blessed influence. These are solid blessings such as cannot well be marred. The machinery is fairly sufficient. It will need only constant use. The tone of the parish—very different from that which I remem-ber in days gone by, is kindly, reasonable, trusting. Prejudices have departed. Church teaching has been proved and accepted.

Thursday, the Epiphany, Jan. 6, 1881.—On this day William John Butler, Vicar of Wantage for upwards of thirty-four years, left his much-loved flock and home to enter on the duties of Canon of Worcester. May God forgive him his many short-comings, failures, neglects, and in His mercy find a place for him at the feet of faithful pastors of His sheep.

He took leave of his parishioners in this letter :

WANTAGE VICARAGE, December 3rd, 1880.

MY DEAR FRIENDS AND PARISHIONERS,—After having lived among you for the long space of thirty-four years in true affection and intimacy, I feel that I cannot withdraw from a connexion so deeply loved and cherished without a word of explanation. I do not, need I say it, wish to leave Wantage—on the contrary, I am well aware that I cannot possibly look to days happier and more full of blessings than those which I have spent among you, still less again to form friendships like those in which I now so greatly rejoice, some of those who have grown up under my eye and care to manhood and womanhood, whom I have had the privilege of preparing for the holy Rites of the Church, others of those who for many a long year have wrought with me and maintained the cause of Christ and His Church, others again in whose homes I never fail to enter as a kindly-welcomed guest. Nor can I forget that in our church-yard lie some of those who are most dear and near to my heart. In truth, I believe that almost nothing would have induced me to resign this charge, save a conviction that my resignation at this time is the best for all. For some years past I have felt that the charge of a large and important parish like this of Wantage is more than I can happily compass. Hitherto, I thank God, I have been able, I think, fairly to meet the many demands on my time and strength—but it is impossible for me not to be aware that, like all others, I must look to old age and infirmity as years roll on.

When then it pleased Her Majesty the Queen to permit a Canonry of a Cathedral Church to be offered to me, I could not but look upon this as an opportunity not to be rejected of seeing the parish of Wantage placed—as I trusted—in the hands of a younger man, who, it might be reasonably hoped, would carry on that work to which most freely and gladly I have devoted all the best years of my life.

Such a one, I rejoice to think, has been designated as my successor—the result, I cannot doubt, of many earnest prayers—one whom all know well, and have already learnt to respect—in whose hands I can trust all, without one shadow of doubt or anxiety.

For myself I can scarcely look forward. I know of a certainty that in the ordinary course of nature I cannot be very long either at Worcester or anywhere else. I trust however that I may be enabled, even in the evening of life, to do some little work for God's glory, before that "night cometh when no man can work": and for this I would earnestly ask your prayers. I would ask you to pray both for me and for him who is about to succeed me, that we may each do our duty honestly and faithfully in our new spheres of service in the Lord's Vineyard. I need not add that, so long as I live, the welfare and interests of this parish will always be most dear to my heart.

Earnestly praying that God's blessing may ever rest upon you, I am, my dear friends and parishioners, your very loving pastor,   WILLIAM BUTLER.

CHAPTER X.

WORCESTER.

WHILE his house at Worcester was getting ready, the new Canon and his family stayed at the Deanery, and there laid the foundations of the closest friendship of his later life :

You ask me to write, says Lady Alwyne Compton, what I can remember of your father, but it is very difficult. It seems as if one should have his vigour to describe him. He must have been nearly sixty when I saw him first, and yet he was full of boyish life and energy, with the keenest interest and enjoyment in everything, and the warmest sympathy for all around him. I never knew any one to whom religion was more the well-spring of his life, that kept it always fresh. 'The breath of daily prayer and praise sanctified his noble mind.' He was vehement, yet very gentle ; stern, yet brimming over with sympathy.

I first saw him at Cambridge, when everybody was talking of *Lothair*. 'The divine Theodora' was blamed for entering into a plot to blow up Louis Napoleon. 'People must be put out of the way,' he said laughingly, "if they interfere with great principles.' I used to tell him that the first thing I learned of him was to do evil that good might come !

In 1880 he was made Canon of Worcester, when we were in the Deanery, and from that time our friendship with him and your mother and you was always growing, if it could be said to grow when it was so perfect from the beginning.

We had great difficulty in believing that he could live or take any interest in a *new* place like Worcester ; but in a very few weeks, I had almost said days, it was full of old friends to him.

He knew the history of every verger and workman about the Cathedral, and threw himself heartily into the interests of all whom he met in the city.

No one ever went to him in vain for help or advice. He often found time for a class once a month, to which he invited some of our servants and others, to talk to them about the Holy Communion. 'I don't believe in your religion,' he used to say, 'unless you say your prayers and go to Holy Communion.' Our servants were always ready to go, and have never forgotten his teaching. He knew all the servants' names, and had a kind word for them whenever he went in and out of the house. When at breakfast about nine, we used to hear the door bang, then a quick step coming up two stairs at a time, and he would rush into the room : 'What! still at breakfast! I've had mine an hour ago.'

He had a marvellous power of imparting his own strength and enthusiasm, and I always remember, on the wonderful day of his funeral, the character of calm strength in the faces of the crowd of friends who filled the Cathedral and the cloisters. There has been a great silence since he went away.

The pastoral spirit which was always alive in him soon led him to form some communicant classes on the old Wantage lines :

W. J. B. TO MRS. WILKINS.

THE COLLEGE, WORCESTER, March 8, 1881.

. . I had a class last week, composed of our servants and the servants at the Deanery, seven in number altogether. I should not be surprised if by degrees I get together something like the old Wantage classes. At least, I mean to try to do so. You see that there is a great difference between a Cathedral and a parish. I have no one exactly who claims my services. A good many people attend the Cathedral, but they belong to some parish or other, and I know nothing about them personally. Still we have a great many people, vergers, bedesmen, singing men, boys of the choir, a grammar school—connected with the Cathedral, and I hope by-and-bye to get hold of some of them. . . .

But he found plenty of work ready to his hand in his new capacity of Canon Residentiary.

Already efforts had been begun to make the restored Cathedral more spiritually useful in the city and diocese. Canon Barry, with the co-operation of the Chapter, had established a Sunday evening nave service, and had secured a better observance of the Holy Week by arranging a special evening service at which Bach's 'Passion Music' was sung.

Canon Butler, being the Canon in residence during the Lent season of 1881, gave a series of addresses at three P.M. in the Lady Chapel twice a week. These addresses were as much appreciated in Worcester as afterwards in Lincoln Cathedral. It was also by his advice that a Thursday Celebration of the Holy Eucharist was then adopted.

From the earliest years of his ministry Canon Butler had always been a great promoter of *real* education, i.e. of education grounded on a basis of definite religious teaching. He was never tired of denouncing in the strongest terms the sham of 'unde-nominationalism.' It was therefore natural that he should at once apply himself to the wants of Worcester in this respect. Beginning with the Cathedral, he observed that the daily attend-ance of the choristers (all of whom were then Worcester boys) at matins and evensong, and at practice, had the effect of drawing them away from the Cathedral Grammar school at important hours of study, thereby seriously hindering their chance of education. By this time the appointment of Canon Melville and Canon Knox Little had brought fresh elements of vigour to the Chapter. Accordingly a scheme was carefully thought out, and approved by the Chapter, by which a separate choir school was set up for the Cathedral choristers. The wardenship of this school was entrusted to one of the minor canons (the present Precentor), who for many years had worked with Canon Butler at Wantage as assistant curate. The classical and mathe-matical instruction of the boys was entrusted to a very able man, whose education and training from boyhood had been personally supervised by Canon Butler himself.

The choir school was commenced in January, 1882, and by the kindness of the Dean was carried on for the first six months at the Deanery, until a suitable house was available in College

Green for boarding the boys. The choir school has now developed into a preparatory school for the sons of gentlemen and professional men; and the list of distinctions and honours won by the boys in competitive examinations shows that to give three hours a day to Cathedral duties in no way interferes with the work of general education.

In the year 1882 the want of some better provision for the education of upper class girls began to be acutely felt in Worcester. While good endowed schools supplied amply the needs of the boys, their sisters were dependent upon private effort, which had proved wholly inadequate to meet the ever-increasing demands of the educational movement of the time. Naturally Canon Butler, who had the genius of a great educationalist, was foremost in promoting a scheme for the establishment of a school which should meet this need.

The leading citizens of the town, attracted by the manly vigour and sound common sense of the new Canon, gave their hearty co-operation to the scheme. A suitable house was purchased for the purposes of the school by the late Lord Beauchamp, who by all means in his power strongly supported the project. And in June, 1883, the work was fairly started on Church principles, and with a conscience clause, under a Head Mistress of the Canon's selection.

Some of those who had known how persistently Canon Butler had opposed the introduction of a conscience clause into National schools were surprised at what appeared to them the inconsistency of his accepting it in a High school. But he saw clearly that the circumstances are wholly different. The adoption of a conscience clause makes it possible to give definite Church teaching, because parents have full liberty to withdraw their children from the whole, or from any part of it, so that the teacher can be true to her own convictions while perfectly loyal to the wishes of the parents, who certainly have the right to determine what form of religion their children shall be taught; whereas in schools where all children must come to the divinity classes, a conscientious teacher is perpetually hampered by fearing that she may be teaching what some of them would disapprove, and finds herself upon the horns of a dilemma, untrue either to herself or to them.

The Canon's clear-sightedness and generosity averted what he felt would have been the real calamity of an undenominational school being started in Worcester; he never used the word 'undenominational' without the modification 'so-called', for he used to say that there could be no such thing as real undenominationalism; that in practice it either means no religion, or something so colourless as to have no reality; no backbone of definite dogma which can enable it to stand against the rising flood of agnosticism.

The success of the school has proved the wisdom of his prescience; but it was not only in laying down the true lines at first, but also by his constant fostering care, that he contributed so largely to that success.

His generous trust in all those who worked with him inspired them with something of his own enthusiasm; it was such a joy to give him pleasure; one could not but long and strive to be what he believed one to be; the sound of his cheery voice, the grip of his friendly hand, seemed to impart some of his own manly vigour, and he thoroughly understood the details of school life. While he detested mere theorising, he had strong and clear views of the true aims and of the right methods of teaching; to hear him give a lesson was worth months of ordinary training; no eye could wander, no attention flag, while he held the young minds 'at tension'; and with absolute accuracy and perfect clearness drove home the point he meant them to apprehend.

Verily had his path lain in that direction he would have been the greatest head master of this century. But there was another side to this strong, and as it appeared to those who knew him only superficially, somewhat stern character; a depth of untold tenderness; a sympathy, womanlike in its gentleness, which was called forth at once by suffering or sorrow; it is difficult to touch upon this without lifting the veil that should cover the sanctities of the hidden life; but those who have felt it, perhaps first learned from him that the word 'comfort' means 'strength,' and think of him as, above all, a very St. Barnabas, a son of consolation.

Closely connected with this was his chivalrous attitude towards all women. His ideal of Christian womanhood was a very high one, and if he strongly deprecated any approach to publicity in woman's work, it certainly was not that he depreciated their powers, but that he feared for them the loss of the delicate refinement, the purity, the humility, which he held to be their distinguishing and characteristic virtues, "the ornament of a meek and quiet spirit."

So write two of those who worked with him at Worcester. He himself wrote to Canon Liddon :

W. J. B. TO REV. CANON LIDDON.

THE COLLEGE, WORCESTER, Dec. 18, 1883.

. . . I have taken an active part here in setting afloat a 'High school'—another hateful word—for girls. I had three alternatives—(1) and worst, to hold my hand and then suffer —— to swoop down upon us, and set up a school which would certainly do much to stamp out what there is of Churchmanship and even Christianity from the city.

(2) To set up a school with what people are pleased to call 'undenominational teaching,' which again means something *against* the Church. For there are only two religions in England with any definite doctrinal faith, ourselves and the Roman Catholics. The others are all covered and included and maintained by the word 'undenominational.'

(3) To have such as our present school, where the teaching is most definite, with a power for parents to withdraw children from the religious instruction. I believe that this will never be exercised. But it satisfies the great mass of those who certainly otherwise would have set going (1) or (2). . . . In the colonies the (R.C.) Sisters and others receive masses of children into their schools, with an understanding that they are not to influence them towards the R.C. religion. Of course this very often results as one might expect, though the promise may be honestly kept. I think that there is a great difference between day schools and boarding schools in this matter. A boarding school is a family where one and one only faith can rightfully exist. . . . But it is very different when you are making arrangements for day-school teaching in a town. We have to deal with masses of Church people, who are themselves not half instructed, and if you refuse to satisfy their scruples, you simply precipitate them into the opposite

camp. Whereas by a little patience you bring them to be strong supporters of the truth. I found this to be the case in Wantage, and I believe that it will be the same here. . . .

W. J. B. TO REV. CANON LIDDON.

THE COLLEGE, WORCESTER, March 3, 1884.

I am driven to write to you on account of the few words of yours which I read in the *Guardian*, lately spoken at Oxford on the subject of women. I am most thankful that you said them. It is to my mind by far, and beyond all comparison, the saddest feature of this generation, that women are claiming, and are encouraged to claim, a position which is not intended for them; and that they do not perceive the inevitable consequence, that while they never can emulate men in men's work, and can at best be but poor imitators, they will lose that most grand power and influence which are really and by God's providence their own.

I am sometimes thankful to think that the end of my earthly life cannot be far off. It seems to me that what with the sentimentality of one set of minds, the recklessness of others, the self-will, the weak abandonment of those great Church principles which men like Mr. Keble held and taught . . . there is a very bad time ahead.

I trust that —— will comport himself reasonably. . . . If men of his type would be *Churchmen* first, and then *politicians*, the case would of course be different. I always tell them to vote and work for those who "love our nation and build us synagogues." That text seems to embody the politics of a true Churchman. . . .

Other letters, illustrating the Worcester period, follow.

W. J. B. TO MRS. WILKINS.

THE COLLEGE, WORCESTER, Feb. 10, 1882.

. . . Depend on it, there is nothing like Church teaching to make children grow up in the right road. What crowds of young men and young women are now, I thank God, doing well. There is something in Church teaching definite and satisfying, which cannot be found elsewhere. Prayer, Church, Holy Communion, these are the means by which God's grace enters the soul, and when people seek and use them, they will not go far away.

No one could have grieved more than I, when I was, as I thought, called upon to relinquish a place and post which I loved so dearly. But I had to look to the future, and it was quite clear to me that it would be better for the future welfare of the parish, that a younger man should be appointed. . . .

W. J. B. TO REV. CANON ISAAC TAYLOR.

THE PALACE, ST. STEPHEN'S GREEN,
DUBLIN, May 5, 1883.

MY DEAR TAYLOR,—I was delighted to get your letter in this wild land, and to hear that your 'magnum opus' is really about to see the light. You must feel the joy of delivery 'that a man is born into the world.' It is most kind of you to offer a copy to such an ignoramus as I am. I shall value it the more on the 'omne ignotum' principle. Nevertheless I do look forward much to the diving into its abysses. I can hardly fail to pull out and appropriate a jewel or two.

I was giving a lecture at Sheffield on Monday, on St. Chrysostom, and I had great pleasure in making acquaintance with our friend Bradley.[1] . . .

We, my daughter Mary and I, arrived here last Wednesday. The Trenches are old friends, and the visit has been hanging over for a long time. I had never before been in Ireland, and so far I am *agreeably* disappointed. Dublin is, to my mind, far more of a metropolis than Edinburgh, and there seem to be much life and business in the place. I went to the trial of Hanlon, one of the conspirators, and was much struck with the freedom and calmness with which the witnesses owned to lying.

Counsel cross-examining: 'Then, when you said that, you lied.' Witness (cheerfully), 'I *did*, sor.' This repeated several times during the course of examination.

Your letter was most àpropos. The Archbishop's son is a partner with Paul, and the bit of Irish lore created much interest.

I stay here over Whitsunday to preach in Cathedral.

[1] Henry Bradley, Esq., now joint-editor of *The New English Dictionary*.

W. J. B. TO HIS SISTER.

LOWER HOUSE OF CONVOCATION, Feb. 13, 1884.

Brothers and sisters do not often write to one another, I fancy, in a general way. They take it for granted that all is right, and so leave matters alone till there is a real reason for doing so. Birthdays are something of this kind, and are specially useful in bringing out old memories and present love. And thus, in the midst of a great deal of talk, and some excitement, of a very long debate on the old vexed question of the 'Conscience Clause,' I am struggling to scribble at the corner of the table, sitting all askew, to write a word of birthday greeting. We are all growing very old, but somehow we keep pretty well together the essence of youth, *i.e.* vigour and cheeriness. (Division is coming, I know not which way it will go. The fight is hard. I rather expect to be on the wrong side, because I have for once taken what is looked upon as the less Churchy line. —— is very fierce and strong, and the house is rather with him in this matter.) We have, I think, much, very much, to be thankful for. Sound health is indeed a blessing second to none, and in spite of occasional creakiness, we seem to have inherited good sound constitutions. I am now two years older than my father was when he left us in 1849, and you are as old as our grandmother when I first remember her. They seemed quite old to us, but I doubt if we should seem so old to the young ones. Then it is a great comfort to see the young ones growing up good and healthy and right-minded, every one of them, settling down into moderate middle life, with conscience "void of offence towards God and towards men." And so, I think, we shall jog on to the end, and when the call comes, be ready to meet it 'without shame,' as Bishop Andrewes calls it, 'and if it pleases Him, without pain.' And so our generation will have done its work and be called to its rest. . . .

W. J. B. TO HIS MOTHER.

THE COLLEGE, WORCESTER, March 23, 1884.

MY DEAREST MOTHER,—Hurrah for March! How well he has treated us this year. This fine soft weather, with wind W. and S.W., will make up for many other years like, for instance, 1883,

and the long protracted bitterness and misery. Now everything
is looking bright and genial. Rooks cawing happily as they build
their nests just opposite to my study window; spring vegetation
clean and healthy, fruit trees covered with bloom, March dust
without its poison. Altogether everything delights the eye and
ears. People say that we shall pay for this by-and-bye. I do
not hold by those croakings. You never can calculate in this
country either on fine or foul weather, and the only plan is
to be happy when one can, and to let the future take care of
itself.

Last week was tolerably busy in one or other way. On
Wednesday I preached at a village . . . where the leading
man Mr. ——, is one of our great iron-masters. He is an
excellent Churchman, and a very well informed and interesting
person. . . . This good Mr. —— has built a church and
schools for his men at his own expense, and takes immense
interest in all that concerns their good. He quite laughs at the
idea of strikes. Living among his men, they realise him as a
friend, and work cheerily under his directions. It is a wonderful blessing to a neighbourhood when a man like that is found
there. On Thursday I was at Upton-on-Severn, a small country
town about twelve miles from this. It was of some importance
at the time of the Battle of Worcester. The Cromwellian party
had to cross the Severn, the cavaliers having broken down
the bridge. They managed somehow, by crawling on their
stomachs along the parapet, occupied the church tower, and
drove the cavaliers back on the road to Worcester. . . .
—Your most loving son,

W. J. B.

His mother died, aged 91, on April 4th, 1884.
This was the last letter of a series written every
Sunday for a period of more than thirty years.

W. J. B. TO MRS. WILKINS.

4 ADAM STREET, ADELPHI, W.C. Feb. 11, 1885.

I cannot think how you and others can be so good and
faithful. I do greatly delight in getting your kind notice of my
birthday. I do not suppose that I shall have many more

for my kind friends' greeting. Wantage always must be to me the spot in the world in which I feel most interested, and it is the greatest blessing out of my many blessings that have befallen me in life, that all goes on quite steadily and satisfactorily. I may say like St. Paul, though with all reverence and humility—I planted, another watered, but God giveth the increase. Yes, I fully hope to preach to you at Eastertide. Though I am growing older, yet my voice has not deserted me. It has plenty of practice, I assure you. I have to preach in no less than five Cathedrals during the coming Lent. . . .

An anonymous writer in the *Church Times* thus summed up the impression left by William Butler on the Cathedral and city of Worcester :

When Canon Butler of Wantage, most energetic among men, was appointed to Worcester, the preaching power of the Cathedral was materially strengthened. Many an eloquent, manly, and downright sermon have we heard from his lips. He threw himself heart and soul into the improvement of the services, especially with regard to the more reverent and devotional Celebrations each Sunday and Saints' day in the year. He preached right and left in the diocese with all the vigour and strength of a man carrying but half his years, not knowing, apparently, what ill-health or weakness meant. In the matter also of the voluntary choir for the Sunday evening services in the nave Canon Butler recognised a valuable means of obtaining a firmer hold over men, co-operating cordially in the movement. Now that he is Dean of Lincoln there are many who look back with gratitude to his work in Worcester. It was suggested in the early days of the Salvation Army movement to Canon Butler the advisability of attempting to grapple with the new force, with the object of diverting the singular organisation into orthodox channels. With characteristic energy he at once condemned the idea. It is impossible, he said, for the fundamental principles are opposed to Church doctrine ; their fierce and dangerous enthusiasm could never be made to harmonise with our system, and any attempt to accomplish this must fail.

In May, 1885, the Deanery of Lincoln was offered

to him by Mr. Gladstone. Curiously enough, on this
occasion also he was abroad, taking his holiday in
North Italy, and the letter lay about ten days or a
fortnight at Worcester. The contents of the letter
were telegraphed to him, and he returned at once to
England. He paid a short visit to the Bishop of
Lincoln, an old friend of many years' standing in
the Oxford diocese, and satisfied himself that his
acceptance of the post would not render it necessary
for him to sever his connexion with the Wantage
Sisterhood. Here are two of his letters in answer
to the kind expressions of friends on his new
preferment :

W. J. B. TO ———

St. Mary's Home, St. Barnabas Day, 1885.

Thank you and your father also for your kind words. Do not
however congratulate me, but pray for me. Church appoint-
ments involve very serious responsibility, and certainly Lincoln
Cathedral not least of all. I would not have accepted it if it
would have separated me from Wantage. This was the main
difficulty. But when I came to talk over the matter with the
Bishop and the Canons, I found that practically I could be here
as much as ever, or even more so. A Dean's residence is quite
undefined, though a Canon's is not. . . . I have been so lovingly
greeted by the Lincoln people that I feel already at home
there. . . .

W. J. B. TO REV. W. G. SAWYER.

The Mead, Wantage, June 12, 1885.

Thank you for your kind words and all your affection and
kindly thought of me. It has been a matter of very serious consideration whether I should accept this charge of the Lincoln
Deanery. I have lived so long in the 'West countree' that
eastern voices and ways are strange to me—though at one time
Middlesex, Hertfordshire, and Essex were my natural habitat.

But the great question was that of severance from the Wantage Sisters, and it was not until I had ascertained that I could hold on there that I allowed my name to be gazetted. After long talk with the Bishop and the Chapter, both of whom received me most warmly, . . . I found that there is little, if any more, difficulty than I have at present, in keeping my charge here. Of course I shall resign everything else, as Rural Deanery, Chaplaincy of the Berks Forces, etc., and so far lighten the ship. . . .

He was not allowed to leave Worcester without some recognition of his work from the inhabitants of the city. A circular letter was put forth by the Dean and the Mayor, of which this is a portion :

WORCESTER, August, 1885.

It has been thought that the friends of the Rev. Canon Butler, who has recently been preferred to the Deanery of Lincoln, would gladly avail themselves of the opportunity to join in some permanent memorial of his work and zeal for good in this city and diocese during his five years' connexion with the Cathedral Chapter. The earnestness with which Dean Butler has laboured amongst us to maintain the highest purposes of our Cathedral service, to foster relations of increasing sympathy between the Cathedral and municipal bodies, to promote the institution and insure the success of the High school for girls; added to the deep personal esteem which he has inspired in numbers by the self-sacrifice and sympathetic devotion of his life and character, have suggested not alone the necessity for some memorial, but that it should take a form which, while being personally acceptable, might permanently connect the memory of his work with a Worcester institution, which he did so much to found and perfect, and in the success of which he is known to be deeply interested.

It is therefore proposed to form a Reference Library at the High school for the use of the teaching staff and the pupils, the books being placed and preserved in a suitable case, a tablet on which may prominently connect the library with Dean Butler's name.

It is also hoped that it may be found possible to present

for the Dean's personal acceptance an illuminated address containing the subscribers' names.

On December 16th the address was presented to him by his old friend Lord Beauchamp. He replied :

Lord Beauchamp, ladies, and gentlemen,—While most gratefully accepting this token of your extreme kindness, I am compelled to say that, in some sense, you have placed me in a false position. I feel as if in some sense I stand before you this afternoon as an impostor. I cannot for a moment venture to take to myself the kind expressions which are conveyed to me in this testimonial. I can only assure you that I have had most earnestly at heart the welfare of this school and city, and whatever little work I have been able to do has been more than repaid by the kind regard you have accorded me. But I cannot for a moment imagine that such a school as this depends in any sense on me. I am sure if I had never been Canon of Worcester, or even if I had never existed at all, a school of this kind must have been formed in the city. It is impossible to suppose that in a city so conspicuous for its intelligence, its cultivation, and its patriotism, the very brightest jewels—the precious pearls I may call them—the sweet young maidens who are growing up among us would have been left without the very best kind of education which this country could possibly afford. Therefore I simply feel myself as one who has just pulled the trigger of a mine already laid; or, if I may take something of a Worcester comparison, as one who just touches the ripe fruit, and it falls without effort to the ground. I may say that the kindness and confidence with which I have been treated in the effort I did make to suggest this school to the city, more than repaid me for any anxiety I may have felt. I should like to be allowed to repeat what I have said on a previous occasion, that I believe there is no place in England where any public effort is so admirably met as it is in this city of Worcester. There is less of that wretched petty jealousy which so often cramps people's attempts; there is so little of that political or religious antagonism which we find in so many places, that any one who has any work of good to do in this city may certainly expect to be heartily and kindly met. Let me say one word as to that which especially delights me as I look upon this school. It has been our own voluntary effort. By our own personal exertions we have done this work ourselves; and as I look on this beautiful room, as I think of the excellent scholastic machinery we have around us, as I think of that splendid staff of mistresses who are teaching your children, and as I think of the results which we are seeing year after year springing forth from this school, it does seem to me that we have here that which I very much desire to see everywhere, a firm and consistent setting forth of what voluntary effort can do. I believe in voluntary effort. I believe it to be consistent with the whole character of the people of this country. We hear in other countries of wonderful State institutions, of schools and other institutions of the same kind manipulated from headquarters; but in England we do everything ourselves. Our hospitals are our own work; our Church—it is true that some people may call it State-supported, but those who know better know it is nothing of the kind. Our army is a great voluntary institution, and we know that when there was some danger to this country from the vapouring French colonels, 250,000 Volunteers started up to oppose the foe. So it is with our schools. It is somewhat the fashion in some quarters to desire to introduce that manipulating system; but I only hope that I shall never see it done. It is true that sometimes voluntary effort begins somewhat clumsily; but in voluntary effort there is heart and will, and after all that is the great thing which gives it spirit and life and genuineness. Therefore I trust we shall never see voluntary effort suppressed in this country by the action of Boards in London, Commissions, or anything of that sort. We have seen something of that, and the evil of it; attempts for instance to deal with the arrangements of land; attempts to interfere between masters and men; and others are threatened, though I trust we shall never see anything of that sort. This school is a clear token to everybody how voluntary effort can send forth its work better, more reasonably, and more lovingly done, than any Board or Commission. I thank you with all my heart for the kindness with which you have received me, not only to-day,

but for all the many, many kindnesses, all the love and affection
and confidence which I have received during the time I was
resident among you. It is a great grief, I do assure you, to
leave you, and I can only say this, that Worcester, this fair
city and its lovely Cathedral, and certainly this most charming
school of yours, will ever find a place in the very warmest
affections of my heart.

Although he held the canonry for so short a time,
his strenuous character and his large sympathies did
not fail to make a deep impression on Worcester.
This was expressed in a letter from a citizen of
Worcester, written on the occasion of the Canon's
appointment to the Deanery of Lincoln :

I am very glad—for Lincoln ! but the faithful city cannot
take a quite unselfish view of your removal. Although I felt
well convinced that you would leave us if the call of duty came
with sufficient clearness and emphasis, the definite acceptance of
the idea of separation is not perhaps the less painful on that
account. You had come to work so good an influence amongst
us—our Church, our municipal life—our external life altogether
were feeling more and more the benefit of your zealous work
for truth and high principle, that to those of us who know how
much this goodly city needs the comfort of such influences, your
removal is more than ordinary painful.

As to the High school, I do not quite know where we are to
look for the steadfast faith and enthusiasm with which you began
and have carried on that great work to its perfect end. That, however, will remain as a link still to connect Lincoln with Worcester.
Of course to very many of us your removal will mean a sharper
wrench still, because a personal one. Those who have been
permitted, as I have, to a share of your deep, loving, and affectionate sympathy, and know how great that sympathy was even
for one's everyday difficulties, will continue to hope that you have
been long enough with us to leave, when you go, some portion of
your large heart behind.

And to the no less deep and lasting impression

made upon the clergy of the diocese, touching testimony was borne after his death nearly nine years later, when an eye-witness related how " at the Diocesan Societies' meeting one after another got up to express a sense of deep personal loss, and of the blessing he had been to Worcester."

He was installed Dean at Lincoln, 15th July, 1885, and on the 26th November following was made D.D. at Cambridge, *jure dignitatis*, as he considered that for the dignity of the cathedral the Dean should hold that degree, and therefore took it as a matter of principle.

CHAPTER XI.

LINCOLN.

[THE REV. A. R. MADDISON, Priest-Vicar in Lincoln Cathedral, who from the earliest days of William Butler's residence in Lincoln was thrown much into contact with him, has contributed the greater part of the chapters dealing with the last nine years of the Dean's life.]

Dean Butler came from a Cathedral of the new foundation to a Cathedral of the old. After a life spent in a country parish he had in 1881 found himself in a Cathedral city where he had much to learn. As Canon of Worcester he threw himself heartily into every work, and made it his business to draw city and Cathedral together. At Lincoln he found another Cathedral with a different history and character. He found himself invested with authority as Dean, but with no one able to say precisely to what limits the authority extended. His very residence as Dean was undefined. Eight months in the year he was bound to be resident, but the terms of the residence were not stated.

There are topographical difficulties too at Lincoln which have been generally cited as obstacles to any cordial unanimity between the Cathedral and the city. 'Above' and 'Below hill' are terms significant of a line of demarcation and two populations. The Cathedral has no parochial jurisdiction. The city itself, although the capital of the county, is very unfavourably situated as a centre. The service of trains is not convenient. Proud as Lincolnshire people might be of their Minster, they certainly did not regard Lincoln as a Yorkshireman does York. Grantham, Boston, Stamford, and Louth had their separate interests and agencies. The Cathedral clergy were looked upon by the parochial clergy as separate from themselves. The Cathedral services might be admired for their musical effect, but any attempt to represent the Cathedral as a spiritual force and activity would have been received some few years ago with a smile.

Dean Butler came with the heart and the lifelong experience of a parish priest. His great aim and object was to utilise the machinery he found ready to his hand. He found a vast Cathedral with only one Celebration of Holy Communion on a Sunday, closed and unused from five P.M. on Sunday to the following morning, and one of the very first things he did was to provide an early as well as a late Celebration every Sunday. He never rested till he established a Sunday evening service. His parochial instinct showed itself in the care he bestowed on the workmen employed in the Cathedral. He sought them out and brought them to Confirmation and the Holy Communion. He was in thorough sym-

pathy with the parochial clergy. He made it known
that he would be always willing, if he possibly
could, to help those who were hard pressed on
Sundays. He did all he could to bring together
the Cathedral and the city. He cultivated friendly
relations with the leading citizens, and threw himself heartily into the welfare of institutions such as
the School of Art, which he held to be a valuable
influence on the manners and characters of the people.
He was never deterred by religious or political
differences from co-operating in any good work with
those who were not like-minded with himself, and he
earned the title which was given him, in a letter
written after his death, of a 'kindly citizen.'

Education, it is needless to say, still occupied his
thoughts, as it had all his life, and he took the
deepest interest in the Grammar school, and also
in the school where the Cathedral choir boys were
taught and boarded.

So much may be taken as a sort of summary of
Dean Butler's life at Lincoln, but no one could gather
from it a true conception of the work he was engaged
in. What one of his colleagues said of him shortly
after his death is literally true : " The Dean has lived
another life and done another work." While he
worked hard as Dean of Lincoln, he was working
equally hard as head of a great religious organisation,
the Wantage Sisterhood. And the work involved
in this it is difficult to estimate. Hardly a day
passed without bringing him letters connected with
it. His frequent journeys to Wantage and to other

places where branches of the Sisterhood were established, of which we used sometimes to complain, as they took him so much away from Lincoln, were enough to have taxed the strength of a younger man. How he did it, how he contrived to preserve his wonderful vigour and freshness through it all, will ever be a marvel.

In trying to give a sketch of his Lincoln life, I am obliged to put it mainly into the form of personal reminiscences. Circumstances threw me much in his company, and the materials are lacking for a systematic detailed account, for there are not so many letters available for biographical purposes as in the earlier part of his life.

He found a good deal to do on coming to Lincoln, for he had his own opinion as to what a Cathedral should be, and Lincoln fell very short of it.

But his powers were limited. He indeed inherited great traditional prestige as Dean of Lincoln ; but he found that practically he had only the power to obstruct. He could not initiate any legislation for the Cathedral without the unanimous consent of his colleagues, although he could effectually stop any himself. Such was the change from the mediaeval Dean whose title was *Dominus Decanus*, and who enjoyed the privilege of a train-bearer within the close, to the modern Dean whose rights (as he was informed before leaving Worcester) were merely ' those which the Common Law gave him.'

A letter from one of his oldest and most intimate friends, who happened to spend a Sunday at Lincoln

x

shortly before Dean Butler took up his residence
there, somewhat prepared him for what he would
find. It is full of good humoured criticism, and
after detailing various points where improvements
seemed needful, it sums up with the remark that
" the worshipping arrangements of the congregation
seriously cry out for the application of a little good
feeling and common sense."

Dean Butler could not but be struck with the
poverty and meagre decorations of the altar, coming
as he did from Worcester, where costly gifts had
been offered for the sanctuary. Certainly Lincoln
Cathedral could not match with any ordinary well-
cared-for parish church. There was but one altar
cloth, a red one, which did duty all the year round.
The altar table itself was a poor thing, furnished
merely with two brass candlesticks containing candles
which were never lighted. A sanctuary carpet
worked by ladies of the county in 1847, could not
be termed a thing of beauty, although age had toned
down the brilliancy of its colours.

The altar rails had been moved eastward from
their original position in order to give more sitting
accommodation, but with the result that the space
within the sanctuary was cramped and confined. It
cannot be wondered at that he felt the change, or
that his first Christmas Day was not a very happy
one. He saw much he wished to alter, and the
question was how it could be done.

I may here without impropriety say that the Dean
always bore cordial witness to the kindness of his

colleagues, without whose consent no change could
have been effected. The changes were considerable,
not only in minor details such as have been enumer-
ated, but also in the multiplication of services.

The Sunday evening service at 6.30 was one of
the principal changes. This he set his heart on from
the very first. He had found it at Worcester and
was resolved to have it at Lincoln. He made himself absolutely responsible for the expenses connected
with it, and although fortunately the offertories
covered the greater part of the cost, leaving him
only a small amount to defray, it is well that this
should be known for he did not speak about it.
Neither should it be forgotten that, so far from using
the Cathedral pulpit on Sunday evenings for the
display of his own preaching powers, he only reserved one Sunday in each month for himself,
leaving the lion's share to the canon in residence.

As hard things were said about him which he
did not deserve, I think it only just to let this also
be known. Undoubtedly the Sunday evening service
was an innovation, and it was only natural that it
should affect at first the congregations of parish
churches which had hitherto had Sunday evening
entirely to themselves; but he could not accept this
as a valid reason why the Cathedral should be shut
up for so many hours when multitudes could be
attracted by a bright musical service in the nave.
He argued that the ordinary steady church-going
people would not desert their parish churches, while

the shifting element of congregations might just as well be drawn to the Cathedral.

Of course this multiplication of services entailed increased work on the executive staff. The Celebrations of Holy Communion were much more frequent. He was himself entirely responsible for the one at seven A.M. on the great festivals and the first Sunday of each month, and it was my privilege to be able to assist him, as it did not in any way interfere with my own parochial duty. I have often thought that those who saw him then saw him at his best. The congregation was one after his own heart, mainly composed of workmen employed in the Cathedral, and domestic servants within the close; and no one who was present can forget the wonderful earnestness with which he used to give a short address immediately after the Nicene Creed on these occasions; words full of pith and vigour, driven home into the hearts of his hearers, uttered without notes, and yet always concise and connected. Once a quarter the Church of England Working Men's Society used to attend and swell the numbers very considerably, yet all would be over before eight o'clock, when a Celebration followed at the altar in the choir.

He was wonderfully rapid in his utterance, and yet perfectly distinct and reverent. On one occasion when by accident he was alone at the seven o'clock Celebration and there were more than seventy communicants, he had concluded the service by eight.

Another addition he made to the services was a short address on Saints' days and festivals given after evensong in the retrochoir. The last words he ever uttered in the Cathedral were heard at one of these a few days before his death. But one change which he effected after he had been at Lincoln some little time, brought upon him a good deal of censure, although his object was simply to relieve the clergy and people from what was thought a wearisome length of service. On Sundays matins in the Cathedral choir consisted of course of a full choral service, with anthem, litany, and introit, and a sermon, which, preached by a prebendary in his turn, did not as a rule incline to brevity; then a Celebration of Holy Communion. Frequently the clock struck twelve before the Nicene Creed was finished, and very often a congregation which went in at half-past ten did not leave the Cathedral till past one. The question arose how it could be shortened. No one had the power to limit the sermon, and the precentor was expected to provide on Sundays a musical service superior to those on ordinary week days, and consequently of greater length.

Dean Butler thereupon proposed to remove the litany from the morning to the afternoon, and in place of evensong at four in the choir, to have the litany with an anthem and hymn at that hour in the nave. He contended that as evensong was now sung in the nave at half-past six, it was not needful to have it as well in the choir at four. Of course

the removal of the litany, and having the shortened
form of matins, ending at the third collect, greatly
reduced the length of the services, but the Dean
came in for a considerable amount of censure ; he
was accused of creating 'fancy services,' which
any one who knew him would know was the last
thing he was likely to do.   Many who had repeatedly
cried out against the length of the morning service
now affected to regard the disappearance of the
four o'clock evensong as a positive spiritual privation, and remonstrances, not always of the gentlest
nature, poured in upon him.   He however held
firm to his purpose and effected it, though the opposition surprised him, and seemed to him, considering
the circumstances, unreasonable.

I have dwelt rather at length on these points,
because they illustrate Dean Butler's mind as regards
the use of Cathedrals.   He was never weary of saying
that in these days public opinion would not tolerate
such institutions unless they were put to a thorough
practical use.   He was much amused, and I think
rather gratified, to hear that some one had compared
Lincoln Cathedral on Sundays to Clapham Junction,
on account of the rapid succession of services ; and in
a letter to the *Spectator*, in answer to a rather depre-
iatory criticism of Deans and Cathedrals, he says :

In one Cathedral with which I am best acquainted the Sunday
services are as follows : Holy Communion, eight ; matins, followed
by Holy Communion and sermon, 10.30 ; sermon without service,
three ; litany and anthem, four ; evensong and sermon, 6.30.
I do not see how much more than this can be got into the day.

Something must be said of the wonderful trans-
formation which he effected in the appearance of the
sanctuary. Any one who can recall the former
condition of things will appreciate the change. He
never rested till a more suitable and dignified altar
had been set up,[1] and by degrees he procured a set
of frontals for the different seasons, as well as a
proper supply of altar linen. Personal gifts came
in, such as vases and candlesticks, and the students
of the Bishop's Hostel gave a splendid cross. The
altar rails were moved westward to their original
position, and Persian carpets took the place of the
ladies' handiwork, which now is in the Lady Chapel
at the east end of the retrochoir. He used sometimes to reckon up with positive glee the cost of the
various gifts and improvements, and rejoice that
there was nothing now mean, cheap, or shabby in
the adornment of the sanctuary. One more change
must be mentioned, for it was very characteristic
of him. He noticed that the prebendaries and
priest-vicars very seldom had an opportunity of
celebrating the Holy Communion, and, indeed, up
to his coming their services were not likely to be
required by a Dean and four residentiary Canons
when there was only one Celebration on a Sunday.
He therefore arranged for a weekly Celebration on
Thursdays at eight A.M., for which a rota of prebendaries and priest-vicars was responsible. This

---

[1] The new altar was set in its place on February 10, 1888, and
he came into the Deanery saying he had kept his seventieth birthday
by helping the workmen to lift up the great marble slab.

was held at the altar under the great east window
in the Lady Chapel, and he never missed attending
it if in Lincoln, as a simple worshipper in his
cassock, only putting on a surplice when his services
were needed.

Turning from the Cathedral to the city, it will be
well to hear Canon Fowler's recollections, who, as
head master of the Lincoln Grammar school, was
frequently brought in contact with the Dean.

Dean Butler was singularly happy in his relations with the
citizens of Lincoln of all denominations; that Church people
should have looked up to him, and not only reverenced him,
but loved him, is natural; but the affectionate regard for his
memory which has been, and is now shown by the nonconformists of the city, speaks, as nothing else could speak,
of that true charity and willingness to recognise good work
of any kind, which were among the noticeable traits of his
character. No man could have been a more staunch upholder
of Church principles, no man could have been more opposed
to the spirit of Dissent, but he knew exactly where to draw
the line, and kept strictly to it. While, on the one hand, he
abstained from anything that might seem in the least degree
an yielding of a vital point, while he was quite ready to maintain
his views in language which from its evident sincerity and
the kindness of its expression, never gave permanent offence;
yet on the other, he avoided that petty and vexatious opposition which tends so largely to embitter the relations between
Churchmen and Dissenters. Perhaps in the city of Lincoln he
found this an easier matter than he might have done elsewhere,
for there are few towns in which the members of various
denominations are more inclined to 'agree to differ,' and to
live together in a friendly spirit; this is, in great measure,
due to the veneration felt by all for the Minster, which is
regarded by the whole body of citizens as belonging personally
to each individual, and to be, as it were, outside the region of
denominationalism; partly, perhaps we may allow, it was this
very feeling that drew Dean Butler towards the nonconformists,

for to love the Minster, and to take an interest in its services, was a sure way to his heart; but on the other hand it must not be forgotten that it was Dean Butler's own action in extending the usefulness of the Minster by establishing the largely-attended evening services, and by the personal interest which he took in the congregations as shown by his strong, direct yet simple sermons, that largely increased the affectionate feelings of the citizens towards the Cathedral.

As an instance of what has been said above, we may perhaps mention the lecture on 'Alfred the Great,' which he delivered to a nonconformist audience at the hall attached to the Newland Independent Chapel, which was very much appreciated by those who heard it, both on account of its interest, and still more perhaps on account of the kindly spirit in which it was given.

Dean Butler took a leading part in the erection of the present Lincoln School of Science and Art, and also in the Lincolnshire Exhibition in the Jubilee year, which accompanied its opening; and he was also a strong supporter of the Free Library movement which has been since crowned with success. While at Wantage he always took a great interest in the Volunteer movement, and for many years he was chaplain to the Berkshire Volunteers; he continued this interest at Lincoln, and used regularly to entertain the officers of the Lincoln companies, with whom he was very popular.

In all matters connected with the education of the city he was always to the fore, and it need hardly be said how strongly he felt with regard to the maintenance of the voluntary system; had he lived, nothing would have given him greater pleasure than the successful issue of the efforts of the Subdean and the educational committee, by which we may hope that the voluntary system has been preserved for Lincoln for many years to come.

At no time in the history of the city have the relations between the corporation and the Cathedral been more satisfactory; this has by no means always been the case, for at times in the past the feelings of the two bodies towards each other have been unequivocally hostile. Dean Butler, in his speeches as well as by his action, always emphasised the necessity of the preservation of amicable relations between the Minster and the civic authorities. It has been said that it

was he who initiated the desirable state of affairs which exists
at present; this is hardly true, for much was done by the
late Archbishop of Canterbury, when Chancellor, and by other
members of the Chapter, and the two bodies have been for
years drawing closer together.   There can, however, be no
doubt that by his geniality and straightforwardness he helped
very greatly to remove any old feelings of soreness, and that
it is to the late Dean and to the present Bishop that the
mutual regard now existing between the Cathedral and the
city is largely due.

Much more might be said with regard to Dean Butler's
public connexion with the citizens of Lincoln; nothing failed
to interest him and call forth his support, which appeared to
him as likely to benefit the city of his adoption.   We must not,
however, forget his private relations with individuals; he had
a keen eye for character, and any man who did his work as
he ought, whether with hand or head, was made to feel that
he had a friend to whom he might go for help and advice at
any time.   How people of all sorts and conditions regarded
him was clearly shown at his funeral, at which the Minster
was crowded with high and low, rich and poor, who by their
evident sorrow expressed the deep sense of personal loss which
was felt by all with whom he had been brought at all closely
into contact.   In this short notice, it is not for me to speak
of the inner life of the Deanery; but the kindly hospitality
and warm welcome ever accorded by the Dean and his family,
are still fresh in the hearts of many.   A Cathedral city is
always reputed to be exclusive, and it was one of the late
Dean's great desires to break this exclusiveness down, and to
bring people more closely together.

As I am only touching briefly upon a partial side of the
Dean's life in Lincoln, I must not write more.   All through
his life, in things secular as well as sacred, his watchword
was 'Thorough'; wherever he found thoroughness and sincerity,
he was ever ready to recognise and encourage good work, even
though he might not agree with the result aimed at; hence
his success in dealing with his parishioners and his fellow-
townsmen.   Whatsoever his hand found to do, he did it with
his might; yet with his simple rugged and loving nature, he
if any man, felt that the might was that of his Lord and

Master, and that the smallest as well as the greatest efforts of his life were dependent upon Him alone.

I have said that letters illustrating Dean Butler's life at Lincoln are not so plentiful as at other periods. His work of course was very different from that at Wantage, and he had not so much to construct as to quicken and stimulate. His great refreshment was his annual six weeks' holiday, which until the last year of his life he spent abroad. He enjoyed travelling intensely. Nothing seemed to escape his eye; and on looking through his letters written to me during these tours I am astonished at the wonderful descriptive power displayed, as well as the minuteness of detail.

In August, 1886, he wrote from Tyrol, and after telling me that "so far all is better than well," he adds, "We have many a good laugh to help digestion, and no lack of topics for conversation. We could not stand 'table d'hôte' meals, and generally contrive to get a separate table, where good behaviour is not 'de rigueur.'"

I think that the Dean's light-heartedness helped to keep him so fresh through his laborious life. A holiday to him was a real pleasure. I remember the first Easter Monday he was at Lincoln, how he enjoyed giving himself a holiday from his letters, and making a complete tour of the Cathedral—an enjoyment as simple and unaffected as that of a schoolboy released from lessons.

In July and August, 1887, he wrote from Switzerland. He was staying for a week or two at Vevey,

which he found " very hot" and the " air oppressive ";
and, he adds, " religion in these parts seems to be
quite a secondary matter, very unlike Tyrol, where
churches and shrines meet you everywhere.   Protestantism is *entirely* dead in Germany and Switzerland."

Shortly after, he writes from Grindelwald.   I
suppose that I had been mentioning some plan of
going abroad early in the following year, for he says,
" I hope that you will be able to make your visit
to Pau after Christmas, so long as you clear Lent.
Perhaps I am over-sensitive about Lent and Holy
Week.   But it always appears to me inconsistent
with our profession as priests to be larking about
the world and amusing ourselves at these special
times.   My practice has always been—one good
holiday.   Five Sundays was the length of my tether
once a year, and perhaps a little run, the inside of
a week, in the form of a visit to my mother or
some relations, after Christmas and Easter, when I was
tolerably used up."

In May, 1889, he wrote from Florence : " We
eased our journey by stopping at Laon, which is
reached at 7.30 P.M.   There is a good deal to see
there of one or other kind, and Mr. Waddington,
the French Ambassador, whom I had met there
before, took us into the French Conseil Général of
the Department, which is interesting just now when
we are introducing the same system into England.
The speakers, to my surprise, were much quieter
than our folk, and delivered their sentiments sitting.
It was frightfully dull."

In the spring of 1890 he wrote to me from Siena and Florence. He delighted in the pictures, especially those of the Sienese school, and says, " I still enjoy the Sienese painters' reverence and simplicity, and I seem to learn more from this school than from any other. But it cannot be denied that in force and colouring the Florentines have the palm."

He visited Pisa and its Campo Santo, Cathedral, and Leaning Tower, "up which I clambered for the first time."

He ends his letter : "Will you kindly look in at the Deanery some day and see how my old butler is. I heard a poor account of him, and I am always afraid of his passing away without spiritual help." This was Charles Page, an old servant to whom the Dean was much attached. He was in his service as a youth before the Dean went to Wantage. He died within a few months of completing fifty years of faithful service, the year before the death of his master, who was away from Lincoln at the time, and I was sent for to minister to him. The Dean returned just in time to see him still alive and conscious.

In April, 1891, the Dean met with a serious accident. He had arranged to go abroad directly after Easter with two of his daughters. They were at the Charing Cross station, their tickets taken, and everything ready for a start. The Dean had gone to a book shop in the neighbourhood, and while returning to the station was knocked down by a cab and had his left arm broken. It is very characteristic of him that directly he rose from the ground he said,

"Take that man's number." He at once told them
to take him to the nearest hospital, where his daughters found him shortly after. It was a severe disappointment to be balked of his pleasant holiday,
but he was not one who fretted against the inevitable. The following letters (written in pencil) to
Sir Charles Anderson, an old friend whom he greatly
valued, and to his sister, describe the situation :

CHARING CROSS HOSPITAL, April 10, 1891.

MY VERY DEAR AND KIND SIR CHARLES,—This is only the
fourth letter that I have attempted to achieve, so that you will
understand that it was from necessity or incapacity only that
your very kind letter has been so long left unanswered. It
cheered me very much. This is a strange, but really not an
unpleasant experience. The kindness and skill of the doctors
and nurses are quite extraordinary. I tell every one that I
have fallen into a nest of angels. I have comparatively little
pain, and all the arrangements here are of the best kind. I
have a very pleasant private room, and Mrs. Butler and my
daughters are here the greatest part of the day. Many old
friends visit me, and on the whole I begin to think myself
rather a humbug, as if I had invited the accident for the
purpose of extracting sympathy. But I must own that to find
oneself with the heels of a horse close to one's head, and the
wheel of a hansom cab close to one's body, is not a delightful
situation.

W. J. B. TO HIS SISTER.

THE HOSPITAL, CHARING CROSS, April 16, 1891.

It seems unnatural not to have written to you before, but
I write under difficulties—and one long stream of kind friends,
day after day, have absorbed the time.

This is a strange reversal of hopes and plans, but I do not
grudge it, for it has brought me into contact with a whole
body of the kindest and most unselfish people that I ever met.
This hospital is very well managed, and there is a tone of
refinement everywhere, from the splendid woman who commands

the institution down to the youngest probationer. The surgeons
too are, I believe, considered very skilful, and most attentive.
So that all things considered I have every reason to be very
thankful. I have moreover a very pleasant room, and so many
flowers arrive that I am able to benefit some of my neighbours.

Still of course this must be a long affair. I allow four
months before I am able to enjoy life once more. At present I
cannot unbutton a wristband, crack an egg, or wind up a
watch.

We hope to settle ourselves on Monday at 19 Sussex
Gardens. One of the nurses goes with us, for without such
help I can do nothing. My arm is in a plaster of Paris case—a
most unpleasant experience. . . .

I saw him in the hospital, and he was full of
interest in the nurses and their spiritual welfare.
He was giving copies of the *Christian Year* to
some, and spoke with the utmost warmth of the
kindness he had met with from the hospital staff.
After he left the hospital he wrote a letter to the
Times, strongly urging the claims of the hospital
for support.

I received what he calls his "first ink-written
letter," dated April 27. He had moved into a
friend's house, and although his arm did not then
pain him so much, he suffered much from coughing
at night; but he adds, "Certainly I have that
solace which Shakespeare suggests for old age, 'troops
of friends.'"

His delayed holiday was taken in August. He
went to Normandy, and I had letters from him
from Rouen, Bayeux, and Falaise.

Writing from Rouen, August 10, he says:

It is very amusing to me to find myself here. In the

year 1840 I came to this place, having just taken my degree,
when railways were almost unknown on the continent, and
one had to travel to Paris in a diligence. . . . Afterwards I
came to Rouen in 1843, a few days after my marriage, and
about this time of year, once since, in 1858, when we made
our first expedition into Brittany. . . . Two of the Wantage
sisters met us with a retinue of schoolgirls, whom they are
taking to various parts for a holiday trip. They had made
acquaintance with the Curé of S. Ouen who had been most
polite, and showed them about. He quite understood our
position ecclesiastically, and wrote for them to the Mother
Superior of the Sisters of S. Vincent de Paul, to whom he
introduced them. I rather hope to see him, and get from
him some idea of the real condition of things in France.

On the 18th August he wrote from Bayeux :

I was fortunate enough to make the acquaintance of the
Curé of S. Ouen.[1] . . . He is a most agreeable and intelligent
man. One of the few who really understand and enter into
the Anglican position. '*Il n'y a qu'un cheveu entre nous.*' And
when we parted he loaded us with good photographs.

At Falaise, on August 27, he writes :

On Tuesday we did well ; we took a carriage from Avranches
and drove to Mt. S. Michel. The day was cold but quite
sunny and bright, and we saw that wonderful place to great
advantage. On the whole I think it the most striking building
in Europe. . . . We have been roaming over the Castle of
Falaise and took refuge from a storm in the bedroom of
Arlette mother of Wm. Conquestor. . . . I lament over the
death of Mr. Raikes. He was one of the few M.P.'s on whom
all the Church could depend.

In 1892 he again visited France. He wrote from
Fontainebleau, July 13 :

We are just opposite the old historical Château full of
memories of kings and queens, and 'mistresses' such as Diane
of Poitiers, for whose honour or dishonour Henry II. built a
splendid salon.

[1] He visited the Dean at Lincoln in the summer of 1893.

This was the last of his foreign trips. In 1893 he went to Scotland. I am indebted to an intimate friend of his for the following account of the days he spent in his company :

I remember the Dean coming to me and saying that he was thinking of going to Scotland for his holidays, and asking for information about the West Coast, as he thought of going north instead of, as usual, to the continent. He said that owing to Mrs. Butler's health he did not like to leave her, and that she was not strong enough to go abroad. I recommended him to the immediate neighbourhood of Fort William, and from my description of the locality he said it was just what he wanted. Shortly afterwards he went there with Mrs. Butler, one of his daughters, and a granddaughter. Some fortnight or three weeks later I followed him with some of my family. I found him delighted with the beautiful country, the equally beautiful church, and the people. It was wonderful how quickly he had made friends with all classes. A few days later we moved on together to Spean Bridge, where we were due to pay a visit to some old friends, the Dean and his party going to the hotel there. As our friends, however, knew the Butlers (having met them at Lincoln), we still saw a great deal of them; and the Dean entered thoroughly into all that was going on, walking with us when shooting, and joining us on the river.

One day he started walking with us at ten o'clock, and although the day was very hot and the ground rough, he walked as well as the best; and at lunch on high ground—over 1500 feet—he was quite fresh. To be out all day under somewhat trying conditions of weather and ground, and to have made a very considerable ascent, was a feat for a man of his age. The following day was Sunday. He was not tired with his exertions, and was quite ready for another hard day's work. He celebrated the Holy Communion at eight A.M., and read the morning service at ten. Soon after that service he said he wanted a long walk, and he, our host, his granddaughter, and I started for a pass in the hills some ten miles off. We had to take our lunch with us, and I made the Dean quite angry because I would not allow him to carry the bag! We had a beautiful, but very hot walk; but the whole way the Dean was in the highest spirits. On our return he said, 'Be quick and change, we have just time for evensong.' Not many men, I think, could do two such days' work at seventy-five.

I remember one afternoon we went to Glen Roy to see the parallel roads, and these interested him greatly. He insisted on going up the hillside and on to all the three 'roads.'

I am sure he enjoyed himself in Lochaber thoroughly. He interested himself much, as I have said, in the people, and he gave great attention to all he heard of the Crofter question, of which he took a very impartial view.

He began to learn Gaelic as soon as he arrived in the Highlands, and he bought a Bible, prayer-book, grammar, and dictionary. He tried to learn something of the language from every one he met, and he succeeded in learning the Lord's prayer. On one occasion he upset the usually grave deportment of a native servant by suddenly repeating it at dinner for the benefit of his family!

When he left Lochaber after a stay of about a month, he went by the coach, which then ran from Fort William to Kingussie, for the sake of the very beautiful drive of forty miles. His care for Mrs. Butler caused him to make all excursions by driving, as otherwise she could not have seen the country, and the fine drive to Kingussie was therefore an appropriate end to a holiday which we little thought then was his last.

Some correspondence belonging to these last years may be introduced here.

W. J. B. TO MISS C. M. YONGE.

THE PALACE, ELY, Sept. 19, 1886.

It was very pleasant to see a letter directed by your hand and addressed to me. I am afraid however that ungratefully I thought how much pleasanter it would be to see yourself in the flesh. We want you more than I can say to visit St. Hugh and all the wonders of Lincoln. Do think about it. I wish that I could have fulfilled your bidding. I should have felt much honoured in doing so. But I never go—when I can get off—

to Church Congresses; and, fortunately for me, the Bishop of
Ripon wrote to me to ask me to speak when all my days were
occupied. . . . I am most glad that you decline to appear
on platforms. These platform women are doing much harm
to themselves, and to society at large. In fact, the line which
some of them [take],—and I fear a good many more,—is one of
the worst symptoms of the present age. Satan is striking at
the *citadel*—which women are. . . .

W. J. B. TO MISS C. M. YONGE.

THE DEANERY, LINCOLN, Feb. 27, 1887.

It is rather remarkable that I was so much exercised by the
account of the Droxfield 'Mission' as incontinently to write to
The Guardian. It is probable that you will see my letter on
Thursday. And I begin, "As one brought up in the school
of Mr. Keble and Dr. Pusey." You are quite right—so far as
I am able to judge—and —— is on a very dangerous tack.
—— is no theologian. He is a very worthy and devout man,
but essentially a 'sentimentalist.' I have seen his little books.
. . . But after glancing at them I saw plainly that they were
not made of the right stuff, but belonged to that dangerous
Lutheran school which has done more harm than any other—
even than Calvinism—because it exactly suits the instincts of
the natural man. If I understand Christianity aright, it is
directed equally against the two great crying sins—pride and
sloth. Therefore first of all it claims that every proud thought
shall be brought down, and next that men should take up their
cross and follow Christ—that is, lead a life of effort and struggle.
Pride is humbled by the institution of the ministry of man to
man—use of sacraments—obedience to the Church. But
Lutheranism ignores all this, and actually stimulates human
pride by enabling them to assert that they *are* saved. And
the attack upon 'works' is the answer to 'take up the cross.'
Thus by substituting a gospel which is not a gospel, it contrives
neatly to neutralise Christianity. Then is it justifiable to claim
forgiveness before repentance is made certain? But how can
this be brought about by merely listening to an ecstatic sermon
—the feelings stimulated—and no 'fruits meet' brought
forth?

'This new development of 'High Churchism' causes me great uneasiness. It is the old story. People will not be patient—forget that 'stare super antiquas vias' is the only safe principle—daub their walls with untempered mortar, and rejoice in the shallow results—forgetting that the 'great hailstones' will sooner or later fall.

For my own part, I should say that in a parish like yours a mission could not be advisable. If the quiet regular pastor's visits, and the well-cared-for schools, and the frequent services will not meet the case, then nothing will. The church may be filled for a certain number of services, and a certain number of people may be stirred, etc. But all the real result could be produced much more healthily and thoroughly, though not so showily, by the regular parochial routine. . . .

This is the letter to which he refers :

EMOTIONAL EXPRESSION AT MISSIONS.

SIR,—As one brought up in the school of men like Mr. Keble and Dr. Pusey and others of the same mind, I feel bound to enter my humble protest against the doings of "the Mission of the very remarkable character," held at Shedfield, near Botley, Hants, and described in the last *Guardian*. I read these words :

"When, towards the close, those who *felt* they had received forgiveness of their sins, and had chosen Christ for their Master, were asked to give a sign by standing up or holding up their hands (while all the congregation were kneeling with their eyes covered) the number was very large."

Have we really descended so low as this? Is this the theology of the Church of England? Did the "extempore preacher of great power and ability" imagine that such demonstrations have anything of real worth? How did these people know that they had received forgiveness for their sins? Must not repentance precede forgiveness, and what proofs had they given of anything like true repentance such as ought to satisfy themselves or others? If the eloquent gentleman who held them "spellbound" would study an honestly written life of John Wesley, such as Abbey and Overton, or Lecky have described it, or if he would make himself acquainted with what is called "Revival work in America," he would find that it is a comparatively easy matter, yet not without considerable danger, to kindle emotional expression, but very difficult to lay the real foundation of a Christian life. WILLIAM BUTLER.

THE DEANERY, LINCOLN, February 26, 1887.

W. J. B. TO MISS C. M. YONGE.

BUCCLEUGH VILLA, FORT WILLIAM,
Aug. 19, 1893.

Let me add my word of mindfulness and love to the many which have come to you at this time. The reason why my name was not among those who sent the address to you was simply because, in the deep affection and reverence which I feel towards you, it did not appear to me sufficient for the occasion. Few can realise like me, who remember you a bonny young maiden riding your pony to Hursley, what you have been and what you have done, how you have maintained the good old ways of Mr. Keble and the *Tracts for the Times*, and how freely you have offered of your best 'pro Ecclesiâ Dei.' I am afraid to say more. You would say that the Keble mind abhors praise. But I just wished to explain what might possibly have seemed to you strange, considering the friendship with which you have so long honoured me, and which I appreciate more than words can say.

We are here in the heart of the Highlands, close to Inverlochy Castle where Montrose defeated Argyll as Sir Walter Scott tells in the *Legend of Montrose*, and twelve miles from Glencoe, which we visited on Monday—a wild, savage glen, though hardly so savage as William's soldiers. We have in face of us Loch Linnhe and the mountains beyond, and at our back Ben Nevis frowns upon us, though he has used us gently, sparing us the cold and wet with which generally he treats his guests. . . . Very earnestly I pray that God's blessing may rest upon you, and give you health and strength and joy and peace in this present time, and the reward of faithful service hereafter.

W. J. B. TO MRS. WILKINS.

THE DEANERY, LINCOLN, Feb. 15, 1887.

. . . In the nature of things I can hardly hope to see many more birthdays. I have now nearly "finished my course." And certainly my greatest happiness lies in the thought that, humanly speaking, Wantage will enjoy good Church teaching for many a long year, and that as one generation follows another the love of Christ and His Church strengthens rather than weakens. There is nothing like it to bring out the best stuff that there is in every one. Not only does it make people *good*, but it makes them clever and capable. See how well our Wantage lads do in London. . . . Why? Because they have learnt the real gospel—not the sham thing that people call the gospel, all feelings and rubbish, but the gospel which Christ taught, which commands men to use the means of grace, to accept the ministrations of God's ministers, and to obey the Church. All this is definite and clear, something that one can understand. But "Come to Christ"—what does that mean? Or "Have you found peace?" to which a very holy man, a friend of mine, replied, "No, *I* have found war," meaning that a Christian man has to fight if he is to hold his own. . . .

W. J. B. to Mrs. Wilkins.

The Deanery, Lincoln, Feb. 11, 1888.

. . . It is now forty-one years since I first settled down in Wantage in bitter cold weather, and deep snow lying on the ground. You remember the old vicarage—a tumble-down old house, with thin walls, through which the snails used to find their way into our drawing-room. My study was upstairs, and the labouring men used to clamber up, and leave plenty of their traces on the staircase and the landing.[1] In 1850 we got into the present vicarage, and a wonderful comfort it was to have over our head a good solid roof, and pleasant rooms to live in. We thought ourselves in great state when we got there. *That* was altogether a remarkable year, for besides the vicarage, we had the new schools opened, and laid the first stone of the Grammar School, and consecrated the cemetery. I little thought in those days of being Canon or Dean. All

---

[1] One of those labouring men, meeting him on one of his visits to Wantage, observed, "Ye be main changed since I remembers you, sir." "Well, Bill, I usen't to wear a shovel hat and gaiters." "Nay, it's not that, sir, but ye be getting an old man." The Dean related this story with infinite delight.

that I asked for was not to be persecuted—just to be let alone, to work out my plans for the Church and parish. . . .

W. J. B. TO MRS. WILKINS.

THE DEANERY, LINCOLN, Feb. 11, 1889.

. . . Certainly there is no place which I love to be in so much as my old parish, and I quite agree with you in loving the old church. There are much finer churches in the county, and there are others in other places more decorated and beautified, but for dignity and homeliness combined I know none which equals ours. It is now $31\frac{1}{2}$ years since it was restored. What a fight I had to get it done! Do you remember how some put about that we were going to "ruin the dear old parish church"? This was said and *printed* by some who did not care a farthing for the church, but who wanted to oppose any attempt to make things better. And then there was that vestry in 1852, when all the roughs in the place came to make a noise and bully. This is a very good example of how "the gates of hell cannot prevail against the Church," for in 1857 the work was done and *well* done. And many of those who had most opposed it . . . were ashamed of themselves and came round. So I believe it will be in the case of our good Bishop of Lincoln. "The waves of the sea are mighty and rage horribly, but He that dwelleth on high is mightier." Yet it is, as you say, a cruel attack. . . . The only move that I shall ever make from this will be, in all probability, to my last earthly home. So that you must not think of Bishoprics for me. . . .

W. J. B. TO MRS. WILKINS.

THE DEANERY, LINCOLN, Feb. 11, 1892.

. . . The old vicarage was a queer old place, parts of it five hundred years old, very draughty and inconvenient. Then that summer came small-pox, and we had many cases. Our nurse had it very badly. She was always marked by it. I got some credit because I visited the people regularly, while the Wesleyan preacher took panic and went away. That was useful in the beginning of my ministry, especially as I took a new line of services and the like, [different] from those who had gone before me. . . .

W. J. B. to his Sister.

THE MEAD, WANTAGE, Feb. 14, 1890.

. . . You are fortunate in not having the avalanche of letters which overwhelms me when my birthday arrives. Half the school mistresses in England (to speak with some little hyperbole) have noted it down, and write kind words which alas! must be acknowledged—to say nothing of the children at the Wantage schools, pupil-teachers, etc. It is certainly very pleasant to be met with affection, but, like good taste, it has to be paid for.

I spent the last three days partly in Convocation, where we carried a bold proposal, viz., 'that the Brotherhoods' which formed the subject of our discussion should be allowed to take 'dispensable vows of poverty, celibacy, and obedience.' We had, as you may suppose, a good fight. Amendment after amendment was moved, argued out and lost, and at last we carried it triumphantly. It is so ridiculous to water down old words, which bear with them a certain attractive ring, likely to draw enthusiastic hearts. . . .

W. J. B. to his Sister.

HOTEL BUDAN, SAUMUR, July 27, 1892.

. . . Well, we have lived for nearly three weeks in the midst of Renaissance châteaux, and towns. We have seen Compiègne and its forests, Fontainebleau and its gardens, Blois and its 'escalier' and murder chamber, Chambord and its 'tristesse,' Loches and its dungeons, besides various pleasant little, though not very little, inhabited houses, de Beauregard, Chevernay, Azay le Rideau, whose owners are good enough to let visitors enter. I must not forget perhaps the best of them all, Chenonceaux springing from the river Cher, and full of Diana of Poitiers and our old friend Catherine de Medicis. We have worked up our French and can very nearly repeat the names of the Valois kings, and we know something of their wives—and of those whom, sad to say, they preferred to their wives. They were a very bad lot—and I must say, that always excepting Henry VIII., and perhaps Charles and James II., our kings and queens look like saints by their side. Still, they knew how to build and decorate and plant, and though

Renaissance work has a good deal of the earthly and carnal in it, one cannot deny the deft-fingeredness or the imagination of its designs. Salamanders, long-backed dogs, swans with arrows in their breasts, pelicans, and porcupines, are the animals with whom we have made most acquaintance. Now we are in a very different region. Plantagenets and Angevins are our hosts. We visited yesterday Fontévrault, where Henry II. and the spiteful Eleanor and Richard Cœur de Lion lie, and we spent the night at Chinon, the favourite resort of that race. The Plantagenet castle is gone, still the foundation remains of the walls, but the huge interior is become a vineyard. But there are still to be seen the salle in which Charles VII. first greeted la Pucelle, and the tower in which the dear saint was lodged during her stay at Chinon. If the Pope would call her a Saint, there would be some more reason than in the case of some of those who bear the name in the Roman calendar. . . . The worst of these French towns is their pavement, sometimes even, sometimes rough, but always and everywhere large stones, half a foot square, which make every wheelbarrow sound like a train. People moreover are early birds, and the noise, which does not cease till near eleven, begins before five. . . .

CHAPTER XII.

THE LAST YEARS.

I WILL try now to describe Dean Butler as he was in relation to the Cathedral; but it is not easy work. He was so entirely unlike the conventional Dean. The charge of 'dying of dignity' could not be laid against him, although he knew perfectly well how to hold his own and check a liberty. It was a surprise to find oneself told not to ring the front door bell when one wanted to see him, but to come straight into the house by the private entrance from the cloister, and knock at his study door. It was his way at Wantage, he said, with his curates. Soon I found that he liked one to come to him between 9.30 A.M. and 10. Naturally one hesitated to interrupt him at such an hour when he would be in the thick of his correspondence, but he liked it, and so one gradually got into the way of it. Even if one had nothing particular to ask or say, he liked the feeling of having some one with whom to discuss matters, to tell his plans, and often to instruct in the way he wished things to be done.

I learnt very early that the conventional attitude
of an ecclesiastical dignitary to a subordinate was
not his. On my once quoting some flippant remark
that curates and national school masters were thorns
in the flesh to the parochial incumbent, he pulled
me up quite sharply, "Why, my curates have been
always my best and dearest friends." No one can
read the verses he wrote on his curates without
seeing how true these words were. At Lincoln he
took pains to seek out and become acquainted with
curates in the city parishes.

Of course he expected one to work, and he exacted
a good deal; but then he set such an example in
himself of unceasing work, that however one might
feel inclined to grumble, one felt one's mouth closed
by the sight of a man of his age, with a position
which invited inactivity, working from morning till
night, and yet keeping bright and cheerful through
it all.

Up at six every morning, he set to work at once.
Working-men, who knew his early hours, would come
to him then with demands on his counsel or help.
After his breakfast at 8.30 till ten he would be
busy with correspondence. Shoals of letters came
from all parts of England. Letters asking advice
in spiritual matters would form a large proportion.
Letters from clergymen in country parishes asking
him to come and cheer them by preaching in their
churches on Sundays. Letters from clergymen in
distress begging for some pecuniary aid. Letters
relating to the numerous branches of the Wantage

Sisterhood, as far away as India. At all these he
would be working hard when one tapped at his study
door at about twenty minutes to ten. I hardly ever
saw him impatient, though the interruptions to even
a ten minutes' talk would be frequent. Sometimes
he would be in the middle of an important letter,
and would tell me to take the paper and sit down.
In a few minutes the letter would be finished, and he
would then jump up and stand with his back to
the fire, or perch himself on the arm of his Windsor
chair, to listen to what one had to say. I never
remember being sent away except when he was
engaged in some important interview. He would
then robe and go to the Cathedral for matins, walking
with a quick firm step across the choir, but never
omitting a brief but reverent inclination to the altar
as he passed. On entering the vestry he would go
to the end of the table, and after a few whispered
words on any necessary business, he would cover his
face with his hand and remain standing in that
posture till the hour sounded. It was all in keeping
with his intense dislike to anything that savoured
of irreverence. He could not endure trivial chat
about the morning's paper, politics, or local gossip,
just before taking part in Divine service. To him
it was a very serious thing, and he earnestly desired
that the choir men and choristers should keep as
quiet as possible in their respective vestries. If he
heard loud talking as he passed by he would stop
and say something. He, at any rate, set the example
of reverence he wished them to follow. Looking

back on the nine years during which I was brought
into close contact with him, I note some characteristics of which the outside world may be ignorant.
His was a very grateful nature.   In my intercourse
with him I could not but be struck with the warmth
of gratitude with which he spoke of all who had
shown him kindness or helped him.   It was after
all so little that one could do, but it was enough to
make him express himself with the utmost warmth
towards all his Lincoln friends, whether belonging to the Cathedral or the diocese at large, who
had supported him.   Again, there was much more
softness in his nature than the outside world gave
him credit for.   Many who only saw him from a
stranger's point of view thought him hard, abrupt,
unyielding, unsympathising.   They did not know
what tender fibres lay under that seemingly hard
exterior.   I can recall now how miserable he was
on being told he had unwittingly wounded the feelings of a lady by something he had said in her
presence, and how he was not to be comforted till he
had personally assured her of his regret.

In speaking of a case where an incumbent was
parting with his curate, I heard him say, "I have
no doubt he is right in getting rid of him, but I
should like it done kindly."   After his death the
father of a family in writing to me said, "I never
knew one who so watched to do kindness to my
boys."[1]   And again, I was always struck with his

---

[1] His love for children was very great, and he delighted in producing
a little silver box from his pocket, and giving a jujube from it to any

indifference to public praise in regard to any of the changes he effected in the Cathedral. Once more, he was by no means so unwilling to confess himself wrong as some have thought who judged him by the dogmatic tone of his assertions.

Certainly he never hesitated to speak his mind, and it was generally made up; but I have known him more than once retract an opinion and candidly own he was wrong, and many times in discussing some subject on which a difference of opinion might be entertained, he has said, "I may be wrong." Of course, with his large experience of parochial life, he could not fail to have a tolerably well-grounded opinion on most matters connected with a parish, but he by no means looked back on his Wantage life as totally free from mistakes. On the contrary, in talking it over with me, he has said sometimes that in some points he should have done differently had his life been lived over again.

I have mentioned these traits in his character because those who only knew him slightly, or who held aloof from him, would probably not recognise them. It cannot be denied that there was something in his manner and mode of speaking which was calculated to make people think him hard and opinionative. He had no patience with sentimentalism, nor indeed with sentiment if it interfered with what he thought was practically beneficial. This

little one with whom he came in contact. The surprise and satisfaction this occasioned to a little French baby in an out-of-the-way village near Compiègne was pretty to behold, as was the way the mother's face lighted up at this unexpected notice from a stranger.

brought him into disgrace with architectural critics
when he insisted on the pavement of the retrochoir
being relaid and made smooth for the benefit of the
congregation who met at 8 A.M. on Thursdays and
at 4.45 P.M. for the short addresses on Saints' days.
He could not conceive the advantage of retaining
the old uneven pavement, and was deaf to all remonstrances. So also with the Chapter-house. He
never could rest till the Diocesan Conference and
missionary meetings were transferred from the
County Assembly Rooms to what he considered a
far more seemly place; but the levelling of the
sloping floor was a grievous offence to many who
did not understand his motive in wishing to make
use of an ecclesiastical building for ecclesiastical
purposes, and the rumour spread abroad that the
Dean was spoiling the Cathedral. He would only
laugh on being told this, and I don't think he
minded it. So long as he was clear on the main
point he did not trouble himself with details.

On another occasion, in a speech on behalf of the
School of Art, he used a phrase which gave offence
to some, when he said that the "people of Lincoln
needed a little civilization." Of course his meaning
was clear enough to any one who understood the
technical sense of the word, but there were some
who insisted that he had insulted Lincoln by calling
its people barbarians !

Little things like these often conspired to give
outsiders an unfavourable impression. His out-
spokenness was often unpalatable to those who might

otherwise have been more drawn to him. He never minced matters. He would tell you plainly that he had no opinion of district visitors, that clergymen's wives often did a great deal of mischief by meddling, or as he would say, by "poking their noses" into parochial matters where they were not wanted; that a clergyman was of little use unless he taught religion daily in the parish school; that large congregations were no proof of a clergyman's efficiency, and such like. Now he would qualify all these assertions if any one entered into conversation with him. What he really meant was that district visitors' work is often inefficient when they are not trained, and will not submit to training. What his sentiments were respecting clergymen's wives can be best shown by the following letter:

W. J. B. to Rev. ——

Lee House, Brighton, January 15, 1888.

. . . So you have met your fate at last. I believe that, situated as you are, you will find that your work will be greatly strengthened by having a partner. Not that I believe in what are called 'clergywomen,' nor in the claim which people sometimes make on clergymen's wives to do parochial work. I do not consider that they have any more call to this than any other ladies. ALL people ought to take their part in good works, and so far, no doubt, the wife of a clergyman ought to set a good example. But I resent the *claim*. Mrs. Jones, the lawyer's wife, and Mrs. Brown, the squire's wife, etc., etc., are just as much bound in the sight of God to do good to their fellow-creatures as Mrs. ——, the vicar's wife. And the consequence of the claim being allowed or recognised is that clergymen's wives are often fussy, self-asserting, and negligent of their own households. The first thing for every married woman to do is to have her house well ordered, whether she be the wife of clergyman or layman. Then, *after that*, let her do what she can for others. I am sure that in this way a clergyman will win more respect, have more πίστις ἠθική, and so be able to do more for his flock, than if his wife went poking about into the people's houses, and giving tongue at temperance meetings, or G.F.S., or mothers' meetings, and the like.

Now I did not mean to write all this yarn. It flowed out spontaneously and would not stop.

I hope that we soon may have the pleasure of seeing you and your future wife. You know how glad we should be to receive you at Lincoln. Only if you come, you must come soon. We are all growing old, and before very long you may be called upon to attend something very different from wedding feasts. . . .

He himself had taught daily in the Wantage schools for thirty-four years, and he never faltered in his conviction of the importance of this duty. The real proof of a clergyman's efficiency he believed to be shown in the number of the communicants, not in the number of those who simply came to church possibly for the music or for the preaching. But strong statements sometimes scared and repelled people. He was not merciful to self-indulgence in any form, and never liked a clergyman to smoke. In answer to arguments he would simply say, "Mr. Keble never did." I think this reference to one whom he reverenced more than any other man in the Church of England, helps to explain his attitude towards what are usually thought harmless indulgences. Every one who reads Dr. Pusey's *Life* must be struck with the austerity, and indeed asceticism, which marked the lives of the Tractarian party. Dean Butler had come in contact with it early, and had found in Mr. Keble a guide and pattern he never refused to follow. Hence, he had one good-humoured answer to all who pleaded for a mitigation of the rigid rule he held against a clergyman smoking, or dancing, or shooting, " Mr. Keble never did it."

But he had also a deeper reason for this strictness. He had a very strong conviction that in these days the Church is on her trial, and that what was tolerated in past days would not be tolerated now. He was fond of saying that formerly people believed in the Church, but that now they believe in the parson—meaning that whereas they once had faith in the Church as a *system*, they now only had in individuals.

No one who knew his daily life as a Dean could possibly think he held up a standard of life which he did not keep to. His life as a parish priest had been such as probably few would have lived who so early met with rich preferment. He told me that when he went to Wantage the living was £800 a year, and that when he had paid his curates, and subscriptions to schools and charities, only £150 remained, so that had he been destitute of private means he could not have carried out his plans. His style of living was of the simplest, and he only had a late dinner on state occasions. Social pleasure he put aside, and seldom dined out in the neighbour-hood. Each day was a day of hard work, spent in the church, in the schools, in the parish. His one relaxation was his annual six weeks' holiday which he always allowed himself, and without which he

would have long before broken down. One cannot
be surprised that Dean Butler, after such a parochial
life, had little sympathy with valetudinarianism, or
clerical apathy or idleness. "Of course it is a grind,"
he would say impatiently, on hearing of some clergyman complaining of work. And he could not endure
discontent. "What is he grumbling about, what
does he want?" he would say; and then, on being
told that so and so wanted to get away to a better
or pleasanter living, he would burst out into strong
condemnation. Of course this laid him open to the
taunt that as he obtained a good living so early, he
could not appreciate the weariness of those who
struggle on for long years on exiguous preferment,
but this is easily shown to be a cavil. His own
life of hard work and rigid self-denial gives the lie
to the insinuation that he could not sympathise with
those who feel the wear and tear of body and mind
in well-worked parishes; and it must also be remembered that the greater part of his Wantage life
was passed ungraced by any mark of favour from
his diocesan. Although Bishop Wilberforce called
him a model parish priest, yet he received his
solitary distinction of an Honorary Canonry of
Christ Church from the hands of Bishop Mackarness.
It was reserved for Mr. Gladstone to have the credit
of relieving him from the toil of a parish by making
him first Canon of Worcester, and then Dean of
Lincoln. Hence, he was never weary of telling
clergymen that if they only did their duty honestly
and single-heartedly, preferment would come in good

time to them, as it had done to him. He had never sought directly or indirectly for it. He could thoroughly sympathise with a man who did his work simply and uncomplainingly; he could enter into his difficulties, and would do all he could to help him; but, as I have said, he could not bear complaints and discontent.

The life he lived as Dean was a continuation of the parochial life under different conditions, but with the same vigour as of old. He would come back on Easter Eve from Wantage, where throughout the whole week most of his time had been spent in hearing confessions and delivering addresses, looking completely worn out; and yet the next morning he would be celebrating Holy Communion in the retrochoir at seven o'clock, giving a short earnest address and later on preaching at matins in the choir with wonderful freshness and vigour; and this at an age when most men crave for rest.

He could not be called a *popular* preacher in the common sense of the term. Nature had not given him a correct musical ear, and there was a curious misplacement of accent which often marred the delivery. He would begin in rather a low-pitched monotonous voice, perfectly distinct; but as he warmed to his subject he would gradually raise his voice, and then, owing to the peculiar acoustic properties of the Cathedral, many words would be lost. But none who heard him could fail to be struck with the intense earnestness, the absolute sincerity of

every word he uttered. His sermons were not, as
I have said, *popular*; they were not flights of
oratory; they were not what is called *comfortable*;
for he realised so deeply the nature and extent of
sin that he could not preach without attacking it in
some shape; but such as they were they made a
deeper impression than the more sugary effusions
of recognised pulpit orators. The remarks of a
Lincoln nonconformist curiously illustrate this.
He was asked whom he liked to hear best in the
Cathedral, and he replied, "the Dean, because he
means business." I do not know that a better description could be given of Dean Butler's sermons.

Although he was a very decidedly High Churchman, yet he did not agree with all the practices of
the High Church party. He always insisted that
there should be a Celebration of Holy Communion
on Good Friday. I remember his dear friend Canon
Freeling, taking the opposite view in conversation
with him, but the Dean was inflexible. His views
on this matter are expressed in letters to a former
Wantage curate.

W. J. B. TO REV. E. J. HOLLOWAY.

WANTAGE VICARAGE, Tuesday in Holy Week, 1880.

I have not much time, but nevertheless your letter must be
answered. Every year I feel more that I have been right in
maintaining the Good Friday Communion. The whole thing
starts from the ignorance of the ritualists, who imagine because
Roman Catholics do not *celebrate* on that day that there was
no Communion. Whereas if they had read and could translate
the "Rituale Romanum," they would have found a special service for the Priest's Communion. Moreover, it is an old English

custom, and though one must take care not to let it supersede, as once it *did* supersede Easter, I do not like to let old traditions drop. We have from twenty to thirty communicants always on that day, and it does not interfere with Easter at all. For my own part I cannot imagine how I could get through the day without Holy Communion. . . .

THE COLLEGE, WORCESTER, March 27 [1884].

. . . I send to you a little pamphlet[1] on a somewhat important subject. The evidence of Tunstal is very striking. For my own part I have never, as you know, abandoned Good Friday Communion. I believe it to be an old English tradition which some of our friends have rashly, in their zeal to imitate Rome, endeavoured to stamp out. I think that you will consider the pamphlet worth perusal.

So, too, he disapproved strongly of the custom recently adopted by many clergy, of refusing to give the chalice into the hands of the communicants. Here he appealed to the rubric, "into their hands," for confirmation of his view.

Although the world had all his life looked upon him as a ritualist, yet he was not one in the ordinary sense of the term. He understood and valued ritual indeed, but only where he conceived it to be intelligible and useful. He once exploded in strong wrath in telling me of a young clergyman who had read the Epistle and Gospel in an inaudible voice, and then defended himself for so doing on the ground that the whole service of the Holy Communion was a mystery! This sort of thing he could not endure with any patience.

[1] "Celebration of Holy Communion on Good Friday the rule of the Church of England," by Rev. A. Wilson, M.A. (George Bell & Sons, 1884.)

In talking with me about confession and Sisterhoods he surprised me by what he said. It is always
hazardous to trust to one's memory, but my impression is that in speaking of confession he said it
was of special benefit to two very opposite classes—
those who had led very sinful lives, and those whose
lives were of singular purity and holiness. The
former, he said, found comfort in an authoritative
absolution, an assurance of forgiveness for their past
sinfulness; while the latter were often distressed by
excessive scruples of conscience, and needed support
and encouragement. But he was not for *pressing*
confession on all. What he said about Sisterhoods
I have more than once heard him repeat. He was
not for the multiplication of such institutions on
separate and distinct foundations. He thought that
they often ran into debt and got into trouble simply
because they were started with insufficient means on
an insecure basis. He never allowed his own Sisters
to beg.

I give these scraps of conversation for what they
are worth, but they serve to show with what openness and frankness he would discuss such matters
with a subordinate. He never shirked a question or
put it aside, but would always do his best to enlighten
one on any point when he was asked. He was very
precise in his views as to the conduct and reading
of the service. He disliked seeing the Bible left
open when once it was done with after the second
lesson. He would say, Our Lord *closed the book*
when He had finished reading. He did not like

words to be clipped in reading the Bible or Prayer
Book ; and I remember on one occasion he asked if
any one ever read the opening lines of the exhortation,
" Dearly *belov'd* brethren." He held that the rhythm
of the sentences required that the "eds" should be
sounded.

His own reading was rapid, but never anything
but intensely reverent. So also his whole demeanour
in church struck one as being that of a man who
realised God's presence. It made him absolutely
intolerant of what he called "sloppiness" in doing
the service. He did not use many modes of expressing reverence which have become common in later
days. He gave a reverent inclination, not a genu-
flection, to the altar. I never saw him use the sign
of the cross in church. And yet the *Paradisus
Animæ* and the breviary were, with his Bible and
Prayer Book, his daily spiritual bread.

His attitude towards nonconformists has already
been touched on by Canon Fowler. I may add
to what has been said that there was a cordial
friendship between him and one of the leading
Lincoln nonconformists, who has earned the gratitude of Churchmen by his munificent gift to the
Cathedral of Queen Eleanor's recumbent effigy. Dean
Butler never passed a Christmas Day without a visit
to his friend's house.

A lecture which he gave to an audience largely
composed of nonconformists subjected him to some
criticism. Of course the matter was exaggerated,
and very soon after his death I found an amiable

clergyman possessed with the idea that he had officiated in a nonconformist chapel.

The Dean never disguised his opinions on the subject of Dissent. He never would allow the stock argument that as we all are trying to go to the same place it does not matter by which road we go. He had no opinion of the 'exchange of pulpits' device by which some have thought our religious divisions might be healed. He would have nothing to do with platform controversy, whereby, he would say, the parson and minister enact "a religious cock-fight" for the amusement of the public. His own view was that, as Dissent had thriven from the Church's neglect of her duties, the only way to make things better was for clergymen to do their duty thoroughly.

Nothing depressed him more than to find a clergyman neglecting his duty. I have known him come back from preaching in remote country villages disheartened and out of spirits at what he had heard of parishes where the clergyman never went near the schools. "How can he expect the people to be other than Dissenters if he does not get hold of the young generation and teach them true Church principles," he would say; and at the suggestion that teaching daily in the school was irksome, "Of course it is a grind. What a grind it was at Wantage getting the children to say their prayers."

In politics he took a line of his own. His feelings and sympathies were, in his later years conservative; but his pet formula, which he was fond of quoting, gives the key to his political convictions: "He loveth our nation, and hath built us a synagogue." So long as a man was patriotic, and a Churchman, he did not ask for more.

His own personal friendships were not affected by political differences. Lord Swansea had been a lifelong friend, and he was on terms of affectionate intimacy with his brother-in-law, K. D. Hodgson, who represented Bristol in the Liberal interest.

On coming into Lincolnshire he had great pleasure in renewing acquaintance with men whom he had been with at Westminster and Cambridge—Canon Welby, Mr. Banks Stanhope, and others. He had an extraordinary memory for faces known to him in early days, and delighted in discussing old times with former school and college friends.

Otherwise, it must be confessed, he never quite cordially 'took to' Lincolnshire. Perhaps few people brought up in the south and coming here late in life, ever do.

He was painfully struck with what seemed to him the want of organisation in the Diocese. Living so long as he had done in a very perfectly organised Diocese like that of Oxford, he could not at first understand why Lincoln should be so different. In vain one used to urge various pleas—that the awkward situation of Lincoln itself, on one side of the county, and not well served by trains, was an obstacle; or that Lincoln never had been held in the same esteem in Lincolnshire as York is in Yorkshire. It was all in vain. The contrasts which he not infrequently drew may have served to repel some from becoming intimate with him ; but as a rule he made friends wherever he went. It was difficult, indeed, to resist such thorough sincerity of kindness, such genuine truthfulness as he evinced in his intercourse with clergy and laity. Some held aloof, but though he was quite aware of their sentiments, he never gave vent to any bitterness in what he said of them. On the contrary, in one case he took special pains to gratify what he knew were the wishes of a clergyman, although he was perfectly aware of the latter's feeling towards him. It was all of a piece with the generosity of his nature to try to satisfy another man's desires without getting any thanks for doing so.

I close these recollections with two letters; one written from Scotland. The first words make one feel ashamed that one should have added to his labours by asking him for help during one's holiday ; but he was always only too willing to give it.

BUCCLEUCH VILLA, FORT WILLIAM, August 14, 1893.

I can manage September 24. We are not at all badly situated here, with a loch and mountains in front, and Ben Nevis behind us. House clean and sweet. We are waited upon by two Miss Macdonalds, daughters of a vigorous Highlander who has all the coaching and other traffic business in his hands—a stout Episcopalian and Conservative. He comes from Glencoe, whither, about twenty miles off, he is to drive us to-day. We went to the church here—built mainly by the exertions of Mr. Davey, friend of Mr. Hutton Riddell—a really satisfactory building. . . . We met many friends in Edinburgh ; visited the Cathedral, which is really a fine building and has good services. The Dean, Montgomery, is a fine old Scotchman. . . . I am poking a little at Gaelic. It is very hard and barbaric.

The other letter is the last I ever received from him:

THE DEANERY, LINCOLN, September 25, 1893.

Before I get to write my paper for the Church Congress, I will write you a line respecting yesterday's services at Burton. The church was full both times, and the singing and general tone all that one can desire. How sad it is that the same cannot be everywhere! It might were it not for that horrid Methodism and other forms of Dissent; yet even they would be in a great degree neutralised if the clergy did their work faithfully and kindly. . . . Mrs. Butler is still at Wantage. She is to join me at Dogmersfield in October, I believe. We stay with the Mildmays, and I am to preach on the fiftieth anniversary of the rebuilding of the church. My first curacy was there, and a great blessing it has been to me. The Dysons were no ordinary people. They were very clever and affectionate, and took a high view of clerical duty. He had been Professor of Anglo-Saxon, and belonged to that famous old C.C.C. lot, which included Arnold, and Mr. Keble, and Cornish of Kenwyn, and various other noble souls. Make the best of your holiday, and return ruddy, round, and reasonable.

In July, 1893, the Dean and Mrs. Butler celebrated their 'golden wedding.' It was marked by various gifts to the Cathedral, notably a beautiful Bible for the choir lectern from their children and grandchildren, and a gold chalice set with sapphires for use at the altar in the Lady Chapel, from many friends connected with Wantage. No one then had the slightest idea how near the clouds of sorrow were. The Dean's health was good, and although Mrs. Butler was no longer equal to taking foreign tours, yet there was no cause for uneasiness about her. The sonnet written in acknowledgement of the tokens of love and friendship on the occasion of the 'golden wedding' shows however that the Dean had *memento mori* ever before his eyes. But this was no recent thought to him. One of his first acts on coming to Lincoln was to get leave from the Home Secretary for the interment of members of the Chapter and their families in the Cloister Garth, and he selected his own place of burial and frequently pointed it out to friends as he was passing through the Cloister.

> A crumbling wall to fall at lightest breath,
>   A bark hull-covered as the waters rose,
>   A city round whose wall the foemen close,
> An aged man who daily looks on death—
>   Such, dearest friends, am I—yet this remains:
>   A heart which beats in unison with love,
>   A heart which love rejoices like the rains
>   Which fall on thirsty soil and quickly prove
> That life remains within. Thus, then, 'tis mine
>   To feel new life in all the love from all
>   Poured forth on me and her, for lustres ten
> Most wise and helpful mate, true oil and wine
>   To vexed and troubled spirit, whom to call
>   Wife, and my own, exalts me among men.
>   With grateful heart,
>   WILLIAM BUTLER.

A letter written at the same time breathes the same spirit:

W. J. B. TO ——

THE DEANERY, LINCOLN, July 31, 1893.

Many thanks to you and to your father also for 'minding' our fiftieth wedding day. It is very wonderful that we should both be alive and reasonably well, fairly able-bodied and not idiotic. Of course this cannot last for ever, nor much longer. But whenever the change comes my only feeling will be of deepest thankfulness to Him Who has poured so many blessings on my life. Few have had a happier life than I. I trust that the poor return that I have made may be forgiven. You and others do not know how much I have to lament—yet so it is—and the thought of so many good things given makes this all the more keenly felt. . . .

In October the blow came. He was to preach in a church at Maidenhead, and shortly before going up into the pulpit a telegram was put into his hands which told him that Mrs. Butler, whom he had left perfectly well at Lincoln, was stricken with paralysis. The shock must have been terrible, but with his strong sense of duty he would not shirk the task he had to do. He preached, although, as he afterwards said, he did not know how he did it; and after making some necessary arrangements at Wantage, he hurried back to Lincoln.

He found Mrs. Butler greatly recovered, for the seizure was not a severe one, but it was an unmistakeable warning, and he seemed to realise for the first time how slender was the thread of life that bound them together.

No one who knew Dean Butler, and saw him in his family circle, could fail to see that, great as was his love for his children, his affections were centred in his wife. She was everything to him. I shall never forget the change I noticed in him when I went into his study the morning after his return. All the brightness had gone out of his face; he spoke in a low subdued voice, and looked like one who had undergone a terrible shock. And yet the days that followed were in some respects unusually happy ones. He at once cancelled all his immediate engagements, and devoted himself to the care of Mrs.

Butler. Sitting beside her bed and reading to her the
first volume of Dr. Pusey's *Life*—so full of interest to
them both—it was an interval of calm peaceful happiness in a life which had been so full of hard work,
and so much interrupted by absences from home.

Few could know how entirely in sympathy with
her husband's work Mrs. Butler had been throughout
her married life. She had resolved at the outset
never to be a hindrance to him in his clerical duties,
and so through the years of toil at Wantage she had
been content to lead a self-denying life ; to forgo
many of the pleasant refreshments which sometimes
sweeten the life of a hard-working clergyman's wife ;
to see but little of him during the day when he was
busy in the schools and in the parish, or in the
evening when he would be holding classes. And
in this retired life not many knew what reason her
husband had to be proud of the intellectual powers
which she never sought to display. She had an
unusually accurate and retentive memory, and had
received a thoroughly good education. Before her
marriage she and a sister had made various translations from Fouqué, among which their *Sintram* was
praised by J. H. Newman. Mrs. Butler had, moreover, a singularly clear head for business, and had
kept not only all the domestic but also the parochial accounts, setting her husband absolutely free
from all financial cares, so that he used humorously
to relate how that, since his marriage, he had only
once drawn a cheque, which was returned with the
comment " Signature not known."

No wonder then that on the rare occasions when he allowed himself to contemplate the possibility of losing his wife, he used to speak of his future life as almost too wretched to be borne. "I don't know what I should do without Mrs. Butler," he said to me not many days before his death.

He was mercifully spared the trial. Mrs. Butler had recovered from the immediate effects of the seizure, but she came downstairs an invalid, and obliged to lead an invalid's life. The Dean had already begun to take up the threads of his interrupted work, and though his heart was heavy he forced himself to go about with an outwardly cheerful face.

But he felt that death was drawing very near. On a Sunday in December "he came out of the Cathedral in his surplice," writes a near relative, "and stood between the greenhouses looking up at the central tower. 'What a grand place it is! Well, I shall soon be lying beneath it.' Then with a quick change of manner, and looking down at me with a half smile, 'And then everybody will say, He wasn't such a bad chap after all.'"

He was greatly grieved at the death of Mr. Edward Stanhope,[1] for whom he had a very warm regard. He looked upon him quite as a realisation of his conception of what a good man should be—a Churchman and a patriot. When then he was asked by Mrs. Stanhope to preach on the first Sunday after

[1] Edward Stanhope, Secretary for War, M.P. for Lincolnshire, died Dec. 1893.

her husband's death, he willingly consented, though he was not feeling well. On Saturday, December 30th, he came into the vestry of the Cathedral to tell me he was going to Revesby that afternoon, and would not be back till Monday morning, January 1st, and spoke to me about the seven o'clock Celebration of Holy Communion, which he would not be able to take himself as usual. I saw him next on Monday afternoon when he came to Evensong, and read as usual the second lesson, but with evident signs of illness. After Evensong, as it was the Feast of the Circumcision, he gave a short address in the retrochoir on " a new heaven and a new earth," with what those who heard it described as something ' unearthly' in voice and manner. His last words— the last he was to speak in the Cathedral—were, " I will go forth in the name of the Lord God, and make mention of His righteousness only." That evening he had the Cathedral choristers to supper at the Deanery, and seemed outwardly bright and cheerful, but he confessed that he felt exceedingly ill and could not imagine what was the matter with him. I said he ought to see a doctor, but he only smiled, and said he should soon be all right again. He took leave of me at the front door, and said something about Mrs. Butler's health which showed how it weighed upon his mind.

The next day he did not leave his room. No one had any feeling of serious uneasiness, and no unfavourable symptoms showed themselves, though his condition remained unchanged till Friday, January

5th, when he caught a chill, and by the following morning influenza, which was already in the house, had declared itself. Still, even though we heard that pneumonia had set in, we did not realise the danger. He had always seemed so strong and made so light of illness that it was hard to believe he could succumb to any ordinary attack. But the pneumonia had affected both lungs, and the doctor really had but little hope.

Up to this point he had still been working in his sick-room, preparing his Revesby sermon for publication, and answering his Christmas letters. The following is one of the last he wrote :

W. J. B. TO ——

DEANERY, LINCOLN, Jan. 5, 1894.

Thank you for your kind Christmas greeting, which alas! I have been utterly unable to acknowledge till now, so vast a heap of business of all kinds which had to be got through was lying on my shoulders. Now I am regularly laid by, with the severest throat and chest attack that I have ever had. I can hardly speak for five minutes without coughing myself to pieces. I am in my bedroom, and there likely to bide, especially if this bitter weather holds on. Fortunately all that I had to do—except letters which I can manage—was done before *I* was done for.

I hope that all went well with you and —— on Christmas day, and that you have taught the folk that Christmas means more than roast beef and pudding. How shocking it is to see how the world has snatched from the Church even its holiest days!

Mrs. Butler (D.G.) continues to mend. You would not, I am sure, perceive that she had ever been ill. She is in very good force and spirits. —— and ——, poor dears, have enough to think about, but they seem to stand it pretty well. . . .

He got worse. On Tuesday, the 9th, I was sent for to administer the Holy Communion to him and Mrs. Butler. He had more than once told me he expected me to come to him if he died at Lincoln, because, as he said, "You know my ways." He was in a small bedroom adjoining Mrs. Butler's, and I only saw him when I went in to give him the Holy Communion. Even then he seemed so strong, took the chalice in so firm a grasp, that I never imagined the end was so near. The next day a doctor from Leeds came to consult with the Lincoln medical man. We heard that if he could get over Sunday he might possibly pull through. In the course of the week the Bishop said to him, "It is worth while to be ill for Dr. Pusey," referring to a Review of Dr. Pusey's *Life* on which he had been working, though feeling the strain in the midst of all his other work; he responded with a bright look.

Through Saturday night I sat up at the Deanery in case he should pass away suddenly. All hope was then over. Early on Sunday morning the doctor told him of his hopeless state. He hardly at first seemed to comprehend it, for his strength was still very great. The fever had gone, but the lungs were both clogged, and the heart was failing.

I went to him soon after eight, and read a psalm and some prayers from the "Visitation of the Sick." At nine I went at his desire to the palace, to tell the Bishop he was dying and to ask him to come.

The Bishop came and read the commendatory

prayer, and gave him his blessing. His utterance was much impeded, and it was difficult to make out clearly what he said, but the few words that fell from him were full of gratitude and affection and calm trust.

I had to go to —— at ten o'clock for the service, and I took leave of him, not expecting to find him alive when I returned at one. But he lingered on in full consciousness, and said farewell to his wife, who was brought from her sick-bed to see him once more. He gave directions that any flowers which might be sent after his death should be given to the patients at the County Hospital. His spirit passed away just as the bells ceased to ring for the four o'clock service.

The next Sunday, January 21st, Mrs. Butler followed him. They lie in the Cloister Garth, in the north-east corner, a spot he had marked out for himself some time before. After his wife's funeral a short bright peal of bells, in accordance with the Canon, was rung; and some people, who were more accustomed to funeral peals, and did not know the reason, were perplexed. A maid-servant who had been a member of his communicants' class told her mistress that she wondered at first, but now was sure they did it for joy, because the Dean and Mrs. Butler were once more together.

Among the many letters which poured in after William Butler's death, one of the most touching was from the Curé of St. Ouen, whose visit to Lincoln

in the previous year has been mentioned. He was
the last of a series of foreign priests with whom a
friendship had been established, on terms of mutual
respect, Christian charity, and no compromise.

St. Ouen de Rouen, le 28 Janvier, 1894.

Très-Honoré Monsieur,—C'est avec des larmes dans les
yeux, que j'ai lu la lettre que vous avez eu la très-grande
bonté de m'écrire. . . . Pauvre Monsieur le Doyen !

Comme je le vénérais, comme je l'aimais et comme je le
regrette ! Et Madame votre si respectable mère, quel délicieux
souvenir j'avais emporté d'elle !

Je crois vraiment que la nouvelle d'un décès dans ma famille
ne m'aurait pas plus vivement impressionné que celle de la
perte si inopinée, si inattendue de deux personnes amies pour
lesquelles j'avais un véritable culte de respectueuse affection.
Comme vous le dites si bien et d'une manière si touchante, ils
sont partis tous deux dans la foi d'une Église qui repose sur
la même fondation que la nôtre.

Oh certes, je n'ai pas l'ombre d'une doute qu'ils n'aient reçu
tous deux dans le ciel la récompense de leur foi et de leurs
admirables vertus.

Vous permettrez pourtant à ma foi catholique romaine, cette
douce consolation de prier pour le repos complet de l'âme de nos
regrettés défunts, en offrant à leur intention le Saint Sacrifice
de la Messe. Pour que vous puissiez vous unir de loin à ma
prière, je compte dire cette Messe à St. Ouen Dimanche prochain
à neuf heures en présence du Très-Saint Sacrement exposé
solennellement. . . .

Agréez, très-honoré monsieur, l'hommage de mes condoléances
les plus sympathiques et les plus respectueuses en N.-S. J.-C.

The late Rev. T. B. Pollock of St. Alban's,
Birmingham, noted down some recollections of
a long friendship before he too passed to his
reward:

. . . What St. Alban's owes to him we can never fully
tell. When we were in lowest depths, and every man's hand
and voice were against us, and we had hard work to keep any
faith in the future of what we were trying to do, he came, and
was the means of turning the whole course of things. He
had preached at Holy Trinity for E. C. U. On the morning
after, he came to the early Celebration at St. Alban's, and breakfasted with us. This was about twenty-seven years ago. He
went into the whole history of our troubles with the kindest
interest, and braced us at once by the contagion of his strong
spirit. He spoke to Lord Beauchamp, who visited St. Alban's,
and offered to be one of the trustees, and was till the day of his
death an active friend of the work, with his influence and his
offerings.

We were in heavy debt, and some of our lay people urged the
sale of St. Patrick's mission-room and schools. Your father was
the means of sending us an anonymous offering of £1500, which
saved what now promises to be a work almost as large as that of
St. Alban's.

We knew well how much he was in demand, and felt diffident
about asking him to come to us as often as he did; but he
always came when he could, and with a readiness that made his
help more valued. Some one wrote, I think in the *Guardian*,
that he was a man "more to be feared than loved." This was to
us most strange. I never met one in his position with whom
one was able to be more absolutely at one's ease, sure of his
warm kindness of heart. He never 'pawed' or fondled people,
either with words or hands, as the manner of some is. He had
stronger and more manly ways of showing affection and winning
it. A born ruler of men, no one ever seemed to me more to
recognise the 'authority' under which he was. He had no
patience with wilfulness and private fancies, and used constantly
to urge the carrying out in its thoroughness of the system of
the Church which entrusted us with a commission. Some years
ago he expressed great concern at the new notions about fasting,
which he said were becoming common. He said he would like
greatly to see Dr. Pusey, who first taught him, and ask what
his feeling was about the change. Fasting used to be looked
upon as a discipline and self-denial, but now, even in religious
houses, it was becoming merely a matter of formal obedience,

and the most dainty and luxurious food was provided, all being thought right, if only meat was avoided.   When the Dean was with us during the week of the Congress in Birmingham, he was as cheery as a boy ; but he often said things that plainly showed a feeling that his life was not to be long.   Talking one day he said, " I only care now for friends and books.   Anything else—give it to Chimham."   And twice before, when he was leaving us he said, " I always think now when my visit to you comes to an end, that it is my last." . . . Many feel with me that his friendship was indeed a blessing for which to thank God.   There are few friends to be found so true and so stimulating, so kind and so strong.   May God raise up for this Church in England men such as he was. . . . He was with us about the time that he left Wantage for Worcester. I remember his saying that people told him that the work at Wantage would go to pieces without him, and that he had replied, " Then the sooner the better, for if so, it is Butler and not Christ."   At his next visit he told us, with delight in his face and voice, that at the last Christmas there had been more communicants than there ever were in his time. . . . But for the help which he obtained for us to save St. Patrick's, our school and other organisations would be now, as far as we can judge, about half what they are.   We indeed owe it to him that we are about to build another church nearly as large as St. Alban's, with its complete organisation.

The great point which he was never tired of urging was the duty of working the Church system as laid down in the Book of Common Prayer.   This he was convinced would, if thoroughly used, meet all needs in a better and more lasting way than the new and exciting methods that are being constantly invented.

It was thought fitting that the Cathedral to which his last years had been devoted should contain a memorial of him ; and on St. Mark's day, April 25, 1896, the Bishop of Ely, in the presence of many friends, unveiled the alabaster effigy on an altar tomb which had been erected in his memory.   The inscription summarises the character which it has been the aim of this book to portray.

In pace Dei requiescat
Pastor animarum
Sagax simplex strenuus
Willelmus Johannes Butler S.T.P.
Ecclesiæ huiusce Cathedralis decanus
Qui natum se atque renatum
Non sibi sed Christo ovibusque Christi ratus
Austera quadam caritate
Labore indefesso assidua prece
Id egit
Domi foris validus ægrotans
Ut amorem Dei erga peccatores testatus
A peccatis reduces in amore Dei confirmaret.

APPENDIX I.

EXTRACTS FROM 'SPIRITUAL' LETTERS.

I suppose that different people find comfort and help in different manners. To me nothing is more stirring than the lives of men who have nobly served our Lord—*e.g.* Bishop Gray, or Patteson, or St. Charles Borromeo, or Gratry (La Jeunesse du Père G.), or Montalembert. They help one, I think, to long and to try. To St. Paul the thought of our Lord "Who loved me, and gave Himself" had an inspiring force.

Wandering thoughts are a trial to every one. The great test of spiritual progress is not, I think, freedom from them, but power to resist temptation. If you find that you have more power over your tongue—more ability to restrain a satirical remark—or at least more consciousness of its evil, and regret for it after giving way; or again, if you find yourself more ready to make sacrifices for others' sake, in one word, more unselfish, or, if you are more careful to give the right time to prayer, whether or not the thoughts may be distracted. All these and such as these are *tests*. Feelings are worth almost nothing. Do you know Newman's sermon "On the Use of Excited Feelings"? It is well worth reading. I think that it is in Vol. IV. The great *help* to spiritual progress is the gaining a deep sense of God's love, referring all to Him, resting on His love. I believe that people become good much more by looking out of, than into, themselves. "Beholding as in a glass the glory of God, we are changed into the same image," etc. We cannot become good by self-analysis. That will indeed show us our own sinfulness, but it is the bringing the soul under the light of God's countenance which enables it to slough off evil, and to develop good, just as the sun, not the gardener's broom, frees the soil from the damp of dew.

Every one makes progress who *means* to do so. This is a great law. The stone is always rolled away at the proper time. But then we must climb the hill. That means effort.

After all, what is food but medicine, and I cannot see why it is more sinful to eat a slice of mutton than to take a dose of quinine or of cod-liver oil. Of course I quite accept that some sort of fasting is needful. We are bound to obey the Church. We are wise to subdue our flesh, and to strengthen the will by such mortifications as we can manage without injury to health. But there I make my stand. I will never give in to the fish and pudding theory *versus* meat. It seems to me both superstitious and dangerous. But there is much to be said on this subject, partly limiting, partly explanatory.

Do not fret about 'deep feelings.' The great thing is simply to be desirous to *do* God's will. Feelings are not under our control, at least they are so only in a limited degree. They are more physical than spiritual, though people lay so much stress on them and imagine because they have susceptible nerves, they are in the road to heaven. "In quietness and confidence shall be your strength." Hurrell Froude somewhere says that he wishes to be a 'hum-drum.' There is a great deal in that. He means that he admires those who just go on from day to day doing their natural work, and not fidgeting or fussing, simply trusting to God as a merciful and loving Father, Who, if He meant to slay us, would not accept "a burnt-offering at our hands."

Lent is an excellent time for a fresh start, and such starts and beginnings do really make up our poor earthly life, and we must be satisfied. "There is no condemnation for those which are in Christ Jesus, who walk not after the flesh, but after the Spirit." Read all that chapter, Romans viii., very carefully. It is a wonderful exposition of the Christian's real condition. To walk after the Spirit does not imply perfectness of life, but the aiming after it—the following such light as we possess with such strength as we possess. I believe greatly in all that unites the soul in love to God—the use of psalms, prayer, meditation, short ejaculations and aspirations, the Holy Eucharist. These, together with humble confession of sins, seem to me such as cannot fail to bring the soul into the divine image. This is why it is very important to make our prayers a *reality*.

God does not mean that His children's lives should be one long fret and vexation, though He does mean them to be a battle. Yes, a battle, but with the *certainty* of victory, if only the struggle is maintained. The victory is of Him and His grace, but our will and effort must co-operate. Or perhaps one should rather reverse the sentence, and say that His grace co-operates with our effort. When our Lord speaks of peace, He means what *we* call happiness.

Touching Holy Communion, do you know Sadler's little book? It seems to me to be remarkably good and sensible, like all that he writes. I always think that the best and safest plan is to make preparation part of daily prayers, adding, it may be, some special devotion on the days when one communicates. This seems to keep the soul in a quiet and orderly condition, ready for whatever comes. In former days, when Celebrations were few and far between, the week's preparation or the month's preparation was greatly needed, but with *our* happily frequent Communions, it is best I think to live *always* in a state of preparation. And what is better than this for us who know not when the Master cometh? To be prepared for Holy Communion is to be prepared for seeing Him as He is.

The truth is that what is called the world, is, like the kingdom of heaven, something *within* ourselves. If our hearts are worldly, we might be worldly in a Trappist monastery. If our hearts are *not* worldly, then, like Mrs. Godolphin, we may be saints in the midst of a profligate court like that of Charles II. Of course there is a limit to lawfulness in amusements, etc. They may be such as injure the soul, or they may be innocent, yet too much sought after and indulged in. In which case we ought to draw in the reins pretty tightly.

There is no patent road to prayer. Nothing but *effort* will attain it, and self-humiliation for failure. Praying is like springing from the ground. Do what we will, except in some very special cases, the earth draws us downwards. And therefore we *can* only pray as it were by *leaps*. But then we know that God accepts the will for the deed; and growth is 'how a man knoweth not.' It is certainly not measured by *feeling*, but by the power of resisting temptation.

I do not know what to say about 'Guardian Angel.' I do not use such devotions myself, nor do I think that any good comes from it; we know so little. Why not cling to our blessed Lord? Pray Him to give His angels charge. Surely that will do.

There are no patent recipes for getting rid of one's faults. French polish looks well, but does not last. Elbow work does. So it is with our characters. Dodges and artifices, like teetotalism, do not hold on. There is nothing for it but watchfulness, effort, and self-humiliation, continually carried on through life.

I do not think that any one can be better off than where God places her. He can save by few as well as by many, and there is great danger in these days lest people should get the habit of *resting* on means of grace, and imagining that if without their own fault they are deprived of them, they cannot get on. God gives His grace to all who are obedient. And obedience consists in seeking means of grace *when they can be had*, and putting up with the privation of them when it is God's will that this should be the case. The meat with which the angel fed Elijah lasted for forty days. I am not at all sure that many of those who are connected with confraternities, etc., are the better for it. There are no better Christians than the old-fashioned folk who made it a point to read every day the Psalms and Lessons.

I suppose that this may be rightly said: that no one who *tries* to be good, or who mourns and humbles herself for sin, can possibly be cast away. God does not look for victory in

us, but for effort.   When there is effort His Holy Spirit is
working with us, and none can pluck us out of His hands.
The best course in most cases is simply to go on working,
praying, striving, and *not* speculating; trusting simply and
implicitly to His mercy and love, by means of which all must
in the end come right.   I own that I dread and dislike
extremely all theories of purgatory and the like.   Be practical and let imagination alone.   The only use of purgatory
in the Roman Catholic teaching has been (1) to fill the coffers
of Leo X.; (2) to bring on the Reformation; neither of which is
satisfactory.

Do not worry yourself about Church matters.   "Pray for
the peace of Jerusalem," and let all the rest alone.   All is
sure to go well.   "The waves of the sea are mighty, and rage,
but," etc.   *I* think that Mr. Keble's sermons, all and each, are
as precious as gold filings.

I never trouble myself about speculative questions.   The
only thing that I care for is to try to be good as far as I
may myself, and to help others to be the same.   Given that
and all will be well.   You know "Justum et tenacem propositi
virum," etc., or if you do not, get ―― to translate it to you.

Who can define or limit the power of the grace of God
in any soul?   This is quite certain, that "to them that knock
it shall be opened," but it does not follow that they may
not have to knock for a long while, nor even that they will
attain in this present life.   Our work is simply to continue
the struggle, to aim at the highest standard which God
presents to our minds, and to leave it to Him to open the way.
I think that it is quite wrong not to believe Holy Scripture,
or to try to tone it down to suit man's feelings and wishes; and
when our Lord says, "These shall go away into everlasting
punishment, but the righteous into life eternal,"—the word for
everlasting and eternal being exactly the same in the Greek—
how can I believe anything but that one is correlated with the
other, the punishment of the wicked with the happiness of the
good?   Such speculations *can* do no good, and may do an infinity of
harm.   Let all alone, and look to God to make all things right.

The prayer for invocation of the Holy Spirit is *not* essential to consecration. What is essential is to use the words and do the acts with which our Lord instituted it. This is admitted on all sides. No doubt such invocation is reverent and right, and it is through the influence of the Holy Spirit that our Lord's Body is with the bread and wine, even as the divine nature was united with the manhood in the Incarnation. This is the opinion of theologians, and it ought to be enough for *us*. Touching the translation of the Bible. Wait a little. Let us see what is to come. Of course it cannot be accepted without the consent of Convocation, and that consent is not very likely to be given. In all these matters the great thing is not to be in a hurry to judge or to form conclusions.

I do not think it necessary to explain the "sun standing still." Perhaps it simply means that there was light even when the sun went down, that the result was as if it stood still. The Bible does not profess to give lessons in astronomy. So also the shadow on the dial might have receded, without altering the actual movement of the earth. These difficulties are the merest nothings when you come to tackle them. They remind me of a donkey who when he read that God created great whales (Gen. i. 21), suggested that therefore He did not create the little ones. I do not say that *you* are a donkey, but that *he* was.

I think that it is quite lawful to attend R.C. churches abroad. *That* is the Church of the country. We have never excommunicated Rome, and it is quite open to *them* to communicate with *us*, if the Pope allowed it. It is true that they will not receive us to Communion. But what they will permit us to advantage ourselves by, *i.e.* presence at Mass, etc., we are quite justified in accepting, so far as I can see.

Why do you ask such questions as Solomon could scarcely have answered to the Queen of Sheba? It is far better to leave all that sort of thing in God's hand. He knows best, and it is quite certain that He will call none away till it is best that they *should* be called away. How can we tell what refining of the soul goes on in paradise, or even in eternity? No one, as I believe, can be lost who acts according to his conscience, or when he fails to do so, laments and repents. Neither will any be lost who commit sin without knowing what sin is. But, as I said, it is useless to attempt to dive into mysteries. God gives us all the knowledge that is needful for our own edification. That is enough for us.

Your paper is very good as far as it goes, but it is incomplete. You omit the most important part of our Lord's redeeming work. He came to sanctify as well as to justify, and this should never be omitted. The world likes to be told that Christ came to die for sinners, and that to believe is to be saved. But they do not like the idea of being made good, because *this* costs *them* trouble. Any statement of our Lord's work therefore which omits this plays into the world's hands. And again, what is the meaning of 'Justification'? How was it brought about? Not by suffering, but by obedience, Rom. v. 19. His obedience involved suffering, but it makes all the difference to our idea of God, whether you state that He must have obedience, or that He required a sort of vengeance on sinners in Christ's sufferings.

After much anxious consideration and consultation I came to the conclusion that it is absolutely impossible, without breaking our Lord's distinct ordinance, for certain people *not* to take some slight amount of food before communicating. If you care to see a letter from Dr. Pusey on the subject, whose opinion I esteem more than Mr. ——, good and learned though he is, ask —— to send it to you. We must not attempt, as things are with us, to be guided by the rules of either the Primitive or the Roman Church. I wish heartily that it were otherwise, and where the old rule can be observed with impunity to health I always recommend and enjoin it.

I am sorry that you have no early Celebration at ——. It is far better to receive early than late. But if you cannot gain this, then take what food is absolutely needful to prevent you from being unwell, and commit yourself to God's mercy and love, owning to Him your weakness, and praying Him to bring about in His goodness a more Christian and reverent state of things in the parish where you live.

It seems to me that St. Matthias's history ought to help us and give us courage. "The lot is cast into the lap, but the whole disposing of it is of the Lord." In other words, all we have to do is our *best*, then quietly to leave the rest to Him, not fretting or vexing at misfortune or ill success. *He* can take care of His own work. *We* must take care that we do our best; if this be so we shall have an equal reward with the most successful. And as in the case of St. Matthias, whose election I daresay disappointed the friends of Barsabas, that which seems to us disastrous often is in truth the very best thing for the cause which we are trying to benefit.

I am inclined to think that knitting, etc., are *not* good works for Sunday. I do not say that there is anything actually sinful in knitting on Sunday. But it seems to me that it is very important to give Sunday a peculiar character, *i.e.* the character of a day set apart, so far as we can set it apart from other days, for enabling the soul to hold special converse with God. It is true that, formed as we are, we cannot keep the mind long in close relation to heavenly things; but it is greatly helped in doing this by external arrangements, such as closing the shops, avoidance of the ordinary daily occupations, etc. Moreover it is very important to do nothing which may be misinterpreted by those around us, which may lead them to take liberties with what is *on the whole* an edifying English custom, even though injured and made grotesque by Puritanism.

APPENDIX II.

ABSTRACTS OF PAPERS READ AT CHURCH CONGRESSES IN 1869, 1877, 1879, 1883, 1888, AND 1893.[1]

AT the Liverpool Church Congress of 1869, Mr. Butler read a paper on the "Improvement of the Church's Services: how to Increase Attendance at them."

In this paper he begins by deploring the large numbers in towns like Birmingham and Liverpool who are untouched by the Church's ministrations; he declines to believe that Disestablishment (which some good Church people were at that time, it would appear, ready to welcome) would make things any better; —Mr. Butler pointed to the Colonies in support of his contention —and then he goes on to advocate a greater elasticity in services conducted in mission rooms and chapels; he would have the litany as a separate service in the evening, or a metrical litany and a sermon, something simple and easy to follow for those (and he admits there are many) for whom matins and evensong are too elaborate.

But the most remarkable part of this paper is undoubtedly his outspoken utterance on behalf of restoring the Holy Eucharist to its proper place in the public services. "Why," he asks, "have we discarded it from this its due prominence and special character, thrusting it into the end of a long morning service of prayers, psalms, hymns, sermon, when both the heart and head are wearied? We complain of the comparatively small number of our attached church-goers: may we not trace it to this fact? Observe I am not advocating that the Holy Communion should be thrust as it were on all, that all whether fit or unfit should be present at that most solemn service; but that all should have the opportunity of taking part in it, according

---

[1] By Rev. Canon Randolph, Principal of Ely Theological College.

to the ancient and catholic rule of the Church, at least once
weekly."

"From Justin Martyr downwards," he says a little before, "in
one unbroken tradition, as every one who has the slightest knowledge of ecclesiastical history cannot fail to perceive, all writers
describe this as *the* service of the Church, that to which all
others are mere subsidiary handmaids."

Among the speakers who followed the reading of the papers
were the Hon. C. L. Wood (now Lord Halifax) and the Rev. Dr.
Littledale, both of whom strongly supported Mr. Butler's utterance about the Holy Communion.

The paper read at the Church Congress of 1877 was on the
temperance question. It is very characteristic of the writer, and
illustrates the line he took throughout his life on this difficult
subject.

After some apology, feeling no doubt that he was in a
minority, he boldly announces himself opposed to all the three
great remedies usually proposed by temperance reformers ; he is
against legislation, against the formation of a Church Temperance
Society, and against those who preach total abstinence for
every one.

He is against legislation, because "sumptuary laws have had
their day. They belong to that against which the free heart of
England will ever rebel, which is called a *paternal government.*
Let us not forget that while swaddling clothes no doubt keep
children out of mischief, they also restrain the free growth of the
limbs. And I venture to contend that there is a certain discip-
lining of man's nature, which is to be found in resisting
temptation, and which cannot be obtained when temptation is
altogether withdrawn." To illustrate this point he contrasts
(following Montalembert in the *Avenir politique d'Angleterre*) the
system of espionage at a French Jesuit College, with the freedom
of an English public school.

He is against temperance societies, for there must always be
a danger in isolating one sin in this sort of way. "Why," he
asks, "are we to inculcate temperance only in drink ? Does not
the apostle bid us to be 'temperate in all things'? What is
there special in drunkenness which places it in a category outside
all other sins? Are we prepared to have special associations
against lying, selfishness, or that sin of the flesh which, if

drunkenness slays its thousands, may truly be said to slay its tens of thousands—I mean the sin of unchastity?"

So again, "the Church herself is the National Temperance Association, and all special temperance societies got up within her, tend, I humbly submit, to obscure that attribute which equally with 'One,' 'Catholic,' and 'Apostolic' is hers, viz., that of holiness, her right to exact from her members to be holy, not in one thing only, but in all."

He is against total abstinence, though as a "kill or cure" remedy he would allow it in extreme cases, where it is in fact the only chance; but he deprecates "the belief that it is necessary or even right that they who would induce others to be sober should themselves entirely abstain."

Constructively Canon Butler considers that higher intelligence and education, bringing with them higher taste and refinement, will do much for the lower classes, as it has already done much for the higher in respect to this temperance question; the lesson will work downwards; he advocates clubs and reading-rooms, "not on too strait-laced principles." "Let lectures be given explaining how the conditions of happiness lie in habits of self-control. . . . Provide two things which too often are not to be obtained, good pure water, and real honest beer, such as our brethren in Germany enjoy, making it penal—*so far* only would I invoke the aid of legislation—to sell the poisonous concoctions which more than anything else cause the drunkenness of the working-classes; and lastly, inculcate early in life that the body is the temple of the Holy Ghost, and not for fleshly defilement of any kind whatever, but for the Lord, and the Lord for the body."

Canon Butler read a paper at the Swansea Church Congress in 1879, on the congenial subject of Parish Organisation. On a subject such as this he was, it need not be said, thoroughly at home. Every word was dictated by recollections of his own experience as a parish priest.

"The longer I live"—these are almost the opening words of his paper—"the more I believe in the rule, 'stare super antiquas vias'; and I look on the following out of such a system as the Prayer Book suggests, in its unpretentiousness and simplicity, as of infinitely more value in the great battle with evil than some of the more showy efforts of the present day."

He passes at once to the great question of the schools, expressing his conviction that "well-organised schools lie at the very foundation of all good parochial work," and that "no cajolement or threat should induce the pastor to suffer his schools to pass from the hands of the Church." He asserts his conviction that the "battle of the Church is to be fought in the schools," that no pains should be spared in making them efficient, that the parish priest should himself take a lively part in their working, that he should see by actual investigation that the Catechism is thoroughly learnt and understood, that the children's private prayers are said; that he should "draw round himself, and not leave merely to the masters' and mistresses' enforced hours of instruction, the pupil teachers, and carefully supervise their religious teaching"; and that he should establish between himself and the head teachers the relation of true and loving friendship, "as between those who are engaged in one great common work for the glory and praise of God."

He speaks appreciatingly of Guilds for deepening the spiritual life, and warns against the snare of "setting quantity before quality"; and he especially emphasises the importance of communicants' classes, that is, of classes called together and regularly prepared for Holy Communion every month: they work towards this special end, and for this reason they have an advantage, he thinks, over ordinary Bible classes. They involve, he admits, "intense and unremitting labour": "they must be carefully arranged and adapted with a view to difference of age, intelligence, and above all, to those nice grades of social position which exist among the people." Such classes will, he thinks, nearly cover the ground of many other possible organisations.

There follows in this paper a characteristic warning against too much organisation: "a fussy beating up of recruits and subscriptions, writing reports and rushing from meeting to meeting." He pleads for loyalty to the Prayer Book specially in the matter of daily service throughout the year. The service, he insists, said daily in the Church "organises the organiser," that is, the clergyman himself. "It keeps him to his work; it provides for his flock an opportunity of finding him at his post; it spreads over his work that character of dutifulness to the directions of the

Church; the lack of which lies, as I think, at the root of our most pressing difficulties." He insists on the importance of regular visiting, and urges that no machinery or organisation ought to be allowed to supersede the pastor's "own regular and loving visits to his flock." "Of this," he says, "I am quite sure that when it may be done, even as Sir Robert Peel pressed on his supporters the famous advice of 'Register, register, register,' so visit, visit, visit, not by proxy, but in person, face to face and heart to heart, should be the parson's rule."

In speaking of Sunday schools he quoted a letter that had reached his hands from an 'earnest and capable master,' which so well illustrates a danger well known to parish priests that it is worth while to transcribe it here:

"I fall in with the work in the day school very well, and as yet I have had no difficulties to overcome. My great grievance, however, is the Sunday school, at which a host of ten teachers attend, five of whom are good ladies from the village. It is hard to see those who know nothing of teaching take the authority out of one's hand, and undo in an hour or two a whole week's work. The kind-hearted ladies are inclined only to smile at the dear little bairns when they are at all refractory, or engage in some paltry little squabble; and Johnny dear is told that his lady teacher will be so very very angry, if he persists in getting over the desks, or speaks impertinently to his kind instructor. I am deposed from the position of head master for the first day of every week."

Mr. Butler's comment is, that on Sunday "the day school should be carried on—*mutatis mutandis*—as on week-days, under its natural teachers, while the Sunday school, under its voluntary teachers, consisting of children who only attend on Sundays, should be held in a separate room, or, better still, as so many separate classes in private houses."

At the Church Congress at Reading in 1883, Canon Butler read a paper on Purity.

The special department of the subject which fell to his lot was the prevention of the degradation of women and children. The paper is difficult to epitomise: it is full of sympathy and tenderness, combined with simple and practical suggestions as to how best to help those who need help.

There is a passage on the general condition of society which shows how keenly alive was the writer to the great dangers in this direction :

"In speaking of woman's degradation," he says, "let us not shut our eyes to the general condition of society. There is other degradation besides that which obtrudes itself in the streets. Those who mix much with the world mourn over a general laxity of tone which seems to be permitted—conversation of a loose and suggestive kind ; theatrical performances taken from the free and immoral literature of France ; that which some years ago would have been scouted, now witnessed and enjoyed ; French novels, where evil is freely set forth and spoken of as good, read even by young girls growing into womanhood ; men whose lives are notoriously profligate encouraged, sometimes even by mothers ; the tie of marriage no hindrance to dangerous intimacies, sometimes not falling short of gross and flagrant sin. If this is not degradation of women, it is difficult to say what it is."

The central portion of the paper is taken up with describing the actual state of the law in regard to the protection of women ; the writer points out clearly where legislation is insufficient, and then goes on to speak of what might be done, apart from legislation, in a preventive direction by private enterprise. He insists on the much-needed improvement of dwelling-houses, and then passes on to speak of the need of great caution in regard to mixed schools. A small tract, entitled "A Few Words to School Mistresses," published by Hatchards, is recommended, for it "may with great advantage be placed in the hands of teachers, with reiterated warnings not to live in what is called a fool's paradise, but to be watchful and even suspicious of every approach to familiarity between boys and girls."

There is a strong plea for the establishment in every neighbourhood of moderately-sized industrial schools where girls may be received for about two years during the critical period between leaving school and going out into the regular work of life, when, as Mr. Butler so truly says, "employers of the better kind decline to hire them, and then they often linger on at home, or accept a low and often very dangerous kind of situation."

In these proposed industrial schools the girls may be well nurtured and trained, "well instructed in the principles of their religion, taught to pray, to respect themselves, to believe in and to love God, confirmed and made regular communicants; and then, and not till then, sent out to fight the battle of life."

In what he says here, as always, the writer is speaking from the background of his own wide experience, for he adds, " I know what can in this way be done, how from such an institution there may be sent forth, year after year, a stream of high-toned, high-principled girls, capable and trustworthy as servants, and, so far as is possible to human nature, raised into a condition of thought and feeling in which they recoil with horror from all that is unmaidenly or impure."

Canon Butler expresses his satisfaction that so many callings are now opened to women which were formerly closed to them, and thinks that the more these openings are multiplied, "the more that women are incited to that which encourages and demands propriety of demeanour and self-respect, and which provides a fair means of living—the more will woman be freed from the danger which so grievously besets her life."

In 1888, at the Church Congress held at Manchester, the Dean of Lincoln read a paper on the "Desirableness of Reviving the Common Religious Life of Men."

Dr. Butler's paper was unfortunately lost before reaching the publishers. There is, however, a brief summary of it given in the Report of the Congress, which we reproduce here with little or no alteration.

The writer dealt with the subject as applied to clergymen. He described what, as he believed, were the needs of the present time in dealing with the large populations of our great towns. In London alone were four millions and upwards of people, to whom about six hundred clergy ministered, and they not distributed in a manner likely to hear the real calls for help. Liverpool in like manner had 600,000 souls, with seventy clergymen. Other towns also told the same tale, showing that the present parochial system was utterly inadequate to meet the demands made upon the clergy. What must, he asked, be the inevitable result? The complete chaos of society, the falling, as too many symptoms already showed, into a condition of materialism and inutility worse than the

worst days of barbarism.   They wanted some means of dealing
more adequately with the large masses of the population.   Was
it within the bounds of reason and common sense to imagine
that the great problem could be dealt with on a large scale
without having recourse to something very different to the
methods that had hitherto been tried?

He suggested that religious houses should be established
among the clergy for the better prosecution of evangelizing
work.   When he ventured to speak of the desirableness of
reviving the common religious life of clergymen, it was because
he was convinced that in no other way could the crying needs
of the Church be met.   Taking the very lowest ground, it
seemed to him that if the Church was in any way to fulfil
her great trust of preaching the gospel to every creature, it
could be effected only by the devotion and self-sacrifice of
men who would consent to lead a celibate life; to give up,
either permanently or for a stated time, much of that which,
to use a common expression, sweetened life; to cut themselves off, at least in a great degree, from the engagements
and expenses of ordinary society, and dwelling together under a
common roof and taking their meals at a common table, would
be in a position to bring to bear common counsel, common
action, and common intercession upon darkness, and ignorance,
and sin.   Men thus living together would be spared the
sense of loneliness and helplessness, which so often weighed
down the spirits and paralysed the energies of men who from
poverty or any other cause, found themselves living alone
with almost no support.

He would suggest that those who would offer themselves
for this common life should bind themselves for a period of
not longer than five years, which might, at will, be renewable;
that they should agree honestly to follow the rule which the
Prayer Book provided, keeping strictly to what was there
laid down, to the feasts and fasts, the daily service, frequent
Communion, with any additional services for which they might
have time and inclination.   The dress should not be peculiar
or demonstrative, and the diet simple and plain, but sufficient.
Such societies should be directly under episcopal supervision,
whether as regarded the central or parent house, or the
districts in which its members laboured.

The Congress held at Birmingham in 1893 was the last at which Dr. Butler appeared.

The subject assigned to him then was "The Ministry of the Laity," and the special department of the subject which fell to his lot was that on which he could speak with paramount authority, viz., Deaconesses and Sisters.

The paper is of special interest, not only because it is the last which the Dean read, but also because it brings out in a very striking and beautiful way his intense appreciation of the 'religious' life, and of all that such a life implies.

He begins by contrasting the favourable and grateful recognition given to Sisterhoods in the present day, with the way in which they would have been regarded before the rise of the Oxford movement. Now nearly all the prejudice against such institutions has passed away; there are more Sisters—more women aiming at the Religious life in England now than there were before the Reformation, and now not merely in England, but throughout the world—in India, Africa, and America, English Sisters are at work.

" A Sister's theory of 'vocation' is that in a very true though ineffable and mysterious manner our blessed Lord calls to Himself certain souls, who for His sake shall give up all; that He infuses into such souls a burning desire to be His, a true love even like the love of man to woman, or of woman to man, only far nobler and more exalted; that when this exists in any soul it finds no rest till it has given itself for the things of God; that this vocation is not to this or that work, possibly not at all to what is called work, but solely to be His, just as the true wife, without reference to house or household duties, finds in him whom she loves all that satisfies her heart. So the Sister is her Beloved's, and her Beloved is hers. Willingly for His sake she labours; but her great aim, the object of all her longing, is to be altogether His."

As to vows, Dr. Butler is clear as to their intrinsic reasonableness and their use.

"Let me be permitted," he says, "to say something on this very delicate and controverted question. I cannot, after much consideration, sympathise with the strong objection which some excellent people hold in regard to vows. I quite agree that where vows are permitted to be taken there should be a discretionary dispensing power. But with this, which surely lies within the range of episcopal jurisdiction, I cannot see, considering the number of vows which are accepted on all hands as right and proper—baptismal vows, repeated in confirmation; ordination vows, marriage vows, and that which is so strongly urged by many, the pledge or vow of abstinence from any form of alcohol—why those vows are to be looked upon as evil things, or at least, as full of danger, whereby men or women of mature age offer themselves to God."

He quotes Jeremy Taylor in support of his contention as to the legitimacy of vows. "It hath pleased God in all ages of the world to admit of intercourse with His servants in the matter of vows."

He insists, it is unnecessary to say, on the wise safeguard of a long and thorough noviciate, during which time every opportunity should be given to those who are thinking of the 'religious' life of clearly understanding the difficulties of such a state; but, after all precautions have been taken, he sees no reason why any who wish to do so should not by a solemn promise or vow dedicate their lives to God.

Further, he insists that a vow has distinct advantages. Like the marriage vow, it settles the question for good and all. It quiets that restlessness from which none of us are altogether free. It helps the 'religious' to bear cheerfully difficulties which "are sure, sooner or later, to crop up." As in marriage, which the religious life closely resembles, the die is cast, and any who have cast it find their happiness in accepting what it brings.

Among the advantages of Sisterhoods on which the Dean insists are such as these—*Continuity of work*: they bring with them a guarantee for at least such perpetuity as is possible in the changes and chances of life.

The moral weight and power which is ensured by discipline: the Sister sets aside her own private likes and dislikes. She goes whither she is sent. All that is given her to do is, in her estimation, God's work, and therefore equally good.

The knowledge which results from the experience which a Community gains in respect to methods of work. Each Sister is trained and taught how to act under various circumstances; how to enter securely the haunts of vice and crime; how to meet rudeness; how to maintain an uniform self-control and gentleness;

how to speak a word in season.   In Penitentiary work especially (which gave the first main impetus to the growth, in these later times, of the Religious life in the Church of England) experience has proved that the influence of Sisters living under a rule is of incalculable value.

At the conclusion of this very remarkable paper the question is discussed how far and under what conditions the Church as a whole should accept such institutions as Sisterhoods and Deaconesses, and the main answer which the Dean gives to this question is as follows : That it is better to leave such institutions to feel their way and to be proved before any direct interference or recognition is given them on the part of the Church. For the present the wise course is to leave these Communities to the care and wisdom of the Bishops, for episcopal supervision is, he thinks, essential; and he does not consider that a Community is formed on a solid basis where the Bishop has been ignored, any more than Communities are justified in altering at their own wish and pleasure the services of the Prayer Book.

The paper concludes with the following words : " It was once said to me by one of another Communion, ' You English are good people in your own way ; you have a good-natured disposition, and therefore do many good things, and abstain from much that is evil ; but you do not accept the idea of grace, or know what it can do for you.'   Here, then, in these religious Communities we have the answer. We may, I think, truly say that they have taken away this reproach from Israel.

" Very earnestly I pray that many living souls may be enabled to join them, to partake with them in that life of union with our blessed Lord, which brings with it true joy and peace, and to aid them in their blessed work of winning souls to Him."

INDEX.

THE END.

Macmillan & Co.'s Standard Works.

ALFRED LORD TENNYSON. A Memoir. By his Son. With Photogravure Portraits of Lord Tennyson, Lady Tennyson, etc.; Facsimiles of Portions of Poems; and Illustrations after Pictures by G. F. Watts, R.A., Samuel Laurence, Mrs. Allingham, Richard Doyle, Biscombe Gardner, etc. Two vols. Medium 8vo. 36s. net.

LIFE AND LETTERS OF FENTON JOHN ANTHONY HORT, D.D., D.C.L., LL.D. By his Son, ARTHUR FENTON HORT, late Fellow of Trinity College, Cambridge. Extra Crown 8vo, with Portrait. 17s. net.

St. James's Gazette.—"No small thanks are due to Mr. A. Fenton Hort, who has performed his task with sympathy and success."

THE LIFE OF CARDINAL MANNING, ARCHBISHOP OF WESTMINSTER. By EDMUND SHERIDAN PURCELL. With Portraits. Fourth Thousand. In two vols. 8vo. 30s. net.

Times.—"These two volumes, bulky as they are, will command universal attention, and in intrinsic interest they will not disappoint expectation. . . . The real attraction of such a biography lies not in the literary skill of the biographer, but in the story he has to tell. Mr. Purcell has wisely recognized this."

Standard.—"This profoundly interesting book."

THE LETTERS OF MATTHEW ARNOLD, 1848-1888. Collected and arranged by GEORGE W. E. RUSSELL. Two vols. Crown 8vo. 15s. net.

Speaker.—"In these letters will be found the genius of his books and the atmosphere of his poetry. . . . Mr. George Russell has edited the letters with excellent taste and judgment. Make two most interesting volumes, to be read and re-read with increasing advantage."

Daily Telegraph.—"Arnold's correspondence is not only deeply interesting because it embodied 'an abstract and brief chronicle of the time' in which two-thirds of his life were passed, but because it set forth with fearless frankness his own views with regard to many questions of moment, as well as those of other intellectual giants, his literary and political contemporaries."

LIFE OF ARCHIBALD CAMPBELL TAIT, ARCHBISHOP OF CANTERBURY. By RANDALL THOMAS, Bishop of Rochester, and WILLIAM BENHAM, B.D., Hon. Canon of Canterbury. With Portraits. Third Edition. Two vols. Crown 8vo. 10s. net.

Saturday Review.—"The interest of the two volumes steadily increases from the beginning to the end."

THE LIFE AND LETTERS OF DEAN CHURCH. Edited by his Daughter, MARY C. CHURCH. With a Preface by the DEAN OF CHRIST CHURCH. A New and Cheaper Edition. Globe 8vo. 5s. [*Eversley Series.*

Guardian.—"The *Life* of the great Dean has been admirably written by his daughter. . . . The book is introduced by the Dean of Christ Church in a Preface admirable alike in its expressions and its reserves."

MACMILLAN AND CO., LTD., LONDON.

Macmillan & Co.'s Standard Works.

FRANCIS OF ASSISI. By Mrs. OLIPHANT. Crown 8vo. 6s.

JAMES FRASER, SECOND BISHOP OF MANCHESTER. A Memoir. By T. HUGHES, Q.C. Crown 8vo. 6s.

LETTERS AND MEMORIES OF THE LIFE OF CHARLES KINGSLEY. Edited by his Wife. Two vols. Crown 8vo. 12s. Cheap Edition. One vol. 6s.

BISHOP LIGHTFOOT. Reprinted from the *Quarterly Review*. With a Prefatory Note by the BISHOP OF DURHAM. With Portrait. Crown 8vo. 3s. 6d.

LIFE OF FREDERICK DENISON MAURICE. By his Son, F. MAURICE. Two vols. 8vo. 36s. Popular Edition. Two vols. Crown 8vo. 16s.

LIFE OF JOHN COLERIDGE PATTESON, Missionary Bishop of the Melanesian Islands. By CHARLOTTE MARY YONGE. In two vols. Third Edition. Crown 8vo. 12s.

ERNEST RENAN. In Memoriam. By the Right Hon. MOUNT-STUART E. GRANT DUFF, G.C.S.I., F.R.S. Crown 8vo. 6s.

THE LIFE AND TIMES OF ST. BERNARD, Abbot of Clairvaux. By J. C. MORISON, M.A. Crown 8vo. 6s.

SPINOZA: A Study. By Dr. J. MARTINEAU. Crown 8vo. 6s.

CATHARINE AND CRAUFURD TAIT. Wife and Son of Archibald Campbell, Archbishop of Canterbury. A Memoir. Edited by Rev. W. BENHAM, B.D. Crown 8vo. 6s. Popular Edition, abridged. Crown 8vo. 2s. 6d.

SAMUEL TAYLOR COLERIDGE. A Narrative of the Events of his Life. By JAMES DYKES CAMPBELL. 8vo. 10s. 6d.

LETTERS OF CHARLES DICKENS. Edited by his Sister-in-Law and his eldest Daughter. Crown 8vo. 3s. 6d.

A MEMOIR OF RALPH WALDO EMERSON. By JAMES ELLIOT CABOT. In two vols. Crown 8vo. 18s.

LETTERS AND LITERARY REMAINS OF EDWARD FITZ-GERALD. Edited by WILLIAM ALDIS WRIGHT. In three vols. Crown 8vo. 31s. 6d.

LIFE AND LETTERS OF E. A. FREEMAN. By W. R. W. STEPHENS. Two vols. 8vo. 17s. net.

LIFE, LETTERS, AND WORKS OF LOUIS AGASSIZ. By JULES MARCOU. With Illustrations. In two vols. Crown 8vo. 17s. net.

THE NEW CALENDAR OF GREAT MEN. Biographies of the 558 Worthies of all Ages and Countries in the Positivist Calendar of Auguste Comte. Edited by FREDERIC HARRISON. Extra Crown 8vo. 7s. 6d. net.

THE LIFE OF JOHN MILTON. By Prof. DAVID MASSON. Vol. I., 21s.; Vol. II., 16s.; Vol. III., 18s.; Vols. IV. and V., 32s.; Vol. VI., with Portrait, 21s.; Index to six vols., 16s.

MACMILLAN AND CO., LTD., LONDON.

www.ingramcontent.com/pod-product-compliance
Lightning Source LLC
Chambersburg PA
CBHW021342110726
47900CB00005B/1576